Drake's Drum:

The Peace of Amiens

Drake's Drum

The Peace of Amiens

Nicholas Sumner

SEA LION PRESS

First published by Sea Lion Press, 2019

ISBN: 9781689121415

Cover artwork by Jack Tindale

For Barbara; who believed in
this book when I didn't.

He goes directly from headquarters to the airport, his car passing swiftly through the streets of the darkened capital, escorted by two motorcycle outriders. They are not really necessary. There is hardly anyone around in the late cool hours of an autumn evening. The light aircraft is waiting for him as they had said it would be, its engine already turning. The pilot is busy with the last of his pre-flight checks; he looks tired, exhausted in fact, but salutes when he sees the Colonel's uniform.

The Colonel makes himself as comfortable as he can in the cramped interior of the aircraft. As they climb into the night, the little plane shakes and rocks in turbulence, the sound of its engine changing as it reaches altitude. His eyes probe the starless darkness outside the window but find nothing to alight on there and come to rest on the tense features of the pilot beside him, his face lit by the green glow of the instruments.

The Colonel's hands rest on the box in his lap. They did not tell him what was in it and, professional that he is, he did not ask. His mission is a simple one; deliver it in person to the General at the beachhead. He wonders what it could contain. It isn't heavy, wrapped in brown paper, tied with string, about sixty centimetres long and twelve centimetres square. Not papers, not maps, but what?

They had called him at eight o'clock, he had been working late. In the conference room, maps of the beachhead were laid out on the tables; he had seen at once that the situation was grave. The General Staff had looked drawn, resigned, when one of them had handed him the box he had held it reverently as if it contained something precious but the look in his eye was serious, gloomy, full of misgiving.

He might have felt annoyance at being treated as a delivery boy, but he is also glad to be going to the front, he feels the old thrill of excitement and fear, he has not seen action for a very long time. Uncomfortable in the silence he says to the pilot: "You look tired." The pilot turns toward him, as if noticing him for the first time.

"Yes, Colonel I am pretty tired." The pilot smiles self-consciously, a rictus grin without a trace of humour. "I don't think I've had more than three hours sleep in the last four days, my squadron has been flying supplies to the beachhead."

1

"In this little plane?" the Colonel asks. He means it as a joke but the pilot's smile is again mechanical, joyless.

"Yes, in this little plane. We've got every aircraft that can carry a load dropping supplies, they've even attached panniers to the fighters. All they've told us is that the situation is critical and our soldiers need every gram we can drop to them." He hesitates for a moment as if wondering if he should continue before he says: "Our losses have been bad. We've lost half the squadron. I'll be honest with you Colonel I'm quite happy to be flying this mission tonight, after we land, I'll have to go straight back." The Colonel does not reply.

*

The first flush of a grey dawn is lightening the eastern sky as he picks his way swiftly along the quay. The dock is in chaos, crates of food, munitions and medical supplies are stacked everywhere, the shouts of soldiers and dock workers, the noise of cranes moving the crates onto vessels of all shapes and sizes. From one of them, a procession of orderlies brings men on stretchers, some of them whimpering in pain even as the cranes move nets filled with supplies over their heads.

He finds the quartermaster's office. It is crowded, blazing with light that spills out onto the dock despite the blackout. Men hurry in and out clutching manifests, harassed, panicky; above the hubbub of voices two are raised in argument.

"Do you not understand? Is it not clear? The medical circumstance is beyond desperate over there; we must send these medical supplies immediately!"

"I'm sorry doctor but my orders are explicit; munitions first, food second, medicine third."

The Colonel interrupts; "Who is in charge here?"

"I am," says the second man. The Colonel tells him his name.

"Ah, you are here Colonel, good. Your transport is waiting for you."

It is a motor torpedo boat, roughly thirty metres in length, two torpedo tubes either side of the open bridge, two twin 20 mm gun mounts, one before the bridge and one aft, its engines throb and it sits in a reeking cloud of diesel smoke. As he walks down the companionway he sees that the crew are lashing crates and boxes to the deck.

The captain, a Lieutenant, is on the bridge, a cigarette dangling from his lip. He salutes and asks if the Colonel is ready. They cast off and as the boat noses its way past the mole, the note of its engine changes from a steady throb to a thundering scream. As the throttles open, the Lieutenant flicks his cigarette over the side, a tiny orange spark spiralling towards the sea as the boat leaps forward into the grey morning.

In the gathering light the Colonel sees that the vessel has suffered damage, there are hastily patched holes from bullets or splinters in the sides of the bridge and on her deck, the men look exhausted; they are unshaven, their clothing rumpled and stained as if they have not changed for many days. The water is choppy now and the boat bounces from wave to wave, he holds on to the cockpit coaming as the deck pitches beneath his feet. Instinctively he hunches into his jacket and pulls his peaked cap down further as the wind of their slipstream blows strong and cold into his face. On the horizon – the enemy coast – a great dark column of smoke rises into the clouds, it looks like a funeral pyre or an omen. They are steering straight for it.

The cloud is beginning to break up, shafts of sunlight stream through its tattered edges from the dawn behind them and suddenly one of the gunners is shouting, "Enemy aircraft, seven o'clock!"

Three fighters in a loose V formation have dropped out of the low cloud and are turning toward them. The formation splits, one aircraft banks away to the port side of the boat, the other two to starboard. The Lieutenant is giving orders to the helmsman, they turn towards the two aircraft, shortening the distance between them, giving the greater threat the smaller amount of time to bring their guns to bear.

They know even as they turn that the enemy fighters are herding them, for while they steer straight towards the guns of the two fighters now in front of them, the third aircraft is angling in behind and their relative speeds mean that the pilot of the third aircraft will have a much longer period of time in which to aim.

The aft guns open up and suddenly the two fighters in front of them break right and left, but the Colonel looks over their stern to the third fighter, the great disc of its propeller seems to float inches above the water, its wings catch a flash of sunlight as they rock, then a ripple of fire spreads along their length and the bullets come whistling around them. The Lieutenant shouts an order and the helmsman slams the throttle back and turns the boat broadside into the enemy fire. The Colonel loses his footing as the boat heels over, he falls to the cockpit floor as water comes foaming white over the gunwales but it is too late, the boat seems to stagger under the thud of bullets striking home and suddenly someone is screaming as the fighter roars overhead seemingly inches from the top of the bridge.

The Colonel scrambles to his feet as the boat rocks from side to side but he slips and falls heavily back to the deck. He has slipped on the helmsman's blood, his body lies crumpled on the deck, one hand still grips the wheel. The side of his face is smashed open. The Colonel can see broken teeth and the white of bone through the ragged hole in his cheek. Pinkish grey brain matter oozes from the helmet that still somehow remains on what is left of the man's head.

Again the Colonel gets to his feet – more carefully this time – he fights down a desire to vomit, he has not seen violent death close–up for more than twenty years. The box has slipped from his hands and fallen into a corner of the bridge, he scrambles to retrieve it but when he holds it again the corner of the wrapping is soggy with blood. The Lieutenant is shouting orders and takes the wheel himself but lets it go suddenly, his hands come away bloody, he wipes them quickly on the dark material of his jacket. Another sailor pulls the helmsman's body out of the bridge.

One by one the crew report back, the damage is light but the aft gunner has been injured, he sobs in pain, a bubbling cry of agony and despair. No one speaks, as slowly the boat moves forward again, picking up speed towards the dark column of smoke. The body is wrapped in canvas and laid out next to one of the torpedo tubes.

Another crewman takes the wheel, the engines open up and the boat once more surges forward. The Colonel fights to bring his mind back under control, he lights a cigarette with trembling hands, 'Try not to think about the dead man, remember your mission...' For him it has been many years since war was more than just an exercise in command and control, an abstract problem. He is a staff officer, he isn't used to this anymore; but then, no one ever gets used to it, not really.

*

They are close to the enemy shoreline now and the Lieutenant is giving him instructions, he holds up a map and is pointing to one of the beaches on which the landings had been made four days previously.

"We can't get too close to the beach – there are too many obstructions in the water – including mines and booby traps, it hasn't been cleared." He looks at his watch. "It's now low tide, we will stay about a hundred metres out, you'll take the dingy..."

The Colonel interrupts him. "But we captured the port on the second day; I was told you could take me right to the dock."

The lieutenant shakes his head; "No Colonel, our HQ is six kilometres east of the port and the harbour is closed, air attacks have been constant, there are several hulks blocking the entrance to the harbour, we can't get in – and if we could there is no transport. Everything has to go over the beach including you."

They can see the shoreline clearly now, high cliffs, peaceful green countryside. The column of smoke is rising from the town behind the port, as the boat speeds closer they can see burning buildings. The Colonel pulls his field glasses from his pack but there is little he can make out through the smoke. The beach is around the next promontory, their speed slows to a crawl, the smoke is thicker here and the choppy water filled with debris; pieces of wood, strips of metal, a life raft half deflated, the bloated body of a horse. A landing barge down at the bows, abandoned, her wheelhouse blazing, the upturned hull of another, the masts and superstructure of a larger ship jutting from the sea.

With the engines throttled back they can hear the sound of gunfire clearly across the water, the rattle of small arms, the thud of exploding shells. It makes no sense, their forces had struck more than thirty kilometres inland, they shouldn't be able to hear the sound of battle at that distance; has the situation degenerated that far?

The Colonel's eyes strain in the direction of the gunfire, the smoke clears in patches showing the beach, the sea wall and the buildings of the town behind it. Then he gasps, for a moment refusing to believe the evidence of his senses as the smoke clears some more to reveal the unmistakable shape of an enemy battleship.

The battleship died fighting and has been deliberately grounded. She has been driven up on the shingle, is listing to port and her prow is only a few metres from the low sea wall. Her ram bow is completely clear of the water and crumpled by the impact, waves break around her stern and there are two jagged overlapping holes beneath her exposed waterline, together they are nearly thirty metres in length.

The main deck is a shambles; the hull and superstructure bear the scars of fire and shell impacts, her guns all point in different directions and her battered tripod foremast, stark against the sky, looms over them like a gallows. The Lieutenant is speaking; there is weariness in his voice but also admiration.

"That happened the day before yesterday, they timed it perfectly, came past the narrows and caught us at sunrise. It was chaos, they went right through the escort and slaughtered our transports. It was a massacre..." As his voice trails off he points to the battleship with his chin. "She took two torpedoes, she was finished but they beached her and it was nearly two hours before we could silence her guns. The crew didn't surrender even when they had emptied their magazines, they fought on with small arms, I don't know if any of them survived..."

His face darkens suddenly, as if his mind is straining to grasp at something that he cannot understand or does not quite believe. "After the torpedoes hit her, everything went quiet, her crew must have been thrown from their positions by the impacts and all our guns stopped firing as well. It was just a moment, not even five seconds I suppose, but... I thought I heard something, a sound from far away, I could barely hear it, as if I wasn't hearing it so much as feeling it..."

The Colonel looks at him; "What? What did you hear?"

The lieutenant shakes his head. "I thought I heard a drum."

6

"A drum?"

"Yes, a drumbeat, regular and insistent like, like... I'm not sure, a heartbeat perhaps, or... I don't know." The Colonel looks at him dismissively. "You heard gunfire, or perhaps they had a band playing to keep the crews spirits up."

The Lieutenant shakes his head; "No Colonel, it was something else."

"You are fatigued, sometimes the mind plays tricks."

"Perhaps Colonel, I don't know." The Lieutenant turns away, unwilling to continue the discussion, unconvinced by the Colonel's rational explanation.

They can see the rest of the beach now; it is pitted with shell holes, crowded with the wrecks of smashed and upturned vehicles. Two transport barges are being unloaded even as shells explode around them sending towering columns of water into the sky.

The Lieutenant straightens and shakes his head as if to clear his mind: "Colonel, it's time." As the boat comes to a stop and drifts for a moment, he again brings out the map, he points to a building behind the sea wall, and then to a point on the paper. "That house is here, the General's Head Quarters are in this building here, three hundred metres east of this point. It's a white hotel; we will hold our position for one hour..."

"No, my mission might take longer, you must wait for me."

"One hour Colonel, I'm sorry."

He rounds angrily on the Lieutenant, about to order him to stay until he returns but something in the man's eyes tells him that it would be a waste of breath.

*

The streets of the town are deserted, some of the buildings are in ruins, most are pockmarked with bullet holes. On one road, some burned–out cars seem to have been assembled into a barricade; an enemy tank with a thrown track blocks another; on a third sits one of his own side's tanks. It appears to be completely undamaged; its hatches are open. The ammunition, hull machine gun and radio have been stripped. It has run out of fuel.

He runs from cover to cover bent double, his service pistol drawn, the oblong box an awkward burden beneath his left arm. Shells are falling on the town and the sounds of battle seem very close. He rounds a corner and sees three paratroopers, a corporal and two privates, recognisable by their cut down helmets and camouflage smocks. With their weapons they are covering four men standing against a wall, they are prisoners, two are in enemy uniforms, but the others wear civilian clothes. It is a firing squad.

"Corporal, what is the meaning of this?"

The corporal salutes; he returns it. "Sir, these are enemy saboteurs."

"Two of these men are in uniform."

"I have orders to shoot all saboteurs in uniform or otherwise Sir, the order comes directly from High Command."

He looks at the prisoners, each of them wears a different expression, one seems resigned, at peace, another meets the Colonel's gaze with a look of curiosity, the third hangs his head fighting to control the sobs that are shaking his frame. As his eyes met those of the fourth, the man begins to shout in his own language; defiance, fury and contempt in every syllable and the Colonel suddenly realises that these are old men, the youngest is in his fifties. The uniforms are twenty five years old or more, they are from the last war – his war.

"Corporal two of these men are uniformed enemy combatants."

"Sir, these men are saboteurs."

"Shooting surrendered enemy combatants is a crime."

"Sir, I have my orders."

He looks very hard at the Corporal, but the man's eyes cannot meet his, the muscle at the angle of his jaw works nervously, his expression wavers between repugnance and resolve.

The Corporal salutes, his gaze fixed somewhere over the Colonel's left shoulder. The Colonel does not return the salute; the enemy prisoner is still shouting as he turns his back, he hears the Corporal say 'Fire.', the quick stammer of the machine guns, the unmistakable sound of bullets hitting flesh. The shouting stops.

*

He is just a few tens of metres from the white hotel now, every window in the building seems to be smashed, part of the roof is missing, the chimneys are toppled, the walls riddled with bullet holes. He walks through the open gate to find the garden full of wounded, they sit or lie on the ground, some are unconscious, a few moan in pain but most are eerily quiet. He bends down to ask one of them where the General is. The man salutes feebly and gestures towards the building's interior. As he turns to go he hears the man ask weakly, "Colonel, please, do you have a cigarette?" He holsters his side arm, gives him the rest of the packet and goes inside.

The corridors too are crowded with wounded, on the stairs and in the passageways. The General is quite alone in what had been a dining room, some tables have been put together and on them a large map is unfolded. The General stands looking through the open French windows, out into what remains of the garden, a cigarette is held in his left hand. The crack of artillery fire seems very close. He turns as the Colonel enters.

"Who the hell are you?"

The Colonel salutes, the General returns the salute perfunctorily. His eyes are distant, dreamy, with a weariness beyond simple fatigue.

"General, I am Colonel Martin Weber, I have come directly from Headquarters; I am instructed to give you this." He holds the box out in front of him; the brown paper wrapping is scuffed and torn. The blood on it has dried.

"What is it?" the General asks.

"I don't know Sir, I was told only to bring it to you and hand it over in person."

The General sighs, stubs out his cigarette and places the box on top of the map on the table. He cuts the string, and tears open the brown paper. The box is made of dark wood, beautifully polished, on the lid a gold eagle with a wreathed swastika gripped in its claws.

"Ha!" An exclamation escapes the General, somewhere between surprise and disdain; "Of course..." But as he reaches

9

for the clasp they hear the sudden snarl of aircraft engines very close. "Get down!" the General shouts and both men sprawl on the floor even as the bombs burst nearby and the room fills with choking dust. They lie there, coughing in the smoke, hearts pounding as the sound of rifle and machine gun fire grows louder under the fading noise of the motors.

They get up and pat down their uniforms in silence. The General brushes dust and masonry debris from the box, the gold eagle is dented. He undoes the clasp and opens the lid, inside is a blue Field Marshal's baton, its shaft decorated with eagles and Maltese crosses, his name embossed at one end, black lettering on a white band. He holds it up and laughs.

"And they say the Fuhrer has no sense of humour." He throws it back into the box angrily, as if the baton has soiled his hand.

The Colonel says; "General, I mean Field Marshal, Congratulations sir, but..."

"Congratulations? For what?"

"For your promotion sir." The General looks at him with contempt and suddenly he is shouting.

"Promotion?" The word hangs in the air between the two men, "Promotion? We have lost this battle Colonel Weber, do you understand that? We have lost it catastrophically; this will go down as one of the worst defeats in history – that fool Goering has ensured it with his meaningless promises and this..." He picked up the baton again, "...this is nothing but a bribe."

Again the baton falls back into the box, the General turns and walks once more to the window. "They sent you too late, I've already given the order to withdraw, my staff are disposing of the papers as we speak." He pauses, "If you have a way out I suggest you use it, we're falling back on the beach near here, but we've no prepared positions, the Kreigsmarine has almost been obliterated, we do not control the skies, we're practically out of ammunition and some of my men haven't eaten in days. Not many are going to get away..." his voice trails off.

When the Colonel speaks he weighs the words carefully; "You realise no German Field Marshal has ever been captured by an enemy?"

The General pauses for a moment; "Well then, I shall be the first." He pauses again, his eyes look outward through the French doors and the clearing smoke. "So be it."

For a moment the two men stand in silence. The Colonel salutes, clicking his heels together in the Prussian way but the General is lost in his own thoughts, looking out through the doors and does not seem to hear. The Colonel turns and walks quickly from the room.

Part 1: The Peace of Amiens

Drake he's in his hammock till the great Armadas come,
(Captain, art thou sleepin' there below?)
Slung atween the round shot, listenin' for the drum,
An' dreamin all the time o' Plymouth Hoe.
Call him on the deep sea, call him on the Sound,
Call him when ye sail to meet the foe;
Where the old trade's plyin' an' the old flag flyin'
They shall find him ware an' wakin', as they found him
long ago!

Sir Henry Newbolt (*Drake's Drum*, 1898)

CHAPTER 1: THE WASHINGTON NAVAL DISARMAMENT CONFERENCE

From 'The British Empire from 1914 to 1948' by Ian Shaw, Longacre 2005

In November 1918, when the guns fell silent on the Western Front after more than four years of unprecedented bloodshed, it was as if the British Empire let out a collective sigh of relief. Victory, though victory at a fearsome cost, had been achieved. It seemed a moment to take stock, to re-appraise the United Kingdom and its Commonwealth and to set a new course into a future that all believed would be free of war. Yet the thirty years that followed that victory were to prove no less tumultuous and no less difficult.

The half decade after the armistice saw a cool, unblinkered analysis of the Empire in peace and in conflict, and the results were unsettling. Before 1914 it had been assumed that the strength of Britain was derived from its overseas territories with their multitudinous populations and vast wealth; yet the crucible of war had revealed a starkly different picture. In fact it was only a small fraction of that Empire that provided the manpower and the money required to defend it at the mother country's hour of need. It had been assumed that British industry and finance could meet the challenges of war, yet as early as 1915 the conflict began to reveal its inadequacies and fissures. It had been assumed that international problems that affected the Empire directly could be resolved quickly and effectively by diplomacy and a show of resolution. Almost a million dead proved that this was not the case.

The British Empire and its Commonwealth was a union based upon trade and a shared system of values. It was the only global power of any real significance between 1918 and 1939. France, Germany and Russia were devastated by the conflict. Japan and Italy were too weak. The United States was isolationist. It was a middle aged polity whose strength grew in peace, and declined in war. What could utterly overthrow it was another war where it would again have no choice but to use up its accumulated capital and become the financial dependent of another power.

Yet Britain was not an Empire in terminal decline. In relative decline perhaps; poorer, yes; weaker, certainly. But still a vital entity, one that had to begin a process of re-invention, one ready to change and adapt its methods and its structures, one ready to grow and to thrive. But how was this to be accomplished?

How was the Empire to proceed? How was it to navigate the troubled waters of the unfolding future? How would it live? How would it defend itself and its peoples? How would it grow? The British Empire had to re-invent itself, to reconcile and consolidate what it had inherited from its past and become something new. That much was evident. The problem was; how was this to be done?

From 'The Rule of the Waves' by Michael Fanshaw, Twelvemonth 1963

The decisive British victory at The Battle of Jutland had a number of unforeseen consequences. Firstly it greatly enhanced the status of the capital ship in the eyes of public and political opinion. Until May 31st 1916, a conviction had been growing in British political circles that the vast resources poured out upon the Grand Fleet had been spent in vain because until that time, it had failed to accomplish its stated aim; the destruction of the German High Seas Fleet. There was a widespread belief before the war began that a large naval battle would take place shortly after the outbreak of hostilities. However, the enemy was reluctant to come to battle, victory proved elusive and several inconclusive engagements in the North Sea caused disquiet in a nation that looked eagerly to underscore its claim to 'Rule the Waves'. The sinking of seven German capital ships and the rout of the High Seas Fleet quite put these arguments to rest.

Secondly it elevated Admirals John Jellicoe and David Beatty to the status of the semi-divine. They joined the ranks of Drake, Nelson and Rodney as first rate British naval heroes.

Consequently, when Jellicoe, in 1920, gave his judgement that a large fleet was a necessity in the Far East after his tour there; or Beatty made his opinion clear on British requirements from The Washington Treaty, they spoke with the voices of gods. This was partly due to the emphasis placed on The Battle of Jutland by the press and political commentators in the immediate aftermath of The Great War. The battle gripped the public imagination. It was far easier and more rewarding for the ordinary people of Britain and the Dominions, having passed through the trauma of the Great War, to contemplate the swift, decisive and comparatively cheap triumph of the Royal Navy. Jutland stood in stark contrast to the long, grinding engagement of attrition on the Western Front.

Writing fifty years after the beginning of the Great War, we can say with some certainty that spectacular though Jellicoe and Beatty's success may have seemed, it altered very little about the conflict. Essentially all Jutland accomplished was the maintenance of the status quo. Its chief significance was that the blockade remained unbroken; but the war was still deadlocked on the Western Front and certainly ended no sooner because of it.

We can also say that Field Marshall Haig accomplished more for Britain by eventually securing the defeat of the German armies on the continent of Europe than either of the two lionized Admirals, despite the almost hysterical adulation that they received. Both men were elevated to the peerage. Beatty took the title of Lord Beatty of Jutland. Jellicoe became Lord Jellicoe of Scapa. Their statues were placed in Trafalgar square, side by side on the fourth plinth.

In 1917, Jellicoe was dismissed from the post of First Sea Lord at the behest of the Prime Minister David Lloyd-George. His sacking was disguised as a promotion (he was made an Admiral of the Fleet) [1] and was almost certainly because of his popularity.

Finally, it is pertinent to note the importance of the thorough review of the effectiveness of British heavy shell after

---

[1] In OTL he was promoted a month later.

their inadequate performance in the battles of Flamborough Head and Dogger Bank. This was initiated by Sir John Fisher, the First Sea Lord, in 1915. He had the able support of Winston Churchill, the First Lord of the Admiralty. Without it, the Grand Fleet might have faced the High Seas Fleet at Jutland with flawed weapons; in which case, Jellicoe and Beatty's triumph might have been no triumph at all.

The victory did not have the same moral effects as had been hoped. Successful though the outcome was, the complete annihilation of the German fleet had not been achieved. Despite the adulation of the press, Jutland was in many ways not the 'New Trafalgar' that Great Britain had looked for. The High Seas Fleet had nothing like the prestige of the Army in Germany and even if it had been completely eliminated, it seems highly unlikely that the Germans would have given up the fight because of it.

Despite the fact of victory, for the RN, the consequences and lessons of the battle caused a great deal of reappraisal. The Grand Fleet became a vastly more efficient and significantly more dangerous force by facing the challenges raised by Jutland. The battle exposed shortcomings in tactical doctrine, signalling and method of command. It also revealed the inadequacy of many aspects of the design process. Jellicoe wrote to the First Sea Lord on 5th June 1916 that: 'There are a great many lessons to be learned.' He did not lose a moment in taking stock of them. Solutions were rapidly and efficiently applied and increased the effectiveness of the Grand Fleet to a level that would not have been considered attainable before Jutland and would not have been possible but for Jutland.

Significantly, the victory of Jutland deprived the U–boats of one of their main supports, since the High Seas Fleet was in many ways the power behind their campaign. Even more significantly, it released a significant part of the Grand Fleet's light forces for mercantile convoy protection.

*

At the Washington Naval Disarmament Conference convened on 12th November 1921 and eventually signed in February of the following year, the British and American delegations disagreed sharply on the issue of new construction of capital ships. A proposition by Charles Evans Hughes, the head of the US mission, to set a ratio of 5:5:3 for the capital ships of the world's three largest navies was embraced very early by the British. However, a further proposal for a ten year moratorium on new construction was rejected by them. This was on the advice of Admiral Lord Beatty of Jutland, Britain's First Sea Lord and the Commonwealth delegation's chief professional advisor. Beatty pointed out that Britain had already undergone a self-imposed building holiday for the past five years. Furthermore, the specialised skills required to construct capital ships in the UK would decay significantly if it went on for another ten years. He also pointed out that upon the termination of the treaty there would, in all probability, be a scramble to build new ships meaning the beginning of a new arms race. Consequently he advocated a steady program of replacement for old ships rather than a complete cessation of battleship construction.

Beatty had consistently opposed cuts in naval strength. Convinced that the Royal Navy was the first line of Imperial defence, he emphasised the need for a strong battle fleet and used his high profile and reputation to press the navy's case to the government. The other Commonwealth delegates were certainly in awe of him and his recommendation was taken very seriously indeed. The victory at Jutland had confirmed the capital ship as the final arbiter of naval power [2] and the Royal Navy's battleships as the defenders of the Empire. Such was his stature, that when a telegram arrived from the British government urging him to proceed more cautiously and not jeopardise the conferences chances of success, he responded that the Cabinet should trust his judgement on the matter. Surprisingly, he was not rebuked.

Thus, from the outset of the conference, the British sought to advocate a final treaty that permitted them to construct or

---

[2] In OTL the disputed and in some ways inconclusive result undermined the status of the battleship

complete new capital ships within an agreed framework. Initially, the American delegation was unwilling to agree and raised the spectre of the talks breaking down entirely. They contended privately that the British were trying to continue the naval race under the guise of disarmament and publicly that this display of recalcitrance indicated an unwillingness to go along with the post-war spirit of peace and reconciliation.

The British delegation reiterated that they had not laid down any capital ships since 1916 and emphasised that this in itself was a de-facto building holiday. Another point they made to support their argument related to the relative ages and the effects of war service on the battle fleets of the United States and the British Empire. Taking war service as double wear (i.e. that one year of wartime service equals two of peacetime service), then the average age of the British battle fleet on January 1st 1922 was almost twelve and a half years. By contrast, the average age of the American fleet was only eight. A third argument was that the British were quite willing to permit the Americans to procure new construction as well.

Both the British and the Americans knew and understood that the United States was capable of winning any building race in the long term. The British were gambling that the Americans were also aware that it would require a ruinous capital outlay to establish this fact. The British shipbuilding industry was highly proficient. It had turned out six or seven capital ships in each year of the decade before the First World War and had built the battle cruiser *Repulse* in nine months [3]. It was also known that the consistently parsimonious American Congress had failed to release funds for the completion of the ships of the ambitious 1916 and 1919 building programs and was unlikely to do so in the near future.

There was also a detrimental side-effect to agreeing to a building holiday. Most of the dreadnoughts to be retained would be due for replacement at the same time and this would result in

---

[3] The British industry had not yet reached the state of atrophy that existed in 1937 OTL – which was a direct result of laying down only three new capital ships (that were completed) in the previous twenty years.

a feast–famine cycle of construction that would be both uneconomical and potentially destabilising from the point of view of industrial capacity. However, the substitution of the age-replacement rule with a steady building programme would be beneficial to all.

Gradually the American negotiators began to warm to the idea of an agreed building schedule with each power permitted to complete a number of ships at intervals within the treaty framework. A compromise was reached whereby the Americans were allowed to complete all four battleships of the *Colorado* class, while the British constructed four 35,000 ton battleships of their own to balance them. Furthermore, the United States Navy retained the right to construct or complete four ships not exceeding 45,000 tons at a later date; while the British were permitted to complete a second *Hood* class ship (HMAS *Endeavour*) plus two more ships of a new design not exceeding 45,000 tons.

This was in part due to Beatty's private emphasis to members of the American delegation that the British Empire and the United States had nothing to argue over. It had become increasingly obvious to the Americans that Westminster's policy was to do business with the US by diplomatic means for the simple reason that there was little or no prospect of strategic competition between the two. The British were comfortable with the Monroe Doctrine, Canada was a Dominion and had reached its own accommodation with America and the policies of the respective governments on most aspects of international relations were mutually supportive. This was understood by the American delegation but Beatty undeniably helped stress it.

Ultimately the American negotiating position was defined by their government's desire for economy. It was argued by some members of Congress that scrapping incomplete ships was wasteful and profligate. Many of the ships of the large American 1919 Program were partially complete. The US government would have preferred not to spend any more money at all on new ships and written off the not inconsiderable amount already spent as a sunk cost. But by agreeing to complete some of these vessels they seemed to have arrived at a less expensive option than permitting the conference to fail. This certainly seemed a sensible alternative to scrapping ships that were half–built, only to lay down new ships a year or two later.

Thus the powers agreed to managed building schedules rather than a moratorium on new construction. [4] Consequently, except in Britain, very few new ships were laid down; the various governments preferring instead to complete ships already begun. There was certainly a widespread belief that the treaty would probably be renewed or replaced by a modified one that also limited new construction.

From 'The Great Submarine Debate 1922 – 30' by Robert Trent writing in Man O' War 2007

At the Washington Naval Conference of 1922, Arthur Balfour, the head of the British Empire Delegation, gave a speech in which he said that the experience of the Great War had shown that submarines were completely ineffective as weapons of war when used against other warships. Furthermore, they were mostly ineffective when used against civilian trade in defiance of the rules of warfare. [5] He based his contention on the fact that the German submarines had been unable to counter the strength of the Grand Fleet, had proved unable to interfere with their operations to any great extent and that they had failed to substantially degrade British commerce and trade after the introduction of convoy and other tactics. He also stated that on a ton for ton basis, submarines cost two to two and half times as much as battleships. He went on to stress that the Germans, in their various submarine campaigns of the Great War had contravened international agreements and international law that restricted submarines to using cruiser rules when preying on

---

[4] There were provisions in the OTL treaty allowing France and Italy to build new ships within the ten–year building holiday period. In TTL the idea is extended to all the powers.

[5] In OTL Balfour's argument was that they were ineffective UNLESS they were used against civilian trade in defiance of the rules of warfare.

24

merchant vessels. He noted that if they had complied with international law they would have been rendered useless as a weapon.

The speech caused uproar in naval circles and the debate, continuing long after the conference ended, was conducted across the pages of The Times and even found its way in to Brassey's Naval Annual. Balfour has been extensively criticised for delaying the general publication of volume III of the British Official History of the Great War. This document dealt with the German U–boat campaign of 1917-18 [6] and restricting its distribution by having it declared secret and placed under the Twenty-five Year Rule was an act clearly designed to support a deception, but he had seized the political initiative and this was crucial.

Clearly, Balfour wanted to counter the perception that submarines were highly effective weapons, but his arguments were relatively weak. He used hyperbole to overstate the points in support of his position while ignoring those that ran counter to it. While German submarines may not have sunk many British warships at sea, they certainly were able to circumscribe the Grand Fleet's operational areas and they made operations difficult for the Royal Navy during the late 1916 sortie by the High Seas Fleet. Similarly, British submarines did manage to torpedo a number of German capital ships on the few occasions that they had the opportunity, even if they didn't manage to sink any.

Nevertheless it paved the way for the conference to include limitations on the total tonnage of submarines. While most professional naval officers had misgivings about Balfour's argument, many of their political masters took an opposite view. Balfour's comment on costs was felt particularly keenly and went to the heart of the reasons the conference had been called in the first place. In peacetime, decisions concerning military spending

---

[6] Naval Operations: History Of The Great War Based On Official Documents By Direction Of The Historical Section Of The Committee Of Imperial Defence. Vol. 3 written by Sir Julian Corbett and published by Longmans, Green And Co, 1923 OTL.

are rarely based on strategic or operational requirements, but on the short- to medium-term availability of financing. Balfour caused a reappraisal of both the potential and significance of submarines and helped divert attention away from them and back towards more conventional avenues of naval thinking.

It is possible that the fleets of the world would have developed in somewhat different ways had Balfour not effectively pulled off a political master stroke. His undoubted mendacity was certainly an attempt to do Britain and the Commonwealth a service, but it must be noted, that of the contracting powers, only France and Italy were greatly affected. The United States and Britain had no plans to embark on large submarine construction programmes. For Japan, on the other hand, the role of the submarine was essential and their actual plans for submarine building greatly exceeded what the treaty permitted. The French signed the treaty before properly formulating a post-war naval policy and, unlike the Japanese, strived to keep within the treaty's limits. The Italians tended to assess their strategic needs with a view to countering the French and were to find their construction priorities severely cramped by the weakness of their economy in any case.

From 'Mackenzie King and the Royal Canadian Navy' by John W. Olds writing in Man O' War 1989

At the Washington Conference, the issue of training ships proved extremely contentious and became embroiled in the issue of the independence of the navies of the Commonwealth nations. The opening British position was that warships under the command of the navies of Australia, Canada, New Zealand and South Africa should not be counted in the Royal Navy's total, an argument that was wholly unacceptable to the United States delegation.

As part of the United Kingdom's efforts to compel the Dominions to bear a greater part of the financial burden of Empire defence; Australia, Canada, New Zealand and South Africa had all been persuaded to fund their own naval forces and had each agreed to purchase and maintain a capital ship. All had been promised assistance from the British treasury and in the case of Australia, Canada and New Zealand ships had already been earmarked for transfer. In the case of Australia and New Zealand, these were incomplete hulls.

The South African's however, seized on American resistance as an excuse to back away from their commitment to Empire defence. Canada also proved reluctant to pursue the matter, but was in the middle of an election campaign as the conference convened. Because none of the candidates wished to be seen as unpatriotic, the British were able to apply a certain amount of leverage on them. One of William McKenzie King's first acts as Prime Minister after his election victory on 6th December 1921 was to send the following letter to the American President.

Dear President Harding

I have the honour to refer to recent events at the current Washington Naval conference and in particular to allegations of gerrymandering made by the American delegation in reference to the formation of independent Canadian, Australian, New Zealand and South African Navies. For my part, I am commissioned and required to speak only for Canada, though the intent of this letter may have some bearing on the conduct of all of these nations.

The people of the United States saw fit to throw off what they perceived to be the injurious yoke of colonial government at a time and in a manner that the people of Canada, presented with identical circumstances, did not choose to emulate. I would submit that at a distance of some one hundred and fifty years from those events, it is not the provenance of the government of the United States to dictate to other nations with a similar history and antecedents, the manner in which they may choose to become independent or pursue the rights that pertain to independent nations.

I would respectfully remind the president that Canada has been an independent sovereign nation and self-governing since 1867, that Australia has been since 1901 and that New Zealand has been an independent Dominion since 1907. I would further remind the president that alliance notwithstanding, the Navy of Canada is at the command of the people of Canada through the medium of its duly elected government.

For more than a century past, relations between the United States and Canada have remained cordial and within the past decade our two nations shared in the great struggle of the war. There can be no doubt that these current minor misunderstandings will be set aside and the happy state of affairs on this great continent which our nations share will continue to pertain.

Very Sincerely Yours

William Lyon McKenzie King, Prime Minister.

For diplomatic correspondence the wording of the second and third paragraphs are quite blunt. Some historians have speculated that Mackenzie King was trying to undermine the British position by forcing them into too aggressive a negotiating stance in the hope that an equally aggressive American response would compel a re-appraisal of Canada's commitment to purchase and maintain a capital ship. The style of the letter is very different from Mackenzie King's normal mode of communication and it seems possible that it was written by someone else with his approval.

If that is the case then the letter backfired in its intent. It was seen in Washington as a reflection of British unwillingness to cooperate on the issue. Instead, the Americans raised the idea of permitting the capital ships to be retained as training ships. After long and occasionally acrimonious discussion, a compromise was reached whereby the Australian capital ship would be included in the Royal Navy's total tonnage, while those of Canada and New Zealand would be disarmed but retained as training vessels. The South African delegation were relieved that their country was to be excused the financial burden of capital ship operation. [7]

---

[7] For a more detailed assessment of the story of the Dominion capital ships see the Appendices.

From 'A New Naval Race Avoided' by Michael Hargeaves writing in USNI Measures 1954

Under the Washington Treaty of 1922, the tonnage allowance for submarines for each power was set at the ratio of 5/5/3/1.75/1.75 (expressed as US/UK/Japan/France/Italy). The actual tonnage figures were approximately 75,000/75,000/45,000/26,500/26,500. While submarines certainly didn't disappear from the world's navies, fewer were built during the term of the Washington Treaty than might otherwise have been the case. [8]

The British Commonwealth was happy to see a limitation on submarine tonnage in place, though disappointed at the failure to obtain an outright ban. There was only a minor effect on their building programmes. The United States on the other hand, had agreed to give up about a quarter of its existing submarine force in number of hulls. However, an appraisal of the oldest subs in the USN in 1922 indicated that this would entail only the sacrifice of small, obsolescent and poorly regarded boats. The H, K, L and N classes were small coastal submarines and suffered from many engine problems, while the T class were a good size but were considered unsuccessful and due to be laid up in 1922 anyway. All of these boats had been designed prior to American entry into World War One and all compared poorly with examples of captured U-boats. All were of only limited effectiveness and the coastal boats could not make long voyages unescorted.

Japan entered into the Washington Treaty negotiations with a large number of submarines that they considered generally satisfactory. In Japanese doctrine they were supposed to cause attrition in the fleet of an enemy before the decisive encounter with the main battle fleet. While this was certainly important, it was judged less important than having a powerful battle line, especially as the IJN wanted to keep as close as possible to 70% of US strength.

---

[8] For a more detailed assessment of the Washington Treaty see Annex 3.

Japanese naval policy was fixated on the notion of a decisive battle and under the Washington Treaty they were permitted to build or retain 12 battleships and battle cruisers. The Kanto earthquake of 1923 forced them to some difficult choices, but their desire to commission the battleship *Tosa*, and two *Amagi* class battle cruisers was an overriding priority. Between 1922 and 1933 the IJN constantly re–appraised its construction programs. [9]

The Marine Nationale was required to keep its submarine tonnage to roughly its pre-treaty level (28,116 tons). However, the French had committed themselves to treaty limitations before deciding on the future direction of their naval strategy. This was yet another symptom of the lack of a coherent French naval policy after the war. [10] Italy, the weakest of the powers,

---

[9] I've approached this problem solely in terms of money, but in considering alterations to the warship building programs of the powers Japan presents a difficult case. Britain, the US and France all had low defence budgets between the wars and consequently increasing them for a piece of fiction is a matter of changing political will. But Japan was spending all it could on armaments and there is no room for financial manoeuvre. (Italy presents a similar problem but not quite so acute.) Therefore, to afford to build their capital ships, other parts of the Japanese naval budget would need to change. To see how this might be done I looked at the costs of various types of warships in the USN, the RN and the various incarnations of the German Navy in the dreadnought era. I have been unable to find more than random bits of information on the building costs of the other powers but the three navies in the sample all show roughly the same trends and from this I was able to get a rough idea of what the IJN would need to give up to get the battleship *Tosa* and the two *Amagi* class battle cruisers (Note here that OTL *Tosa* was launched and the guns and mountings for *Tosa* and all but one of those for two of the *Amagi* class had been completed. Eight of these turrets were installed in the battleships *Nagato* and *Mutsu* when they were reconstructed in the 1930s and six were transferred to the Army. Three of the turrets for the Army were installed in land based forts to cover the southern entrance to the Sea of Japaa at Iki, Tsushima and Pusan and three were kept in reserve).

[10] In OTL this more than tripled to 91,052 tons by 1932, but the plan that provided for this explosive growth was not submitted until 1924. It was at first rejected by parliament but remained a policy goal and the submarine part of it at least seems to have been largely completed. In TTL the French, having foregone a large submarine fleet, will have ample resources to build the new capital ships they were permitted under the OTL (and TTL) Washington Treaty.

enervated by the conflict and convulsed by political upheaval went along without too much protest. [11] Thus the limits placed on submarines at Washington perhaps forestalled the start of another naval race where submarines became proxies for battleships. [12]

From 'The British Empire from 1914 to 1948' by Ian Shaw, Longacre 2005

British defence policy allowed the nations of the British Commonwealth and their immediate neighbours to enjoy the benefit of what the economist Peter Pugh calls 'common goods'. This refers to benefits that all the individuals in a group enjoy, whether or not they contribute to providing it. Although a 'common good' is advantageous to all, paying for it is not, because from the point of view of each individual, the advantages of the common good are not lessened if they do not pay for it. In fact, the avoidance of paying for a 'common good' is a definite economic advantage for those other than the main supplier of the benefit, because the funds saved can be used for other purposes.

A closely integrated economic and military alliance, such as the British Commonwealth, is unquestionably a common good for all its members. But, for each individual within that alliance the most advantageous strategy is to spend as little as possible for its own security while depending on the others for it. However, there invariably comes a point when such reliance by an individual nation compels its allies to re-appraise the terms of their protection and possibly remove that protection entirely.

---

[11] Freed resources permit the completion of the battleship *Caracciolo*. In OTL Italy's submarine construction program did not begin to gain momentum until after the French began to expand theirs. It would seem that they might have just been trying to keep up with French building.

[12] Examples of every class of vessel that was built in OTL will be built in TTL – though many at a reduced number of units – so the overall level of technology will not be greatly changed.

At the Imperial Conference of 1930, which was held in London in the autumn, Admiral Lord Jellicoe delivered a speech to the delegates that had these truths firmly in view. He began by pointing out that because of the underlying strength and broad base of her economy and because she was able to float Government Bonds at a lower rate than all other nations except for the United States. Britain was therefore still able to finance a major war against two Great Powers. However, she was no longer monetarily or militarily able to win a global war against three. He went on to say that although the government and people of Britain felt strong ties of sentiment and of trade (in many cases these were quite literal family ties) to the independent Dominions of Australia, Canada, South Africa and New Zealand, all of these had, (compared to the mother country) very modest defence budgets. While these nations were certainly effective allies in time of war, they sought in peace to deflect as much of the financial burden of defence onto Britain as they could.

He closed by saying that throughout the British Empire, maintaining the Washington Treaty was seen as a positive stratagem. He also stressed that from the point of view of those territories which were in, or adjacent to, the Indian and Pacific Oceans, the Treaty was the best safeguard against Japanese expansion. The Royal Navy was the mainstay of Empire defence and he sought to persuade the Dominions to persist with the work begun prior to the Great War to enlarge both their naval forces and their areas of responsibility.

Jellicoe's speech was the start of a concerted diplomatic effort on behalf of the British to get the Dominions to bear more of the costs of Imperial defence. Canada had made some strides in that regard and in the past had resisted pressure to expand her naval squadron even more, despite having announced a desire to acquire three battleships before the Great War and even set aside funds for two of them. But Canada's new Prime Minister, Richard Bennet, was prepared to accept that the Dominions should bear more of the burden of Empire defence. He overcame strong pressure from United States President Hoover and Canada eventually matched the levels of spending on the Navy that Australia and New Zealand maintained.

If the British could be satisfied with the contribution made to defence spending by the Dominions bordering the Pacific, the same was not true of those bordering the Indian Ocean. The governments of India and South Africa, emphasising the political sensitivity of heavy defence expenditure in their territories, never managed to substantially raise their spending. This was perhaps a blessing in disguise. Until the crises of the mid 1930's, the RSAN was neither the most enthusiastic or effective member of the RN's family of fleets and the Royal Indian Marine was little more than a farce.

CHAPTER 2: WEDNESDAY

19th OCTOBER 1993

"And now for part seventy-nine of Radio 4's 'Voices From the Past' an oral history project for the BBC produced by Hermione Miller. Today we are at the home of Warrant Officer Arthur Leighton in Weymouth, Dorset. Good morning Mr. Leighton…"

"Morning."

"Now we are here today in your home and I understand that you have recently had a birthday?"

"Yes, I'm ninety five years old."

"That's wonderful Mr. Leighton, congratulations."

"Thank you, yes, but you better be quick with this interview, I might not make it to the end.

(Laughs) "That's wonderful Mr. Leighton. Now you also have a son who was in the Royal Navy too."

"Yes, my son John was a pilot in the Royal Navy Air Arm."

"You were on HMS *Revenge* during the German Invasion, but you also served in the Great War…"

"Yes I did, I was in three major actions during that time. I was a steward on the battle cruiser *Lion* which was the flagship of the battle cruiser force under Admiral Beatty at Dogger Bank and at Flamborough Head and a while after that, I was transferred to the *Revenge* and I served on her at Jutland and for the rest of the war."

"So you served on the *Revenge* twice?"

"Yes that's right; she was named for Francis Drake's flagship you know…

"Oh really…"

"…yes that's right. I left the Navy in 1920 and got a job at The Dorchester in London, it was better for my family but I missed the sea and I joined up again in 1938, my son was about grown by then – he joined up around that time."

"Can you tell us about the battles you were in Mr Leighton?"

"Which one?"

"Well, what was that one you mentioned er… Flamborough, er…" (Papers rustling.)

"Flamborough?"

"Yes, er yes, Flamborough, tell us about that…"

"Well, that was when I was with the battle cruiser force. We were off Scarborough, well outside the minefield, guarding the gap in it. It was early afternoon, I was below decks. When we were at action stations most of us stewards made up first aid parties. It could be quite nerve racking. We had no idea what was going on. Of course you could hear the guns firing and you could feel it if the ship was hit, but not being able to do much set your nerves on edge until the call came. Then you had to go and try to help the injured. There was a heavy sea that day and the ship was rolling a lot. It was just past six bells of the afternoon watch, that's about ten past three, and we were sailing south west when we sighted the enemy."

"Why were the German ships there?"

"They had been bombarding Whitby, Scarborough and Hartlepool, everyone on *Lion* was furious about it actually. It was an outrage, they were making war on civilians. Nowadays that doesn't seem so strange, but then it was shocking, absolutely shocking. Anyway, we were already at action stations so we opened fire and they started shooting back. All us lot in the first aid parties could do was sit tight and wait for the call and sure enough I was ordered to the bridge about ten minutes after we started firing. I remember running up the companionway and into the open, it was winter and the cold air just hit you right in the face as you came out of the ship. It was raining and I looked over and saw the German ships about six miles away, they were pitching pretty bad and their bows were digging right into the sea sending up showers of spray – wonderful sight really, I'll never forget it…

"Anyway, there were three or four men injured from shell splinters, none of them badly but one of the lookouts had a gash in his forehead and blood was running into his eyes. He wouldn't leave his post so I bandaged it right there and as I was finishing putting the dressing on him I looked up and I saw a hit on the third one in line, the third German ship. A great big sheet of flame seemed to come out of her. I thought she'd blown

35

up. Everyone on the bridge was cheering, but when the smoke cleared she was still there and she was still firing at us. Same thing happened a few minutes later with one of the others.

"I suppose I should have gone back below but I was just a young lad and I'd never seen action before, I could see that we were getting hits, the wind was blowing a full gale and was behind us, which helped our guns and made it harder for theirs. Our shooting was getting better and better, theirs was getting worse."

"Why was that?"

"Well our guns used a simpler fire control system than the Germans. You've got to remember that in a battle, everyone is under terrible stress and frightened out of their wits. Your mouth's dry and your hands are shaking, you just want it to end – or I always did – so if you're trying to do a complicated job it's a lot harder than if you've got a simple one to do."

"I should perhaps say here for our listeners that you were decorated several times."

"That doesn't mean I wasn't scared though."

"No I suppose not, can you tell us more?"

"Well, about fifteen minutes after the action started, we saw another squadron of ships off to the south, at first we thought it might have been more Germans but when they started shooting we knew it must be Vice Admiral Warrander with the Second Battle Squadron.

"Anyway, the Germans didn't stop around long, they turned and sailed east as fast as they could, still letting fly at us with all they had. Of course night was coming down by now. In mid-December the sun sets before four at that latitude and what with the weather and the cloud cover it was coming on full dark even though it was only about half past three. Anyway, one of the PO's chased me off the bridge…"

"Sorry, what's a PO?"

"Oh, it means Petty Officer – a non-commissioned officer – he saw me hanging about and told me to hop it. Anyway we were all pretty disappointed I can tell you, when we stood down from Action Stations I went back to being a steward and I had to take some tea and sandwiches up to the bridge. Admiral Beatty was talking to Captain Chatfield, I remember he shook his head and he said he just couldn't understand why we hadn't sunk some of the German ships, he said: 'Either the Germans have much thicker armour than we think, or our shooting isn't as good as it looks, or there is something wrong with our shells.' And that was it – that was exactly it. We didn't know it but there was something wrong with our shells. Our shells weren't working properly. That big flash I saw was one of them bursting on the German's armour, but they weren't supposed to burst on the armour, they were supposed to go right through you see.

"Anyway, about a month later, right after another battle – the Battle of Dogger Bank – there was a luncheon party in the wardroom."

"Wardroom?"

"Yes, that's the room where the officers eat their meals and suchlike. Anyway, this luncheon party was given in honour of Vice Admiral Sturdee who had just got back from the South Atlantic where he'd given the Germans a bit of a pasting at the Battle of the Falklands. When it got round to the main course, (which was a lovely bit of roast lamb as I remember) the Admiral started talking about the action at the Falkland Islands and the interrogation of some of the captured German officers afterwards. Well, he said that the Germans were saying that our shells were rubbish, that they usually broke up on impact and they couldn't get through the German armour. Well, I looked at the captain and he just about looked as if he'd been hit by a sledgehammer. Thunderstruck wasn't the word. He and the Number One – the first officer – they started in asking the Vice Admiral all sorts of questions, I don't really remember what was said but after the meal was over and the Vice Admiral left, the captain, the first officer and the gunnery officer came back into the wardroom while I was clearing the table.

"They were pretty excited, the captain was absolutely furious, he was saying that their worst fears were confirmed and the Royal Navy couldn't face the Germans with any confidence. He was effing and blinding and calling it a scandal and a disgrace. I'd never seen him so angry; never heard foul language pass his lips before, not even in battle and the other two were almost as bad. The poor old *Lion* was pretty banged up after Dogger Bank and we were in dock for repairs. The captain left the number one in charge and went to see Admiral Beatty and Beatty sent him straight down to London to the Admiralty.

"Anyway, to cut a long story short it got right the way up to Jackie Fisher – who was First Sea Lord – and Winston Churchill – who was First Lord of the Admiralty. They were the commanders of the Navy, the top men, top jobs in the Navy and Jackie Fisher, he wasn't one for mucking about, nor Churchill neither. They ordered all sorts of tests and firing trials, an inquiry, everything. Still it took more than a year for us to get new shells, more than a year – well there was a war on I suppose, they had all kinds of problems manufacturing shells in 1915, they didn't have enough of them for the army you see, but Churchill and Fisher they got the ball rolling and what with the invasion scare that was on, the navy got top priority.

"Of course both of them were out of a job pretty soon after because of Gallipoli, but they set the wheels in motion and Fisher, he wouldn't even let it go after he'd resigned. I don't know what would have happened at Jutland if our shells hadn't been working properly by then. It's hard to say, we might have lost, it might have been a German victory, I might not be sitting here talking to you…

CHAPTER 3: THE BATTLE OF
FLAMBOROUGH HEAD

From 'The Rule of the Waves' by Michael Fanshaw, Twelvemonth 1963

The Raid by the High Seas Fleet on the Yorkshire coast of 15th – 16th December 1914 caused the first civilian casualties on British soil since the French attack on Fishguard in 1797. Admiral Friedrich von Ingenohl, the commander of the German High Seas Fleet, wanted to pursue an aggressive strategy, and on 3rd November 1914 had led a raid on Great Yarmouth. He selected the Yorkshire coast line as his target in part because it lay between two British fleet bases, on the Tyne and the Humber. In the early months of the war minefields had been laid off both rivers, leaving a gap opposite Scarborough. The region was also a comparatively short distance from the German naval bases. Compared to Yarmouth however, it was much nearer the British Grand Fleet's Scottish anchorages and there was a possibility that the British might trap the German raiding force which consisted primarily of light forces and Admiral Franz von Hipper's battle cruisers. Consequently Ingenohl decided to take the van of his fleet out, to protect the battle cruisers if the British should attempt to intercept them.

In Britain there was a fear that the Germans might attempt a landing somewhere on the eastern coast. The Army estimated two divisions could safeguard the coast against raiders, but all of its regular troops were fighting in France. The Royal Navy was compelled to spread out along the East Coast, with battle squadrons at Rosyth, on the Tyne, the Humber, in the Wash and at Sheerness. It was believed that such small forces would be able to delay the High Seas Fleet if it attacked, permitting the Grand Fleet to deliver the coup de grace.

Unbeknown to Ingenohl, the British had advance warning of the raid. Room 40 of Naval Intelligence had just broken the German naval codes and the British fleet was already well out to sea by the time the Germans left their bases. However, they were unaware that the battleships of the HSF were involved in the raid also.

At noon on 15th December, the British 2nd Battle Squadron and the Battle Cruiser Squadron rendezvoused off the Scottish coast, and began to steam south. Later that afternoon the HSF made its first general rendezvous and began its journey west with the German battle cruisers in the lead. Hipper's force, the First Scouting Squadron consisted of the battle cruisers *Seydlitz*, *Moltke*, *Von der Tann* and *Derfflinger* and the armoured cruiser *Blücher*. The 2nd Scouting Squadron, consisting of light cruisers came next, followed by the van under Ingenohl, some distance behind.

The British 2nd Battle Squadron was commanded by Vice Admiral George Warrender, his force consisted of the battleships *King George V*, *Ajax*, *Centurion*, *Orion*, *Monarch* and *Conqueror* and the cruiser *Boadicea*. The Battle cruisers were commanded by Admiral David Beatty, from his flagship HMS *Lion*. At 15:00 on 15th December they were joined by the Third Cruiser Squadron from Rosyth. The British fleet was screened by seven destroyers, steaming on the port side of the main body.

The first exchange occurred at 05:20 on the following morning between two groups of destroyers. This could easily have led to a major German naval victory, six British battleships and four battle cruisers were within a short distance of the main body of the German Fleet. But Ingenohl had no way of knowing that he wasn't entering a trap and at 05:45 he ordered his ships back to port. He received sharp criticism for this, but if he were to safeguard Germany's 'fleet in being' he had little choice. Both Ingenohl and Warrender assumed that the destroyers were screening larger forces. Even if the two forces had come into contact, the British squadrons were faster than the Germans and could have tried to escape. It was still dark (sunrise was not till 08:13) and it seems unlikely that anything other than a confused and scrappy action could have taken place.

Hipper's bombardment force had passed through the gap in the minefield but the weather was deteriorating and his light cruisers were obliged to turn back. At 08:00 the German battle cruisers were off Hartlepool and Scarborough and began a brief barrage. The force that attacked Scarborough then steamed north to bombard Whitby, before all five ships turned for home reaching the western entrance to the gap in the minefield by 11:00.

Hipper assumed that when he emerged from the safe passage at the south west corner of the Dogger Bank he would have a choice of going either south or north but unbeknown to him, Warrender was heading to block the southern route and Beatty the northern.

At 11.25 Beatty's cruisers, (which were to the north of his main body of battle cruisers) found the German light cruisers, steaming east. They opened fire on the German force, but Beatty attempted to signal that two of the four British cruisers should disengage and return to their scouting duties. Unfortunately, the signal was misdirected and all the British cruisers broke off the engagement upon which the Germans turned south.

At noon Hipper had reached the middle of the safe channel when disaster struck. Because of the danger to his ships from mines that might have drifted into the cleared passage, lookouts and marksmen had been posted on their forecastles with rifles to fire on any mines they saw floating in the water. Several drifting mines were observed (probably freed from their moorings by the bad weather) and fired on, but because the sea was choppy and the visibility poor these were not seen until they were very near the ships and the pitching of the bows threw the marksmen's aim off. Consequently the German squadron was forced to slow down to a crawl and they did not emerge from the cleared passage until 14:15. [13] Warrender and Beatty were now in an ideal position to intercept them. At 14:17, almost at exactly the same time as Hipper's force was through the channel and free to manoeuvre, Warrender sighted the German light cruisers through the mist and assuming the German battle cruisers must be nearby, turned north east to intercept them. In response, Hipper turned south east, in an attempt to draw the British away from the vulnerable cruisers.

---

[13] In OTL Hipper was through the swept channel by 13:05.

When Beatty received a signal from Warrender informing him of these developments he turned west – this was the crucial moment in the hunt for Hipper. [14] At 14:30, Warrender lost the Germans in the mist, and turned east in the hope of re-acquiring them. Hipper, believing that a gap had now opened to the north, turned to a north easterly course at 14:37 and ran straight into Beatty's battle cruisers.

Hipper turned to a south easterly course with Beatty in pursuit and both sides began to exchange fire at 14:42. The British had a slight advantage in that the wind was behind them and they scored seven hits in all before Warrender's force came in to view at 14:51. Hipper was now steering east-south-east with Beatty on his port quarter and Warrender closing from his starboard bow at an angle of about 30° variance from his own course, but the weather was becoming even worse and the light failing rapidly. Sunset was due at 15:37, but heavy cloud cover, squalls and patches of mist made visibility very poor and Hipper now turned due east and lost the British in a bank of mist making good his escape.

Despite the success of the raid, Grand Admiral Alfred von Tirpitz, the Commander-in-Chief of the Kaiserlich Marine, felt that Ingenohl had lost a chance to inflict a catastrophic blow against the Royal Navy. He conveniently forgot that Ingenohl was under orders not to engage with a superior force and on the morning of 16th December had no way of knowing if he was about to run into the entire Grand Fleet. Ill-founded though the criticism was, it actually strengthened Ingenohl's desire to conduct more offensive operations and led directly to the battle of Dogger Bank five weeks later on 24th January 1915.

British public opinion was outraged by the German breach of the rules of war in bombarding an undefended port. Some of this anger was also directed at the Royal Navy who had allowed the raiders to get away with it. The apparent ease with which the Germans had got through to the east coast did little to dispel disquiet about an invasion and it is fortunate that the public

---

[14] In OTL he turned east on the assumption that the Germans must have got past him.

were unaware that the fleet was in possession of advanced warning of the German sortie or confidence might have been even further damaged.

From 'The Ordnance Crisis of 1915' by Peter Hamilton writing in The Journal of British Metallurgy *volume 26 part 3, 1962*

It was not only the British Army that found that it had malfunctioning shells. Although deficiencies in the performance of British heavy naval shells were known prior to the onset of hostilities, a mixture of complacency, incompetence and vested commercial interests prevented any decisive action being taken with regards to their effectiveness.

The naval actions that occurred in the opening six months of the conflict however, caused the British Admiralty a great deal of disquiet. At the Battle of the Falkland Islands, Sturdee's battle cruisers were compelled to expend most of their ammunition in subduing a German force whose thin armour should have yielded very quickly to the heavy calibre guns carried by the British squadron. HMS *Inflexible's* gunnery officer, Commander Verner wrote that 'Although our shots were obviously falling all over the *Sharnhorst* we could not stop her firing and I remember asking my rate operator: "What the devil can we do?" German prisoners taken at the action even stated under interrogation that the British shells had not worked properly. [15] Winston Churchill, the First Lord of the Admiralty and Jackie Fisher, the First Sea Lord, were both made aware of the situation and expressed their concerns. However, there was a general feeling that the results obtained at the Falklands might not have been typical. The 'experts' and the manufacturers resisted all criticism and refused to entertain the idea that something was wrong.

However, the Battle of Flamborough Head on 16th December again called the performance of British shells into

---

[15] As they did OTL

question. The conclusion drawn in Naval Operations by Sir Julian Corbett and Sir Henry Newbolt is poignant.

"In all the war there is perhaps no action which gives deeper cause for reflection on the conduct of operations at sea... Two of the most efficient and powerful British squadrons, having bought the enemy to action, then failed to greatly damage him or impede his escape despite repeated hits by our guns." [16]

Beatty, in a letter to Jellicoe, wrote; "There never was a more bitterly disappointing day. We were within an ace of bringing about the complete destruction of the enemy cruiser force – and failed. I cannot help but feel that there is some serious materiel defect in our heavy shell." [17]

A month later, the battle of Dogger Bank reinforced a growing feeling of dismay in the fleet at the inadequacies of British shell and the spur for action eventually came from the fleet itself. In early February 1915 at a luncheon party held on HMS *Lion* in honour of Vice Admiral Frederick Sturdee who had led the British force at the Battle of the Falklands and had just been appointed to command the Fourth Battle Squadron of the Grand Fleet.[18] Captain Chatfield and *Lion's* other senior

---

[16] The OTL version reads; 'In all the war there is perhaps no action which gives deeper cause for reflection on the conduct of operations at sea... Two of the most efficient and powerful British squadrons, with an adequate force of scouting vessels knowing approximately what to expect, and operating in an area strictly limited by the possibilities of the situation, had failed to bring to action an enemy who was operating in close conformity with our appreciations and with whose advanced screen contact had been established.'

[17] The OTL version quoted in Marder's *From Dreadnought to Scapa Flow Volume II* reads; "There never was a more bitterly disappointing day as the 18th (16th) we were within an ace of bringing about the complete destruction of the enemy cruiser force – and failed. There is no doubt whatever that his (Goodenough's) failure to keep touch with and report the presence of the Enemy Cruisers was entirely responsible for the failure..."

[18] As he was OTL.

officers learned from Sturdee the unwelcome news that the German prisoners interrogated after the Battle of the Falklands considered British naval shell ineffective to the point of being laughable. Not only had British shell failed to penetrate German armour it had frequently broken up on contact. [19]

Chatfield immediately made the connection between this information and the disappointing results of the Flamborough and Dogger Bank actions. This was very bad news for the Royal Navy and confirmed the worst fears about British projectiles. Chatfield went to see Beatty that afternoon and obtained his blessing to travel at once to London to inform the Admiralty.

Both Churchill and Fisher were alarmed at the situation, there was a clamour for decisive action and an air of crisis motivated the convening of an inquiry. This proceeded under the presidency of F. C. Dreyer, one of the Navy's foremost gunnery experts, assisted by his brother Captain J. T. Dreyer of the Royal Artillery. The inquiry concentrated on shell performance, the committee members worked tirelessly and quickly submitting their conclusions in March 1915.[20]

Although both Churchill and Fisher left the Admiralty over the Dardanelles debacle, their prompt action in mounting and pressing forward with a comprehensive and unflinching investigation into shell performance did the Royal Navy a great

---

[19] In OTL the stimulus for action was the visit of a Swedish naval officer to the wardroom of HMS Lion two months after the Battle of Jutland. The officer had been the Swedish naval attaché in Berlin and told the British officers flatly that their shells didn't work.

[20] In OTL a committee under Dreyer was set up four days after the Battle of Jutland. Its purview was somewhat generalised and a subcommittee presided over by Vice Admiral R. B. Farquhar did not begin work until more than two more months had passed. Farquhar was a poor choice for this assignment, as a former Chief Inspector of Naval Ordnance he had a vested interest in showing that British shell was not substandard. The final report of the committee was not received until March 1917. Worse than this, the report seems to have been essentially a fudge and it was not until Admirals Beatty and Jellicoe took matters into their own hands that firm action was undertaken.

service. [21] Even after his resignation, Fisher took an active interest in the issue and the respect he commanded within the fleet ensured his attention propelled the committee's work. The final report was damning and sent shockwaves through the upper echelons of both the Royal Navy and the British Government, at a critical juncture in the war the Grand Fleet was not equipped with any shell on which it could absolutely rely and the provision of new shell for the Navy was accorded the highest priority.

Partly because of the shell crisis of the summer of 1915 deliveries of new projectiles were slow but by the Battle of Jutland some 80% of the ships of the Grand Fleet were equipped with the new 'Greenboy' shells.[22]

A wider result of both the Army and Navy shell crises of 1915 was a re-appraisal of British manufacturing and materials testing. The crises acted as a clarion call and showed that for Britain to remain an effective industrial power then much had to change. Though the process of change was interrupted by the recession and was not to fully bear fruit until the 1930s, the crises marked the nascence of a realistic approach to industrial policy from the British government.

From 'Salt Water Legends' by Rachael Belstaff, Halder and Stratton 1986

Francis Drake took a drum with him on his voyage to circumnavigate the world which he undertook between 1577 and 1580. As he lay on his death bed off the coast of Panama in 1596 he ordered that the drum be taken to Buckland Abbey in

---

[21] In OTL there was no widespread general concern over shell performance at all until after the Battle of Jutland. Unfortunately the First Lord and First Sea Lord at this time were not decisive men like Churchill and Fisher.

[22] In OTL it took twenty months from the final report of the committee until 100% of the ships of the Grand Fleet were re-equipped with 'Greenboys' (the name given to the new shells deriving from the fact that they were painted green) in October 1918. In TTL the process is 80% accomplished in 14 months.

Devon, where it remains to this day. He vowed that if England was ever in great danger then the drum was to be beaten to summon his return to defend the country.

People have claimed to have heard the drum beating on several occasions: in 1815 when Napoleon was brought into Plymouth Harbour as a prisoner; in August 1914 at the outbreak of the Great War and when the German navy surrendered at Scapa Flow in 1919. On this occasion a victory drum roll was heard on HMS *Royal Oak*. The ship was searched three times from masthead to keel but neither a drum, nor a drummer, were found on board.

The last reported occasion on which the drum was heard was during the German invasion of Britain. Several of the survivors of the crew of HMS *Revenge* claim to have heard the drum at different times during their passage from Rosyth to St Mary's Bay and there was a report that some German sailors claimed to have heard it as well.

CHAPTER 4: SUNDAY

13th DECEMBER 1931

The New York City streets are dark with winter rain. The shows are closing; the crowds that pour from the doorways of theatres hunch into their overcoats and hurry through the gusty wind that blows cold raindrops into faces and turns umbrellas inside out. Taxis jostle one another at traffic lights, their drivers scanning the mass of people for fares. Tyres hiss as they turn on the wet tarmac and the reflections of headlamps shine yellow from the black surface of Broadway.

A match flares suddenly in the dark interior of one of the cabs; its glow catches briefly in the thousands of droplets of water that coat the outside of the windows. The man who holds it lights a cigar and shakes his hand to put the match out. He rubs at the condensation on the inside of the cold glass, shifts impatiently in his seat and leans forward,

"Driver!" he growls "Do you know where you are going?" The woman who sits beside him places a gentle hand on his arm. "Winston, don't berate the man."

"I'm not berating him Clementine, we appear to be lost."

"Winston, we are at the junction of Fifth Avenue and Broadway, one can hardly be lost if one is on Broadway."

They stop for a moment; the man's eyes meet the drivers momentarily in the rear view mirror.

"Fifth Avenue..." he speaks slowly, as if to a fool, "...the apartment of Bernard Baruch."

The driver sighs, this jowly Englishman with the steady gaze and the haughty demeanour is becoming annoying.

"Look Mister, Fifth Avenue runs half the length of Manhattan Island, are you sure you can't remember the exact address?"

The Englishman scowls as the taxi moves forward again, then suddenly he sits bolt upright and strikes the back of the driver's seat, pointing triumphantly.

"There, there it is, stop driver I recognise that doorway." The woman is uncertain; she stares in the direction the man is pointing and frowns.

"Winston are you sure, Winston, wait..." But he is already pressing money into the drivers hand and opening the door. He leaps from the vehicle looking the wrong way, the sudden shriek of tyres on the wet road makes the woman catch her breath, she hears the thud as the skidding car hits him, sees the body fold over the radiator. She screams.

CHAPTER 5: THE RISE
OF OSWALD MOSLEY

"The man's a Cad and a Wrong-un". Stanley Baldwin, speaking of Oswald Mosley [23]

From 'A Concise History of British Politics' by Tom Shaed, Gloucester University Press, 2007

Oswald Mosley's leadership of the Labour Party probably prevented not only a split in its ranks but also a heavy defeat in the general election of 27th October 1931. [24] From his re-entry to the House of Commons under the Labour whip (he had previously sat as a Conservative) on 21st December 1926, he had devoted much energy to build a personal following in the Party. He championed radical 'New Deal' style interventionism and Keynesian economic policies, but failed to win over the party leadership. His resignation speech, on leaving his role as Chancellor of the Duchy of Lancaster on 19th May 1930, was a bold claim to leadership pitched at the political centre. It was one of the most ardent and stirring speeches the House of Commons had ever witnessed. [25]

---

[23] All quotes in this book are genuine (i.e. they were said by the person they are attributed to in OTL) unless otherwise stated.

[24] I am indebted to Ed Thomas and his excellent book *A Greater Britain* (Sea Lion Press, 2017) for showing how Oswald Mosley could have become the leader of the British Labour Party. What's set down here by me owes much to his work but lacks the level of detail he achieves in *A Greater Britain*. (See the Acknowledgements)

[25] It was in OTL too – the following are all genuine quotes: 'The best and most constructive speech I have heard in the House. It was fair and it was splendid.' – Clement Davies. 'It was, I suppose, the greatest parliamentary tour de force this generation will hear.' – Robert Boothby. 'A really great parliamentary performance ... I was enormously impressed by it... I don't believe there is anyone else in this House who could have done it.' – Violet Bonham–Carter.

As the recession dragged on, so the internal divisions within the Labour Party grew. At the party conference in the autumn Mosley revealed his 'manifesto'. Although it was rejected by a narrow margin, [26] the support it garnered confirmed the growing discontent within the party and the existence of a credible alternative to the leadership within its ranks.

Over the winter of 1930 to 1931, Mosley's attacks on the direction of party policy became increasingly vociferous. While this irritated some and incensed the Cabinet, it confirmed the fact of his support among the rank and file and their mounting discontent with the Prime Minister and Labour leader, Ramsey Macdonald. At this time Macdonald was already a sick man and Mosley seemed to be everything that he was not; charismatic, energetic, eloquent and swift of thought and purpose.

In April, Mosley decided to leave Labour and establish a new party, but his close political allies persuaded him that his grass–roots support would not follow him.[27] He decided to bide his time and in the event, did not have to wait long. 'The Economy Committee on National Expenditure', chaired by Sir George May issued the 'May Report' in July 1931. It immediately precipitated a political crisis from its conclusion that by 1932 the country would be running a deficit of £60 Million.[28] Its recommendation was trenchant cuts in the budget. It was the final nail in the coffin of the Labour government as the May Report split the cabinet. Macdonald resigned as Prime Minister the following day and a Conservative–Liberal emergency government under Stanley Baldwin took office on the 27th August 1931. Less than a fortnight later, Macdonald had also resigned as party leader. The competition for his replacement

---

[26] In OTL, under Labour's block vote system, it was defeated 1,046,000 for, to 1,251,000 against. In TTL Mosley's greater authority and status in the Party make the vote closer.

[27] In OTL Mosley founded the imaginatively named "New Party" at this time. In TTL he thinks he has a better chance of gaining power by staying with Labour.

[28] In OTL it was £120 million, Churchill's decision to keep the pound 'off gold' greatly improves, but does not entirely remedy the situation.

was between Mosley, championing a radical change of policy and Arthur Henderson, a veteran of Labour's establishment. Mosley won.

The Coalition government was financially orthodox and when parliament reconvened, it announced its intention to return to the Gold Standard which the pound sterling had left during the Great War. Mosley attacked this as 'muddled thinking' and in the following months he used his position as Leader of the Opposition to make searing attacks on government policy. He presented the new prime minister, Stanley Baldwin, and the members of his cabinet, as out of touch and hide-bound. In other words, he did to them exactly what he had done to Ramsey Macdonald and the Labour leadership.

Mosley's impassioned rhetoric and lucid explanation of Labour's new policies struck a chord in the country as a whole. His reception at the Labour party conference in early October was ecstatic and even as Labour met in Scarborough, the government was in the process of deciding to call an election. Baldwin was convinced that his handling of the budget crisis meant that the Conservatives could attain an overall majority. The Liberal Party was split into three factions at this time, Labour had just crashed out of office and he didn't believe Mosley was a credible candidate. On 5th October, he called the election.

In the campaign, the Conservatives attacked Labour as ineffectual and 'Bolshevic'. Mosley himself was characterised as a disingenuous poseur; but the negativity of the Tory campaign stood in stark contrast to Labour's message of revitalisation. Mosley, an accomplished speaker, seemed to embody it. He toured the hustings tirelessly, his vigour galvanised the Labour Party and his message of renewing the country was compelling. However, many Labour supporters were aware that he was changing the party's direction, philosophy and outlook and were uncomfortable with Mosley himself. The result of the election was a Conservative victory but without an overall majority. The results were as follows:

Conservative: 289 (+29)

Labour: 249 (–38)
Liberal: 33 (–26)
Liberal National: 35 (+35)
Independent Liberal: 4 (+4)
Others: 5 [29]

With the exception of Sir John Simon's Liberal Nationals and David Lloyd George's Independent Liberals, all the parties were disappointed by the results. Stanley Baldwin found himself in a situation much the same as before the election, in that he was still compelled to maintain a coalition with the Liberals. The protectionist lobby within his own party was becoming increasingly vocal, while their coalition partners were staunch advocates of free trade. Consequently he had to accept that his government was more fragile than ever. [30] By contrast, Labour's position was a strong one. As the Opposition they could afford to wait for Baldwin's Government to falter, a task made simpler by Labour's backing of Imperial preference. The divisions within the coalition were so deep that they had the potential to bring it down.

On the 14th of December the news of Winston Churchill's death at the age of 57 in a traffic accident in New York reached the UK. [31] In the House of Commons, mourning was led by Sir Archibald Sinclair, the Secretary of State for Scotland and a rising star of the Liberal Party. He had been a personal friend of Churchill's and served with him on the Western Front in the Great War. Obituaries for the former Chancellor and First Lord

---

[29] In OTL the 1931 election was a Conservative landslide and a Labour rout. The Labour vote was split (Macdonald ran with National Labour, a separate party from Labour) and election pacts designed to keep Labour out of office were rife.

[30] In OTL there was also disagreement within the National Government on the question of trade protection, but the Liberal advocates of free trade were vastly outnumbered by the enormous intake of new Tory MPs. Here, the coalition cannot endure without them.

[31] In OTL Churchill was merely injured.

of the Admiralty dwelt regretfully on a career that had failed to live up to its early promise, but all mentioned his bold, but controversial decision to keep the pound sterling off the Gold Standard in 1925. [32]

From The Edinburgh Times *3rd January 1932*

Clementine Churchill looked drawn and pale today as she attended the inquiry in New York into the death of her husband, the late Winston Churchill M.P.

Mrs Churchill was dressed entirely in black and showed dignity and poise while answering questions on the accident which took the life of her husband on 13th December last year. Most noticeable about the proceedings was Mrs Churchill's refusal to attach any blame to the driver of the car, Mr. Mario Contasino, an unemployed truck driver from Yonkers.

In contrast to Mrs Churchill's calm demeanour, Mr. Contasino seemed at times distraught and at one point said "I never want to drive again." Nevertheless Mrs Churchill's insistence that her husband had left the taxi in which they had both been riding; "...in a hurry and while looking the wrong way." has ensured that Mr Contasino will be held blameless in

---

[32] In OTL he decided to get the pound back on the Gold Standard at the pre World War One rate. Churchill's decision, announced at the budget on 28th April, was to return to gold. It was greeted by cheers in the House of Commons but John Kenneth Galbraith has described it as; "Perhaps the most decisively damaging action involving money in modern time." Sir Robert Boothby said of it; "With the exception of the unilateral guarantee to Poland without Russian support, this was the most fatal step taken by the country." D. E Muggeridge in British Monetary Policy 1924 – 31 (1932) speculates that the balance of (visible) trade would have been better off by £80 million (1.8% of GDP) and 750,000 jobs might not have been lost. The return to gold was certainly one of the causes of the General Strike of 1926, contributed to the rise of trade's union militancy in Britain and was a factor in the start of the Great Depression. The main beneficiary of the UK's return to gold was the United States. Stabilisation under the gold standard offered American capital the chance to begin an economic invasion of Europe.

the matter of her husband's decease.   The inquiry recorded a
verdict of 'Death by Misadventure'.

*From 'British Economic Growth' by Simon Reece, Gloucester
University Press, 1985*

Winston Churchill's decision to keep the pound off the Gold
Standard was an extraordinary one. In Britain's heyday, sterling
and gold were interchangeable, and the one was not thought
inferior to the other. For a nation determined to recapture its
past economic eminence, the re-establishment of the
relationship between the pound and gold seemed a natural step.
No-one was more aware of this than Churchill. In his capacity
as Chancellor of the Exchequer, he was subjected to the
conventional wisdom by Montagu Norman (Governor of the
Bank of England) Austen Chamberlain (the Foreign Secretary),
Phillip Snowden (the Shadow Chancellor) and others who
believed a return to gold would stimulate international and
intra–Imperial trade.

British financiers, in both the Treasury and in the City, were
convinced that England's future prosperity could be assured only
if London were re-established as the financial centre of the
globe. This, they held, would be impossible until 'the pound can
look the dollar in the face.' Otto Niemeyer of the treasury asked
doubters: 'How are we, a great exporting and importing country,
to live with an exchange fluctuating with gold, when the United
States of America, Germany, Austria, Sweden, Holland,
Switzerland, the Dominions and Japan have a stable gold
exchange?' To bankers, re-establishing the credit of the pound
was worth any risk.

Yet Churchill was instinctively against going back onto the
Gold Standard despite the clamour and in reality their
arguments were weak and focused on tradition rather than
practicalities. Any precious metal or even a flourishing economy
can serve as well as gold; Niemeyer, Norman and Snowden were
living in the past, when the pound was regarded with awe in the
world's money markets. They assumed that the restoration of
sterling's equivalence with the dollar would re-establish Britain's

pre-war prosperity. None of them were aware that Britain's financial position after the Great War and shrunken export trade could no longer provide the surplus needed to re-establish London's financial ascendancy over the rest of the world. Churchill's instinct was supported by the arguments of Keynes who reasoned that by returning to gold at the old rate, Britain would accept a painful recession of prices and wages with accompanying stagnation and unemployment which would be a rich source of social stress.

The meeting that chiefly influenced the final decision took place on 17th March 1925 over dinner at Number 11 Downing Street. The case for returning to the Gold Standard was made by Otto Neimeyer of the Bank of England and the case against by John Maynard Keynes. Churchill was not as sure of his ground on most financial issues as he was on those of history or strategy and he could be bullied or at least cajoled on the subject. Keynes however could dominate any argument concerning finance or economics and was on top of his form. He was able to make a compelling case and sterling never again returned to gold. [33]

Churchill was jeered in the House of commons when he made the announcement but launched into a typically fiery oration where he overcame the booing with speech harking back to the hard years after Waterloo. At that time governments had done what had to be done, while building the Empire. Churchill finished by proclaiming that a flourishing economy was a better buttress for British prestige than sacrificing sound fiscal policy by cleaving to a symbolic gesture in defiance of common sense and British interests.

But what would have been the consequences of a return to gold? The pre-war exchange rate was 123.27 grains of fine gold and \$4.87 to the pound Sterling. In 1920, the pound had fallen to as low as \$3.40 in gold-based dollars. Though it had since risen and had continued to rise, the pre-war gold content and dollar exchange rates were far too high and in consequence British prices would be far too high. At the pre-war parity – if it

---

[33] In OTL Keynes was not on form and failed to make convince those present, he may even have been ill.

had been again adopted in 1925 anyone who had gold or dollars would have been able to do better by exchanging them for the money of one of Britain's competitors and buying their goods. Exports were essential to Britain and at the pre-war exchange rate British coal, textiles and other manufactured goods would only become competitive if their prices were to fall by 10 per cent. This in turn would mean a cut in wages to keep British goods competitive and unemployment would remain high.

As it was, the unemployment rate among insured workers rose from 11% in 1925 to 12% in 1926 and reached as high as 17.5% in 1932. [34] Churchill, in his capacity as Chancellor calculated that each unemployed person in Britain cost the exchequer roughly £150 per annum, £50 in doles and £100 in lost revenue.

We may also speculate that had the powerful British economy been encumbered by the pressure to keep the value of the pound at its pre-war parity, the effect might have been to deepen and lengthen the recession that overtook the world in 1930 and was preceded by the Wall Street crash. [35]

---

[34] In OTL it went from 11% to 12.5% in 1926 and to a catastrophic 22.5% in 1932.

[35] The world recession will be shorter and less deep in TTL, particularly for the UK.

CHAPTER 6: MONDAY 3rd JUNE 1940

When the reserve tank runs dry as well, the engine coughs twice and the needle on the rev counter flickers before it falls below zero. He feels the drop in speed and the abrupt change of pitch as the nose of the aircraft sags towards the sea. The cockpit is suddenly silent and one blade of the stopped propeller sticks directly upwards above the cowling, dividing his view in half. He is about four nautical miles from his ship, the aircraft carrier HMS *Courageous* and has perhaps three thousand feet between the belly of the aeroplane and the white tipped waves beneath.

He pushes the stick forward to pick up momentum. The aircraft, empty of fuel and ammunition, feels light and playful, as if it were skittering and slipping through the air. He must judge his speed and altitude with care, he has just enough of both, but only just. Each time he puts the aircraft into a shallow dive to keep its air speed up he loses precious height, but if he flies straight and level his speed bleeds away until it teeters at the threshold of a stall. He thumbs the microphone button.

"Hello Goodwood, this is Haystack leader, can you slow down a bit, my engine's packed up."

It is ironic to have the call sign 'Haystack Leader'. Just yesterday he had been a lowly sub-lieutenant, one of the junior pilots in 843 Squadron of the Royal Navy Air Arm. Now he is the senior officer in a unit that has only two surviving aircraft, but even as he forms the thought another comes to mock it 'Perhaps only one if you cock this up.'

As the slanting sunlight comes clear and brilliant through the low clouds, he sees the pitching deck of the ship and the white water foaming behind the hull. It is somehow beautiful, but there is no time to appreciate it now. He looks quickly at his watch – almost midnight, though at this time of year, in this northern latitude, the sun is still above the horizon. His wingman is landing on; the aircraft is almost stationary above the round down, poised like a sparrow over a bird table, then he sees it bounce and roll to a stop.

His hands move around the cockpit automatically. The prospect of a dead stick landing on a carrier in a rough sea is a frightening one, but he is too tired to be afraid. His body aches and his eyes feel sore and gritty. This, for him, is the second day of the war.

*

That morning Sub Lieutenant John Leighton had risen at 5:00 and gone to the hanger deck. The air had a dead, flat taste and the machine smell of oil and petrol clung to every surface. The artificers were readying his aircraft for flight. They had worked through the night, repairing damage it had sustained in the actions of the day before. The thin, red-eyed crew chief, Petty Officer Dent, was nursing a mug of coffee and a cheese sandwich.

"How's your breakfast Dent?"

"Tastes like feet sir."

"Excellent. What's for lunch?"

"Mutton again sir."

"Nothing wrong with a bit of mutton Dent."

"That's what that bloke on the *Rodney* said, sir."

"Which one?"

"The sheep shagger."

Leighton smiled and looked at his aircraft. "Is this contraption going to get me home?"

"You've made a will have you sir?"

"I've left everything to you chief."

"Will I be rich, sir?"

"It'll buy you a couple of pints and a packet of fags, if you're careful." They were still so new to war that they could joke about death. Dent paused for a moment chewing thoughtfully, then he said;

"I expect you'll be going after that German aircraft carrier again will you, sir?"

"Yes I expect so. Perhaps I'm the one who better be careful."

He walked around the aircraft slowly, checking it carefully, noting the patches over the bullet holes, squeezing his body through the narrow spaces between it and the other aeroplanes in the hanger. It was a Hawker Sea Hurricane, a single seat shipboard fighter with the code letter 'R' painted on the fuselage. Once he was done, the aircraft had gone up to the flight deck on the lift. He had taken off and climbed into formation with the five other fighters that had survived the previous day's encounters with the Germans. It was an absolutely clear day and the sea below them was a sheet of glass. As they reached fifteen thousand feet he fancied he could see the uneven shapes of the Lofoten Islands silhouetted against the sun's glare as it traversed the eastern horizon.

A thousand feet below and a mile ahead of them was the strike they were escorting. Six Fairey Albacore torpedo bombers and four Blackburn Skua dive bombers. These sixteen aircraft were all that remained of *Courageous'* air group, she had set sail with forty eight – twelve Albacores, twelve Skuas and twenty four Sea Hurricanes. The reconstruction she had just finished had equipped her to carry sixty, but the FAA was expanding less quickly than aircraft carriers were being commissioned. The situation was so grave that they were being deployed with half air groups and sometimes less.

His squadron had received their orders the day before the ship had sailed. They had landed on her for the first time as she left the Firth of Forth with two escorting destroyers. Both the Albacore and the Sea Hurricane were new aircraft, untested in combat and inclined to produce unwelcome surprises, but there was no time for the leisurely training of peace. The Sea Hurricane in particular had been rushed into service. It lacked the usual naval equipment, being unable to use either the ship's catapults to take off or its arrester wires to land. It didn't even have folding wings for stowage, but in the air it was a huge leap forward in capability from the Hawker Nimrod biplanes the squadron had flown before.

The ship too was unfamiliar; it was so large and so complex that he was often lost. It seemed full of cold, echoing metal corridors that smelled of potatoes or fuel oil and rang with the shrill of boatswain's pipes. So complete had been her reconstruction that even men who had been on her before found her baffling.

Their task was to cover the evacuation of allied troops from Norway. On the morning of 2nd June they had rendezvoused with the French battleships *Martel* and *Charlemagne* and the cruiser *Algerie*. The mood on *Courageous* was cheerful, resolute and tense. *Glorious*, another British carrier, was already patrolling fifty nautical miles to the south. They ate their meals in a hurry, tensely waiting for the call to action. He had found it hard to sit quietly in the stuffy ready room, harder still to listen to the chaplain who came and gave them communion as it was Sunday. By 08:00 the tension had driven him from the chair and he had gone for a walk on the flight deck.

Lieutenant Commander Higgins, the ship's Commander (Flying) and Surgeon Commander O'Rourke, the ship's senior physician, stood near the port aft guns. They watched three biplanes flying quite slowly towards them over the water. The aircraft were about two miles away to the north. As Leighton walked over to them Higgins was saying; "They must be Albacores, but from where? *Glorious* is south of us…"

O'Rourke interrupted him, "They look remarkably Germanic to me, I think they're Fiesler 167 torpedo bombers."

"No, No." replied Higgins, "Those are definitely Albacores – there's been no alarm."

"I don't think so…"

"My dear chap, there is no doubt about it, those are…" but his words were drowned by the sudden crash of the destroyer *Icarus'* guns. She had been keeping station on *Courageous'* port side; now she leaped forward, spray exploding from her pitching bows as they bit deep into the sea and across the water the sound of her Klaxon rang out as she opened fire. The black shapes of torpedoes fell from beneath the approaching aircraft and machine guns in their wings opened up to send bullets ricocheting across *Courageous'* flight deck in showers of sparks. The three men threw themselves flat. There was a thunderous explosion, then another and the aircraft roared above them, so close Leighton was afraid to lift his head though he saw the black crosses painted on the light blue of their wings. As he leapt to his feet and ran for the catwalk around the flight deck he saw the shattered *Icarus* falling behind the stern of the carrier. She was staggering beneath two towering columns of water that slowly fell back onto her decks and her hull was breaking in two. Her bow was listing hard to starboard and turning into *Courageous'* wake, but her engines were still racing, driving the stern forward, jack–knifing the hull as the ship broke in half at the ragged hole where the torpedoes had gutted her. Leighton winced at the horrible shriek of tearing metal and he realised that had *Icarus* not taken those two torpedoes they would have struck *Courageous*.

As he jumped down off the flight deck and on to the catwalk, he landed next to Higgins and O'Rourke, Higgins was shaking his head in disbelief.

Quietly O'Rourke said; "Albacores?"

*

"Haystack leader, this is Goodwood, we are slowing to twelve knots, you've got about forty-five knots wind speed coming over the flight deck, do you want to ditch?"

"No thanks Goodwood I'll bring her in. Tell the deck crew to take cover; oh, and tell the gunners not to shoot at me would you."

"Roger Haystack Leader and good luck."

He blinks and shakes his head to banish the weariness that seems to want to pull him down to the cockpit floor. As he pushes back the canopy the roar and buffet of the slipstream fills his senses. He is close now and changes the trim again, adjusting for the reduction in the carrier's pace. He lets the nose of the aircraft drop a little to gain momentum and pushes the goggles down onto his face.

*

They had launched two fighters, but the Fiesler 167s had made a clean getaway. The other destroyer stopped to pick up *Icarus'* survivors while *Courageous* was suddenly abuzz with frantic activity as they readied their first strike. The German aircraft carrier *Graf Zeppelin* had somehow slipped through the allied ships and was operating to their north. By 09:30 they had launched eleven Albacores (one went unserviceable as she warmed up), all twelve of the Skuas and the twelve Sea Hurricanes of 843 Squadron.

The strike searched to the north for three hours but found nothing but empty sea. When they returned, feeling let-down, they could see the disappointment on the faces of the deck crew as they landed with the tape still covering their gun ports.

Clouds came up during the afternoon, the sea grew bigger and the ship drove through sudden squalls and patches of rain. They were right in the middle of one when the alarm sounded. *Courageous* had turned away from the rest of the squadron and into the wind to launch her aircraft when the squall engulfed them. As Leighton ran from the ready room in the base of the island superstructure across the wet slippery deck, he could see the French ships in clear weather three miles away on their port quarter. Water spouts reared up as bombs burst around them, he could see the tiny shapes of aircraft above them and the sudden glint of sunlight on wings.

He leaped into one of the six Sea Hurricanes ranged on deck, their engines kept warm by being run every twenty minutes thundered in to life. The first two took off straight into the teeth of the gale, then the next two, one after the other. Now it was his turn and the wind was so fierce that the tail came up as soon as he opened the throttle and she was clear of the flight deck and climbing before he had time to realise that he could barely see through the rain lashed windscreen.

He pulled the aircraft into an ascending starboard turn that bought him back across *Courageous'* wake. The radio was dead and the other Sea Hurricanes nowhere in sight, but suddenly he was in sunlight and the slipstream was blowing the water droplets off the cockpit canopy. Ahead and below him, two of the French ships were heeling in circles while the third was stopped and down by the bows in a spreading patch of oil.

Even as he realised that the damaged ship was the *Algerie*, he heard a sound like a handful of stones thrown hard against a tin roof and felt the tug as bullets hit his aircraft's wings and tail. He winced, as instinctively he pulled the stick back and to the left and his head snapped around to look astern.

So close it seemed as if he could almost touch it, a Messerschmitt 109T fighter was right on his tail, following him into the turn, gun flashes rippling from wings and fuselage. As he fought down the tide of panic that clutched at his throat his mind groped for what the intelligence officer had told them about the 109T. 'Don't try and turn with her. Those extended wingtips will make her a good turner at all attitudes, but they will also make her a poor roller.'

He snap rolled the Sea Hurricane onto its back and sent it into an inverted dive. The '109 tried to follow, but wasn't quick enough and as the Sea Hurricane corkscrewed away the German pilot half rolled back in the opposite direction and started to climb. As Leighton came out of the roll he saw why. Two Sea Hurricanes were on the '109s tail, but there was no time to see the results of their attack. He was at a thousand feet and Ack-Ack was bursting around him. He felt a sudden annoyance. Why were they shooting at him? He noticed that two of the French ships seemed to be stopped now and as he started to climb he saw the scuttling shapes of two Fiesler 167s low off his port wingtip heading in the opposite direction. He turned into them, hoping to attack from their port quarter but he didn't have enough speed and found himself closing from astern. Their rear guns sparkled and tracer arched towards him. He selected one of them, fired a long burst and the water ahead of his target churned with bullet splashes but he saw no hits.

He pulled the aircraft into a climbing turn to renew the attack, but the Fieslers were climbing too and disappeared into low clouds. He gained altitude and looked around. Two of the French ships were definitely in trouble. *Algerie* had lost her bows from forward of 'A' turret and was stopped and wallowing. One of the battleships was also stopped and had developed a list to starboard, a destroyer was closing, but he could not concentrate on the scene below him. His eyes swept the sky in every direction and he was suddenly conscious of his racing heartbeat and his hands clammy inside his gloves. He was flying alone in the empty air. He climbed to five thousand feet and the ships were like toys below him, one of them looked squarer than the rest – *Courageous*.

After landing, he learned that all three of the French ships had sustained damage and would have to withdraw. *Martel* could only make ten knots, *Algerie* barely seven. She had taken two torpedoes almost simultaneously; they had struck in the same place as well, blowing off her bows. The ship should survive, but her speed and ability to manoeuvre were gone. *Martel* had taken three torpedoes all on the starboard side. Her list had been corrected by counter flooding, but she was low in the water and would have to be repaired before she could re-join the fight. All three of the French ships had suffered bomb hits but none of the bombs had been armour piercing so they were largely ineffective. However, *Charlemagne* had been struck by one on the bridge at the base of her main director and the blast had rendered it useless.

As the French ships limped westward at their best speed, *Courageous* took up station to their north, zigzagging to throw off submarine attack. Twice more that day they sent out strikes. The first, in late afternoon, failed to make contact; the second, in the evening, went without 843 Squadron who were tasked with standing patrols above the damaged ships. It was nearly 11:00 when they returned. Leighton was dozing in his flying gear in the ready room when the thud of the first aircraft landing on woke him. He ran out onto the flight deck as the crew pushed the Albacore forward to clear it for the next.

This time they had found the *Graf Zeppelin*, had hit her with at least two bombs and a torpedo and were certain that she must be sinking; they reckoned they might have sunk her escorting destroyer as well. The air crews were euphoric, though their losses to the German ack-ack and fighters had been heavy. Their jubilation was infectious, he had gone to bed elated and risen in a mood that bordered on the joyful.

Sending all sixteen of *Courageous'* surviving aircraft out on the strike was a risk, but Vice Admiral Slatter, who was in command of the British ships, was prepared to believe that *Graf Zeppelin* might be too heavily damaged to launch a strike of her own. They searched until their fuel ran low but found nothing and wondered if the German carrier had sunk already.

When they returned to their own ship they were greeted by ack-ack fire from the nervous gunners and were horrified to see the black scars of two bomb hits on her deck. Each time one of them tried to land, the ship fired on them. When Commander Higgins finally managed to get his Albacore down on the fourth attempt, he jumped out almost before it came to rest, stormed across to one of the midships pom–pom gun mountings, grabbed the Lieutenant in charge by the throat and almost throttled him.

The ship had been attacked by six Junkers 87C 'Stukas' from the German carrier. Neither of the hits had penetrated *Courageous'* new armoured deck. Again, the bombs had not been armour piercing, so they had only left dents, scorched paintwork and a severed arrestor wire. Two of the Stukas had been seen to crash.

As soon as they landed, the flight deck crew began the task of refuelling the aircraft. They were going straight back out. In the night they had been joined by the cruiser *Bristol* and she had launched one of her Walrus spotter planes to chase after the retreating Stukas. The Walrus hadn't been able to keep up, but had carried on the same course and had found the German carrier to the east between them and the Norwegian coast. She was hurrying southwards in a bold attempt to slip home unnoticed. The pilot of the Walrus had signalled that he was under attack, then they had lost contact and could only assume that he had been shot down, but he had given a position that put the *Graf Zeppelin* a hundred and seventy miles to the south east of them.

They took off and flew below heavy cloud that had rolled in from the north. They found the German carrier moving slowly on the dark ocean, launching her fighters, while a single escorting destroyer kept station ahead of her. The Albacores manoeuvred into position as the Skua dive bombers attacked. One of their bombs hit her, blowing the aft lift bodily into the air and sending a taxiing '109 careening over the side. Four of the German fighters had managed to launch and were clawing for altitude when Leighton heard 'Tally Ho!' over the radio and the Sea Hurricanes peeled off one by one as each pilot rammed the throttle forward and dived into the attack.

His speed was touching three hundred and fifty knots as he singled out a German fighter and fired a long burst from eight hundred yards. The whole aircraft juddered with the recoil of the guns, but he missed and the Messerschmitt jinked to port and rolled into a shallow dive. Leighton pulled the nose of his aircraft up sharply, his vision turning to grey at the edges as the G forces pushed him down into his seat, but he still had so much momentum that he was easily overhauling the '109. He fired again, this time from four hundred yards, but the German anticipated his shot and side slipped.

The '109 flicked into a starboard bank hoping to entice him into a turning fight and he took the bait because he had enough velocity to stand the Sea Hurricane on a wingtip and turn inside the slower moving German. Now he was practically on top of the enemy aircraft and it seemed to fill the whole windscreen. He pressed the firing button and saw his bullets shred the aircraft's tail, slam into the fuselage and throw chunks of metal outward. Suddenly smoke was pouring from the engine and he could see the stroboscopic effect as the '109s propeller slowed.

He eased the throttle back and pushed the stick over to the left. The Sea Hurricane straightened and he watched the stricken Messerschmitt roll slowly onto its back as fire streamed from its underbelly. He saw it hit the sea, saw pieces of it go spinning in all directions. He felt a sudden heady exultation that overwhelmed him for a moment until it was crowded from his mind by a wave of nausea as the realisation struck him that he had just killed another human being.

He dragged his eyes away from the patch of disturbed water where the '109 had gone in and as he climbed he looked around. The air was full of the black smudges of ack-ack and there, about three miles away, was the *Graf Zeppelin*. She was stopped and settling. Tongues of flame licked upward through her after lift well and smoke poured out of her superstructure. Even as he watched a great column of water rose from her port side as a torpedo found her. She was dying, but her shroud was a sparkling web of tracer and bursting shells setting light to the dark cloudy sky, lacing it with a mesh of fire.

The crew of *Courageous* were lining the catwalk and cheering as they landed, but the day was far from over. Only eleven aircraft came back; three Albacores, four Sea Hurricanes and four Skuas. They kept two Skuas and two Sea Hurricanes on standing patrol and the rest ready to scramble. They scrambled five times that afternoon. German snoopers came over in ones and twos and then a full size raid of twenty Junkers 88s bombing from altitude, too high for accurate aiming and too quick for the British fighters to catch.

So often did *Courageous* have to turn into the wind to launch or recover her dwindling air group that she became detached from the rest of the squadron. At 19:00 that evening they received the terrible news that *Algerie* and *Martel* had been torpedoed by a submarine and sunk. It fell like a blow, bursting the bubble of elation that had borne them up after the events of the morning.

Two more Sea Hurricanes were lost, one to defensive fire from a German Focke-Wulf 200 patrol aircraft, another because her engine failed as she was launched. Neither pilot was recovered. At 23:15, after patrolling for three hours, Leighton and his wingman bought their fighters back to land for what they thought must be the last time that day. The ship was scurrying for home, but he had not even undone his straps when the order came to scramble again.

It was a Heinkel 111 bomber this time. It broke away almost as soon as the Sea Hurricanes launched, but they gave chase at full power, climbing to an attacking position behind and underneath it. Leighton fired a long burst at six hundred yards and missed. His wingman closed to four hundred yards and also let go a long burst, also to no effect. The Heinkel 111 began to jink and sideslip to throw off their aim, they fired again and again, expending all their ammunition and even saw bullets strike the bomber, but it flew on in spite of them. Disgusted they turned for home and it was only then he realised that he was practically out of fuel.

*

The aircraft is gliding fairly comfortably, though the weight of the now useless engine tends to pull the nose downward and he needs to give it a little stick to keep the port wing up. There is a jagged hole in the dragging wing close in by the root, the '111 must have returned fire. He is losing height at four hundred feet per minute, but *Courageous'* deck is very close. He looks out over the right side of the cockpit and drops flaps and undercarriage just as he loses sight of the edge of the flight deck beneath his starboard wing. The ship is rushing up at him; he waits a second, then pulls the stick into his stomach to lift the aircraft's nose. He feels it lurch downwards as he stalls, the Sea Hurricane slams heavily into the flight deck and rolls forward until the force of the wind coming over the bow brings it to a stop nearly level with the island superstructure. As the crew push the aircraft towards the forward lift, be clambers down onto the wing and half falls onto the deck. They help him up with friendly words and slaps on the back, his knees have turned to jelly and the wind is tearing across from the bows sending splinters of spray into his face. He walks to the door into the island, where Lieutenant Commander Higgins is waiting for him, smiling. He says: "Well after that landing I don't know if I should make you fill out Form A 25 or not." Leighton is so weary that he can only manage the faintest of grins at this joke. A 25 is the crash form.

He cuts through the almost empty hanger to reach his cabin, his feet like lead on the companionway steps, for some reason he wants to look at his aircraft. It has already been struck down into the hanger and the fitters are beginning to work on her damage, rearm and refuel her. Petty Officer Dent is looking at the hole in her wing root.

"Another job I'm afraid chief."

"Never mind sir, at least she bought you home."

"Yes, yes she did." He pauses thoughtfully for a moment then goes below to his stuffy cabin, he takes off his 'Mae West' life jacket and his flying boots, lies down in his clothes and does not wake for eleven hours.

CHAPTER 7: THE BRITISH GENERAL ELECTION OF 1932

From 'A Concise History of British Politics' by Tom Shaed, Gloucester University Press, 2007

Perhaps inevitably, it was the issue of economic protection that finished Baldwin's government. The coalition collapsed in June after a series of by elections bought the tariff issue to the forefront of the public consciousness. It was impelled there by the newspapers. Lord Beaverbrook, the Canadian born owner of the Daily Express and The Evening Standard had cooled towards Baldwin and, despite his misgivings about the Left of the Labour Party, had formed a positive opinion of Mosley. He particularly liked the prime minister's support of economic 'insulation' within the Empire.

Beaverbrook had met Mosley in May and the newspaper tycoon's reservations about the Labour Party were ameliorated. Like many within the party itself, he realised that Moseley had completely changed its direction. Mosley too had been compelled to change an opinion after the meeting with Beaverbrook. Where before he had regarded the press with suspicion, he now realised that he had prospective allies in Fleet Street. Later in the month he met with Lord Rothermere, owner of the Daily Mail. Although the two men didn't get on well personally, Rothermere found Mosley's appreciation of the Empire very much in tune with his own and there was a pronounced change in the way the Labour Party was represented in British journalism. [36] Previously it had been seen as a party close to the lunatic fringe, now it was made to look main-stream.

The election campaign of 1932 was brief and rancorous, but it proved decisive; economic protection was its main issue. The two largest parties in the house, Labour and the Conservatives, both understood that an absolute majority was crucial for the

---

[36] In OTL Rothermere endorsed Mosley's British Union of Fascists in 1934.

survival of any new administration the election might bring about. Baldwin, freed from his coalition with the Liberals, promoted a policy of Imperial Preference, but his previous stance had damaged his reputation in the eyes of the protectionists and none of the factions within his party could be said to trust him.

Mosley relished another campaign. His unremitting vitality exhausted his assistants, and on the hustings he continued to stress the need for a clean break with the past and the revitalisation of the British state. His message resonated with working-class Tories who supported protection; but in the end it was their discord over free trade that propelled the swing away from the Conservatives and Liberals and saw the first majority Labour government take power. Mosley's rallying cries of patriotism, economic 'insulation' and social reform had paid off. The results were as follows:

Labour: 317 (+68)
Conservative: 245 (−44)
Liberal: 22 (−11)
National Liberal: 18 (−17)
Independent Liberal: 1 (−3)
Others: 12 (+7)

*

In its first year in office, the Labour Government increased taxes, set in motion policies that would encourage the City of London's financiers to invest more in Britain and the Empire, and put in hand a range of public works. These included a long overdue modernisation of the UK telephone system, a substantial programme of motorway building and increased expenditure on the Armed Forces. The centre piece of economic policy, however, was signalled by the passage of the Import Duties Bill. This created new tariffs on imports and signalled Britain's new stance on the protection issue to the Dominions. It was timed to come into law immediately prior to the Empire Economic Conference to be held in Ottawa. The legislation sailed through parliament with little in the way of difficulty. It was impelled both by the general sense of crisis and a large degree of support from the Tory backbenches.

Mosley knew that the changes set out in the bill were not as far-reaching as his party desired and he stayed in London to oversee the formation of the new government while the Chancellor, Hugh Dalton, travelled to Ottawa in August. [37]

The negotiations were reasonably successful. Mosley visited the conference briefly a few days after its start and made a significant impact with the other Commonwealth leaders. The contrast with his predecessor was stark – and refreshing – but the dour Dalton certainly drove a harder bargain than they were expecting. Overall the result was fair and foreshadowed the much tighter trading bloc the Sterling area evolved into in the different circumstances of 1941 to 1945.

The tariff established at Ottawa protected British farmers from Dominion as well as foreign competition and Britain made roughly equal trade concessions to the Dominions compared to those she received in return. For the British, this safeguarded the value of exports to the Dominions (including Canada, which received the benefit of empire status without being a member of the Sterling bloc). These remained at roughly their 1925-29 level until 1939. In the same period, net imports as a whole fell sharply, while net imports from the Dominions rose slightly. Trade with India and the crown colonies experienced a similar trend. Exports from Britain to the Dominions rose by about 10%, whereas the concessions she made may have added 7% to her imports from the Dominions. Britain's balance of trade deficit with her empire widened slightly. The downside was that the UK had to give up some of the benefits of trade with other countries in the Sterling area that were not within the empire such as Argentina, Estonia and Denmark. Although the Imperial Free Trade Area desired by the British proved

---

[37] This TTL legislation will be close in spirit and intent to OTL's Import Duties Act. However it will be more comprehensive and will introduce higher tariffs. See Annex 3.

unattainable, the British negotiators made a deal that could be seen as a success for the Imperial ideal. [38]

From 'The British Empire from 1914 to 1948' by Ian Shaw, Longacre 2005

The Labour government elected in 1932 enjoyed a remarkably smooth run in its first months in office. The one hiccup in this period was the cancellation of the D'Arcy Concession by the government of Iran. This was announced by the Shah of Iran on 27th November 1932 and caused dismay in both the Foreign Office and the offices of the Anglo-Iranian Oil Company. Because of the recession, royalties paid by Anglo-Iranian to the Iranian Government had been falling and this bought to a head several matters that caused Iranian pride some offence. Too few Iranians were employed by the company in senior positions; oil was sold to the British Admiralty at a discounted rate; the Iranian Government were kept ignorant of the Company's accounts making their true profits unknowable. This last issue meant that the Iranian Government could neither confirm nor dismiss its suspicions concerning the methods by which profits and royalties were calculated. In short, Reza Shah believed that he was getting a raw deal.

The D'Arcy Oil Concession agreement stated clearly that Anglo-Iranian were supposed to pay Iran an annual royalty of

---

[38] In OTL the British settled for a much poorer deal making more generous trade concessions to the Dominions than they made to her while receiving fewer benefits in return. Exports to the Dominions fell in 1934–8 by 22% compared to 1925–9, a poor result for British exporters. Net imports from the Dominions actually rose from £183m to £189m in the same period. Trade with India and the crown colonies demonstrated a similar trend. Exports from Britain to India and the crown colonies declined by 44% in 1934–8 compared to 1925–9.

In foreign policy terms, Mosley is very much an Empire-centric figure, and the Empire is at the heart of his conception of Britain as a Great Power. His policies ITTL don't only support Imperial preference, but also the establishment of strong ties between Britain and the Dominions. See Annex 3 for an appraisal of what these changes might have meant to the British economy.

16% of the company's net profits. However, they did not include profits made by subsidiary companies owned by Anglo-Iranian, profits that the Shah believed he was entitled to a share of. Furthermore it was known that they paid almost twice as much to the British government in taxes.

None of this mattered to Britain's new Prime Minister, who saw the dispute not in terms of commerce, but as an opportunity to assert Britain's moral right on the world stage, announce his arrival in international diplomacy and bring a recalcitrant British puppet into line. Reza Shah had revoked Imperial Airways concession to fly in Persian airspace the previous year, giving it instead to Lufthansa. If one of Britain's client states could simply renege on its agreements with British companies, it was clearly damaging to British prestige and others might be tempted to follow suit. He was also livid at the ingratitude displayed by Reza Shah who had been installed on his throne by the British only 11 years previously. Unsurprisingly, he sent a gunboat. In fact he sent two; the cruiser HMS *Devonshire* and an aircraft carrier, HMS *Furious*.

The cruiser moored at the tiny British colony of Bushire which was the location of the British Persian Gulf Residency, an outpost of the Indian Raj that looked after British interests in the region. Meanwhile the carrier continued on up the Persian Gulf so that its aircraft could demonstrate British resolve by overflying the oil refinery at Abadan on 20th December. The following day, a flight of six Blackburn Ripon aircraft overflew Tehran dropping leaflets and flying low over the Shah's palace, a round trip of 850 miles that took eight hours. The implications were unmistakable.

Britain's ambassador in Tehran, Sir Reginald Hoare, acting on Mosley's instructions, went to see Shah Reza the following day. He gave the Shah to understand that while the British would consider a re-negotiation of the Concession it had to be realised that Anglo-Iranian invested millions of pounds in expanding its operation in Iran. Furthermore, even larger sums were spent in developing new sources of supply in Iran and in constructing pipelines, tankers, refineries and storage facilities throughout the world to market, process and distribute Iranian oil. In addition to this, Iranian security was guaranteed by the

British presence in the Gulf and in India. In short, Reza Shah was getting a bargain and had better conform to British expectations or face the consequences.

Suitably cowed, the Shah agreed and the concession was renegotiated the following year with terms slightly more favourable to Anglo-Iranian than before. The upturn in the world economy ensured that more oil was purchased and the revenues of the Iranian Government from oil were buoyed. The British hoped this might ameliorate any lingering annoyance from this rough treatment; however, unbeknown to the British, the Shah harboured significant resentments and began incremental improvements to Iran's ramshackle armed forces. [39]

This minor international crisis gave way to one of much greater significance in the spring of 1933. The newly elected National-Socialist government in Germany wrecked the Geneva disarmament conference with its assertion that it had decided to enlarge its military unless other countries were disarmed to the level set for Germany in the Treaty of Versailles. This was completely unacceptable to the French but the British saw it as an opportunity to press for general disarmament and consequently endorsed the German proposal. [40] This annoyed the French and was not the outcome the Germans were looking for. They pulled out of the talks in June and declined invitations to return.

From 'A Concise History of British Politics' by Tom Shaed, Gloucester University Press, 2007

It was realised immediately in Britain that the German attitude to disarmament, as demonstrated at the Geneva conference,

---

[39] In OTL, instead of taking any direct action, the British appealed to the League of Nations. The renegotiation resulted in slightly better terms for the Iranians but there was no show of force from the British government.

[40] The the reaction of the British government towards the German demand is consistent with Mosley's stance towards disarmament in OTL.

signalled a more aggressive approach to foreign relations from Berlin. There was also concern in Britain at the Mosley government's apparent weakness in the face of this more robust German policy. The Prime Minister was forced to realise that a political strategy that pursued disarmament would not work. It was not merely Germany that troubled him, both Japan and the Soviet Union were aggressive, acquisitive states whose territories were adjacent to those of the British Empire. From this flowed the conclusion that the British armed forces, which had declined in strength and effectiveness since the Great War, must now be built up again. This certainly went well with the programme of public works the government was pursuing. Increased spending on the military must inevitably lead to more employment, but the reaction of the pacifist element in the Labour Party was wholly negative. The new policy bought into sharp focus the fact that Mosley had radically changed the Party's direction.

The Labour left had always been fractious and cherished their image as being political outsiders and guardians of the Party's soul. They were as likely to attack the Labour leadership as they were to attack the Tories. They tried to trap Mosley with the disarmament issue, but the press and public were becoming progressively more alarmed by both the belligerent character of the new regime in Berlin and reports of Japanese aggression in the Far East.

Mosley met with Mussolini during the Austrian emergency of 1934 and helped draft the Three Power Statement of 17th February. In this France, Britain and Italy avowed their shared view that Austria should remain independent. This was directed at Germany and constituted a warning to Hitler not to interfere in the affairs of Austria.

From 'The Rule of the Waves' by Michael Fanshaw, Twelvemonth 1963

The Austrian emergency was over by the beginning of March 1934, but in April a new crisis arose when the London Naval Disarmament Conference collapsed. This had been talks designed to extend the limits on naval expansion set by the

Washington Treaty of 1922. They had convened at the height of the commotion in naval circles caused by the reconstruction of the Russian battleship *Frunze* (See Appendices) and her subsequent reclassification as a battle cruiser. In addition to this, there was the announcement of the construction of two new capital ships in Japan (one of which was subsequently cancelled) and the plans announced in Germany for the construction of a second 'Panzerschiff' (armoured ship), much larger than the first. Plans for the new construction of capital ships were also well in hand in France, Italy and (it was believed) the Soviet Union.

It was obvious that the world situation was becoming more dangerous. The British called the London Imperial Defence Conference to convene later in the year. Its purpose was to formulate an Empire policy to the rapidly changing world situation after the collapse of the Geneva Disarmament Conference and the London Naval Conference. There it was announced that in the opinion of the UK government, the prospects for war had become much more likely than they had previously appeared. This caused surprise and consternation among the delegates but after some debate there was general agreement that the rising power and latent expansionism of Germany, Japan, Italy and the Soviet Union were all real and immediate threats. The only dissenter was the delegation from India.

From 'The Mosley Years' by Andrew MacDonald, Little Day and Co. 1995

In April 1932 Harry St. John Bridger Philby, a former British colonial officer who had been dismissed for misconduct, arrived in London a hero after his crossing of the empty quarter of Arabia. Philby was a mercurial character whose dislike of the British government was already well known in Whitehall, though strangely the attitude of the British government to Philby was a mixture of tolerance and ambivalence. [41]

---

[41] As it was OTL.

Philby's views were a rag–bag of petty resentments and schoolboy politics and he had 'gone native' by adopting Arabian dress, customs and converting to Islam. Nevertheless he was known to be Ibn Saud's most trusted advisor and his influence over the ruler of most of the Arabian peninsular was considerable.

Mosley understood the potential advantages of securing the rights to the Saudi oil exploration concession for Britain then being sought by the British company Anglo-Persian Oil which represented British Petroleum and Shell. He was eager to close the deal and beat out the American company Standard Oil which was also showing a keen interest in it. Shortly after taking office on 3rd July 1932, he urged his Foreign Secretary, Harold Nicholson [42], to impress upon Andrew Ryan (the British Minister in Saudi Arabia) and Stephen Longrigg (the chief negotiator for Anglo-Persian) the importance of gaining the concession. It wasn't so much the possibility of finding oil that was significant to the Prime Minister; it was the progress of British interests and influence in the world. To Mosley the Saudi oil concession was a trophy and a way of sending a message to the international community. It was imperative that Britain did not lose out to another power – in this case the Americans – who were also in the hunt for it.

One of the ways Mosley changed UK politics was in his respect for strength and his willingness to use it to further his ends. Nevertheless, with Philby he decided to take a more subtle approach. He arranged a meeting with Philby at 10 Downing Street on 20th July 1932, ostensibly to congratulate him for his journey across the Empty Quarter and inform him that he had been awarded a KCSI (Knight Commander of the Order of the

---

[42] In OTL Harold Nicholson was a diplomat, author, diarist and politician. He was also the husband of the writer Vita Sackville-West and for a time one of Mosley's cronies. He joined Mosley's New Party in 1931 and edited the party newspaper 'Action' but ceased to support Mosley when he formed the British Union of Fascists in 1932. In OTL Nicolson did not enter the House of Commons until the 1935 election when he became the National Labour MP for Leicester West. He was one of the small number of MPs who voiced concerns over the threat of Fascism and supported rearmament.

Star Of India) in honour of the achievement. The meeting was necessarily brief and unbeknown to Mosley it came shortly after Philby had accepted a bribe from Standard Oil through Francis B. Loomis a former US Undersecretary of State. Loomis was representing Standard Oil's agency SoCal, and the bribe was to ensure that Philby acted on their behalf in the negotiations. [43]

Philby was impressed by Mosley. Mosley's re-born Labour Party seemed to hold out the promise of the kind of hard-edged Fabianism that Philby had embraced in his youth becoming the main force in the British political landscape. Better still, the new Prime Minister seemed determined to turn Britain into what today is known as a 'meritocracy' rather than a class-bound society based on privilege. Resentment of what Philby felt was his exclusion from that privilege was his overriding obsession in life and the justification for his betrayals.

Mosley does not mention the meeting in his memoirs and refused to be drawn when asked about it by journalists and biographers until his death in 1980. Philby describes the meeting in his diary as 'cordial'. Unusually, the meeting was in private so no official record exists of what was said, but it is known that Mosley offered Philby 'a high position' with the Foreign Office in the Middle East. He also promised to see that the Tamini affair, which had recently re-surfaced, be swept under the carpet, easing Philby's re-inclusion in the British Foreign Service. All this was conditional on Philby using his influence over Ibn Saud to secure the Saudi Oil concession for Britain. [44]

Philby left the UK on the 19th October 1932 with his wife Dora to drive back to Saudi Arabia through Europe. He was driving a car which he had bought with the bribe that SoCal had

---

[43] Just as he did OTL.

[44] In OTL, even as Philby was accepting the plaudits of The Royal Geographical Society, the Tamini affair (in which it was revealed that he had stolen secret Foreign Office files with the intention of undermining British policy in the Middle East) had come to light confirming the already serious doubts that existed regarding his loyalty. The theft was discovered in 1917 but, negligent though it seems, the affair was swept under the carpet to avoid a scandal.

paid him. The six weeks drive offered him ample time to consider his position and he must have weighed his options carefully.

On the one hand, the Americans were offering a good deal for his friend Ibn Saud, a way in which he could solve his considerable personal financial problems and a way he could thumb his nose at his political enemies in Britain by ensuring American success. His antipathy at this time was less with Britain than with individuals – later he became genuinely anti British.

On the other, the British were also offering a good deal for his friend Ibn Saud, also offering a cure for his financial problems and also offering a way that he could thumb his nose at his political enemies by being re-instated to the British Foreign Service.

The Philbys arrived in Jidda in mid-December and negotiations began in mid-February 1933. Philby's loyalty was to Ibn Saud and the various offers he had received were seen by him as a way to increase the bidding. In the end he did not want to return to British service. Philby always bit the hand that fed – if it were a British hand – and he worked unceasingly against British interests in the negotiations. These were concluded on the 8th May, the concession, the greatest commercial prize in the history of the world, went to the Americans.

When news of Standard Oil's success and Philby's part in it reached London, Mosley flew into a rage. He regarded Philby's actions as an affront and a deliberate insult, as well he might, and immediately began to think about revenge. Mosley's obsession with strength meant that he could not, in these circumstances, show weakness to the world or to his colleagues. He had to send a clear message and that message must be that you did not cross Oswald Mosley. There was also a deeply personal dimension to his anger. Mosley, the arch seducer, had tried to politically seduce Philby and been rejected. Now he reacted with all the fury of a jilted suitor.

The Tamini affair was bought back into the light and a thorough investigation of Philby's activities was ordered; in fact not just Philby was to be investigated, but every member of his family also. Mosley planned to do the political and social equivalent of burning Philby's crops and sowing his fields with salt. Word went out in the Foreign Office that the Prime Minister wanted any and all evidence that could be used against Philby to be found.

There was certainly no want of proof. Philby's animus for the government he served was well-known and little that was new came to light but, taken in sum, Philby's many misdemeanours amounted to a damning body of evidence. The case against him was sufficiently strong that a warrant was issued for his arrest on charges of espionage and treason. While Philby was in Saudi Arabia he of course enjoyed the personal protection of Ibn Saud, but the warrant meant that not only was he disgraced, but that he could not set foot in any British territory without risking arrest. Although Mosley was unable to 'see that blackguard Philby hanged' as he put it, he was utterly discredited and St John Philby never left Arabia until his death in 1960.

Philby's brother Tom, a nautical advisor to the government of India, came under investigation too, as did Philby's son Harold, an undergraduate at Trinity College, Cambridge, who was known to his friends as Kim. No blame could be attached to Tom, but the investigation of Kim had wide repercussions.

In addition to Mosley's desire for revenge against Philby senior, there was his desire to neutralise the far left of his own party and reduce the influence of Communism in Britain. Kim Philby might have been less thoroughly disgraced had not problems with Communists within the Labour Party been endemic. Labour's far left were always Mosley's strongest opponents and in attacking Communism in British society generally, the Prime Minister sought to address the specific problem of extremism in his own party.

The loss of the Saudi oil exploration concession did not, of course, leave Britain without oil. The vastly lucrative Iranian concession was safely in British hands as was part of the Iraqi concession. Oswald Mosley was to remember the importance of oil later in his career when crafting the Mosley Report, the committee of which he chaired in 1942.

From 'The Apostles Scandal' by Mark Halliday, Pantillera Publishing 2003

One incident from Mosley's first year in office illustrates his temperament and the profound changes he bought to British politics and British government. What has sometimes been characterised as 'Oswald Mosley's anti-Communist witch hunt' took place at a time of expanding Communist influence in British society and within Mosley's own Labour Party. The King and Country debate of 9th February 1933, in which the Oxford Union accepted the resolution: 'That this House will in no circumstances fight for its King and Country' by 275 votes to 153, had shaken patriotic confidence and it was easy to see the debate as a symptom of the influence of the far left.

Mosley, a decorated veteran of World War One, had thundered against the Oxford Union, declaring it 'Despicable, base and cowardly.' In 1933, in the wake of the loss of the Saudi Oil concession due to the activities of St. John Philby, the investigation by MI5 of Philby's son Kim (which Mosley had directly ordered to gather evidence against his father) revealed that he and his circle of friends were Communists. [45] Worse still, one of them, Donald Maclean, was about to enter the British Civil Service.

Because of this, Mosley issued a directive that no-one who had been found to have, or to have had Communist sympathies would be eligible for recruitment to any branch of the Civil Service. This edict was almost certainly designed to exclude not just Donald Maclean, but also Kim Philby, as it was known that Kim's parents hoped that he would make a career in the Foreign Office like his father before him.

This caused consternation within the Labour Party. It seemed unfair and arbitrary that people should be punished for 'youthful indiscretions', but Mosley did not relent. If the Prime Ministers initial motive was petty revenge on St. John Philby by getting at his son Kim, it was soon eclipsed by more pressing imperatives. Mosley wanted to neuter the power of Communism

---

[45] This was well known OTL also.

in his own party certainly, but in the Apostles Scandal he also saw a way to confront the establishment and consolidate his power. The academic world, which was initially broadly supportive of Mosley, was beginning to turn on him. To them, he was a thug and a brute; he had been educated at Sandhurst rather than one of the hallowed seats of learning at Oxbridge and he showed little in the way of respect for academia.

To Mosley the fight was a way to confirm his authority. If academia and the establishment didn't like it, then so much the better. Though a product of upper-class privilege, Mosley drew much of his support from the lower and middle class. In attacking the country's vested interests, he was not just championing the cause of his supporters; he was consolidating his own power.

Mosley used his friends in the press to break the scandal and stir it up. Lord Rothermere's Daily Mail, at the time an ardent supporter of Mosley and his policies, went public with the scandal in mid-August at the height of the 'silly season' (the summer recess of the UK parliament when newspaper circulation is low and papers are traditionally likely to publish stories that would not normally be broken). In many ways it was blown out of all proportion. The subjects of the scandal were callow and immature young people of limited abilities and uncertain prospects. Kim Philby was not even a member of The Apostles. [46]

As well as Kim Philby and Donald MacLean the men implicated by the scandal were: Guy Burgess – an alcoholic and indiscrete homosexual; Anthony Blunt, a fellow of Trinity College and also a homosexual; and Michael Whitney Straight, the son of an American publisher who had been Blunt's lover for a time.

The details were unpleasant and quickly stirred up anger and disgust in the public. The Apostles were presented by the press as a group of self-appointed know-it-alls who had come from a

---

[46] St John Philby, who met his son's circle of Cambridge friends including Burgess, MacLean and Blunt describes them in his diary as being 'Pretty second-rate'.

background of wealth and advantage, lived a hedonistic lifestyle and had turned on the society that nurtured them. They were 'Vipers in our Bosom' 'Ungrateful Prigs' and 'Bollinger Bolsheviks' to quote just some of the opprobrium heaped upon them.

The homosexuality of three of them also figured heavily. Homosexuality was then a criminal offence in the UK, and the salacious revelations that accompanied the political aspects of the scandal did nothing to decrease the popularity of the story.

The battle lines then, were drawn. It was Mosley versus academia and the establishment, two groups who were showing signs of turning against him. He relished it; it pitted him against some of the highest in the land.

Guy Burgess was the son of a Royal Navy officer; Maclean the son of a former cabinet minister (now deceased); Blunt was related to Elizabeth Bowes Lyon, the wife of the Duke of York who later became King George VI.

Along with the King and Country debate, Mosley presented the Apostles Scandal as more evidence that the universities were turning out 'worthless men'. At the Labour Party conference in the autumn of 1933 in his address to the delegates he said:

> 'The universities are breeding men without loyalty and without honour, as we in the Labour Party work to create a country where all may rise on the basis of merit rather than favour, where all may partake of the rewards of opportunity if they have earned them; these vested interests seek to hold back those not gifted by accidents of birth and furthermore they seek to undermine the very nation that nurtured them.' [47]

It was explosive stuff and in hindsight it was completely fair. Mosley was trying to create a meritocracy – a society where engineers and entrepreneurs could get the acknowledgement they deserved. He posed the question; 'Was academia still an asset to the Great Britain?' The academics, who had been uncertain about Mosley up to this point, now hated him. They

---

[47] Not a genuine quote.

accused him of being anti free-speech and anti free-thought. They branded Mosley's crusade as 'persecution', 'a pogrom' and 'a squalid attempt to muzzle conscience'.

The consequences of all this were far reaching. The scandal died down by Christmas and with it the debate. By early 1934, the Austrian Emergency completely eclipsed all other stories in the news. But Mosley had made a mark in British political circles and used the scandal to set out his agenda. Philby, Burgess, McLean, Blunt and Whitney Straight were just collateral damage in Mosley's crusade to consolidate his power by reducing that of academia and the establishment.

All of those implicated in the Apostle's Scandal were disgraced. Whitney Straight fled back to America; Antony Blunt went to live in France where he made a career in the art world. Kim Philby was in Austria when the scandal broke, he never returned to the UK. True to his beliefs perhaps, he died in Russia in 1942 while reporting on the fighting there for an American newspaper owned by Whitney Straight's family. Guy Burgess was murdered while drunk in an Illinois brothel by a jealous former lover in 1951.

MacLean drifted and did various jobs all the while protesting his innocence. But the story of the Apostles Scandal was to have a Coda. In 1943, because of the chaos in Russia, a defecting Soviet agent bought his way into Britain with the revelation that Mosley's 'persecution' was in fact of individuals who had been recruited by Soviet intelligence to become spies. He also revealed that the fifth member of the cabal was John Cairncross, a British civil servant, then working at Bletchley Park, the code breaking centre of British Intelligence.

Mosley, though no longer Prime Minister by this time, was utterly vindicated. Blunt, Burgess, Philby and Maclean as well as those who had supported them were completely discredited. Cairncross was thrown out of the civil service and both he and Maclean were tried for Treason. They were convicted and executed in 1944. The policy that no one tainted by an affiliation to Communism could serve in the British Civil Service was almost reversed in 1939. However, the unsavoury character of the Soviet regime in general and Stalin in particular; the Molotov-Ribbentrop pact (that saw Communist Russia align itself with fascist Germany) and the subsequent Soviet invasion of Poland in concert with the Nazis, made the reversal seem imprudent. [48]

---

[48] Kim Philby, Donald MacLean, Guy Burgess, Anthony Blunt and John Cairncross are the infamous 'Cambridge Five' spy ring. The Cambridge Five all worked for MI5 in OTL WW2 and ran the most successful penetration of the West's intelligence service by the Soviet Union. They passed atomic and other secrets to the Russians, it is estimated that they probably saved them five to ten years in atomic weapons development. In OTL Kim Philby died in 1988 in Moscow having defected in 1963. Donald MacLean died in Moscow in 1983 having defected in 1951, Guy Burgess also defected in 1951 and died in Moscow in 1963. Anthony Blunt stayed in England and became Master of the Queen's Pictures. He confessed in 1964 and was exposed publically in 1979. He died in London in 1983. John Cairncross made a full confession in 1963 but was never prosecuted. The confession was given in Cleveland, Ohio, and thus was not made within British jurisdiction or under Police caution so was ineligible in court. Cairncross moved to Rome and worked for the UN as a translator. In December 1979, a journalist named Barrie Penrose confronted him and he confessed again. His confession was corroborated by Oleg Gordievsky, a KGB defector but he was never prosecuted. He retired to the south of France and died of a stroke in 1995 at the age of 82.

CHAPTER 8: SUNDAY 8th SEPTEMBER 1935

The fetid heat of the Louisiana night hangs heavy around the walls and shutters of Our Lady of the Lake Hospital; the rhythmic sound of cricket's throb in the still air. Doctor Arthur Vidrine stands on a third floor balcony. One hand is pushed into the pocket of his white coat, the other holds a lit cigarette. He looks out into the blue darkness and in the distance the lights of Baton Rouge cast a yellow glow on the low clouds. Above his head, moths swirl like snowflakes round the light. He can hear the wavering buzz of their wings as he draws the last of the cigarette into his lungs, grinds the butt beneath his heel and exhales. There is no more time to be lost; he is going to have to operate. He turns and walks back into the sick room.

The patient is a forty-two year old man; he has been shot in the abdomen. Over the past hour his pulse rate has slowly risen while his blood pressure has fallen and fallen again, he is haemorrhaging internally and if the bleeding isn't stopped he is going to die. It is a simple prognosis and a simple decision, but what makes Vidrine hesitate is the fact that the patient is 'The Kingfish' – Senator Huey Long, the former Governor of Louisiana, one of the most powerful men in the state and an absolute crook.

He is conscious but growing weaker, lying in bed, his face is clammy, his breathing laboured and his skin ashen; he has the inward, preoccupied look of a dying animal. Vidrine smiles, it is a smile he does not feel, he is trying to look confident, Long looks up and his eyes are suddenly bright as he says, "Getting about time to operate is it Doc?"

Vidrine nods, "I'm afraid so Huey, I don't think we can wait any longer."

Long's eyes fall. "No word from Maes or Stone."

"I'm sorry Senator, no. Do you have any objections to my performing the operation?" Long looks crestfallen for a moment, then shakes his head.

"No, no." he murmurs weakly then closes his eyes; his voice is barely more than a whimper. "Dear God don't let me die, I have so much to do…" The doctor is about to turn away when

Long grabs at his arm and pulls himself upright in the bed. His grip has surprising strength and his eyes are suddenly ablaze, he is talking wildly, as though he sees something beyond the hospital walls. Instinctively the doctor tries to pull himself away as a nurse rushes over to ease Long back to a prone position, but the words seem to tumble from his mouth in a torrent as if he has no control over them and could not stop them if he tried.

"I can see the people out there doc, America's poor, I can see their faces looking to me, they need me doc, they need me, they want to give *me* the power, they want to give *me* the power so I can help them..."

Long's voice trails off, he is gasping for breath, Vidrine is shocked at this outburst, "Senator, you've got to try and relax..."

But the desperately sick man is merely gathering strength for a new verbal onslaught "...the sharecroppers in the cotton fields of the South, the debt–ridden farmers of the Great Plains, the unemployed factory workers tramping the streets of the North East, small businessmen all over the country pushed to the wall, pathetic elderly couples in countless towns and villages whose lifesavings disappeared when the banks collapsed, the fresh-faced young, eager to get an education, they look to me, they trust me, it's them, them – they are the ones who will give me the power..."

Abruptly he lets go and falls back onto the pillow as if spent. Vidrine eases the Senator's hand from his arm and quickly begins to prepare. He tells the nurse to call an anaesthetist, a pathologist and to begin taking blood tests of the various people in the room for a transfusion should one become necessary.

To his dismay, he finds that the operating theatre is filled with people. Associates, supporters and employees of the Senator throng the walls and the crowd stretches out into the hall. Vidrine wants to shoo them away and remarks to one of the nurses; "Here's a man maybe dying and the room is full of politicians." But in the end he decides the commotion that will accompany the act of making them leave will delay the operation still further and he lets them stay. He has to ask several of them to put out cigarettes.

As he begins, he glances at the clock on the wall. The cigarette smoke hangs around its face. The time is 11:20. The room is absolutely still as the mob of Huey Long's cronies falls silent, craning their necks to see. There are two wounds, one beneath the ribs on the right side, the second in the lower back near the spine. Working swiftly, Vidrine opens the abdomen looking for damage to the internal organs, to his relief there seems to be little. The liver, gall bladder, and stomach are unharmed but there are two perforations in the colon, the bullet has gone through one fold and then another. To his surprise there seems to be only a small amount of blood in the abdominal cavity and a blood clot in the small intestine. He sutures the wounds in the colon then hesitates.

Something is wrong. The operation has lasted about forty minutes: he has found the wound, repaired the damage and he should be closing the abdomen but his hands remain still. There is too little evidence of bleeding to explain the symptoms. What has he missed? Seeing him pause the anaesthetist looks up.

"Dr. Vidrine?" He shakes his head helplessly, he just cannot think. A nurse stands at his elbow, there is urgency in her stance.

"Yes, what is it?"

"Dr. Maes has arrived and has asked if he may assist you." Vidrine is uncertain for a moment and then says; "Yes, yes of course. Ask him to come in."

Dr. Urban Maes walks quickly to the operating table adjusting his surgical gloves while a nurse running behind him ties the cords of his gown. His eyes above the mask are intent; he barely glances at Huey's cronies. In a low voice he questions Vidrine and looks up sharply when he learns that Vidrine has not catheterized the bladder. Quickly he inserts a catheter to find the bladder filled with blood: a renal duct to the kidney has been hit by the bullet. Maes works quickly and precisely to repair the duct. Vidrine can only look on, his gloved, bloodied hands held upwards before him, a gesture of helplessness.

He stands by as Maes closes the abdomen. The two physicians wash their hands side by side in the preparatory room. Maes glances towards the younger man, whose professional pride is hurt. He can see in the darkness of his frown and the obsessive way he runs the soap through his fingers again and again that he is angry with himself for missing so important a detail.

As Maes dries his hands he says; "You did good work here today, Doctor. If you hadn't begun the procedure when you did, Senator Long might have been too far gone to save."

Vidrine shakes his head, his voice is flat, an exhausted monotone. "I missed it. It was staring me in the face and I missed it. If you hadn't arrived when you did and checked his bladder…" His words tail off as he finishes drying his hands.

Maes' voice is conciliatory, forgiving. "You've had a difficult day Doctor. They tell me you witnessed the assassination attempt?"

"I don't know as you can say I witnessed it. I was there alright, but when the shooting started I just hit the floor…" again his voice trails off, again Maes is kind,

"But you administered first aid, did you not? Come now Arthur, don't be so hard on yourself. The Senator has a good chance of recovery and much of the credit for that must rest with you. Well done Doctor." Maes reaches out a hand. Vidrine hesitates a moment then takes it. The men's eyes meet for a second as Maes turns to leave. "Doctor Maes."

He turns back. "Yes Doctor?"

"Thank you." Maes smiles and walks away. [49]

---

[49] In OTL, Huey Long did not survive the assassination attempt. Vidrine knew from the first that an operation would be necessary, but he had hoped to delay it until Dr. Urban Maes and Dr. Russell Stone, more experienced surgeons than he, could arrive from New Orleans. Long had asked for these two as well as Dr. E.L. Sanderson to be sent for and his associates had chartered an aeroplane to bring them. Maes decided that he could reach Baton Rouge more quickly by car than by taking the aeroplane but on the trip he had an accident that caused a long delay. He only arrived after Vidrine had finished operating on Long and his questioning revealed that Vidrine had failed to catheterize the bladder to see if it contained blood. When this procedure was done it was found that a renal duct to the kidney had been hit by the bullet, and the patient was experiencing internal haemorrhaging from the injured kidney. But all the doctors agreed that in his weakened condition another operation to tie off the kidney would be fatal. Long died shortly after. The speech given by Long before the operation is adapted from a passage in the biography *Huey Long* written by T. Harry Williams. This speech (or its import) is attributed to Long after the operation as he lay dying. I have used it here for effect.

CHAPTER 9: THE 1940 AMERICAN
PRESIDENTIAL ELECTION

"I was born into politics a wedded man, with a storm for my bride." Huey Long

From 'The Roosevelt Era' by Francis Greyson, Stevens and Samuel, 1973

Senator Huey Long's recovery from the wounds he sustained on September 8th 1935 in a failed assassination attempt was a slow one. His injuries were severe and the time spent in recovery mellowed the man to the extent that he was forced to limit his forays into national politics and concentrate on his power base in his home state. The Kingfish (as Long was nicknamed) retained his seat in the Senate and while his brush with death did nothing to diminish his popularity, it almost certainly turned him into a more dangerous and more ambitious political opponent than he had previously been. There was a change in his style of rhetoric; famous for being abrasive, his tantrums during speeches became rarer and less extreme, though he still at times indulged in berating political opponents in the foulest language. To the surprise of all who knew him, he began to mention God more often in both his speeches and in his personal life, and it seems that his recovery helped to convince him that he was a man of destiny whom God had chosen to rescue America from all that ailed it.

According to the generally-accepted version of the assassination, on September 8, 1935, Huey Long was shot once by Dr. Carl Weiss in the Capitol building at Baton Rouge. Weiss was then shot dead by Long's bodyguards, but a stray bullet from one of them also hit Long. Long died two days later from internal bleeding following an attempt to close the wounds by Dr. Arthur Vidrine. However it seems likely that the two wounds were an entry and an exit wound, suggesting that he was only hit once. The walls of the capitol hallway are still nicked from the bullets fired in the shootout.

By the autumn of 1936 Long was once more campaigning in the senate, but his radical rhetoric and antagonistic style meant that few of his proposed bills, resolutions or motions were passed. During one debate, a Republican senator told Long that "I do not believe you could get the Lord's Prayer endorsed in this body." Despite this he was undismayed, convinced that he was building a reputation among America's poorer voters as a forceful standard bearer of their cause. He skilfully manipulated his many defeats and setbacks in the senate to assume the image of the trodden down crusader who alone could relate to and speak for America's poor.

Long began to lay out the groundwork for his presidential campaign in the autumn of 1938. The kind of campaign that Huey wanted would be expensive, but he believed that he would have ample funding, for in addition to his revenues from Louisiana he had been promised help from an unforeseen quarter. Representatives of some of the largest banks and corporations in the country came to him in secret and promised substantial contributions. These ranged in amounts up to two million dollars if he would oust Roosevelt from the White House. Huey was amazed at the depth of their antipathy for the President and reminded them that he was more radical than Roosevelt. But, as he remarked to an associate, "They're not for me either, but I don't care about that so long as they give me the money. Why these conservatives ain't no smarter than the ones in Louisiana."

By early 1939, he was both well enough and confident enough to once more intensify his war on the administration of Franklin Roosevelt. The President's policy makers were becoming increasingly alarmed at reports of the Kingfish's growing strength. A poll conducted in secret by the Democratic National Committee indicated that Long, as a third-party "Share Our Wealth" presidential candidate, might draw off enough votes from FDR to throw the race to the Republicans. Reports that the GOP was offering illicit financial backing to Long's campaign did nothing to assuage their fears. Long began to boast about his ability to oust Roosevelt. At one rally he was heard to say to a group of his associates: "I can take him. He's a phony. I can take this Roosevelt. He's scared of me. I can out-promise him, and he knows it." [50] It therefore did not come as a complete surprise when Long offered himself as a candidate at the 1940 Democratic convention. Long knew that the party was unlikely to turn its back on Franklin Roosevelt but he hoped to sway a substantial number of delegates from the South, and perhaps from some of the Plains States as well.

The convention itself was tumultuous, with rancour aplenty and massive press and radio coverage of Long and his 'Share Our Wealth' plan. But after Roosevelt's inevitable nomination for a third term, Long announced the formation of a new party, The American National Party, that he described as free of Wall Street's influence and dedicated to ending what he termed "Roosevelt's Depression," by redistributing the wealth of America. [51]

Long began making personal appearances in various American cities where he nearly always he spoke to large and enthusiastic crowds. His plan to form a new party dated back to before the assassination attempt; in fact, to before the previous presidential election. In 1935, the Kingfish had been uncertain about who would become the third party's candidate. Then he had doubted that a Share Our Wealth ticket had a realistic chance of taking the White House. But though he still had occasional doubts, Huey had begun to trust in the idea of his God given destiny and firmly believed that at the age of forty-six, he would win the Presidency and save America.

Leaders of the Democratic Party grew increasingly apprehensive that Huey's strategy might allow the Republicans

---

[50] The quotes in this section are all genuine, though they were said at different times.

[51] Long created the Share Our Wealth program in 1934, with the motto "Every Man a King," proposing extreme income redistribution measures in the form of taxes on large corporations and the wealthiest individuals. He had been advancing this programme in his Senate speeches since 1932. It was completely unworkable and derided by anyone who understood the workings of the American economy, nevertheless it gained him significant support. There is evidence that even Long came to realize that wealth could not be as easily dispersed as he thought.

to win. Another secret public-opinion poll authorised by the Democratic National Committee in the Spring, conducted for the purpose of determining how much of a threat Huey Long posed, found that approximately 11% of American voters preferred the Kingfish over Roosevelt or a Republican candidate. DNC chairman Farley believed that Long might garner as many as six million votes and thereby "...have the balance of power in the 1940 election"). "This country was never under a greater menace," exclaimed New Dealer Hugh Johnson in a radio address on March 4, 1939, referring to the political alliance of Long and Father Charles Coughlin, a broadcaster who had given Long his support. [52] Roosevelt himself, having unleashed Internal Revenue investigators on Long, even considered placing Louisiana under federal military occupation. He shelved the idea because such action would probably have revived bitter memories of Reconstruction across the South. Nevertheless Roosevelt again had Long's finances investigated by the Internal Revenue Service, again they failed to link Long to any misconduct and again a few of Long's cronies were charged with income tax evasion.

In terms of foreign policy, Long was a convinced isolationist and even argued that The United States' involvement in both the Spanish-American War and the First World War had been errors committed on behalf of American bankers. The GOP's leaders almost certainly wanted an isolationist candidate in the 1940 election because Long seemed to have struck a chord with many voters on the issue of involvement in the war in Europe.

However, Wendell Willkie became the Republican candidate beating such isolationists as Robert Taft and Thomas Dewey. In

---

[52] The possibility of a Long-Coughlin alliance had been a topic of increasing political discussion during 1935. If it had come about, it would have had a significant effect on the election of 1936, bringing together as it would, two masters of radio oratory. Most commentators doubt that Long and Coughlin could have joined together and even if they had succeeded, they were two men of overbearing personalities and would have found it difficult to work together. Nevertheless they were known to be personally friendly. Long always denied that he and the priest had an alliance but admitted that they were fighting for "the same general objectives."

his final appearance before the convention, he said in a speech that England now was "...standing in imminent fear of being crushed..." and called for Americans to rally to its defence with all aid short of war. "America, instead of being afraid," he declared, "Should grow stronger and measure up to its true destiny." [53]

But most Republicans held the opposite view. New York Congressman Hamilton Fish, grandson and namesake of Ulysses S. Grant's Secretary of State, invited fifty of his isolationist colleagues to Philadelphia and paid their expenses so they could testify before the platform committee. On Tuesday, June 25th, Fish signed full-page advertisements in a half-dozen leading newspapers, including the New York Times, urging Republican delegates to "Stop the March to War! Stop the Interventionists and Warmongers!"

Alf Landon, chairman of the platform committee's foreign affairs subcommittee, worked to achieve a pro-Allies plank. He found it extremely difficult to overcome the committee's hard-line isolationists, headed by Senator Henry Cabot Lodge Jr. of Massachusetts and Illinois and Senate nominee C. Wayland Brooks. In the end, the committee declared: "The Republican Party is firmly opposed to involving this Nation in foreign war. The Republican Party stands for Americanism, preparedness and peace. We accordingly fasten upon the New Deal full responsibility for our unpreparedness and for the consequent danger of involvement in war." Landon was unable to insert an amendment that read: "We favour the extension to all peoples

---

[53] German agents were using subterfuge to try and influence the Republican's choice of candidate. The conspiracy was not made public until 1956 when the State Department declassified captured documents of the German Foreign Ministry. Hitler's spies had been working for months to bring about the defeat of Franklin Roosevelt and the election of an isolationist President. These efforts were directed by Dr. Hans Thomsen, Germany's chargé d'affaires, in Washington. The plan had been conceived by George Sylvester Viereck, the most enterprising and dangerous German spy in America. His cover was as Washington correspondent for a Munich newspaper, but he was, in fact, the chief of intelligence at the German embassy. Viereck established working relationships with many isolationist senators and congressmen and even managed to get paid German spies on some of their payrolls.

fighting for liberty, or whose liberty is threatened, of such aid as shall not be in violation of international law or inconsistent with the requirements of our own national defence." [54] Britain could derive little encouragement from the GOP's foreign policy plank.

Despite this, Willkie's popularity with the party rank and file surged. Gallup described Willkie's rise as the most astonishing phenomenon in the brief history of polling. One of the reasons for the Willkie boom was the European war and the fact that he, alone among the Republican contenders, was an advocate of aid to Britain. In late September, a Gallup poll apparently indicated that the majority of Americans favoured assisting England at the risk of war.

Willkie's campaign however became notorious for its ineptitude. Republican leaders, already cool to his candidacy, complained about unanswered phone calls, letters, and telegrams. He nearly lost his position on the Wyoming ballot by failing to respond to GOP counsel Henry Fletcher's letter with the official registration form. Furthermore, his staff seemed permanently on the verge of mutiny. Experienced political observers began to question Willkie's competence. Raymond Clapper wrote in his column on September 20th that; "The Willkie campaign falls so short that grave doubts are raised about the kind of job he would do as President. Seldom has there been more chaos in a presidential campaign."

At the beginning of September, Willkie was in a virtual dead heat with Roosevelt in the Gallup poll and actually led in projected electoral votes. But on the same day that Clapper's column appeared, the Gallup poll reported that FDR had moved in front by ten points. In an off-the-record conversation with reporters, Willkie conceded that he would probably lose the election if the war in Europe continued. Another public opinion survey showed Willkie winning the election by 5.5% if the war ended, but losing by 18 percentage points if there was a possibility the United States might enter it and the majority of

---

[54] In OTL he managed to get the amendment approved.

the Willkie press corps thought his chances were fading fast. Significantly, these polls ignored Huey Long.

Willkie seemed unable to find a central theme for his campaign. Republican leaders urged an all-out offensive on FDR and the New Deal, but Willkie dismissed this as being too negative. At a chance meeting in the barber shop of the Waldorf-Astoria in New York, James A. Farley pressed him to emphasize the third term as his major issue. Beyond quoting the founding fathers a few times, Willkie chose not to argue the question of a third term. [55]

Walter Lippmann (the Herald Tribune Columnist) advised that Foreign policy was the fundamental issue. "Your opportunity arises out of the fact that people feel insecure and want the assurance of a strong, competent man," he wrote Willkie. "Roosevelt is not a strong, competent man and that is where you can beat him if you take the hard line and summon the people rather than vaguely trying to please them all." At the start of the campaign, Willkie followed this advice and attacked FDR as too soft, an appeaser.

Willkie's main differences with FDR were in domestic affairs. He believed that government should not be in competition with private enterprise, that federal regulations should be rolled back to provide incentives for industry, help create more jobs and stimulate the economy. He believed that private capitalism would be sufficient to revive the economy where supporters of the New Deal believed that private capitalism alone was inadequate to the task and must be accompanied by public spending.

In later years, Willkie would be praised as a man who would rather be right than President of the United States, but when confronted with a test of principle in the fall of 1940, he bowed to expediency. From the GOP convention on, Republican

---

[55] Franklin Roosevelt's pursuit of a third (and fourth) term as president was not technically illegal at the time but went against a precedent established by George Washington that a President should serve only two terms. In March 1947 OTL Congress approved a 22nd Amendment to the US constitution that specifically forbade any individual to run for a third Presidential term. It took until February 1951 to get enough states to ratify the amendment

leaders were urging him to condemn Roosevelt as a warmonger, but he continued to refrain from withholding bipartisan support. However, as his popularity began to slip he became less inflexible in his principles and more amenable to compromise. Abruptly he reversed his position and began echoing the isolationist line.

At Shibe Park, in Philadelphia, Willkie accused Roosevelt of causing "...a drift toward war." He then went on to say; "We must stop that drift toward war. We must stop that incompetence. Fellow Americans, I want to lead the fight for peace." In a nationally broadcast speech, he alleged that Roosevelt had made covert pacts which would commit the nation to war. "We are being edged toward war by an administration that is careless in speech and action," he said. "We can have peace but we must know how to preserve it. To begin with, we shall not undertake to fight anybody else's war. Our boys shall stay out of Europe."

Throughout the isolationist Midwest, he kept reiterating that if Roosevelt's assurance to keep Americans out of foreign wars was no better than his 1932 promise to balance the budget, then "They're already almost on the transports." In St. Louis, he shouted, "We do not want to send our boys over there again. If you elect me President, they will not be sent. And, by the same token, if you re-elect the third-term candidate, I believe they will be sent."

Willkie's foreign policy reversal brought him into alliance with people for whom he had contempt, including such isolationist stalwarts as Hamilton Fish, Charles A. Lindbergh, and Colonel Robert McCormick, but it disappointed a great many of his backers. Political analyst Richard H. Rovere wrote: "By the time the campaign was over, Willkie was as much in opposition to the man he had been a few months earlier as he was to his opponent." And in a 1981 interview, Oren Root, one of Willkie's staunchest allies, admitted that his sudden change on the war issue was nothing more than a cynical appeal for votes.

Questionable though the tactic might have been it revived his candidacy and alarmed Democratic strategists. Within, two weeks, the Gallup poll reported he had trimmed the President's popular vote margin by half, had moved ahead in five Midwestern states and was surging in the industrial North East. The New York Daily News poll indicated the Empire State was a toss–up. On Wall Street, the betting odds against Willkie dropped from twelve-to-five to seven-to-five.

As the results came in on election night what later became known as 'The Long Effect' was quickly obvious, crucially the industrial states of New York, New Jersey and Pennsylvania with a combined total of 99 Electoral College votes declared for Willkie because of the split in the Democrat vote. [56]

Only in his home state did Long actually succeed in winning but its small contribution of 10 Electoral College votes could not make a difference to the final result. In the end Roosevelt won 28 states and Willkie 19, but even with Louisiana's votes thrown to Roosevelt he only succeeded in securing 257 Electoral College votes, the remaining 274 going to Willkie.

---

[56] In OTL these three declared for Roosevelt but in New York and New Jersey the margin was less than 4% and in Pennsylvania less than 6%.

CHAPTER 10: SATURDAY

14th SEPTEMBER 1940

Number 506 Squadron lifts from the scattered web of cloud and into the searing light at seventeen thousand feet. There are seven Spitfires in a loose 'V' formation, Sub Lieutenant John Leighton is flying one of them, its code letters are FS–G and his call sign is Red Two. The sun is low and there are less than three hours of daylight left, he has been with 506 Squadron for three weeks.

Summer is slipping into autumn and though the hours of daylight have grown mercifully shorter, almost every day has given perfect flying weather and the enemy have come at them relentlessly. The pilots of 506 are scrambled three or four times every day. Exhausted, they drag themselves into the air each dawn and by nightfall are too tense to rest. They drink too much in the mess, laugh too loudly and talk too quickly. They do it to blot out the roar of engines, a sound that rings in their ears long after the engines themselves have been switched off, but when they finally crawl into their beds, sleep eludes them. Their minds range back over the day, over who had lived and who had died, reliving every terrifying moment of the fight.

When *Courageous* returned from The Battle of Lofotten, he had fully expected that the task of rebuilding 843 Squadron would begin immediately, but to his surprise and annoyance he and the other surviving pilot had been posted to the Naval Air Station at Donibristle in Scotland. There it seemed that the Admiralty had forgotten about them. Throughout July, the Battle of Britain had raged in the sky above southern England and Leighton chafed at his enforced inaction until in mid-August he was ordered to number 17 Operational Conversion Unit to convert to Spitfires. So desperate was the RAF for fighter pilots that in the memorable words of his instructor, 'Fighter Command are even prepared to consider you Navy types.'

Leighton loved flying the Spitfire, the dull brown and green camouflage could not disguise the aircraft's beauty, and while there was nothing wrong with the Nimrods and Sea Hurricanes that he had flown before, the Spitfire was something special. Even the rather worn example on which he converted was a delight to fly and perform aerobatics in.

From the newspaper and radio reports, as well as the inevitable rumours, he had learned that the battle was hard fought. Still, when he arrived at Hawkinge aerodrome in the last week of August he was shocked by its condition. It had been attacked repeatedly by the Luftwaffe, most of the buildings had been destroyed and the pilots and ground crew slept in tents. He had been posted with two other replacements, both straight from flying school; neither had flown high-performance fighters for more than a dozen hours. The other pilots in the squadron were taciturn, almost curt, Leighton put it down to the strain of constant operations, it was only later that he realised that it was simply a defence mechanism designed to insulate them from the inevitable sorrow of loss.

The commanding officer, Squadron Leader Huntingdon, welcomed them briefly and showed them their aircraft. They were brand new, straight from the factory in Southampton with only a few tens of hours on the air frames, but they barely had time to stow their belongings in their tents when the squadron was scrambled.

And so it has gone for three weeks. Fewer than half of the pilots that made up the squadron when Leighton arrived are still flying. The strain tells on those that remain, they are worn out, nervous, irritable. In just four days they are due for rotation out of the combat zone, but each man asks himself if he will live long enough to see it.

The formation of Spitfires climbs into the bright blue summer sky, the clouds spread out below and through them can be seen patches of Kent, the radio crackles in his headset, Huntingdon is practically shouting;

"There they are! There they are! Straight ahead! Echelon starboard – go!"

Leighton's eyes search the sky as the seven Spitfires move into a ragged line behind and to the right of their leader, his heart races and he counts thirty Dornier 17s in six 'V' shaped formations of five aircraft each. They are passing in front of them, going west across their noses from right to left. About two thousand feet above and behind the bombers, a mixed formation of fifteen Messerschmitt 109s and 110s in groups of twos and threes, wheel and zigzag like hovering wasps.

Huntingdon rocks his wings for the squadron to close in tighter, they are still climbing but he levels out and leads them into a left-hand turn.

"Now! Keep in! Keep in! And keep a bloody good look out!"

The German formation keeps straight on, though they must see the British fighters angling in from their port quarter, at the last moment the fighter escort breaks right and left wheeling into the attack and the two formations meet and split into a wild melee.

Leighton banks hard to the right and selects the rear aircraft of two Messerschmitt 110s in line. The '110 breaks from his leader and turns to port, but the Spitfire flicks over and easily turns inside him. Leighton waits until he is within fifty yards, but the Messerschmitt rolls out of the turn and is suddenly flying straight and level. The Spitfire shudders as he fires a short burst at three-quarter deflection and to his amazement, a mass of pieces fly off the German aircraft – bits of engine cowling, lumps of the canopy – and he watches in a kind of fascinated horror as the '110 goes into a spin, its tail suddenly swivels sideways and tears off and he feels an unaccountable relief as he sees the sudden puff of white parachute and a figure swaying beneath it.

He pulls the stick into his stomach, engages the boost override and climbs into the blue at full power as his head swivels from side to side. Close by, a '110 is climbing at forty-five degrees in a left-hand stall turn, a Spitfire is on its tail firing into it and a series of flashes and long shooting yellow flames erupt from its engines. It hangs for a second in the air and then tumbles end over end towards the earth.

Above him he can see three Messerschmitt 109s climbing in line astern to get above the fight and pounce. There are three more off to his right closing fast. He turns towards them, firing. They break right and left and he hauls the Spitfire into a starboard turn as he tries to target the exposed belly of one, but it is moving too quickly and he cannot turn fast enough to catch the twisting shape in the web of his gun sight.

The '109s turn back towards him, two from the right and one from the left. He twists and turns, kicking the rudder to send his aircraft slewing sideways to put off their aim. One fires, but his shooting is wild. Leighton can see tracer flashing well above his canopy and he turns tight to starboard to fly straight at his opponent. There is time for only a half second burst. He pushes the stick forward and dives under the Messerschmitt's nose, then pulls up in a steep climbing turn to meet the next attack.

His mouth is dry as he again sees two '109s coming straight at him head-on. He fires almost simultaneously with the Messerschmitts and at the last possible second he pushes the stick forward violently and there is a sudden bang right behind him and the Spitfire staggers in the air. For a moment his mind is blank, the aircraft seems to be falling, the controls are limp, black smoke is pouring from the nose and enveloping the canopy. Suddenly there is a hot blast and a flicker of reflected flame is creeping into the cockpit.

He pulls the pin from his harness, wrenches back the canopy and hauls himself out to the left. The slipstream presses his body tightly against the fuselage, his legs are still inside. He sees that his aircraft has lost its tail and he grabs at the trailing edge of the wing and heaves. He falls free and somersaults, whirling round and round through the air, fumbling for the rip cord, until at last he finds it and with a violent jerk the parachute opens above his head.

There is no sensation of movement, just a slight breeze as he swings gently to and fro. Two '109s are circling, he looks at the ground and sees a shower of flaming sparks as his aircraft explodes in an orchard, then another in a nearby field as the '109 he collided with also goes into the ground. His is the only parachute. The German fighters turn and fly off.

*

When he returns to Hawkinge after hitching several lifts, it is nine o'clock at night. The sound of rowdy singing spills from the blacked out windows of the mess, the only building apart from the control tower to have been repaired.

He goes to his tent to get a change of clothes and to his surprise sees the angular shape of a Royal Navy Swordfish parked at dispersal. The Swordfish is a bi-plane bomber, used mostly to launch torpedoes but sometimes to drop bombs. It is unusual to see a Swordfish on an RAF base in the south of England, the domain of the Swordfish is the Naval air stations in Scotland and the north. This one has suffered damage, there are bullet holes in the fabric of the wings and tail. He walks over and finds a soldier standing guard by the cockpit.

"It came in about an hour ago Sir, one of the crew was injured. It was getting quite dark and we had to line the cars and lorries up with their lights on either side of the runway to show the pilot where to land, I think the crew are in the mess, but I can't say for certain Sir."

Two naval fliers are by the bar. One of them is a Royal Navy Commander of about thirty; the other, is a Lieutenant, younger by two or three years. His hair is curly and his rank insignia is in the gold wavy lines of a member of the Royal Navy Volunteer Reserve. There are pint glasses in their hands and cigarettes dangle from their lips. Most of the 506 squadron pilots are crowded round them, their faces are weary, but elated and they both smile when they see Leighton's naval uniform. Huntingdon sees Leighton and says, "Where the hell have you been? We thought you were dead."

Leighton responds; "Sorry to disappoint you Squadron Leader."

"Get one?"

"Thanks, I'll have a pint."

"No you scrounging bastard – did you get any Germans?"

"Two Messerschmitts, a '109 and a '110, but I had to ram one of them and bail out, so I don't know if it counts."

"Oh it counts, it counts Leighton. Two – one to us. Well done; I'll have to invoice the Admiralty for that Spitfire though, I expect they'll take it out of your pay."

Huntingdon offers him a cigarette and gestures to the older of the naval fliers. "Leighton, this is Esmonde."

Leighton salutes, the Commander returns the salute and offers his hand, his voice has an Irish lilt and he says; "Call me Eugene." Huntingdon turns to the RNVR Lieutenant,

"This is another one of your own; his name's Brabner." As they shake hands Esmonde grins and says,

"Wait now, let's introduce the man properly shall we," Brabner, closes his eyes, shakes his head slightly and says, "Not this again." But Esmonde is clearly enjoying the moment.

"This is the Honourable and Gallant Lieutenant Rupert Brabner, MP…" Huntingdon looks confused.

"What, hang on, Brabner? You're Military Police?" Esmonde laughs,

"No, no, Squadron Leader, he's a Member of Parliament." Huntingdon looks askance at Brabner,

"Get out of it, you're not a Member of Parliament…" Brabner grins ruefully.

"For my sins, yes."

Esmonde is still laughing, "Yes, by God, the Honourable and Gallant Member for Hythe no less, which is just down the road about five mile if I'm not mistaken; the Honourable and Gallant Member for Hythe is having a pint with us fortunate souls in this very place. Honourable *and* gallant mind you, one of the elect no less, in fact, one of the elected."

Huntingdon is still confused. "Honourable and gallant? What?"

Esmonde is pleased to clarify, "'Honourable and Gallant', is the correct style of address for a member of the House of Commons who is also serving in the armed forces. So you people better be careful what you say to this one; Leighton and me, we can say what we like, we're Navy, but you Air Force boys…"

Amid the general laughter Leighton asks; "What brings you to Hawkinge? You know the beer's better on naval bases."

Esmonde smiles, takes a long pull on his pint and shakes his head ruefully. "We were lost, just plain lost; our navigator was injured, shrapnel, in his leg; in and out of consciousness, not saying a lot, but he's going to be alright. We were running out of fuel, leaky tank, had to put down. I think Brabner here wanted to get back to his constituency and say hello to them all…" Brabner grins and says,

"I was flying the aircraft, Commander Esmonde was leading the raid."

Esmonde interrupts, "If you can call it leading, mostly I was just leaning out of the side of the cockpit with a map trying to figure out where we were."

Leighton says, "Were you on an operation?"

Esmonde hesitates before he responds, "Yes, yes we were – I suppose I shouldn't tell you, but the secret is out now. We hit the fighter bases in the Pas de Calais, the ones near the coast. Quite a big show actually, air groups from three carriers, over a hundred and fifty 'planes, plus a couple of RAF fighter squadrons that could be spared, flew down from Scotland yesterday, left the carriers behind…"

"Which carriers?"

"The Home Fleet's. *Fearless*, *Formidable*, *Victorious* and odds and ends from *Ark Royal*, *Indomitable* and *Courageous* – I was on *Ark* you know, most of us got off when she sank…" There is a pause, then Leighton says;

"I didn't know *Indomitable* had commissioned yet."

Brabner interjects, "She hasn't. I'm from *Indomitable*, our air group is forming up and we need the practice. It was just a couple of flights, twelve Albacores and some Sea Hurricanes, I was one of the spare pilots for the Sea Hurricanes but Commander Esmonde's pilot went sick yesterday. Appendicitis or something…"

Leighton interrupts him, "I was on *Courageous* – which squadron came from her?"

Esmonde shakes his head, "Just a flight – I'm not sure which one, led by a chap named Higgins. Know him?"

"Higgins, yes he was the Commander (Flying)."

"Yeah, that's the fellah. We had to hit Audembert, went in just before sunset. We were right down on the deck, as we planned, though we were a wee bit late. Some of our 'planes had already gone in, but we caught most of the Germans on the ground. I suppose they weren't expecting us, only a couple got airborne…"

It is Huntington who interrupts now, "From Audembert?"

"No, from all of them I suppose – all the German fighter bases. There are seven of them to the south west of Calais, within five miles of the city and all less than four miles from the coast. We left Audembert pretty banged up, and I flew over

Wissant on the way back, it looked a mess as well. You know, I think Babner shot a Messerschmitt 109 down there…"

The room falls abruptly silent. Huntingdon, incredulous, says; "With a Swordfish?" Babner shakes his head,

"I know, I can scarcely believe it myself. We came over the treetops and we were flying right over the airfield when I saw a '109 halfway through it's take off run. The sun had gone down and I could hardly see him, but I lined the Swordfish up and had a pop at him with the machine gun. Had to really, if he'd got up, he'd have come after us. He was just airborne and I managed to hit him, he belly flopped back onto the runway, his undercarriage collapsed and he skidded off sideways. Esmonde saw it, I'd call it a 'probable'."

"Wait now," said Esmonde, "damaged is about all I can give you, probably destroyed is a bit too much." Huntingdon is aghast.

"I didn't know Swordfishes had forward firing guns?" Esmonde takes a pull on his pint and says;

"Oh yeah, just the one though, a three–oh–three Browning, the back of it is right next to the pilot so you can give it a thump if it jams. When I'm flying, I keep a bit of stick in the cockpit just for that." Esmonde takes a long pull of his pint and Brabner takes up the story.

"The fighters that escorted us shot up everything in sight on strafing runs, while we put bombs all over the place. Two fifths of the bombs we dropped were booby trapped flares with delayed action fuses, they're supposed to send in bombers later on, after dark. The idea is that they will bomb on the flares and smash the German air fields up a bit more. If it works. Well, even if it doesn't I don't think you'll be seeing as many German fighters tomorrow as you may have today." He turns to Huntingdon; "If you don't you can thank the Navy."

Huntingdon smiles; "So can we blame you if we do?"

Esmonde interrupts him, "Well perhaps, but that isn't what's concerning me right now, what's concerning me right now is the emptiness of my glass and the fact that it's your round…"

They laugh and for a moment the war seems very distant.

*

107

The next day is Sunday, 15th September 1940. As usual the pilots of 506 Squadron are ready before dawn, but the long waiting silence of sunrise passes into morning. By eleven o'clock the breeze is bringing the scent of honeysuckle and roses across the airfield to mingle with the smell of oil, rubber and petrol that seeps from their aircraft. They lie down on the grass beneath the wings to escape the hot sunshine. Some sleep, their heads on parachute packs, as Squadron Leader Huntingdon paces up and down looking irritably at the sky.

The day is so still, so quiet and perfect that Leighton even allows the hope that peace might have been declared into his mind for a moment. But then the dispersal telephone rings, the howl of the siren dispels the beauty of the late summer day and they are running towards their aircraft as engines roar into life and turning propellers scythe the air.

Leighton's Spitfire leaps forward, faster and faster across the bumpy grass until suddenly everything becomes smooth and it lifts into the air. As he adjusts his flying helmet the headphones crackle; "Badger to Red Leader, scramble, ninety plus bandits, angels fifteen, vector two-one-zero, buster." This gibberish is code for 'Ground Control to Red Section, there are 90 enemy aircraft at fifteen thousand feet, steer a course of two hundred and ten degrees to intercept them'.

The squadron is circling the airfield as the last few aircraft become airborne, then quickly they form into sections and climb into the cloudless sky. Far below, the English countryside stretches lazily into the distance, green and enticing. They level out at twenty thousand feet. Leighton's call sign is Red Two once more; he looks over at Red Three, the Spitfire of Pilot Officer Soames. His oxygen mask is moving on his face – he is probably singing again – sometimes he forgets and leaves his radio on 'send' so the rest of the squadron have to listen to cracked renditions of 'Night and Day' or 'Danny Boy' over the voices of the controllers.

They fly straight and level for a tense fifteen minutes, then Huntingdon's voice crackles in his headphones;

"Bandits dead ahead! Line astern everyone and watch out for fighters."

The enemy aircraft are about two thousand feet below. For once, 506 Squadron have the advantage of height. There are more than a hundred of them, Heinkel 111s and Dornier 17s, wave upon wave. They are moving away from them, it is a perfect attacking position.

"Echelon starboard" came Huntingdon's voice, "Going down – Now!"

One after another they peel off in a power dive. Leighton picks out a Heinkel 111 and switches his gun button from 'Safe' to 'Fire'. At 300 yards, he has him in his sights; at 200 he opens up in a three-second burst and sees tracer slamming into the fuselage and tail and then he is pulling out so hard that he can feel his eyes pressing into the bottom of their sockets and his vision is greying at the edges until he comes round in a fast climbing turn to port. He looks over his left shoulder, to his annoyance the aircraft he had targeted is apparently unharmed, another Spitfire is attacking it and Leighton opens the throttle and climbs to get above and behind the enemy formation again.

He selects a new target, another Heinkel 111. This time he waits until he is a scant 150 yards away before he opens fire. He has barely let go a two-second burst when it explodes. He pulls the stick back and hard to the left to try and avoid the fireball. As he flies through it, the Spitfire shakes in the turbulence and he can hear thuds and bangs as pieces of the German aircraft ricochet off the underside of his own. He levels out, throttles back and looks at his instruments. Gingerly he rocks the aircraft to right and left looking at the wings and what he can see of the tail in the rear view mirror for signs of damage. His heart leaps into his throat as he sees another aircraft right on his tail but it is Spitfire. He hears the excited voice of Soames.

"Is that you Leighton? You alright?"

"Hullo Soames, I think so – did you see that kill?"

"I think they saw it in Blackpool Leighton, you must have hit his oxygen tanks or his bomb load."

Though the aircraft seems to be unharmed, they have flown right through the middle of the German formation and are now alone in the sky. They begin a climbing turn to Starboard and see perhaps a dozen black specks several thousand feet above and about 5 miles away. Focusing more intently, Leighton realises that it is a formation of German aircraft travelling in roughly the same direction as the two Spitfires. Eight Heinkel 111s and three Messerschmitt 109s. Without taking his eyes from them he turns to port and begins to climb parallel to the course of the enemy formation urging as much speed as his screaming engine will give him in order to stay in front of them. Soames follows; they are in a bad tactical position, caught below and in front of the enemy. For a precious minute the Germans do not see them, but just as they reach the same altitude at a point roughly two miles to the right of the enemy formation and about a mile in front of it they are spotted. The leading bomber executes a violent turn and begins to dive away followed by the rest of them.

The 109s fan out and angle towards them. The Spitfires turn towards the attack and Leighton begins firing, more to try and throw the Germans off their aim than with any hope of hitting anything. But they peel off unnerved, allowing him to push the aircraft over into a dive to follow the bombers.

Leighton hurtles towards the ground, throttle wide open, engine howling, He looks to right and left but Soames is nowhere to be seen. His speed is touching four hundred knots when suddenly he spots a shadow moving across the ground below. He focuses on it for a second; it is a Heinkel 111 skimming low across the surface of the fields, racing back for France and safety.

It is moving diagonally across Leighton's line of flight from the right, he flattens out just above the treetops and banks to starboard to ease into a firing position when he realises that he has picked up too much speed in the dive and is going to overshoot unless he slows down. As he cuts back on the throttle and side slips to brake his speed instinctively he looks over a shoulder and sees two '109s diving towards him from an angle slightly off to his right. Their intent is obvious enough; they want to kill him before he can kill the bomber.

In an instant his mind becomes strangely detached from the danger and he sees it only as a problem in time and distance. He feels suddenly, inexplicably obstinate and decides to make the most of the one good shot he will get. He fires a long steady burst across the bomber's line of flight and as it flies through the bullets its port engine begins to burn, its wing drops and it hits the ground, cart wheeling across a field as its fuel explodes.

Leighton banks hard to the left just as the 109s open fire, he sees their shells churn up the earth but like him they have built too much speed up in their dive and they overshoot. As they pull up Leighton slams the throttle through the emergency gate and turns back towards them. He is now behind them but they too must have throttled back because he is overhauling them, they stay close to the ground as slowly he closes the distance.

Fields of wheat and hops, hedgerows and cottages flash beneath his wings. When he is two hundred yards from the nearest Messerschmitt he opens fire, the guns only work for two seconds before they stop firing and he hears the rapid clicking of the hammers in the empty breeches. He has run out of ammunition, but the '109 staggers in the sky and drops abruptly towards the ground. The German fighter pulls up just over a village but the edge of one wing catches the steeple of a church and it goes into a flat spin, bounces once in a field and drives a furrow through a hedge, there is a flash of light and the wreckage breaks up in whirlwind of flame and fragments scattering into the sky.

*

He lands and taxis back to dispersal. In the debriefing tent the chatter of exited voices swells into a hubbub of elation that threatens to burst through the canvas. Only one 506 Squadron aircraft has failed to return and a parachute was seen when it went down. Almost every pilot is claiming at least one kill except Soames who looks dejected as the others laugh at his downcast face.

The Debriefing Officer shakes his head. "Never mind son, you'll probably get one tomorrow."

Soames looks up; "Can I claim one frightened?"

"No you bloody well can't!"

CHAPTER 11: BRITISH POLITICS, FROM THE IMPERIAL DEFENCE CONFERENCE OF 1934 TO THE ABDICATION

From 'The Imperial Defence Conference of 1934' by Erwin Steiner, Economic History Chronicle Volume 11 Part 6

Like the British Empire Economic Conference held in Ottawa in 1932, the Imperial Defence Conference of 1934 was born of a crisis. In 1932, the cause was the depth and duration of the recession; in 1934, the collapse of both the Second London Naval Treaty and the Geneva Disarmament Conference had stimulated a sudden and unsettling reappraisal of the Empire's defensive posture.

Up until this point it had been hoped and believed that a major war had become very unlikely between the developed nations, but the reason for the conference was made abundantly clear as it opened in July against the backdrop of the Austrian Emergency, the confirmation of a new militarist government in Tokyo under Admiral Keisuke Okada and the ominous boasting of Soviet industrialisation at the Communist Party Congress. In January the Foreign Office had received an analysis of the situation in Germany from its Ambassador in Berlin, Sir Neville Henderson.

"Here it may be said that nothing has so enhanced the prestige of Herr Hitler in Germany as the behaviour of the ex-Allies since he took office. All reasonable and cautious opinion in Germany foretold disaster, occupation of the Rhineland, sanctions, perhaps blockade, if Germany reverted to nationalism. The Nazis seized power, and nothing happened. Herr Hitler left the League and still nothing happened. On the contrary, the statesmen of Europe were represented here as having been galvanised into running after Germany. The fear that force may be used against Germany exists, but it is rapidly disappearing, and the man, particularly the young man, in the street thanks Hitler for the removal of a distressing bogey. It is therefore not surprising if the Chancellor pursues methods which hitherto have brought him success." [57]

While the Dominions had been persuaded in the early 1920s to bear a more equitable share of the cost of Empire defence (particularly naval defence), it is fair to say that between the armistice in 1918 and the end of the Imperial conference of 1934, it is difficult to find evidence that any of them had a real grasp of the economic implications of a new war. This was also true of the United Kingdom itself, but to a lesser extent.

This is hardly surprising as up to this point Imperial conferences, when they considered strategic issues at all, tended to be both optimistic and conciliatory in their outlook. However, in this case Prime Minister Mosley and his Foreign Secretary Clement Attlee (who had replaced Harold Nicholson the previous year) clearly expressed their dismay at the collapse of the disarmament conferences and their fears for the future in no uncertain terms. Henderson's assessment was circulated among the delegates as well as an appreciation of the continued expansion of the Japanese fleet. The news of the re-commissioning of the Soviet battleship *Frunze* and the resolutions of the XVIIth Bolshevik Party Congress (adjourned on 16 March 1934) signalled a resurgence of Russian military and industrial strength to the entire world.

Various scenarios including the possibility of an alliance between Soviet Russia and Imperial Japan, as well as one between Soviet Russia and Nazi Germany were analysed. It is interesting, but perhaps not surprising, to note that with the Austrian Emergency underway, analysis of the possibility of an alliance between Nazi Germany and fascist Italy was not pursued. The conclusions drawn by the delegates were unsettling. While the prospect of a war involving the British Empire had drawn much closer, it was woefully unprepared to meet the threat.

---

[57] This communication is reproduced here exactly as it was OTL.

From this basis the two main issues in the economic discussions of the conference were addressed. First, was the need of the United Kingdom to guarantee supplies (especially of food) from Empire countries. Discussions had been opened with the Dominions, the colonies and India as to the procedure which the United Kingdom would follow for the purchase of food in the event of a major war. A special warning of direct importance to Australia and New Zealand was that the need to economise on shipping was likely to dictate import from the nearest available sources of supply, even though these might not be the cheapest or might not be Empire countries.

Second, was the stress by the United Kingdom on the need for the Dominions and India to free themselves of dependence on Britain for supplies of arms and munitions by developing their own production. It was made clear by the UK delegation that its own rearmament programme was straining the country's ability to produce munitions and that it was imperative that the Dominions and India should build up manufacturing infrastructure with a view to promoting a greater self-reliance in armaments for the future, because a major war might mean that supply from Britain would be subject to interruptions. However, the United Kingdom indicated that it was prepared to give aid in the expansion of Dominion and Indian munitions industries by placing orders for some of its own supplies in these countries. At the same time stressing that it could not implement this policy at the expense of the planned development of its own industrial structure.

An especially thorny question was that of aircraft. The Dominions were relying almost wholly on Britain for supplies of aircraft and Australia in particular made the point that long delays in completion of their orders were the norm, because British factories were accepting orders from foreign countries (in some cases for commercial aircraft) rather than filling Australian orders. To accommodate these concerns the conference passed a resolution that:

"To the utmost extent practicable, having regard to the difficulties involved, His Majesty's Government in the United Kingdom should endeavour to ensure that the

114

requirements of the Dominions and India are given priority over those of foreign countries."

And also that:

"Such technical and financial assistance as may be necessary and prudent for the British government and British firms to provide to enable the manufacture of British types of aircraft shall be forthcoming."

The Dominion governments therefore obtained from the Imperial Conference not only a clear-cut guide for the formulation of their own policies but also a commitment from Britain to aid in the manufacture of weapons (particularly air weapons) in the Dominions. This meant that while they would have to rely to an increasing extent on their own sources for the production of munitions, they could count on Britain for financial and technological assistance in facilitating that change.

Nevertheless, of the four Dominions, essentially only Australia, concerned about the danger represented by Japan, reacted as strongly as the British, although the Canadian government under Richard Bennett and then Mackenzie King also took firm steps to increase Canada's industrial preparedness for war. Financial preparedness was less of a problem for Canada than for the other Dominions.

In New Zealand, decisive action in the pre-war years was directed to welfare provisions, public works and housing, rather than to preparation for war. George Forbes, the Prime Minister at the time of the Imperial Defence Conference, is described as "apathetic and fatalistic", and his reaction to the conference was attended by very little vision or purpose. His loss of power to Michael Savage in 1935 also did little to improve the situation as Savage's Labour Party of New Zealand held strongly pacifist views and they too did not take sufficiently seriously the mounting evidence of military preparation by Germany, the USSR and Japan. The net effect was that the British suggestion to prepare for war met with a marked lack of New Zealand Government enthusiasm. The same was true in South Africa, though for different reasons, and that country too was woefully unprepared for war when it came. [58]

From 'A Concise History of British Politics' by Tom Shaed, Gloucester University Press, 2007

Mosley's lack of success in his efforts to reform the House of Lords in 1935 is widely regarded as the point at which his luck began to turn. Later in the year, the coming of the Abyssinian crisis and his apparent ambivalence toward the Italian invasion further damaged his credibility. These events seemed to confirm that the engine of his success was running out of steam.

Another issue on which Mosley seemed unable to form a coherent policy was that of the rising power of Nazi Germany. While he had sponsored re-armament, he believed that conflict with Germany could be averted. Effectively, he saw Hitler as a problem which could be managed, but his conviction was undermined by the failure of the negotiations for an Anglo-German Naval agreement. The French perception of the Mosley government was severely tarnished by the collapse of the Geneva disarmament conference and had been cool ever since. [59]

Although these setbacks were serious, the Labour government entered 1936 confident in its popularity. The economy was buoyant, unemployment was down and the prospects of winning a second term seemed good. The

---

[58] This reaction of the Dominion Governments in TTL is essentially similar to that OTL; the crucial difference is the timing of the conference, in OTL these issues were raised at the Imperial Conference of 1937. Here they are addressed three years early.

[59] This will not last as TTL Britain is beginning to re-arm earlier and more enthusiastically then OTL, although Mosley is going to face quite a political struggle within the Labour Party to get certain sections of it to accept this. Weapons research will get a little more money than OTL, government expenditure is far higher in real terms but only slightly higher in proportionate terms (because of the markedly stronger economy). Higher government expenditure will also mean more money to go around, by producing a Keynesian style early recovery from the Depression.

Conservatives had a new leader, Neville Chamberlain, and had recovered from their defeat four years previously. The Liberals too had a new leader, Sir Archibald Sinclair and had re-absorbed David Lloyd-George's Liberal Independents, though reunion with the Liberal Nationals was still elusive.

The reoccupation of the Rhineland by German forces in March was greeted by the international community with a strange mixture of astonishment and dithering. The French reaction, or lack of one, meant the other powers also failed to act against Hitler. The French Cabinet shrank from a military response and instead opted to oppose the German move politically through the medium of the League of Nations. Their attitude eventually persuaded Mussolini to align Italy with Germany. Il Duce was one of the few who realised that the reoccupation was a bluff, but if the other powers could not, or would not, oppose Hitler; then Italy was better off on his side.

In Britain, the reaction to the news was mixed. While some of the more excitable newspapers published pessimistic editorials, the main political parties urged restraint in dealing with Germany. In the general climate of inaction the story was soon eclipsed by other events.

Mosley believed that war with Germany could be avoided and that the dictators could be contained by diplomacy and a strong commitment to the defence of the United Kingdom. There was virtually no anti-fascist sentiment from the leadership of the Labour party, but many voices condemning fascism arose from the rank and file. Appeasement was government policy. The Conservative leadership under Neville Chamberlain essentially agreed, though again, notable voices within the party strongly condemned the dictators. Anthony Eden, for instance, resigned as shadow Foreign Secretary in protest at the party's stance on the issue. The deeply unpopular John Simon of the National Liberals was an 'arch appeaser' and it was only the Liberals under Sir Archibald Sinclair that resolutely condemned fascism as party policy.

Sinclair was a member of the League of Nations Union and served on the Executive Committee of the Peace Ballot. His consistent opposition to rearmament made him a darling of the pacifist movement. But both pacifists and militarists failed to understand his position. He was an ardent opponent of arms proliferation, but he was certainly not a unilateralist; he believed that disarmament had to be part of the course of international conciliation and that the one could not proceed without the other. In other words, he worked for general disarmament, but believed that the United Kingdom had to maintain its military strength until other nations could be persuaded to disarm in concert with Britain. Cooperative security and disarmament had been important Liberal foreign policy objectives since the end of the First World War; but as the threat of the dictators grew ever stronger and the League of Nations ever feebler, the Liberal Party were compelled to admit the need for rearmament. A change of direction had somehow to be charted and it was Sinclair who persuaded his party that it was a necessity.

Under Labour's policies, unemployment continued to fall and the stock market continued to rise. In these favourable circumstances it is hardly surprising that in early July Mosley went to Buckingham palace and asked the King to dissolve parliament.

From the start of the 1936 election campaign, there was little doubt as to the eventual result. The vote was presented by the Labour Party as a vote of confidence in their policies of the previous four years. Turnout was down on the previous election and in many constituencies the reorganised Conservatives were able to present a strong challenge to Labour. However, where they tried to focus the debate on the subject of policy, Labour was often able to shift the emphasis to the two leader's personalities. Here the patrician, schoolmasterly Chamberlain was clearly at a disadvantage to the youthful, dynamic Mosley.

Though the Conservatives did better than the other parties; Mosley's government was returned with a reduced overall majority of 5 seats. The Liberals also made small gains, while the Liberal Nationals continued their decline. The results were as follows:

Labour: 312 (−5)
Conservative: 259 (+14)
Liberal: 25 (+3)
National Liberal: 11 (−7)

Others: 8 (–4)

Having won a historic second term, the Government oversaw the passage of the gigantic Government of India Act. This was the outcome of a long and often caustic process of negotiation between the British Government, the princely states of India and the Indian politicians. It foreshadowed the elevation of India to Dominion status and laid the groundwork for the formation of a Federal government. It was the longest bill ever passed by Parliament. [60]

Another vitally important innovation at this time was the setting up of a Ministry of Supply to oversee Britain's re-armament. [61] Led by Herbert Morrison it was a very small Ministry, but its role was significant in facilitating co-operation between the services, the manufacturers and the banks. [62]

The Berlin Olympics were put on in August over the objections of its critics. A British newspaper, the Manchester Guardian, demanded a boycott and strongly objected when Mosley visited Germany during the games to hold talks with Hitler. The talks were a success, but nothing of practical importance was decided. Relations between the two men were business-like but cordial. It seems that each admired the other despite their differences in purpose and outlook. Some have gone so far as to describe the relationship between the two as friendship but this is stretching what we know of them and it is probably more accurate to describe them as 'being on convivial terms'.

While in Germany Mosley was invited to attend the ceremonial opening of a new section of the Rhine–Main–Danube Canal, the central European waterway that was soon to link the North and Black seas. It is possible that Mosley saw this

---

[60] The Act is different than OTL's version. The subcontinent will evolve differently in TTL. See Chapter 21 and Annex 7.

[61] In OTL the Ministry of Supply was not set up until July 1939.

[62] See Annex 4

extension of Germany's eastward communications as further proof of Hitler's commitment to eastward (rather than westward) expansion.

From 'The Abdication Crisis' 1982 'O' Level essay by Samantha Cunningham, Bourne Priory School, Leicester

In the autumn of 1936, the entirety of the British Empire became embroiled in a constitutional crisis that was to shake it to its foundations. The new King, Edward VIII, announced his determination to marry Wallis Simpson, an American socialite who had divorced her first husband and was in the process of divorcing a second.

The Prime Minister, Oswald Mosley was quite comfortable with the notion of Edward's marriage to Mrs. Simpson and made this known in a speech in Parliament on Tuesday 17th November. But he had completely mis-read the mood of the House, the Country and the Empire. There was an immediate storm of protest and he found himself sharply at odds with most of the chamber, including a large section of his own party. The opposition denounced him and Labour's whips proved unable to contain a back bench revolt. The governments of the Dominions and those of the Commonwealth countries were also implacably against the union.

The grounds of opposition to the King's proposed marriage were religious, moral, political and legal. Edward, as British monarch, was the nominal head of the Church of England. At the time, divorced people could not remarry in church if their former spouse was still living. Consequently, they held that Edward could not marry Wallis Simpson and expect to retain the crown. Mrs. Simpson was politically and socially unacceptable as a queen consort. She was perceived as shallow, vain and hedonistic; a social climber, compelled by a desire for wealth and prestige rather than by genuine love for Edward.

By 20th November Mosley realised that his support for the King was undermining his position and was therefore a mistake. The government's majority of 5 seats began to seem fragile as the Conservatives used the issue to damage their credibility. Shaken, Mosley saw only three options:

1. The couple could enter a morganatic marriage (one where Edward's titles and privileges would not accrue to Wallis or any children they might have). In this case Wallis would not become queen but would be given a courtesy title.

2. Edward and Wallis could remain unmarried. In this case Edward would remain King but he and Wallis would presumably continue their affair.

3. Edward could abdicate.

In considering the first two, Mosley realised that their outcomes were dangerously unpredictable, particularly the first. The second, relied on co-operation from the press, which might be forthcoming but was far from being guaranteed. Most of his ministers strongly felt that option one was a non-starter. It was constitutionally dangerous and would undermine the government. It was now obvious that Edward could marry Wallis Simpson or remain on the throne, but not both.

Mosley met with Edward again on Sunday 22nd November. The King was not willing to give Mrs. Simpson up and also not willing to do anything other than marry her. As far as Mosley was concerned it was now a question of him or Edward. He informed the King that he had grave misgivings over both the idea of a morganatic marriage and the idea of him not marrying Wallis.

There was no way out for Edward other than to give up the throne. There was too much opposition to the marriage in the country and the Empire for it to precipitate anything other than a disaster. He signed the instrument of abdication at Fort Belvedere on 10th December 1936. His brothers, The Duke of York, The Duke of Gloucester and The Duke of Kent were all there to witness it. The following day, his final act as King was to give the royal assent to the instrument of abdication. In the evening, he made a broadcast to the nation and the Empire, giving the reasons for his decision. During this broadcast he uttered the famous words, "I have found it impossible to carry the heavy burden of responsibility and to discharge my duties as king as I would wish to do without the help and support of the woman I love."

The Labour government breathed a collective sigh of relief. But the Abdication Crisis was an important milestone in the story of its decline.

CHAPTER 12: TUESDAY

25th JANUARY 1938

"Please state your name and occupation for the record."

"Me name's Sergeant George Morris of the Wiltshire Constabulary."

"Sergeant Morris, please describe the events of the night of Saturday the third of July last."

"I was the sergeant on duty at Chippenham police station when we received a telephone call at about one o'clock on the Saturday morning."

"Who was the call from?"

"It was from Tytherton 'ouse, Lord Ormford's residence."

"What was the nature of the call?"

"One of the servants, a man, 'ad telephoned to inform us that two people 'ad been shot at the 'ouse."

"Did he say who they were?"

"No he didn't, 'e seemed quite distraught."

"What happened then?"

"Constable Giles and myself took the car to Tytherton 'ouse to investigate."

"Why did you go yourself? Why not just send two constables?"

"Well sir, it's not every day two people get shot at the Tytherton manor, I thought I 'ad better go meself. When we got there, the place was in uproar, all the lights seemed to be on and people were milling around in their night attire."

"Why were there so many people there?"

"Lord Ormford was entertaining guests; there were about twenty guests as well as eleven servants and the members of Lord Ormford's family."

"What did you do then?"

"As soon as we arrived, Lord Ormford informed me that we had to restrain Senor Alvares. 'e led us to 'im. Senor Alvares was on the first floor landing, three men 'ad him pinned on the carpet but 'e was struggling like a goodun an' shouting in Spanish. A woman was holding his face in her 'ands..."

"Was this Senora Alvares?"

"... yes it was, she was a weeping 'ysterically and speaking to Senor Alvares, but whatever she was saying just seemed to make him more and more angry. When we got Senor Alvares to his feet she tried to throw 'er arms around his neck but he made to strike 'er and so we had to wrestle 'im to the ground again. At this point Lady Ormford ordered one of the servants to restrain Senora Alvares and then she slapped 'er face quite 'ard. Senora Alvares fell to the ground, she was still weeping, and the servant picks her up bodily and carries 'er out. Constable Giles 'andcuffed Senor Alvares and led 'im to the car, though 'e needed some 'elp to do it, as Senor Alvares continued to struggle."

"What did you do then?"

"I ask Lord Ormford what 'ad 'appened and 'e says that a shotgun gone off while it was being cleaned. I ask 'im 'ow many times it gone off and 'e looked a bit sheepish and said 'Twice I think.' which struck me as an odd response."

"Did you ask why a shotgun was being cleaned in the middle of the night?"

"I din't, no. I thought to ask, but it seemed a bit impertinent."

"I see. What did you do next?"

"I ask Lord Ormford to take me to the injured parties."

"What did he do?"

"Well, 'e seemed very agitated and displayed considerable reluctance to do as I asked him."

"What did he say to you?"

" 'e said that I needn't concern myself and that 'e would deal with the matter. I replied that I would have to make a report and 'e said; 'We really can't let ourselves get bogged down in all this red tape can we Sergeant?' I said that it wasn't a matter of red tape but a matter of my duty and I asked him again to see the injured parties, but at this point the doctor arrived."

"This was Doctor Greene."

"Yeah, Dr Greene from the village, 'e was led into one of the bedrooms so I followed him. I 'ad to be a bit sharpish like as I got the distinct impression Lord Ormford would have been happier if I didn't."

"What did you see in the bedroom?"

"Well I saw the Prime Minister – which was a bit of a shock! 'e was in a dressing gown lying in bed but 'e looked very pale, 'e 'ad an injury in his right arm, just below the shoulder, it had been bandaged and there was quite a bit of blood on the bedclothes. I was quite surprised I can tell you..."

"I dare say you were. Who else was there?"

"The Prime Minister's bodyguard was standin' by the bed. As soon as I come in he walks over and introduces 'imself, Detective Sergeant Benson was 'is name."

"What did Detective Sergeant Benson say?"

"Benson said that there had been an accident and that the Prime Minister and a servant 'ad been shot but he would deal with it. I said that I would 'ave to make a report and 'e said that I would need to submit it to his office for verification before it could be filed."

"Is such a request unusual?"

"Unusual? It's 'unheard of, it's totally contrary to procedure and I said so."

"What did he say to that?"

"'e said there was extenuatin' circumstances and that I needed to be discreet, 'e says the investigation would need to be conducted by an 'igher authority than the Wiltshire Constabulary an' the Prime Minister's wound wasn't life-threatening so I says 'Well what about the other one then?' and 'e says that she's unconscious but 'e's sure that she'll be fine. So I asks him where the gun is and he says not to worry 'e 'as it in safe keeping. I ask what kind of gun it was and 'e says it's a pistol."

"But didn't Lord Ormford describe it as a shotgun?"

"Yes 'e did."

"What did you make of all this Sergeant Morris?"

"Well I tell you sir, I've been a copper – man and boy – for nigh on thirty years and I know when I'm being given the run-around so I said I needed to see the other person."

"Now this was Nora Smyth?"

"Yes sir, Nora Smyth, God rest her soul, she was a chambermaid at the 'ouse."

"And did you get to see her?"

"Yes I did sir, the doctor, who had been examining the Prime Minister's injuries, was just finishing up with him and was also asking to see the other injured person so when they led him away I followed."

"Where did they take you?"

"They took us to the servant's quarters in the attic, to Mrs Smythe's room."

"Now Sergeant, where in the house was Mrs Smythe's room in relation to the Prime Minister's bedroom?"

"It was directly above it sir. Nora Smyth was lying in her bed, it was obvious to me that she was dead the minute I laid eyes on her. She'd been shot through the 'eart, lot of blood, the doctor examined her then said that there was nothin' he could do and so we went back downstairs."

"Were you able to examine the room?"

"No sir I wasn't, Lord Ormford insisted that we leave immediately, I informed Lord Ormford that I would have to investigate and he said that as there was nothing more that could be done and as his guests needed their sleep it could wait till morning. I insisted that he seal the room so as not to disturb the evidence and he said that he would see to it.

"Were you surprised at Lord Ormford's attitude?"

"Surprised? I was appalled, but, well, he is a Lord..."

"Did you do as he asked?"

"Yes I did sir, it's not my place to be contradicting a peer of the realm and there didn't seem to be anything else to do. So I returned to the car."

"What was Senor Alvares condition at this time?"

" 'e had settled down and was a lot calmer. As we drove back to the station 'e begun weeping and carrying on, he was the worse for drink. I 'adn't noticed before but in the confines of the car the smell was quite strong. He kept muttering a phrase in Spanish over and over again."

"What was that phrase Sergeant?"

"La puta."

"And do you happen to know what that means Sergeant?"

"Yes sir I looked it up, it means 'whore'."

"Did you return to Tytherton House the next day?"

"Yes sir I did, I got there at nine o'clock in the morning."

"And were you able to investigate the shootings?"

"No sir I was not."

"Why was that Sergeant?"

"I was met at the door by a Chief Superintendent Mitchell who said he was from Scotland Yard. 'e informed me that he was taking over the case personally, that I'd done a good job and that 'e would see to it that 'e mention it to my superiors."

"And what did you say to that Sergeant Morris?"

"I said I 'adn't done any sort of a job, I 'adn't been allowed. But 'e just smiled at me."

"What happened to Senor Alvarez, were you able to question him?"

"When I got back to the station Senor Alvarez had been transferred."

"On whose authority?"

"Chief Superintendent Mitchell's…"

CHAPTER 13: THE ALVAREZ AFFAIR

"I knew that woman was trouble from the minute I laid eyes on her." Violet Attlee, speaking of Consuela Alvarez. [63]

Taken from 'The Fall of Mosley' by Nigel Wintergarden, Journal of Twentieth Century History, Volume 4, April 1988

Consuela Alvarez was renowned as being one of the most beautiful women of her age. She was born in the small town of Villarica in Paraguay and married, at the age of 17, to Ernesto Alvarez – a minor official in the Paraguayan diplomatic service. Three years after this, in the Spring of 1936, he was posted to Paraguay's London legation and brought his young wife with him. This pushed what was essentially a very young and inexperienced girl into contact with a world of power and glamour that must have seemed overwhelming. With her mane of dark hair and compelling eyes she was impossible to miss at the parties and functions that she and her husband were required to attend in the capital city of one of the world's richest and most influential nations.

It was almost inevitable that her husband would grow jealous of her popularity and it is probable that he began to suspect that he was invited to many functions, not so much on his own merits, but for the sake of his wife. Certainly, Consuela inspired both lust and adoration in many of the men who met her, but she also inspired jealousy and contempt in quite a few of the women. It was rumoured that she had many affairs, but she is chiefly remembered for her central role in forcing Britain's Prime Minister, Oswald Mosley, to resign from office. [64]

---

[63] Not a genuine quote.

[64] Mosley was a vastly intelligent, highly motivated and prodigiously talented man, but he was also impulsive, rash, conceited, narcissistic, and arrogant; tended to a short–term outlook, chased headlines and was capable of almost total self–delusion. Here he is essentially destroyed by his own vanity.

It was at a private party in July 1938 that the incident that led to the revelation of what became known as the Alvarez Affair to the British public, occurred; but it is certain that it had been going on for some time prior to this. The party was held at Tytherton House, Lord Ormford's residence in Wiltshire; but the young South American beauty had caught the Prime Minister's interest at a reception given for members of London's Diplomatic Corps in May. He was unable to keep his eyes from her and she was obviously flattered by his attentions.

Mosley's first wife, Cimmie, had died in December 1934, and while Diana Mitford became his mistress the following year, Mosley continued to have affairs and was a prolific philanderer. He was not unmindful of the danger this might do to his career however, and avoided the wives of colleagues – his motto at the time was "Vote Labour; Sleep Tory". Mosley was blasé about his conquests – on one occasion, after being told that a group of angry debutantes' fathers were coming to deal with him, he merely commented "Well I suppose I should wear a balls protector then." [65] During his time in office such things were common amongst the elite and easily covered up. It is probable, that had it not been for the accidental death of a chambermaid, killed by a stray bullet from the gun of Ernesto Alvarez, a bullet meant for Mosley, that his liaison with Alvarez' wife would also have been covered up.

Certainly as much as possible was done to prevent the story becoming public. Mosley sustained a gunshot wound in the arm when Ernesto Alvarez, who was drunk and suspected his wife's betrayal, burst into the Prime Minister's room and caught him in 'flagrante dilecto' with Consuela. Fortunately for Mosley the room was dark and Alvarez' intoxication affected his aim. Wakened by the shot Mosley's bodyguard, who was asleep in the adjoining room, burst in and attempted to grapple the gun away from Alvarez, but before he could wrest it from him it discharged at the ceiling, the bullet then instantly killing Nora

---

[65] In 1933 when he told his friend Robert Boothby that he had told his first wife Cimmie about all his other women Boothby responded; "All of them?" Mosley replied; "Well, all apart from her step–mother and her sister".

Smythe who was asleep in the servants quarters on the floor above.

Mosley's injury was only a flesh wound but he was obliged to wear a sling. This, as well as the death; were officially explained as having been caused by careless cleaning of a shot gun by one of Lord Ormford's servants. The essential problem, however, was not only the death of Mrs Smythe, but the fact that so many people had been staying in Tytherton house on the night of the shooting. It wasn't long before rumours began to circulate about what had really happened at Tytherton House and the story began to take on the air of a particularly salacious scandal.

In his time in office, the Prime Minister had made many enemies and fallen out with not a few friends. One such was Lord Rothermere whose newspaper, the Daily Mail, had been a supporter of Mosley up until the abdication crisis. Lord Rothermere had never warmed to Mosley, but had viewed him and his Labour Party as the least unpalatable fixture on the British political landscape. Nevertheless, Rothermere was outraged by what he viewed as Mosley's immoral stance on Edward VIII's relationship with Wallis Simpson and there was a noticeable cooling in the Daily Mail's support of the Prime Minister from that time. It is possible that Lord Rothermere was looking for the right issue on which to reverse his support of Mosley, and if so, he must have counted himself fortunate that the Alvarez Affair landed in his lap.

Lord Rothermere assigned two of his most thorough reporters to look into the story and they quickly unearthed several suspicious aspects to the case. Firstly, there was the fact that Ernesto Alvarez had been transferred from his post with unseemly haste and sent to the Paraguayan embassy in Mongolia, his wife accompanying him. Then there was the unusual way in which Lord Ormford had dealt with the police. Although both the police officers who had attended the incident claimed to have been ordered not to answer any questions on the subject one of the reporters was able to find a witness who had seen and apparently had contact with Ernesto Alvarez in the cells at the Chippenham police station. The witness had been arrested earlier that evening after getting into a fight outside a pub at closing time but remembered that Alvarez had appeared to be under great emotional strain and continually repeated the word 'whore' in Spanish. The witness had spent some months with the International Brigades in Spain and in consequence was able to understand Alvarez. From these details it wasn't difficult to piece together a hypothesis concerning what had really happened at Tytherton House and the real cause of the Prime Minister's injuries. Discreet enquiries, helped in some cases by inconspicuous 'donations' to various members of Lord Ormford's staff provided most of the remaining specifics.

The most devastating revelation, the aspect of the case that certainly sealed Mosley's political fate, however, was not the Prime Minister's lecherousness, but the fact that in this instance his lover was also conducting an illicit relationship with the German Naval attaché, Korvettenkapitän Oscar Mannerheim.

When the story broke on the 23rd of August, Mosley tried to deflect attention from it, but his efforts were futile. Once the whiff of sex and scandal was out, the media would not let it go. Even the pro Mosley papers, sensing the unlikeliness of his political recovery from the humiliation, ran the story.

State visits to France and Italy kept Mosley away from Britain for two weeks but if he had hoped that the story would have blown over by the time he returned he was to be disappointed. On the 8th of September, he made the crucial mistake of temporising in the House of Commons, telling the chamber: "Mrs Alvarez and I were on friendly terms." and refusing to either confirm or deny the story of their affair. However, the knives were out even within his own party which many felt that Mosley had taken too far to the right. Even the whips, who were thuggish bullies and would use all manner of coercion to get Labour MP's to vote with Mosley's policy, found resistance within the party ranks hardening.

On 30th September 1938, Mosley signed the Munich Agreement with Adolf Hitler. He tried to present it as a diplomatic triumph and one of the fruits of his policy of 'Accommodation' with Germany. He promised the country that: 'There would be no war over insignificant territories, far from our shores.' However, it diverted attention away from the Alvarez scandal only briefly, the focus of the press was on Mosley, not Eastern Europe.

A month later, after the opposition (who seized on the twin opportunities of scandal and questionable foreign policy to discredit him) tabled a motion of no confidence, and facing a back bench revolt of unprecedented proportions, a beleaguered and humbled Mosley appeared before MPs again to say "With deep remorse," that he would resign as Prime Minister, though he did not subsequently resign his seat as many expected.

The government survived the motion, but barely, and promised a public enquiry. On 10th January, 1939, when the report was released at midnight, hundreds of curious members of the public queued to buy a copy. Although it contained few salacious details and criticised the government for not dealing with the affair more quickly, it concluded that there had been no breach of national security.

From The Edinburgh Times *Tuesday 21st June 1938*

ENGLAND PLAYERS BRING HOME FOOTBALL WORLD CUP

England's World Cup football squad arrived home yesterday at Croydon aerodrome to a rousing welcome from several hundred delighted fans. Many of the fans had waited several hours for a glimpse of their heroes. Eddie Hapgood, the captain, and the rest of the team stopped for half an hour to sign autographs and pose for photographers before returning to their homes for a well-earned rest. Hapgood made no attempt to conceal the black eye that he received during the final from Italian centre forward Gino Colaussi. The match has been described as 'passionate', 'robust' and 'physical', but fortunately was not marred by violence to the same extent as the infamous 'Battle of Highbury' four years ago which saw scenes more reminiscent of gladiatorial combat rather than the game of Association Football.

England was undefeated in the four games of the World Cup finals. They beat Hungary 3–1 on the fifth of June, Switzerland 1–0 in the quarter–finals on the 12th of June, Sweden 4–0 in the semi–final on the 16th and finally Italy 2–1 in the final on Sunday.

This is the second time that England has played in the World Cup finals; their surprising exit in the semi finals of the 1934 World Cup is now a distant memory. [66]

---

[66] In OTL England were invited by FIFA to play in the 1930, 1934 and 1938 world cups but declined the invitation. In TTL they take the place of the Netherlands East Indies team in the 1938 tournament, who in OTL were defeated 6–0 by Hungary in their opening match and eliminated. Between 1936 and 1939 England only played Hungary once and the result was 6–2 to England. England played Switzerland once in the same time period losing 2–1 in a close game in Zurich. They played Sweden once winning 4–0 in Sweden. They played Italy on 13 May 1939; the result was a 2–2 draw in Milan. The battle of Highbury took place on the 14th of November 1934. It was billed by the British press as the real World Cup final and Benito Mussolini offered each Italian player an Alfa Romeo car if they won. The match was extremely violent from the start but England won 3–2.

CHAPTER 14: SUNDAY

18th NOVEMBER 1940

How could it have come to this?

The limousines move slowly down Whitehall. Past the silent Houses of Parliament, across Westminster Bridge, then east along Borough High Street and Jamaica Road. There are nine of them altogether; flags flutter from the front wings of a few. The clouds part for a second and their highly polished flanks gleam in the momentary sunlight. Motorcycle out-riders pause at each intersection to stop traffic, but there is no traffic; London's streets are almost deserted.

Clement Attlee, Britain's former Prime Minister, now Foreign Minister, looks out at the grey anonymous day from the back of one of them. Defeat had meant his resignation but ensured his place in this drama. And why not? The can is his to carry. Despite his overcoat he can feel the coldness of the leather seats on his skin. Through his mind a stanza of poetry passes again and again

> Unreal City,
> Under the brown fog of a winter dawn,
> A crowd flowed over London Bridge, so many,
> I had not thought death had undone so many…

There is a face in Attlee's mind too, a face that he cannot banish. Cape Hellas, a morning in 1915, a boy dying in his arms. Shrapnel had pierced his lungs and severed his spine. His body immobile, his confused eyes form a question that the blood foaming from his lips will not let him ask.

He had lied to the boy, he had said; 'It's alright lad, we'll get you out of here, try and relax.' What else could he do? The boy had been an unmemorable soldier; he had done his job well enough and laughed at the other soldier's jokes though he had few jokes of his own to tell. He had held him close like a child and waited till he had gone before he let the body slip down to the ground, but the boy's face would be with him always.

On Evelyn Street a stray dog noses through the rubbish and a lone man walking hurriedly, glances up as the cars pass him by. He hunches into his overcoat as the cold wind whips autumn leaves into small tornadoes at his feet, the convoy of cars cross the bridge at Deptford Creek, turn left onto Horseferry Place and stop at the pier.

The German cruiser *Prinz Eugen* is anchored in the Thames, her colours snapping in the fitful wind. Men are stepping from the cars now; the doors open and close. Dark overcoats, a few uniforms, the red tabs and gold braid of high command. They stand in resigned knots, few words pass between them. They avoid each other's eyes.

Attlee leads them down towards the pier and the waiting boats, there is little point in prevarication, he must do what he has come to do and be damned for it. On the quarter deck of the ship they are waiting for him, an honour guard, a table with a pen and a great bound book open at a page. The German officers give nonchalant salutes, their greetings are studiously relaxed, the meticulously observed formalities underpinned by their cockiness, there is laughter in their eyes and smiles come readily to their lips.

He has seen German soldiers before, long lines of them marching back from the front; starving, broken men, with the haunted eyes of defeat. In the summer of 1918 the British Army had shattered the German, sent them reeling from one defensive position to another. They surrendered in droves and Major Attlee watched them go with quiet satisfaction in his heart. How different they looked now.

Men of his generation had justified that war with the hope that it would be the last of its kind. It was the only way they could find to make sense of it, the idea that all the carnage and suffering, the pain and futility of it, had somehow changed the world for all time. How could it have come to this?

Here on the deck with his legs wide apart, a hand theatrically placed on one hip, his lips pursed and his chin jutting outward is the dictator of Italy, posturing like a third rate actor. Absurd, ridiculous; his grey and black uniform reminds Attlee of a vulture's plumage. Well, the vulture shall have its carrion today and much good may the fly blown wastes of British Somaliland

and a couple of miserable settlements in the Sudan and Egypt do him.

There is one civilian, Ribbentrop, the German foreign minister, the Führer himself does not have the time to accept Britain's surrender, for surrender this is, though it does not go by that name. It will be called the Treaty of Leamouth, it will be sold to the British public and the peoples of the world as a success, peace with honour, an opportunity to end the war, stop the suffering. But it will be none of these things. And the word will get out, it will not be long before the truth will be obvious, the facade of British power has been stripped and the Treaty of Leamouth will not hide the fact of defeat.

One by one, those required to sign shuffle forward, sit and write their names. He is the last. One of the German officers gestures to the chair, the movement is a command. The book lies open before him; the pen is poised in his hand. He hears the whirr of the cine camera, the pop of flashbulbs, signs his name and stands up. The officer dabs the signature with a blotter, snaps the book shut and inclines his head. He does not disguise his smirk. "Thank you Herr Attlee."

As he turns away and begins to walk back toward the gangway he tells himself again that there is no choice, that his hand has been forced, that by doing this he is preventing a worse defeat, a greater ignominy. He must think of other things now, he must reunite a party that is tearing itself to pieces, try and prepare it for an election that must come within a year, but the face of the dying boy will not leave his mind and in his heart he knows he has betrayed him.

CHAPTER 15:

THE UNTHINKABLE VICTORY

"The world believes only in success!" Adolf Hitler, addressing his generals 22nd August 1939

From The Edinburgh Times *22nd March 1970*

CABINET CONSIDERED ATTACKING FRENCH FLEET IN 1940

Documents released today under the 30 Year Rule show that a suggestion was made to attack the French Navy at its bases in North Africa in June 1940 after the capitulation of France. The proposal was rejected out of hand by the Prime Minister, Hugh Dalton, despite warnings that the French Fleet – if it fell into the hands of the Nazi regime – would seriously affect the balance of power in the Mediterranean and the Atlantic. This surprising revelation has caused some ruffled feathers across the Channel, though no statement has been forthcoming from the Elysee Palace.

From 'A Concise History of British Politics' by Tom Shaed, Gloucester University Press, 2007

By 1938, the French government were growing increasingly irritated with British reticence on the issue of the rising power of Germany. Essentially Mosley had abandoned the traditional British policy of the 'balance of power' – one to which the United Kingdom had adhered for some two-hundred years, believing instead that the influence of the League of Nations could grow sufficiently to replace it. Mosley was happy to see Germany expand to the south or east if it wished, believing as he did that it deserved a sphere of influence like any other Great Power. It was Mosley's hope that a Germany satisfied in the East would provide a counter balance to the threat from Russia and would be happy to rejoin the League. Stability, he believed, would therefore follow. Even at the time, this policy was seen as questionable and many members of his own party, as well as the opposition, were uneasy with its potential consequences. Mosley was content to see the Germans absorb Austria; 'rectify' their frontier with Czechoslovakia; even to be the masters of central and eastern Europe. His one concern was that the West wasn't attacked.

The policy of the Conservative opposition was similar to that of the Labour Government. The term 'accommodation' was used to describe it, but in the press it was derided as 'appeasement'. Of the three major parties, only the Liberals took a position that was not one of pacification towards the dictators. Sir Archibald Sinclair's was one of few voices raised against Britain's policy though his was 'a voice crying in the wilderness'.

The French were deeply alarmed by the Anschluss (Germany's annexation of Austria in March 1938) and even more so with the seizure of the Sudetenland in September 1938. The Anschluss seemed to mark a reversal of the position Britain had taken four years previously in the Austrian Emergency of July 1934. At that time the British had given the French to understand that their policy included the preservation of Austria as an Italian satellite for Mussolini's security, their sudden willingness to negotiate this away prompted the familiar outcry in the French press against 'Perfidious Albion'. But the fact that Italy was now in alliance with Germany left the French diplomatically isolated.

From 'The British Empire from 1914 to 1948' by Ian Shaw, Longacre 2005

The Sudeten Crisis as it became known, came at a time when the British government was heavily distracted by the Alvarez affair. The French were once again unwilling to act without British support. Partly in an attempt to divert attention from the sordid details of his personal life Oswald Mosley flew to Berlin for talks with Hitler on the issue. This meeting cemented in Hitler's mind something that he already strongly suspected; that the British Prime Minister, and indeed British policy in general, was essentially unconcerned by German expansion. This was not strictly true, Britain had begun serious re-armament from 1935 onwards, initially on concerns about Japanese and Russian expansionism. Firstly the Royal Navy and later the Army and the Royal Air Force had seen a marked increase in their budgets and were undergoing growth. This was partly as a result of the Labour Party's efforts at job creation, but also because Mosley firmly believed that the Germans would be reluctant to attack a well-armed Britain and would avoid conflict to the west on that basis. This notion of deterrence was also central to British policy on the containment of Japan, Italy and the USSR [67]

Clement Attlee's elevation to Prime minister on Mosley's resignation in late October 1938 marked a distinct change in Britain's attitude towards Germany. The event unleashed vicious infighting within the Labour party. The battle for Labour's soul, a battle that was to tear it apart, was just beginning.

Although Mosley's basic policy was still followed, Attlee gave a personal assurance to the French Prime minister Edouard Daladier in January 1939 that Britain would stand by France if it were attacked. It was only at this point, however, that the British and French began to draw up joint plans for the eventuality of a war with Germany. Then, on 15th March 1939 when Germany Annexed the rump of Czechoslovakia (something Mosley had essentially sanctioned), Britain gave a guarantee of military assistance to Poland that it would support it in the event of German aggression.

The Polish crisis of late August 1939 and the subsequent invasion of Poland by Germany in September prompted an Anglo-French ultimatum to Hitler and when this was rejected a state of war existed between them. The French request that the British send forces to help secure its eastern frontiers prompted a gradual build-up of British ground forces in France over the

---

[67] There is substantial improvement in British forces in TTL, especially the Royal Navy, as Mosley has initiated better funding and an earlier rearmament programme. The effects of a stronger economy and the different TTL Washington Naval Treaty are also marked. See Annex 8.

winter of 1939 – 40 to a total of nine divisions by 10th May 1940 supported be elements of the RAF including ten squadrons of light bombers and ten squadrons of Hurricane fighters. [68]

There was much criticism of Attlee subsequently for his reversal of Mosley's policy. He was accused of mismanaging Britain's relations with Germany and in so doing leading Britain to the humiliation of defeat. The War of 1940 was branded 'The Unnecessary War' in some circles, particularly on the back benches of the Labour Party. But we can say now with some certainty that Mosley completely misunderstood the true nature of the threat posed by Nazi Germany, that his attempts to 'manage' German expansion were doomed to failure and that eventually Britain would certainly have been forced to oppose Adolf Hitler no matter what.

From 'The War of 1940' by Evelyn Bailey, Macallister, 1989

When the German armed forces defeated the Allied armies in the Spring and Summer of 1940 it was a victory without precedent in the history of war. In a matter of weeks Germany took control of Denmark, Norway, Holland, Belgium, Luxembourg and France, leaving only Britain and the Commonwealth still opposing them. The world was staggered by the scale of the German success and while the more hysterical commentators prophesied Britain's swift defeat, those with a clearer grasp of strategic realities pointed out the difficulties of crossing the English Channel against the strength of the Royal Navy. Some even called as examples the events of the Napoleonic Wars where the British built a coalition to fight on land and slowly strangled France with the time honoured tactic of naval blockade. The Battle of Britain was a serious setback for Hitler's Luftwaffe and the disastrous losses of mid-September meant that the invasion of Britain failed to materialise before the

---

[68] Exactly what was committed on 10th May 1940 OTL.

storms of Autumn made such a venture impossible. [69] The operations carried out by a joint Royal Navy Air Arm/Bomber Command strike force on the evening of 14th September and the full moon night of 16th September meant that the Germans were able to commit only a greatly reduced number of fighters to the attacks of 15th and 17th September. The execution done among the German bombers that day was so fearful that Hitler ordered a drastic reduction in operations over the British Isles and by the end of September the battle was over. [70]

Why then was Britain compelled to seek terms from Germany in November 1940? There was the obvious fact of British military defeat, despite prevailing in the skies over southern England the humiliating reverses in Norway and France and the enormous loss of war materiel was inescapable. The decisive result of the Battle of Britain gave His Majesty's Government a scrap of clothing to disguise the nakedness of the rout and even claim success, but nothing more.

There was the less obvious but more pressing reason that the United Kingdom was simply out of money. Before both the Great War and the Napoleonic Wars, British Finances were on a sound footing. Money was the foundation of the war effort in both cases but the strain of 1914–18 had eroded much of Britain's wealth leaving the country with substantial debts. Furthermore, the recession of the early 1930s as well as the slow recovery from it had inhibited growth. Modern economists agree that the Mosleyite program of job creation in the late 30s meant the contemplation of a long war extremely problematic in 1940 because Mosley's schemes had been partly funded by digging into Britain's gold and foreign currency reserves. Meanwhile the

---

[69] Mosley's build up of British defences means a slightly larger Fighter Command. The production network built up in OTL (the shadow factories) to manufacture weapons is in place and the training programs of the RAF are expanded compared to OTL meaning a slightly better flow of trained pilots (and better trained pilots) to the squadrons. Some of the extra training capacity TTL will of course have been absorbed by the substantial increase in the size of the Royal Navy Air Arm.

[70] See Annex 4

United States, which had financed part of the British effort in the Great War through loans, was now, because of default, determined not to lend belligerents money. President Roosevelt's offer to loan weaponry to the British in exchange for basing rights had created a storm of controversy in what was an election year in the United States.

The influence of one of the presidential candidates (the former Governor of Louisiana, Huey Long) was particularly malign for Britain. Long ran as a third party nominee, his campaign was resolutely isolationist and while he was never really a serious contender for the Oval Office (except perhaps in his own mind) his apparent initial success forced a policy review by the Republican candidate, Wendell Willkie. Willkie's subsequent reversal of his previously interventionist position came as a profound shock to the British government and caused an abrupt re-assessment of strategy.

There had been a suggestion as early as 1937 that the vast manufacturing power of the United States could be used to produce weapons for Britain in any future war. The French had embarked on a similar programme, but in the British case the suggestion had to be rejected because it would mean even greater calls upon the already depleted gold and foreign currency reserves. [71] 'Self-reliance' had to be Britain's motto in weapons

---

[71] Due to the earlier abandonment of the Gold Standard Britain will be much wealthier and her gold and dollar reserves will be much greater TTL than OTL. Manufacturing industry will also be healthier, allowing greater and more rapid expansion of war production. However, interventionist financial policies tend to require high spending from governments that attempt them and the ways in which income can be secured are limited. While the 1941 OTL sell-off of enormous British assets at cheap prices will not take place in TTL, Mosley's extravagance, combined with the policy of self-reliance in weapons procurement has compromised Britain's ability to fight on effectively. It is worth noting here that in OTL, once Britain's gold and cash had all been handed over to America, the country was compelled to divest itself of £5.3 billion worth of high-yield foreign investments which were sold to American interests for about 20% of their book value. The appalling strategic position in which the country found itself meant that the British had to permit the Americans to fleece them. In financial terms it was one of the worst bargains ever struck, in geopolitical terms it was better than surrendering to the Nazis. This also has a huge effect on the American economy.

procurement though of course a limited programme of buying American weapons and materials was undertaken in the wake of the Polish crisis.

Critically, the British cabinet was forced to its decision by the defeat of Franklin Roosevelt in the Presidential election, for with his dismissal from office faded Britain's last hope of securing the finance and the manpower to ensure final victory over Germany. It is important to note that because of the innate strength of the economy, Britain was well able to fight on defensively using only her own resources. But in the strategic position of 1940, with Germany in control of the continent and seemingly on friendly terms with Russia, the old British tactics of coalition building and blockade looked to be utterly futile. The only route to a meaningful victory was the invasion of Europe and the military destruction of the German war machine. A daunting prospect to say the least.

President elect Willkie seemed to have become an implacable opponent of measures that might entangle the United States in a European war and thus there seemed no prospect of securing either the alliance or the money to invade Europe and liberate it from the Nazis. Willkie's chaotic campaign and ambiguous statements on the subject had caused despair and incomprehension in the British Government. Was Willkie an isolationist or not? His party certainly was. Thus, the British Cabinet saw no clear way forward other than seeking an armistice.

The German terms were not wholly ungenerous and many of the promises the Germans made in their discussions with the British on the wording of the treaty were in fact fulfilled, though recently released cabinet papers show that for their part the British believed none of them.

The symbolism that attended the signing of the document was unmistakable. A German warship moored in Greenwich Reach opposite the twin cupolas of the Royal Naval College sent a powerful signal to the world. Nevertheless the Treaty of Leamouth was essentially meaningless. In drawing it up, the German high command knew that because of the still unbroken strength of the Royal Navy and Royal Air Force they were not then capable of the military subjugation of Britain.

In the end the Treaty of Leamouth was merely an opportunity for each side to pause. On the 1st of November 1940, Neville Chamberlain, leader of the opposition Conservative Party, rose to make his last speech in the House of Commons. Desperately ill with cancer and barely able to speak, he had to be supported as he stood to address the house which listened in absolute silence as he denounced the treaty as "... nothing more than the Peace of Amiens." [72] He died a week later.

---

[72] The Treaty of Amiens was signed on March 25, 1802 by Joseph Bonaparte and the Marquis Cornwallis as a "Definitive Treaty of Peace" between France and the United Kingdom. It lasted for one year.

CHAPTER 16: FRIDAY 28th AUGUST 1942

The flagship, the battle cruiser *Frunze*, has already left the dock and is nosing past the mole led by the destroyer *Bodryi*. The ancient, salt-bitten light cruiser *Krasnyi Kavkaz* and the newer *Molotov* have cast off their lines, drawn in their gangways and are belching palls of thick smoke into the hazy sky. Only the large destroyer *Kharkov* is still tied up right at the end of the quay. It is close now, only another sixty yards.

It is a long time since John Leighton has had to run anywhere. Two months cooling his heels in Istanbul and another three weeks waiting in Tehran for transport to Russia has taken the edge off his fitness and besides, it is years since he went through basic training. His breath comes like the rasp of a saw as his shoes pound the worn concrete of the quay but the crash of bombs falling on the town of Batumi is drawing closer and lends urgency to his feet. He looks up to see a Heinkel 111 roar low overhead, bombs spilling from its belly. One of the warehouses that line the dock disappears in a sheet of flame and the shock wave knocks him down.

When he wakes up a moment later he is lying on the ground with his eyes full of dust and smoke and a ringing in his ears. His minder, Gergiev, is shouting beside him, at least he is trying to shout but the ringing is so strong that Leighton is unable to hear what he is saying. The camera clenched in his left hand is undamaged. It is a Leica III and was given to him by an army Major at the consulate in Tehran, along with thirty rolls of film, a brief explanation of its workings and an admonition to 'Take as many pictures as you can – we need to know what's going on over there in as much detail as possible'.

"Come on get up, let's go, come on…" Gergiev is hauling him to his feet but his voice seems to come from a great distance away. "Get up John, come on, move…"

Gergiev had been waiting for him on the dock at Baku on the Caspian Sea, where the boat from Rasht in Iran had left him. He had introduced himself as an official translator though they both knew that he was not there to help Leighton communicate, but to watch everything he did. An officer in the

Narodny Komissariat Vnutrennikh Del – the secret police – there is no getting rid of him, the man has dogged his steps for the past six weeks. He is friendly enough but his English is as limited as Leighton's Russian.

After being shuffled from one unit to another, Leighton's requests to be posted to a Soviet warship had got him as far as Batumi, where the surviving vessels of the Soviet Black Sea Fleet had fled after their bases in the Crimea and Ukraine were overrun by the Germans. The ships were streaked with rust, their crews dispirited and indifferent, worn down by inactivity; they had not put to sea for nearly a year.

Again Leighton found himself cooling his heels, his billet this time was in a ramshackle hotel. Weeks had passed without a hint of action, but that morning the base was in uproar. The listless crews of the decaying warships were suddenly galvanized by purpose. Orders had come for the squadron to put to sea, the Germans had made a landing seventy miles to the north at Ochamchire.

He had gone at once to the administration block to get permission to go on board one of the ships, but in the commotion no-one had the time to listen to his request and one sour-faced clerk had given him a fifteen page form and told him to fill it out. He had thrown the form straight back at the man – the squadron was already raising steam – and left the office at a run with Gergiev following in his wake calling out plaintively for him to wait. He had no clear idea how he was going to get on one of the ships, only that he must try and as he ran towards them the wail of the air raid siren started and the first bombs began to fall.

In the chaos, even the guards seem to have deserted their posts, though a mass of soldiers, sailors and civilians are milling about on the docks. As he runs up the gangplank of *Kharkov* the sentry on deck levels his rifle and challenges him in Russian. Leighton's hearing is only beginning to come back but the message of the rifle is plain enough. The sentry is a freckle-faced lad and looks terrified.

Leighton is wearing his Royal Navy uniform which must be unfamiliar to the boy. He is about to try and respond when Gergiev pushes past. His voice is hoarse from exertion.

"He's with me, he's an English observer. Here, here are my papers." Gergiev brandishes the wad of documents he carries but the boy shakes his head and holds the rifle steady.

"English observer? What are you talking about?" This time Gergiev shows his party ID and when he speaks, even though he is breathless his voice has an edge like steel;

"I am Captain Vassily Nikolayavitch Gergiev of the NKVD and you will let us aboard, that is an order." The boy blanches and stands aside, coming neatly to attention as he does.

"Who the hell are you?" An officer is coming down the companionway from the bridge, he looks angry, confused, Gergiev answers him;

"I am Captain Gergiev of the NKVD, I and my companion are here to observe the workings of this ship." The officer frowns, his expression is part anger, part fear. The NKVD are loathed by everyone Leighton has met. Not that he has been allowed to speak with many people, but the expression on their faces when they see Gergiev's identity card is more eloquent than words.

"What do you want with us?" Gergiev pauses, sighs and shrugs as if exasperated. Then he says softly;

"To observe Lieutenant, you can let us do that can't you?" The man hesitates, uncertain, shakes his head.

"You can go up to the searchlight platform, we won't be needing that just yet, but stay out of the way of my crew and obey any orders they give you – do you understand?" Leighton nods.

The searchlight platform is a good vantage point for photography; it is a raised dais amidships, between the two funnels, where the movement of the ship will be less marked than at the ends. As they pass the mole the sky begins to clear, the sea is calm with only a gentle swell and the *Kharkov* accelerates to what Leighton estimates must be a speed of over 30 knots. Behind them smoke rises from Batumi, it seems to mingle with the smoke that surges from the funnel above them. They will be off Ochamchire in just over two hours.

It is good to be on the sea again, smelling the salt in the air and listening to the shriek of the white gulls that wheel above him. He checks the camera carefully, polishes the lens with his handkerchief and feels in his pocket for the spare rolls of film. It is a bright day and he sets the aperture and the shutter speed accordingly, his hands are trembling a little.

Kharkov slows to keep pace with the cruisers as they catch up. They are moving at about 28 knots in line ahead, led by the destroyer *Bodryi*, then the flagship, followed by *Molotov* and finally *Krasni Kavkaz*. *Kharkov* takes up station off *Frunze'* starboard beam. The sky is mostly clear now and the sun warms his face. Gergiev sits down on a tiny metal seat that folds flat against the side of the cylindrical wall of the searchlight mounting, he reaches in to his coat and offers the flask he always keeps there. Gergiev lights a cigarette. "It has turned in to a beautiful morning John."

Leighton asks; "Do you know where the life jackets are?" Gergiev smiles;

"Can't you swim?"

"Yes of course…"

"Good, because I can't." for some reason Gergiev finds this amusing and his voice tails off into a wheezy laugh.

*

They see the aircraft one hour and fifty two minutes after sailing from Batumi. They are north west of the ship's position, black dots high against the wispy pattern of cirrus cloud above them. The klaxons ring out and the crew, already at action stations, look tensely at the sky. Leighton estimates that there are more than seventy of them; he asks Gergiev; "Ours or theirs?"

Gergiev makes no answer, then one of the aircraft peels off into a dive, then another and a third; "Theirs."

They are Junkers 87s and 88s. They come streaking down, black shapes like diving crows, as the guns on the Russian ships open up and the bright summer sky is stained with bursts of smoke. Above the crash of the guns comes the banshee howl of the Stuka's sirens and the sea around the cruisers begins to churn with explosions. Towering columns of water tinged with brown and grey from the explosives leap upwards and suddenly *Krasni Kavkaz* disappears in a column of flame that seems to break the ship in half, her stern – with its still thrashing screws – rears out of the water for a moment, then disappears beneath the waves. The bow section stays afloat fractionally longer but a massive explosion obliterates it, sending pieces of steel spinning outwards from the fireball to splash all around them and rattle off the funnel and the decks.

Leighton gasps in horror and tries to frame the picture, he closes the shutter and twists the wind on knob with unnecessary force, he shoots again and again, then as the cloud of smoke falls astern he frames the flagship. Their speed has increased and *Frunze'* white wake goes curling away from her hull, cutting a foaming furrow across the face of the bright ocean, her battle ensigns are snapping at her mast and her guns thunder in unison, spitting great gouts of fire at the sky.

She is magnificent. Her forward turrets, unable to elevate enough to engage the German aircraft, traverse right and left then abruptly she takes a hit aft of the bridge, she seems to stagger under the blow and a great column of white steam roars out of her forward funnel followed by black oily smoke as she slows. A second bomb strikes forward of her rearmost turret, then a third amidships causes a huge detonation that shatters the superstructure and tears her aft funnel and her mainmast from their mountings to send them tumbling into the sea.

The ship lurches to starboard and careers towards them as the dark smoke gushes out of her, she is losing speed and cuts across their wake just yards from *Kharkov's* stern. Leighton can see the frantic figures of her crew swarming across her deck, over the side into the water. He frames another picture and another, then the wind–on stops. He is at the end of the roll, fumbling with the film release and his shaking hands can barely move the tiny handle that rewinds the film. He opens the back of the camera and the cartridge falls to the deck. He stoops to retrieve it and gropes in his pocket for a fresh roll of film, loads it, closes the camera and winds on. As he straightens and looks again for the flagship he sees it astern off their port quarter well down in the water and still pouring smoke into the sky.

Kharkov is heeling in a hard starboard turn. He hangs on to one of the handles on the searchlight as she straightens and rights herself before heeling into a port turn that is just as hard. They are the target now. A great column of water leaps out of the sea twenty yards off their port beam. Instinctively Leighton winces and turns his back as a curtain of spray drenches him. Another hits the water to their starboard closer than the first, then another directly after that and closer still. He hides the camera inside his uniform jacket and falls to the deck throwing his free arm over his head and praying for it to end.

After a moment he looks up, but as he staggers to his feet he sees a Stuka closing rapidly from astern, ripples of fire flicker at the bend of its crooked wings, two lines of splashes converge on the ship. But even as the bullets pop and buzz around his head rattling off the steel he raises the camera and exposes a frame, twisting the wind-on knob as he again throws himself flat. The glass in the searchlight disintegrates into tiny shards that rain around him in glittering pieces, bouncing off the deck catching rays of sunlight.

He lies with his eyes tight shut for what seems an age. He can feel the throb of the engines through his prone body but the ship's guns have fallen silent. As he gets unsteadily to his feet he sees from the position of the sun that they are steering south. The sky is empty and they are alone on the still surface of the ocean.

He brushes broken glass from his clothes and looks around. Gergiev is slumped face down on the grey steel of the deck. A patch of dark blood is spreading around his body. He shakes him by the shoulder but the man does not move, he turns the body over and sees the piece of shrapnel jutting from Gergiev's chest, the glassy, sightless eyes, the broken cigarette still stuck to his lower lip.

Leighton stumbles down the steps from the searchlight platform to the deck and falls to his knees, the camera is still in his shaking hands. He closes the shutter and twists the wind-on, he does it again and again, staring into empty space, eyes unfocused, looking at nothing, taking pictures of nothing, until he comes to the end of the film and the lever will advance no further.

CHAPTER 17: THE COLLAPSE

OF THE SOVIET UNION

"If I don't get the oil in Maikop and Grozny, I'll have to liquidate this war." Adolf Hitler, addressing his generals, June 1942.

From 'The Path to War in Asia' by Michael Stravinski, Halifax University Press, 2001

The German attack on the USSR caught Japan diplomatically flat–footed. Japan's Ambassador to Germany, Oshima Hiroshi, had got wind of the plan two weeks before it was unleashed and reported it to Tokyo. But the warning was too late; no more than two months earlier, Japan had concluded a neutrality pact with the Soviets.

Japan's Foreign Minister, Matsuoka Yosuke, had followed the example of Germany in befriending the Soviet Union. He believed that improved relations with the USSR would bring an end to their aid to China's Nationalist regime as well as sending a signal to the Americans that Japan was not isolated. Now, he was forced to admit his misjudgement and he went on to propose that Japan join the Germans in their attack on Russia. The Imperial Navy however, affirmed its wish for Japanese forces to strike south.

Japanese government at this time was characterised by confusion and misunderstanding. Each actor within the administration was working towards a different goal while all had their direction of purpose led by a sense of honour that tended to be different with each individual. In the Japanese constitutional system the Supreme Command was independent of the Prime Minister. This meant a chaotic and uncoordinated approach to the formation of policy and the determination of the Generals to control national destiny (and murder anyone who opposed their aims) made the work of civilian politicians both impossible and hazardous.

The whole messy edifice was notionally loyal to the Emperor, but his refusal to state a direct preference for any particular faction, policy or line of reasoning, did nothing to clarify matters. Hirohito, the Showa (Enlightened Peace) Emperor, could have brought Japan's slide into war to a halt with a few well-picked words, but chose instead to let his generals posture and bicker, while he communicated his thoughts through sonnets and haiku.

After conferences between the Army, the Navy, the Foreign Ministries and the Prime Minister's office; the Japanese leadership decided to leave the South alone for the time being and concentrate on the Russian Far East. [73] They did, however, decide to call for the occupation of Indochina and for the secret mobilization of one million reservists and conscripts.

Unbeknown to the Japanese, the Americans had broken their top-level diplomatic 'Purple' code in September 1940 and were able to read their despatches. Consequently, the Japanese unwittingly handed the US Administration an outline of what was to be expected, by informing their Washington embassy of the future direction of policy.

At the ensuing meeting of the US Cabinet the question of an oil embargo was discussed. Both the State Department and the Navy's analysts argued that an oil embargo meant war. President Willkie postponed any decision but on 4th July, 1941 sent a message to Japan's Prime Minister Konoe Fumimaro, asking him, point blank, whether rumours of the Japanese intention to attack the Soviet Union were true and threatening dire consequences if further Japanese aggression occurred. Konoe replied that Japan had no intention of attacking the Soviets, and professed Japan's desire for peaceful relations.

On July 18th, Willkie informed his cabinet that the code-breakers believed that the occupation of the parts of Indo-China not already controlled by the Japanese would take place within the next three to four days. Queried as to the possible reactions

---

[73] The opposite decision (to go south rather than west) was made in our time line.

that the United States should consider, Willkie responded that they should do little; especially not embargo oil. [74]

On July 24th, the President received a memorandum from the Chief of Naval Operations, Admiral Harold Stark, in which the Navy's position was clearly put as opposing an oil embargo for fear of the possible results of such action. That very same day, Japanese and Vichy French authorities arrived at an understanding regarding the use of air facilities and harbours in Southern Indo-China. This was thanks in no small part to Japanese threats of violence and from July 29th on, Japanese forces began to occupy the area.

President Willkie's response came on July 30th; he gave in to the prodding of the Treasury and War Departments and froze Japanese assets in the United States. He also federalized the Philippine Armed Forces, putting General Douglas MacArthur in charge of the newly established United States Army Forces Far East. However, on 6th August Willkie issued another directive permitting the release of funds sufficient to allow the Japanese to purchase oil up to pre-war levels, although he embargoed high-grade aviation fuel. While this was not quite a reversal of the Roosevelt Administration's position, its significance was noted in Japan.

The reluctance with which Willkie treated the oil embargo spoke clearly of his conviction that it would not help to curb Japanese aggression. But the comparatively small economic pressure exerted by the decision for government control of Japanese spending in the US allowed for an increase later on, if there was no sign of Japanese cooperation.

The American embargo was essentially a hollow gesture as the Japanese were able to obtain petroleum products from the Netherlands East Indies via Thailand. The British attempts to stop tin, copper, rubber and oil exports from South East Asia to Japan were equally futile for the same reasons.

However, the survival of Prime Minister Konoe's government was a direct result of the perception that he was able

---

[74] In OTL and TTL the Japanese had occupied most of French Indochina in September 1940.

to achieve a rapprochement with the Americans. The Willkie administration's volte-face was seen by the Japanese as weakness. Konoe's replacement by the Army Minister General Tojo Hideki did not take place until 1945. [75]

Taken from 'Japanese Operations in Far Eastern Russia 1942–43' Piotr Yevseyev, writing in the Morskoi Zhurnal, *1993 volume 2*

After their defeat at Khalkin Gol (Nomohan) in 1939, the Japanese chose to bide their time for a strike against the Russian Far Eastern provinces. In the Summer of 1942, with the Soviet Union reeling from a renewed German offensive the opportunity arose and on July 23rd 1942, as news of the German capture of Rostov reached Stalin, the Soviets were struck from behind.

The Japanese avoided the Khalkin Gol area and concentrated their efforts farther east. With their left flank covered by a thrust at Belomorsk, the main Japanese drive struck north east up the Amur valley from Harbin. The Japanese Navy's Special Landing Forces rapidly invested the Komandorski Islands, the major towns on Kamchatka and those around the perimeter of the sea of Okhotsk. The main fleet covered Japanese Army landings on Sakhalin (Karafuto), and on the eastern shore of the Maritime provinces of Russia's Far East. Vladivostok was progressively cut off and then completely isolated when the Kwantung Army cut the trans-Siberian railway.

Vladivostok and Sov'govan were heavily defended with in-depth fortifications, the Red Army had around 35 divisions in the trans-Baikal region and initially they stopped the Japanese from advancing very far. But for the Soviets, the situation quickly became grim. Although they thoroughly outfought the Japanese, the calls placed on their resources by the demands of the war in the west meant that the eastern armies lacked the assets needed for a decisive victory. Still they fought doggedly

---

[75] In OTL Konoe was replaced by Tojo in October 1941 precisely because he seemed unable to manage Japan's relations with America in a way the militarists deemed satisfactory.

and Vladivostok, besieged for almost a year, was the scene of a defence as determined and bitter as that of Leningrad.

The Soviets planned a counterattack in the winter of 1942-1943, but the collapse of the USSR put paid to the operation, and by 1943 the Japanese had occupied all of Karafuto (Sakhalin), the Kamchatka Peninsula, and the Russian Pacific Coast;

The decision to move against the Soviet Union represented a victory of the Army over the Navy in Japanese governance. Unfortunately, the gains made in eastern Siberia did nothing to solve Japan's real problem: the strength sapping war in China. The resources they had seized were difficult to exploit and the British and the Americans were still opposed to Japan's presence there. However, Thai business interests continued to act as brokers, supplying Japan with petroleum products throughout the Axis-Soviet war, despite some diplomatic pressure from the UK.

Taken from 'Operation Lehrer' by Richard Gage, Aldermann, 1973

Hitler reduced the scope of the 1942 Summer campaign (Operation Blue), deciding to ignore Moscow and make a single major push towards the oilfields of the Caucasus as well as driving on Stalingrad. It is uncertain as to whether or not he grasped the true importance of the natural resources of this region and their significance to the Soviet economy. Before the operation started he interfered in the disposition of his forces, dividing them between two different objectives. Capture of the oil producing region in the south and the destruction of the Red Army's reserves west of the Volga.

In comparison with the rest of Operation Blue, Operation Lehrer (Teacher) was very minor, but it proved to be Operation Blue's most significant element. The initial landing of the 21st Panzer and 90th Light divisions on the eastern shore of the Black Sea at Kabuleti and Ochamchire was conducted with the assistance of units of the Italian and Romanian navies supported by elements of the Kreigsmarine. The assembly of the fleet that facilitated and supported the landing was a major undertaking in itself. The Romanian and German components being largely composed of a mixture of captured Soviet vessels and craft that had come down the central European canal system from Germany, some of them disassembled and transported on barges.

British intelligence strongly suspected that an Italian naval force had passed through the Bosporus and into the Black Sea disguised as merchant vessels. However, when this information was passed to Stalin he rejected it out of hand as a figment of someone's imagination. Nevertheless when the guns of the cruiser Pola opened fire on the town of Supse on the morning of the 25th August, its shells were very real indeed.

The Germans had been planning the assault for more than a year. The embarrassingly piecemeal nature of their preparations for Operation Sealion and the lack of confidence that attended the planning of the invasion of Britain had bought the backwardness of German tactical abilities in this area into sharp focus. Both Grossadmiral Raeder and Hitler agreed that the ability to land troops over hostile beaches could bring a new tactical dimension to the German armed forces. The Kreigsmarine, with little to occupy it in the interval between the Treaty of Leamouth and the beginning of Operation Lehrer, had studied and practised the art. The Black Sea was in many ways an ideal theatre in which to attempt a major seaborne assault. German forces had occupied several towns on the eastern coast of the Black Sea in 1917 after the treaty of Brest–Litovsk so the area and its environs were not unknown to the Germans. It would have been impossible to move German heavy naval units into the Black Sea without arousing the notice of the entire world. But Hitler was able to call in a favour from his ally Mussolini after rescuing him from the embarrassing humiliation he suffered in the Balkans.

The ruse of disguising a squadron of Italian warships as Greek merchantman had been thought of by Admiral Iochiani of the Regia Marina. The disguises themselves were simple structures of wood and canvas and were highly effective. Even so, the Italians had some bad luck when the force was observed by a British Naval officer while anchored in the Sea of Marmara following an engine room mishap. He deduced correctly that they were disguised warships and his report was passed to the Foreign Office in London but, as we have seen, once it reached the Russians it was dismissed as fantastical.

Hitler ceased vacillating and made the decision to concentrate resources with Generals Paulus and Hoth's drive on Stalingrad on the 23rd of August at the expense of Von Kliest's thrust into the Caucasus. Unbeknown to him, on the following day (24th August), Stalin ordered that the city that bore his name must be held at all costs and directed General Georgy Zhukov to supervise the defence. With the sudden demands on Soviet forces caused by the Japanese attack in the Far East, there was no choice but to draw forces for the defence of Stalingrad from General Tyulenev's Transcaucasus front and the defence of the Caucasus was fatally weakened.

The Black Sea landings themselves met only light opposition. Soviet forces were caught completely off-balance and fell back on Tblisi. Von Kleist, in command of the First Panzer Army, attacking into the Caucsas from the north suddenly found that resistance on his right was evaporating as the Russians desperately tried to realign their forces. Novorissisk fell on 28th August, Tuapse two days later and the German column racing down the coast road reached Sokhumi on September 2nd.

Heavy fighting in Tblisi slowed the Germans down, but once the city was secured on 11th September the second phase of Lehrer went into effect. This time lead by the fresh 15th Panzer division with elements of the motorised Italian Ariette division in support, the Germans covered the 280 miles in a week. Soviet resistance had effectively collapsed and with the capture of Baku by the German 'Falshirmjaeger' (Airborne) division on 15th September it ceased entirely. Russian forces retreated into a pocket around Grozny and Makhachkala where they were ordered by the enraged Stalin to make a final stand. Attempts were made to supply them by ships from Astrakhan (there was no railway line along the western shore of the Caspian Sea) but the pocket surrendered on 5th October.

In comparison with the titanic struggle to the north, Operation Lehrer was a sideshow, the German attack and the Soviet defence were both under-resourced and not perceived as an important component of the struggle unfolding in the southern Soviet Union. Nevertheless it was one of the most significant military operations in history.

From: 'The USSR and Total War: Why the Soviet Economy Collapsed in 1942' by Mark Harrison, Gloucester University Press, 2005[76]

The history of other wars and other countries can offer us clues as to why the Soviet economy collapsed in 1942. In World War I, Imperial Russia struggled to mobilize itself and eventually disintegrated. The disintegration was as much economic as it was military and political; it can be argued that Russia's economic break-up was the key factor in both its military defeat and the Russian revolution. Later in the same war and under similar stresses, both Austria-Hungary and Germany went the same way. In all these cases the tendency of shrinkage ended in economic collapse.

A country's war effort will fail when its people decide to invest effort elsewhere. In wartime the citizen may choose to allocate effort to patriotic service of the country's interest or to service of self-interest. In economic terms, the Soviet Union in 1942 was a dictatorship of the 'stationary-bandit' type. In this system, the dictator manages his assets through agents. Each agent will remain loyal to the dictator's interests as long as that agent's share in the dictator's expected revenues from the assets he manages surpasses the anticipated value of the asset if the agent were to steal it. If and when the agent steals from the dictator, he becomes a 'roving bandit'. This reduces the value to all agents of serving the dictator loyally and increases the incentive of other agents to rove too.

---

[76] This passage is adapted from 'The USSR and Total War: Why didn't the Soviet Economy Collapse in 1942?' by Mark Harrison, in A World at Total War: Global Conflict and the Politics of Destruction, 1939–1945, pp. 137–156, edited by Roger Chickering, Stig Förster, and Bernd Greiner (Cambridge University Press, 2005).

War production was a crucial factor in the Soviet war effort, but in 1942 its foundations were already crumbling. In fact, they started to crumble in 1941. Soviet factories could not operate without metals, machinery, power, and transportation. Their workers needed to be fed and clothed, and competed for the same means of subsistence as soldiers on the front line and farmers in the rear. As war production climbed, civilian infrastructure fell away. While Soviet factories turned out munitions, civilians were starving and freezing to death. The German success in the Caucasus and consequent capture of a large proportion of Russia's oil production districts and refineries pushed the crisis of resources passed the point of recovery and made 'roving banditry' a pre-requisite for survival.

Once Baku and Grozny had fallen, the USSR was doomed by shortages of fuel and the attendant dislocation of communications and transport, the inability to sustain a war on two fronts down the immense distances of the Trans-Siberian Railway was critical in exacerbating the strain but the inevitable disintegration of the country into minor satrapies and their subsequent coalescing into larger post collapse economic units was a direct result of the loss of the fuel producing areas.

CHAPTER 18: MONDAY 9th FEBRUARY 1942

Commander Mike Brevard, USN, watches the light gather on the eastern horizon, a sliver of blinding yellow sun breaking through the low clouds and touching the grey bulk of Table Mountain across the bay. He is standing on the bridge of the cruiser USS *Wichita*, moored by the inner mole at the Royal Navy's Simonstown naval base. It is five o'clock in the morning and already he can feel the moist African heat beginning to build.

It is time to get the ship ready to depart. The smoke from *Wichita's* funnel rises vertically in the still air as they begin to raise steam. They have been away for four months but are sailing today for their home port, Norfolk, Virginia; there is not a man on board who is not anxious to be off.

They leave Simonstown in the late morning, round the headland into the Atlantic and steer north-north-west, sailing past Cape Town and the long swathe of white beach to the north of the suburbs until the shoreline falls beneath the horizon and *Wichita* seems alone on the dark ocean. They are glad to leave the heat of the land behind them. The wind freshens from the north and the raucous gulls that have followed them out of the harbour turn back toward the shore.

They see the shadow of smoke on their starboard quarter in the middle of the afternoon. It is a British escort carrier. Both ships 'dip' the flags at their main mast in salute as is the common courtesy of the sea, Captain Richards steps out of the Chart House onto *Wichita's* bridge, Brevard looks up from the message chit he is signing as he hears him say, "What is *that*?"

Brevard follows the direction in which the captain's binoculars are pointing with his eyes. "That sir, is the British escort carrier HMS *Activity*."

"Not the ship, commander. That thing on its flight deck."

Brevard takes his own binoculars and focuses on *Activity*. He hesitates a moment, but he is fairly sure that he knows which aircraft the captain is referring to. "It's a Fairey Swordfish, sir."

"A what?" Brevard is about to repeat himself but Richards cuts him off.

"It looks like something out of the Great War."

"They are phasing them out I believe, Sir. They're used mostly for anti-submarine work now." Richards lets the binoculars fall to his chest and stares at the aircraft with distaste.

"Ya know Brevard, if the Germans and the Japanese don't start behaving themselves we could wind up allied to the British – and they're using goddam' *biplanes*?"

"Apparently they are quite effective anti-submarine airplanes, sir."

Richards snorts contemptuously. "Would you want to go to war in a plane named 'Fairy' Brevard?"

Brevard is about to answer him but a noise from astern is beginning to drown out the sounds of the sea. It is a rhythmic thumping, an endless series of pulsating reports like a broken drum being beaten at a very fast time. They turn and see that it is an aircraft, but instead of wings it has two pylons jutting out of the sides of the fuselage and at the end of each pylon a huge upward pointing propeller thrashes the air. As it draws closer the noise becomes deafening. Like the Swordfish it is painted in greys and greens and wears British markings, the carrier has slowed to three or four knots and turned into the wind. Richards shouts above the din, "And what the hell is *that*?"

Brevard answers him, "An autogyro Sir...'

"I know it's a goddam' autogyro Brevard."

"I'm sorry sir. *Activity* is being used as a trials ship I believe, but more than that I can't tell you..."

The autogyro lands on the carrier, a graceless belly flop of a landing that compresses the oleos and shakes the machine's entire frame but mercifully the noise begins to fade as its rotors slow. The captain shakes his head and goes below decks.

*

Two hours later, the wind has turned around and is now coming from astern of them, another shadow of smoke darkens the horizon directly ahead. The ship that is making it is travelling on a reciprocal course to their own; as it draws closer they see from her fittings that she was once a whaler. She is painted in the colours of Norddeutscher Lloyd and flies the flag of Nazi Germany.

Brevard is on the bridge, though it is not his watch when he hears one of the lookouts say, "Sir, I think you should take a look at this."

"What is it?"

"They seem to be burying dead Sir but... I don't know, I can't quite make it out. It looks as if some of them are women and children."

Brevard raises the binoculars and looks for himself. An involuntary exclamation escapes his lips. "What the hell?"

The crew of the ship are throwing corpses overboard, but you could not call what they are doing 'burying the dead'. The bodies have not been prepared in any way. They have not even been wrapped in cloth, some of them are half naked. There is no care or respect in the way the crew of the ship are treating them, they are just slinging them without ceremony into the water. Boxes, suitcases and possessions are also thrown over the side to bob in the ship's wake like flotsam. Quickly he takes in the rest of the ship, the nameplate; *Sonderburg*, the cranes and rig. He notes that she is flying the quarantine pennant and has not dipped her flag in salute.

The two vessels close at roughly twenty-five knots. They pass, port side to port side, about two cables distance from each other. As they pass, Brevard orders the helm to come about. The cruiser crosses the ex-whaler's wake and begins to overhaul her. It is only now that they are downwind of the other ship that the smell reaches them across the water. It is a stench so vile that Brevard feels his throat contract involuntarily.

It is hard to describe, a co-mingling of the smells of death, disease, vomit, excrement and decay. Brevard says to the signalman, "Send – 'Do you require assistance?'" The *Wichita* slows to around nine knots so as not to pass the other ship, they wait, Brevard reaches for the telephone that will connect him with the captain's cabin but before he can lift the receiver he hears Richards behind him.

The captain scans the *Sonderburg* quickly. He says, "Are you familiar with that smell, commander?"

"No Sir and I would be glad to be less familiar with it to be honest."

"Commander, sound general quarters, prepare a boarding party and signal that ship to heave to and prepare to be boarded."

Brevard looks at the captain sharply.

"Yes, sir. Sir – they're flying the quarantine pennant, and Sir, may I ask what grounds we have for boarding them?"

"I don't give a damn if they're flying Adolf Hitler's lederhosen Mr. Brevard, give my order."

"Yes Sir."

He gives the order. The klaxon howls as the ship comes to action stations, the signal lamp rattles in one corner of the bridge as the message is sent. They wait. The party on *Sonderburg's* deck cease what they are doing and seem uncertain what to do next. The ship does not slow down or lower a ladder. Finally *Sonderburg* replies, "We are going about legitimate business. By what authority do you stop us?"

Captain Richards does not lower his binoculars, he barely waits a moment, then says, "Mr Brevard, have the forward five inch gun put a shot across their bows."

Brevard is shocked, but he gives the order, he hears the crash of the gun, sees the waterspout leap up a mile beyond the *Sonderburg*. For a moment she continues and then they begin to overhaul her. *Wichita* slows too. They come to a dead stop and lower the boat which begins to cross the gap between the two ships. Again *Sonderburg's* signal lamp begins to flash. "We do not consent to your search. Be advised there is cholera on board."

Richards lowers his binoculars. "Commander, have our boat keep station but signal they are not to board until they receive my order. Send to the other ship, 'What is your business in these waters?'"

Again they wait. The three vessels rise and fall on the ocean swell. The stench is worse than ever. At last the reply flashes out from *Sonderburg's* bridge wing. "We are a passenger liner transporting Jews to Madagascar."

Brevard looks over at Richards. He can see the anger in his eyes, his knuckles are white against the black coating of the barrels, but again the captain hesitates. He brings the binoculars back to his face and Brevard can almost feel the intensity with which Richards is scrutinising the other ship. Again he brings the glasses down. His eyes beneath his frown are diamond hard pinpricks that would bore a hole through the steel of the other ship if they could. He stands motionless for what seems an age. When finally he speaks his words are choked by an impotent rage. "Send to the other ship – 'Your failure to show respect for the dead is offensive.'"

Again the signal lamp rattles, but Richards does not wait to see what the response will be, as he turns to leave the bridge he says, "Commander, recall the boarding party and get us out of here."

*

That evening, as is his habit, Richards invites Brevard into his cabin where they discuss the ship's business and the day's events over a drink. The United States Navy is a 'dry' service, but the captain keeps a bottle of Tennessee whiskey in his desk. He pours two glasses and hands one to his executive officer. Never one for small talk he launches straight into the subject that is uppermost in his mind. "Will the British fight Brevard? What did you make of the officers you met in Simonstown?"

Brevard takes a sip of his drink before responding. "I'll be honest with you, sir. Some of them seemed dispirited; their collapse in 1940 weighs on them. Most of them seem positive about their new Government and they are getting a lot of new equipment, some of it is quite innovative – as we saw this afternoon."

"That contraption looked like some unholy cross between a bedstead and a couple of sycamore seeds. Perhaps they're hoping the Germans will surrender because they'll be laughing so hard. But the question is, do you think they have the stomach for another round?"

"I really couldn't say sir. I've always been impressed by the professionalism of the British Navy men I've met. I think most of them would very much like to get back at the Germans. It's their Government that is going to hesitate."

"The Germans beat them pretty badly."

"The Germans beat their army, not their navy My opinion is that the British won the battle in the air too, but they came to an agreement with Germany right after the Battle of Britain so the Germans got to claim it as their victory. That's one for the historians to figure out."

"Brevard I'm going to be honest with you, I wasn't joking this afternoon. I think America is going to be at war with Germany within the next three years, perhaps Japan too, and if that's the case we are going to need allies. The British are the only power left that aren't in alliance with Germany. I know they made some sort of treaty in 1940, but will they be bound by it? I don't know. I hope not, but I don't know."

There is silence for a few moments. Then Brevard says, "Captain, you asked me if I knew what that smell was? The smell from that German whaler – or whatever she was. What was it, what was that smell?"

Richards places his glass on the desk and looks at him evenly. "That's the smell of a slave ship commander. It's the smell of torment and fear, misery and despair. I've only smelled it once before, but it's not the kind of thing you forget. I was an ensign on the *Marblehead,* maybe twenty years ago now. We were cruising in the Red Sea off Al Hudayah, it was a large dhow out of Aseb. We boarded her – they had no cargo – but the smell… that smell gets right into the fabric of a ship. Once it's been used as a slaver a few times there's no way to get rid of it."

Brevard thinks for a moment. "Sir, do you think they did have cholera on board?"

"I doubt it, but I wasn't prepared to take that risk. Or set off an international incident." He reaches once more for the bottle. "Have some more whiskey Commander; it will help get the stench out of your nostrils. It won't get it out of your mind though, it'll take more than whiskey to do that."

CHAPTER 19: NAZI GERMANY
IN THE INTERBELLUM

"Germany now stands astride the prostrate body of Europe like some dark Colossus, brooding over its success and plotting the perpetration of yet further outrages." Sir Archibald Sinclair, speaking in the House of Commons in January 1945 [77]

From 'Germany After the War of 1940' Piotr Yevseyev, writing in Morskoi Zhurnal, *1994 Volume 4*

As 1942 drew to a close, the power of Nazi Germany appeared to have reached an unassailable apogee. Hitler's domination of Europe stretched from the Ural Mountains to the Atlantic Ocean, but his ambition was not yet sated. Once again, one of the principal causes of German aggression was the Nazi's ongoing mismanagement of the German economy and the strain of the vast projects undertaken, such as the rebuilding of Berlin and the enlargement of the Kreigsmarine.

Yet despite the general climate of hysterical rejoicing in the Axis countries, a few voices were raised in caution. Prinz Rupprecht, the Crown Prince of Bavaria, who had been forced into exile in Italy by the Nazis in December 1939, wrote to his friend Marie, Baroness von Weinbach in a letter dated 11th January 1943 that,

"It may be that the Nazis have utterly overreached themselves. I cannot help think that this is the high point of the tide, now it must surely flow the other way."

Switzerland, with its large gold reserves [78] looked a prime target, much as Austria and Czechoslovakia had done in 1938

---

[77] Not a genuine quote.

[78] Over US$1 billion OTL and TTL which is roughly RM 2.5 billion at the 1938 exchange rate and current (1938) prices. To put this in context; after the Anschluss and the subsequent seizure of Austria's gold reserves, Germany roughly doubled its gold reserves to just under US$90 million using the 1938 exchange rate and current prices.

and 1939. The invasion of Switzerland (Operation Tannenbaum) in 1943 was successfully mounted and Hitler's power stretched across the entire continent of Europe with only a supine Sweden, a friendly Finland, a nervous Portugal and an apparently marginalised Britain not directly under Nazi rule or in the Axis alliance. German was declared the official language of Europe. English and Russian were outlawed while Danish, Dutch, Polish, French, Norwegian and Swedish were to be tolerated for a decade.

The fact of the German conquest of Europe served to mask the tremendous problems the Nazis had created for themselves. The Nazification, depopulation and exploitation of the new conquests became Hitler's principal goal, but his sadistic racial policies alienated the subject populations and inspired an insurgency campaign unparalleled in history for both its scale and its viciousness. Partisan activities in the newly created 'protectorates' of Ukraine, Muscovy, Gottengau (Kherson and the Crimea) and the Caucasus were widespread and (particularly in the Caucasus) difficult to counter. More and more of the SS and Army were embroiled in the hunt for partisans who knew that they had nothing to lose and whose numbers grew with every brutal reprisal. Hitler was inclined to see this as an advantage, claiming that it would speed the depopulation of those areas for German colonization, but his generals and political advisors were increasingly dismayed by the casualty lists. Inevitably, front line strength suffered and Hitler's refusal to reverse the sharp decrease in war production that occurred after 1942 exacerbated the problem. The newly created German state of Schweizmark (Composed of the German and French speaking areas of Switzerland) was also a hotbed of partisan activity. At first reprisals were limited, but as the insurgency dragged on, the slaughter of Swiss civilians in revenge for partisan attacks became almost as bad as that of Ukrainians or Poles.

The 'Vassalzustand' (Vassal states) of Denmark, Norway, Belgium, Holland and France were less of a problem. In a direct imitation of Bismarck's policy in 1870, Hitler withdrew most of his forces from French territories after one year, limited the size of the French armed forces by treaty, compelled France to pay vast 'indemnities' and surrender the most modern ships of its fleet. In all cases the Vassalzustand were allowed to retain their colonies though their foreign policy was dictated from Germania. [79] Pillaged by their German overlords and hemmed in by restrictive trade practices and the decimation of industries that might compete with German manufacturers, the Vassalzustand suffered severe economic decline.

Luxembourg was annexed outright by Germany in 1942. Belgium on 1st January 1944. Holland, Denmark and Norway were to be similarly seized by 1950. Hitler believed that the Dutch, the Flemish, the Danes and the Norwegians were Aryans and therefore 'Germanisable'. He also believed the French, Spanish and Italians were Aryans but had a severely diluted gene pool. Nevertheless, significant numbers of German soldiers had to be stationed in these territories, lest their populations prove ungrateful for the Third Reich's munificence.

Hitler's attitude toward the United Kingdom was characterised by ambivalence and contempt. He believed that Britain and the Commonwealth were defeated foes and would be bound by the Treaty of Leamouth, which had a non-aggression clause. In this, he was guided by Rudolph Hess who, upon the cessation of hostilities, resumed his frequent trips to England and pursued his many friendships with members of the British aristocracy. Hitler often referred to the war of 1940 as 'Der triumph der Ubermenshen' and his view was reinforced by the inept British showing in that war.

The British sent supplies to the Soviet Union from Barbarossa until its collapse. This fact was not lost on Hitler but the support was more moral than material. A small amount of weaponry reached the Soviet Union from the UK through the port of Murmansk and across the Iranian border. This included some aircraft and armoured fighting vehicles, but consisted mostly of humanitarian supplies and was seen by the Germans as insignificant. It is not unfair to say that the Labour Party in Britain was inclined to vocal backing of the Russian war effort to assuage its own conscience. Astonishing as it may seem today it

---

[79] Hitler planned to change the name of Berlin to this.

is certainly true that many elements of Britain's Labour movement – not only the most radical – held common cause with Stalin's regime. The Liberals and Conservatives were appalled by the Soviet Union and saw it as essentially another kind of fascist state. However, after the German attack in June 1941 sent Soviet forces reeling, Britain began sending food and medicine to alleviate the suffering of the Soviet Union's ordinary people as well as military and civilian observers to learn as much as possible about the situation there and the course of the war.

Hitler's attempts to export Nazism were not as successful as he hoped. The Finns for instance, though valuable allies in the war against the Soviet Union declined to join the Axis Pact. Italy too was a not entirely content member of the Pact. Il Duce's appetite for conquest had been left un-sated by the Treaty of Leamouth. He had gained very little at the expense of the British and his ambitions in Egypt, the Red Sea, East Africa and the Western Indian Ocean were unsatisfied. Mussolini also made plans to offset the power of Germany and his erstwhile partner Adolf Hitler by creating an Italian leaning faction within the Axis. In Il Duce's fancy this would consist of an alliance of nations under Italian guidance which would include Spain, Portugal, Romania, Hungary and even France. But from the tentative feelers put out through private channels Mussolini was quickly to discover that there was little appetite for any changes in the pecking order within the Pact.

Spain eventually did become a member of the Axis after the disintegration of the USSR.[80] Franco, having resisted bringing Spain into full membership of the Pact, essentially succumbed to bribery. Though both the British and the Germans made extravagant promises to win his support, it was the proximity and success of The Third Reich that proved the deciding factor. That, and the tempting prospect of a return to the days of

---

[80] In OTL the advice of Admiral Canaris, the head of the Abwher – the German intelligence service – was one of the principal causes of Franco's refusal to be drawn further into alliance with Hitler who wanted to pressure Franco into one. Canaris had long–standing ties to Spain and his personal relationship with Franco meant that even as Nazi Germany's official position was being presented, Canaris was whispering cautionary words in Franco's ear.

Spanish glory, at what seemed a low cost, held out by an alliance with Germany. Encouraged by his Foreign Minister Serrano Suñer, it is certain that Franco had little idea of the consequences of his actions, believing in 1943 that the peace would continue for at least a decade.

From 'The Nazi Religion' Larry Ledbetter, writing in The Anglican, *May 4th 1986*

The Nazi ideology was an amalgam of German ultra-nationalism and a neo-Germanic heathenism. From its earliest expression in the völkisch clubs and wandervogel groups and its development via eugenics and race-theory, it was permeated with an obsessive sense of national/racial superiority that inspired a revival of a romanticised Teutonic paganism. Hitler himself said:

> "Those who see in National Socialism as nothing more than a political movement know scarcely anything of it...It is more even than a religion. It is the will to create mankind anew. The old beliefs will be brought back to honour again. The whole secret knowledge of nature, of the divine, the demonic. We will wash off the Christian veneer and bring out a religion peculiar to our race."

The Nazis' favourite cultural expression – the operas of Wagner – fitted this idea well. The Ring Cycle can be seen as an idolisation of Teutonic paganism while Parsifal, with its mixture of magic, occultism and Christian symbolism is more ambiguous but fundamentally apostate in its outlook. [81] The Chief architect of this blasphemous usurpation of Christian imagery was Heinrich Himmler.

---

[81] It is also possible to view Parsifal as an allegorical expression of Christianity. Wagner's commentary on the opera is contradictory but this very ambiguity suited the Nazis' plan.

One of the methods designed to help convert the German population (who generally thought of themselves as Christian) to the new Nazi religion, was to arrogate Christian concepts, beliefs and symbols and incorporate a twisted version of them into it. In the Nazi iconography, Hitler was a kind of Messiah, the thousand-year rule of the Third Reich a sick parody of the Messianic Era on earth mentioned in the book of Revelation. The Aryan race took the place of the Jews as the Chosen People and racial purity – blood purity – assumed the place of the Holy Blood of Christ as the means of salvation.

Religion is often an expression of the desire of individual human beings to find peace, yet the leaders of the Nazi party, despite their success, found no peace at all. The deaths of Heinrich Himmler and Joseph Goebbels in the purge of 1943 meant that plans to displace Christianity with the new Aryan religion were slow to be implemented. Martin Bormann, the victor of the political infighting within the Nazi party, was certainly anti-Christian and the Kirchenkampf, his war on Christianity within The Third Reich, continued. It left a spiritual void in the hearts of the German people that can scarcely have been any better than the regressive heathenism the Nazis were intent to foist upon them.

From 'The Economy of the Third Reich' by Wilhelm Offenbach, Macallister 1962

Prior to 1939, the Nazis had made a series of decisions that reduced Germany's engagement with the global economy. They preferred autarky and bilateral agreements to trade. German industry experienced difficulties in obtaining many raw materials that could only be sourced outside Europe, and in many ways could be considered as living hand-to-mouth. The situation was not helped by the Nazis habit of allowing manufacturers to pursue too many technically difficult projects simultaneously. A good example of this is the development of aircraft engines which was catastrophically mismanaged and failed to produce results as good as those of Britain. Albert Speer, the head of the Armaments ministry for much of 1942 wanted to cull the multifarious projects being undertaken by the engine manufacturers, but the success of German arms in the east meant that his colleagues were disinclined to interfere with what seemed a highly successful organization. [82]

Within Germany itself however, money was plentiful, especially after the conquest of Switzerland and the appropriation of Swiss gold and foreign currency reserves. These amounted to the sum of 2.5 billion Reichsmarks but this enormous quantity of money paled into insignificance next to the Nazis spending plans.

These included the reconstruction of the five 'Fuhrer' cities – Berlin, Munchen, Nuremberg, Linz and Hamburg. The plans for rebuilding Berlin alone were estimated at 5 billion Reichsmarks! The expansion of the Kreigsmarine was due to absorb almost as much. The fifth iteration of 'Generalplan Ost', the German plan for the subjugation of eastern Europe and its transformation into a settler area, was extraordinarily ambitious and was estimated at costing 67 billion Reichsmarks! The scheme included the construction of many new highways, large hydroelectric projects and a new train system, the Breitspurbahn. This was a broad-gauge railway which required the complete replacement of much of central Europe's rail lines with a new 3-metre gauge track. In addition to this, the Germans were lending money to their allies – most notably Spain where it was used to fund Franco's large programme of naval construction.

Hitler, up to this time, showed a marked reluctance to place too heavy a tax burden on the German economy. This was not a product of any financial orthodoxy, but was due to his paranoid fear that the German people were 'soft' and unable to tolerate hardship. Only in 1942 was the task of matching the German economy to the demands of the war undertaken seriously, but with the peace, military spending (particularly on the Army and Luftwaffe) was severely curtailed. So even this delayed expansion

---

[82] In OTL the dismay at defeats on the Eastern Front caused a wide reaching re-appraisal of the armaments industry. In TTL success leaves its inadequacies entrenched.

was not as far reaching or as successful as it might have been had the war continued into 1943.

Due also to the entry of Swiss gold into the German economy inflation began to grow. Indeed, like Phillip II's Spain, Nazi Germany found the economic adjustment necessitated by the influx of new wealth caused many difficulties. The Nazis response was price fixing by decree, but this caused shortages, sharp growth in the Black Market and sharp decline everywhere else. Corruption was rampant at every level of the Nazi administration and the Reichsmark began to devalue steadily against both the pound and the dollar.

The deportation and murder of vast numbers of persons the Nazis considered undesirable caused shrinkage in the overall size of the German economy and, unlike the regime in the Soviet Union, which in economic terms the government of Germany began to resemble, the Nazis mounted direct and efficient attacks upon the German education system. In general, Communist regimes have tended to fund and encourage education whereas Fascist ones have tended to undermine it. In the German case the educational malaise was much deeper and more significant than the burning of books by the SA in the late 1930s. Germany underwent a severe brain drain prior to the war of 1940 and by 1942 graduates were emerging from German universities knowing much about eugenics, the mathematics of artillery and the Nazi version of history, but next to nothing of the skills that would be useful in building a modern diversified economy.

Germany was able to continue economically for three reasons. Firstly, it had an enormous reserve of talent built up over many years because of its strong tradition in science and research. Although this tradition was being deliberately eroded by the Nazis in their search for a racially pure German science, it represented intellectual capital. A wasting asset certainly, but a considerable one nonetheless. Secondly, the enormous territories that Germany had conquered provided both economies of scale and primary resources that cushioned the impact of educational and economic decline. Thirdly, the widespread use of slavery which caused general economic shrinkage but gave the impression to those not enslaved that they were wealthier. The prospects for Germany's economic future however were extremely bleak.

From 'The Madagascar Plan' by Chanoch Cohen writing on jewhist.com [83]

Initial Nazi plans to address what they so euphemistically called 'The Jewish Question', consisted of the establishment of a 'Jewish reservation' for all Jews from Poland and the other conquered territories. It was to be located in the Lublin district of Poland, and was one part of an extensive resettlement project that Hitler had selected Heinrich Himmler to oversee. Hundreds of thousands of Jews were expelled from eastern Europe to make way for German settlers, but the plans for an 'ethnic new order' in Poland were unworkable. In June 1940, they were supplanted by the 'Madagascar Plan' under which all Jews were to be deported to the French colony of Madagascar, a large arid island off the west coast of southern Africa.

The idea of evacuating the Jews of Europe to Madagascar was not a concept that originated with the Nazis. The German scholar Paul de Lagarde put forward the idea in 1885, and in 1926 the Polish government investigated using Madagascar to settle its Jewish population. The commission set up to investigate the possibility, found that it would be feasible to settle 40,000 to 60,000 people in Madagascar, but Leon Alter, the director of the Jewish Immigration Association in Warsaw, believed the island could only handle 2,000.

The idea was considered again in Germany in 1931 but it wasn't until 3rd June 1940 that an ambitious bureaucrat named Franz Rademacher, head of the Judenreferat der Abteilung Deutschland: (Jewish Department of the Ministry of Foreign Affairs) set the plan in motion with a memorandum to his superior Martin Luther. Rademacher advocated the separation of eastern and western Jews. The eastern Jews, he felt, were principally responsible for the "militant Jewish intelligentsia",

---

[83] At the time of writing there was no such website as jewhist.com.

and should be kept in a specially constructed ghetto in Lublin to be "used as hostages to keep American Jews in check." The western Jews, he went on, should be expelled from Europe entirely, "to Madagascar, for example."

On receiving this memorandum, Luther brought the subject up with the Foreign Minister, Joachim von Ribbentrop. By 20th June 1940, Hitler spoke of the Plan with Grand Admiral Erich Raeder and had mentioned it to Mussolini on the 18th. The plan was turned over to the RSHA (Reich Central Security Office) and Adolf Eichmann (who was in charge of the Office of Jewish Evacuation within it) became involved. With the surrender of France on 21st June, one of the principal obstacles to the plan was removed. On 15th August, Eichmann released a draft titled Reichssicherheitshauptamt: Madagaskar Projekt (Reich Security Main Office: Madagascar Project), which intended the forced resettlement of one million Jewish people per year over four years and relinquished the idea of retaining any Jews in Europe at all.

Most of the Nazi hierarchy viewed the forced relocation of four million Jews to Madagascar as being better than the gradual extradition to Poland. As of 10th September, all deportations were cancelled and construction of the Warsaw ghetto was stopped.

Rademacher proposed the setting up of a special bank tasked with overseeing the liquidation of all Jewish assets in Europe to pay for the Plan. This bank would then play the role of financial intermediary between Madagascar and the rest of the world. Jewish people would not be permitted to have monetary transactions with anyone outside the island and they would only be allowed to take their money out of Germany in the form of German goods. The desired perception of the outside world would be that Germany had given 'autonomy' to the Jewish settlement in Madagascar. However, Eichmann made it clear in his draft, that the SS would manage and regulate every Jewish organization that was created to govern the island. With some changes the plan was approved by Hitler in October 1940 but was not put into operation until February of the following year.

The first deportation, 'transportation' as the Nazis described it, took place in March 1941. A group of 7000 Moravian Jews who had been deported to Lublin were forced to board trains bound for Danzig where they were herded onto a 12,600 ton German steamer the *Sonderburg* which then set sail for Madagascar. Conditions on board were indescribable. The *Sonderburg* had been launched in 1899 as the Potsdam, a passenger liner for the Holland-America Line but had been operating as a Norwegian whaling ship when taken as a prize in 1940. She had been designed to carry 2500 passengers and the overcrowding on the ship was appalling. Little provision had been made to feed the ship's 'cargo' and none of them were allowed on deck during the 26-day voyage. One of the survivors, Mordechai Bronfman estimates that 65% of the people who boarded the *Sonderburg* died on the journey from a combination of malnutrition, disease and general abuse. The bodies of the dead were simply tossed overboard.

The *Sonderburg* made five voyages to Madagascar in the following year, inevitably the cruelty and barbarism that attended these 'voyages of death' became known throughout the world and sparked international outrage. In February 1942 the *Sonderburg* was intercepted in the South Atlantic by the American cruiser USS *Wichita* and the disposal of bodies, was observed by her crew. Her captain contemplated sending a boarding party to the *Sonderburg* but she was flying the yellow quarantine flag and he was reluctant to cause an international incident.

Once the survivors of the *Sonderburg's* voyages disembarked in Madagascar, life was scarcely any better than it had been on the ship. Housed in camps, without money or resources, the Jews were expected to grow or procure their own food, but they were given no tools, no seeds, no livestock and no assistance of any kind. Furthermore the goods that they were supposed to receive in exchange for their money were usually pilfered by the SS before they ever left Germany.

The plan was suspended in April 1942 by directive of Adolf Eichmann, not for any reasons of human decency, but simply that the Nazis decided that there were simpler and less expensive ways to kill Jewish people. The Madagascar Plan was deliberately under resourced, haphazardly implemented and showed unequivocally that the Nazi 'territorial solutions to the

Jewish Problem', were not only conceived to bring about the end of the Jewish presence in Europe, but to kill as many Jews as possible in the process. The failure of the Madagascar Plan and the logistical problems of deportation in general, would ultimately lead to the conception of the Holocaust as the 'Final Solution of the Jewish Question.'

From 'The Night of the Lance' Gunter Schmidt, writing in Die Nachrichten, *June 1951*

It was perhaps inevitable, given the predatory character of the regime, that once victory had been achieved and a kind of peace once more held sway in Europe, that the Nazis would begin to turn on one another. In the early spring of 1943, shortly after the collapse of the last organised Soviet resistance, Himmler began pressing for the founding of the new state of Burgundy which conformed roughly to the outline of the medieval kingdom of the same name. It was to be carved out of parts of France, Belgium, Luxembourg and Switzerland. The capital city was to be either Ghent or Dijon and its chancellor was to be Léon Degrelle, the Belgian Fascist leader.

Although Himmler was certainly blindly loyal to Hitler, by 1943 the SS was beginning to resemble a private army with eight motorized divisions and more forming including several Panzer divisions. Himmler wanted the status of the SS within the German Reich to become that of a kind of new nobility, ruling it as a military-religious order, like the Teutonic Knights who had their own fiefdom in Prussia. The State of Burgundy was to be governed by a Reichsverweser (Regent), who would also be the Reichsfuehrer SS (Himmler's position). He was supported in this aim by Joseph Goebbels, but both men were aware that to achieve this goal they would have to weaken the influence of the party bureaucracy, which bought them into direct conflict with Martin Bormann. In fact, the main reason for Goebbels' support of Himmler was to marginalise Bormann.

By this time Bormann had skilfully turned himself into the second most powerful man in the Third Reich, he was effectively Hitler's deputy and closest confidant. Disparagingly referred to by other members of the regime as the 'Brown Eminence' his brutality, crudeness and apparent insignificance led many of them to misjudge his subtle perseverance and ability to make himself indispensable. He had an uncanny knack of exploiting the Fuhrer's weaknesses and idiosyncrasies and thus increasing his own power. He seemed always to be in attendance on Hitler, taking care of tedious administrative detail and expertly steering him into approving his own schemes.

As a result of his machinations, Hitler had dismissed Rudolf Hess in 1942. Hess' increasing distraction with high living and the trappings of authority had enabled Bormann to present him to the Fuhrer as too flippant and superficial to be trusted with power. This opened the way for his 'transfer' from head of the Parteikanzlei (Party Council) to the role of Germany's Ambassador to Britain. Bormann was, of course, appointed in his place.

Hitler's trust now resided in Bormann, whom he once called 'my most loyal Party comrade' but Bormann did not cease his Machiavellian intrigues against his rivals. He began to gather the reins of the Party into his own hands and progressively undermined all his competitors for power. Working in the anonymity of his modest office, the diminutive, thickset Bormann showed himself to be a master of intrigue, manipulation and political in-fighting. Always the guardian of Nazi orthodoxy, fanatically anti-Semitic and a keen exponent of the Kirchenkampf ('War on the Church', the Nazis attempts to destroy Christianity in Europe), he increased his grip on domestic policy until he decided most issues concerning the security of the regime. The rising power of the SS concerned him greatly, and he viewed the notion of a separate SS fiefdom in Burgundy as an intolerable schism within the party that would undermine his own authority. Himmler and Goebbels, frustrated by the waning of their own influence over Hitler, began to make clumsy attempts to sideline Bormann.

The leaders of the armed services, Reichsmarshal Herman Goering, Field Marshal Wilhelm Keitel, and General-Admiral Rolf Carls (heads of the Luftwaffe, Army, and Navy respectively), already felt that the SS was greatly exceeding its authority and becoming an over-powerful state within the state.

[84] There were hundreds of SS-controlled corporations and large numbers of its members in political posts. [85] Even the Gestapo was an SS organisation and the growth of the SS was not only a potentially destabilising influence but could be seen as an attempt at a 'slow coup'. Bormann had little difficulty persuading Carls that action would have to be taken. Carls had recently taken over from Raeder and was not really a political animal, whereas Bormann was a shrewd and wily plotter. Goering, on the other hand, was more ambivalent; while lesser members of the party saw which way the wind was blowing and made their alliances accordingly. The example of Albert Speer, Hitler's chief architect, is illustrative of this trend; he simply opted for the faction he felt was most likely to win.

In implementing his plans against the SS leadership, Bormann enlisted Admiral Wilhelm Canaris (head of the German intelligence service, the Abwher) whom he found most helpful. There was little love lost between Himmler and Canaris. The Reichsfuhrer SS distrusted the spymaster and believed him to be in contact with the MI6 branch of the British intelligence service. [86] Both Reinhard Heydrich and Heinrich Himmler, had done a detailed investigation of Canaris' sources of information on Operation Barbarossa and had arrived at the conclusion that there had indeed been contact between him and the British. Canaris wanted to protect himself from Himmler and in collusion with Bormann he manufactured evidence that

---

[84] In this timeline Raeder is replaced in January 1943 by General-admiral Rolf Carls who would be 57 years old. In OTL the choice was between Carls and Doenitz, Doenitz, a U-boat man was the obvious choice, Carls was a former 'flottenchef' and had more surface navy experience so is a better choice TTL.

[85] This happened in OTL as well, for instance SS-Obergruppenfuehrer Dr. Werner Best became the Reich's Plenipotentiary in Denmark, SS-Brigadefuehrer Professor Dr. Franz Alfred Six worked in the Foreign Office training the new generation of diplomats, SS-Gruppenfuehrer Dr. Stuckart was State Secretary in the Interior Ministry, SS-Gruppenfuehrer Otto Ohlendorf was Undersecretary of State in the Economics Ministry etc.

[86] As Himmler did in OTL.

Himmler and Goebbels were planning to murder the Fuhrer. He was also very careful to cover his trail, the forgers and even the typist who created the documents were killed as soon as they were complete.

Bormann acted quickly to present this 'evidence' not only to Carls, Kietel, and Goering but also to several of the more fanatical and impetuous middle ranking officers of the Liebstandarte 1st SS Panzer Division. The division was reforming at Warschau (formerly Warsaw) but the decline in munitions manufacture in Germany after 1942 meant that this was a slow process. Originally constituted in 1933 as Hitler's bodyguard, the formation had grown into a motorised division and had distinguished itself in the fighting between 1939 and 1942. It drew the most fervent and bloodthirsty soldiers in Germany to its ranks and was responsible for many war crimes and atrocities.

After meeting with Kietel and Carls on the afternoon of 19th November 1943, Bormann took a scheduled overnight train to Warschau (some 500 kilometres from Berlin) and met with Major Kurt Meyer, Captain Gerhard Bremer and Major Wilhelm Mohnke the following day. [87] He had consulted Kietel and chosen the men he wished to carry out his plan carefully. They were ruthless, fanatically loyal to Adolf Hitler, would obey orders without question and could be relied on to be discrete. It is also worth noting that in any state other than Nazi Germany, they might well have been considered to be criminally deranged and Mohnke was actually a morphine addict.

The resulting operation was known as Betreib Kaninchenfell (Operation Rabbit Skin – a reference to Himmler's hobby of breeding rabbits) took place just after midnight on the 23rd November. Units under the command of Meyer, Bremer and Mohnke arrested most of the senior leadership of the SS. The incident was to become known as 'Die Nacht der Lanze' (The Night of the Lance). Keitel had mobilised all Wehrmacht formations within Germany in case the SS rank and file decided

---

[87] These were three of the five SS officers responsible for the murder of more than a hundred surrendered Canadian soldiers in Normandy, 1944 OTL.

to oppose the arrests of their senior officers, but while there was some fighting, the basic loyalty to the person of Hitler of most of the junior and middle ranks of the SS meant that it quickly ceased. Nevertheless, more than 300 SS men were killed, Bormann, Carls, Keitel and Goering [88] presented the 'evidence' of the plot to Hitler at his Alpine retreat on the following morning while the operation was still taking place.

At first, Hitler did not believe that his trusted lieutenants were capable of treason, but Bormann was persuasive, and explained his unilateral action with the reason that he had acted only to protect his Fuhrer and the need to act quickly was pressing. Hitler was swayed by the deception and had thirteen of the implicated SS officers – including Himmler, Goebbels and Heydrich – tortured to death. Meyer, Bremer and Mohnke were all decorated and promoted, the idea of a separate SS state in Burgundy was dropped.

While Bormann's actions on Lanze Nacht were certainly risky, his daring paid off. Crucially, he had used SS officers as the instruments of his plan, making the coup seem a matter of internal SS house cleaning. If he had used Army or Luftwaffe troops the outcome might have been civil war.

Having dispensed with his most dangerous opponents and consolidated his power and influence, Bormann continued to 'rule from behind the throne' through management of the Party administration. This inevitably led to an increase of the authority of the Gauleiters (regional party leaders), who remained an important prop for Bormann. Unsurprisingly, in the fallout from the neutering of the SS as a political force, they were quickly purged of elements Bormann deemed to be disloyal. The Reich became more and more bureaucratised and, in that respect,

---

[88] It's important to note here that Herman Goering is not the somewhat marginalised figure within the Nazi hierarchy of our timeline. The German victory in 1940 has largely disguised the poor showing by the Luftwaffe in the Battle of Britain and their shortcomings have been largely forgotten in the general rejoicing over victory. Furthermore, there is no bombing campaign by the Allies and Germany has been victorious on the Eastern Front further enhancing Goering's prestige.

became even more like the regime in the USSR that the Nazis claimed to despise and had so recently destroyed.

What can best be described as a reshuffle followed the violence of 23rd November, and many SS men were removed from important posts, such as SS Obergruppenfuhrer Dr. Hans Kammler, who had taken over from Albert Speer at the Armaments ministry in late 1942, was replaced by his deputy, Karl–Otto Saur. Those that remained in important offices, like all holders of the Party's most eminent posts, became members of the Reichsenat, Germany's newly formed Senate. This was a legislature that wielded very little real power. Its main function was to enable Bormann to keep an eye on any potential rivals. The Reichstag was also preserved, though it too was little more than a rubber stamp assembly. Bormann, as head of the party bureaucracy, was in many ways the most powerful man in Germany.

CHAPTER 20: WEDNESDAY

18th AUGUST 1943

"Stalin? I killed him, I killed him with my own gun, I looked into that bastard's eyes and I shot him in the guts. I watched him die, I enjoyed it, he cursed me with his dying breath. But the last thing he saw on this earth was me, it was my face, smiling at him. I hope he burns in Hell."

The teahouse is crowded with men. Their clothes are ragged, their heads wrapped in black turbans, dark faces worn by hardship and fatigue. The broken window has been patched with newspaper. They sit on cots that stand around the room. The yellow walls are painted with simple patterns in blue; a fireplace in the corner heats a dented brass samovar. The man reaches again for his glass of tea. His hands shake as he takes a bottle from inside his jacket. The lip of it rattles against the glass as the clear liquid creates a swirling pattern in the green tea.

Lieutenant Commander John Leighton looks at him evenly. He says,

"That isn't the only thing that I came to ask you about."

The man's eyes narrow. He rubs his hand over the stubble of his shaved head. As he speaks his Adam's apple bobs noticeably up and down in his thin throat.

"What is it that you want?"

That was a good question, and the answer wasn't as clear as it had seemed when Leighton had set off from England two months previously.

The third man at the table looks at him, his name is Carstairs, he is the local British Consul.

"I wanted to ask you…" He stops, groping for the words "I wanted to ask you about the 470th rifle division?"

"I was in the first Regiment. What about it."

"Were you in the action around Patomnik?"

"Of course. The division was almost wiped out, hardly any of us survived but God wanted me to live, he had a purpose for me, he wanted me to kill Stalin."

Leighton waits for a moment then comes to a decision and stands up.

"I'm sorry, I shouldn't have come."

"Yes, yes you should have come, God brought you here. Don't say you shouldn't have come. It is blasphemy."

Blasphemy? Perhaps it is.

"Tell me, tell me why you are here, you are from England? That is a long way. Tell me why you are here?"

*

Leighton had not been happy about his transfer away from Istanbul and his new fiancée in July of '42. Still he did as he was ordered and took the BOAC flight to Teheran and from there an RAF transport to Kraznovodsk to become one of the British military observers attached to the Russian forces. The Russians had been cruel in their taunts, mocking the British and French for their capitulation, affirming that Russia would fight the Germans to its last drop of blood. He had swallowed these insults with outward equanimity, but inward chaffing, and concentrated on his job, which was to gather as much information about the war, the tactics used by each side and their methods and equipment, as he could.

In 1941 when operation Barbarossa had started the government in Britain had sent almost a hundred observers, as well as some aid. All of the observers were career military men, many of them specialists and the information that they gathered had proved vital in rebuilding Britain's armed forces after 1940.

Leighton had expected a post on a Soviet ship or at least to a naval base. He was surprised when he was ordered to report to a line infantry regiment, the Third Regiment of the 470th rifle division. It had been a long train journey across the steppe to Stalingrad, but the commanding officer was a captain in the Red Navy and his soldiers had all been ratings in the Soviet fleet. Their ships had been sunk or trapped in harbours and Russia's desperate need for manpower meant that they were required to fight as infantry. The captain had been impatient, condescending;

184

"You want to see what the Red Navy does? This is what we do: we fight the Germans. We fight them any way that we can."

To his surprise they had let him talk to the men, after the morning parade. The captain had interpreted, they had seemed confident, self-assured, laughing and joking like schoolboys. Leighton didn't doubt that many of them had been schoolboys until very recently. If he had been asked to guess their average age he would have said sixteen. As the two men had walked towards the officer's mess afterwards he had complimented the captain on his troop's élan. The captain's response had been flat, matter-of-fact, brutal.

"We are leaving for the front tomorrow, I have eight hundred and fifty rifles and a thousand men – a week from now they will probably all be dead."

He had not gone with them. He was transferred to Batumi and was on board the destroyer leader *Kharkov* during the action of 28th August 1942 when the Soviet Black Sea Fleet was almost annihilated by the Luftwaffe. He was transferred again to Guryev on the Caspian Sea.

The transfer had perhaps saved his life. In the chaos and confusion as the Soviet Union unravelled in the autumn of 1942, some of the British observers were killed. He had stolen a sailing boat and piloted it back to Bandr-I-shar on the Persian shore. It had taken him two weeks staying close to land, travelling mostly at night, hunger and the cold had almost killed him. Dorothy, his fiancée, barely recognised him when he saw her again.

He had tried to find out about the fate of the 470th Rifle Division. As far as he could tell they had been thrown into a counter attack south west of Stalingrad near a town called Patomnik and the division had been destroyed. And that had seemed to be an end of it, until he had received orders to travel to Mazar-I-Sharif in Afghanistan to investigate the story of a man who had deserted from the Red Army and slipped over the border. A man who claimed to have killed Stalin, a man who had been a lieutenant in the 470th.

Leighton had barely recovered from the ordeal of his escape and had been hoping for a seagoing commission on a carrier. The brand-new *Indefatigable* was working up. *Intrepid* was about to return to the fleet after her reconstruction, but he was going to one of the wildest and most inaccessible regions on earth. The orders came from MI6, along with his promotion. The fact that the 470th had been one of his postings in Russia had selected him for the job. "You might even have met him," as the briefing officer said. He also said that the man he was going to see might be completely insane, or simply telling a story in the hope of notoriety, asylum or both.

What had happened to Stalin was one of the mysteries of the war, it was certain that he was dead, but how he had died was not known.

The journey had taken weeks: a flight to Istanbul, another to Karachi, the train to Lahore, then another train to Peshawar and from there the tiny train of the Khyber Railway as it puffed laboriously up the switchbacks to Landi Kotal below the pass where he met the two men who would guide him through the Hindu Kush on horseback to Kabul.

The guides spoke some English and had a suit of local clothes for him to wear. He had allowed his beard to grow and almost looked the part. The men were Pashtuns, smiling and affable. Leighton had been assured that they would guarantee his safety for two reasons: firstly, there were the laws of Moslem hospitality; secondly, they had been handsomely paid. Still, on the fourth day of the journey they had unnerved him. When they had come to the village of Gandamak they had delightedly shown him the hill where the 44th Regiment of Foot had made its last stand a hundred and one years previously. Laughing and slapping his back they had said, "Many British killed here!" but he had kept his face impassive, and waited until the joke wore thin even on them.

Two weeks later he had finally reached Mazar-I-Sharif and the tiny house that served as the British Consulate. The Consul – Carstairs – was pathetically glad to meet another Briton. He begged Leighton for news of home and he answered the questions as best he could until finally the questions came to an end and Leighton asked to be taken to the man he had come so far to see.

*

Leighton sits down again and looks at the man carefully. "How were you able to get so close to Stalin?"

The man sneers as if responding to a foolish question. "After Patomnick, I was posted to his bodyguard."

"By whom?"

"Beria, who else?"

"Why did you kill him?"

The man smiles, takes another drink from the glass. Leighton searches the lines of the tired, cynical, prematurely aged face in front of him. He cannot reconcile its expression with the faces he remembers. The man gets up, opens the window. Outside the street is crowded. The sound of the call to prayer comes drifting across the rooftops: distant, ethereal, achingly beautiful. He remains standing.

"Why do you ask me why I killed him? Everyone in the country had a reason to kill him. I just got to be the lucky one. What you are trying to ask me is who put me up to it. Well, who do you think? Who stood to profit the most?"

"Beria?"

"Yes Beria, and Kaganovitch too, and Bulganin – those three, the bosses now. Beria came to me personally, offered me money. I took it, but I would have killed Stalin if he had offered me nothing. It was God's purpose for me. My family died because of Stalin; my wife, my son, gone because of him. Our village was overrun by the Germans because we weren't ready, because he had a pact with them, because he killed all the officers who knew what they were doing. My regiment, my friends – they died because of Stalin. They died because the only way we had to fight the Germans was to throw half trained men at them: men with no weapons, men with no hope, only rage, rage at the enemy, at what they were doing to our country. What was Stalin hoping? That eventually the Germans would just run out of bullets? What trade was he making? One Russian soldier for every Nazi bullet? My country came apart because of him. But it isn't over. They will go on fighting. The Germans will have to kill every Russian, every last one. And perhaps they will, but that is the only way they will win, the only way."

He pauses, Leighton says, "Why did you desert?"

The man smiles.

"To make it harder for Beria to kill me. They don't want the world to know that they bumped off the boss. I've been on the run for seven months – seven months – but they will kill me, sooner or later..." He looks straight into Leighton's face, "And what of England? Will you fight? Will you fight the Germans? All we hear is rumours. They say you have a new Government now, but there are always new Governments and they always lie. Will you fight? Will you fight alongside Russia or not?"

Leighton pauses. "I don't know."

There is silence for a moment. They hear the hubbub of voices from outside and the twittering of birds. "I think you will... yes, I think you will." He is looking straight at Leighton as he lifts the glass of tea to his lips but before it reaches them the side of his head explodes and a wet red splash of blood spatters across the wall next to it. The report of the shot reaches them a moment after and Carstairs cries out. The glass slips from the dead man's fingers to shatter on the floor as his knees buckle and his body collapses sideways onto the table, a dark pool of blood spreading across its surface.

The room is suddenly filled with shouts and cries as the men in the teahouse rush the exits, overturning the cots and tables, their glasses smash on the floor. Leighton throws himself to the ground and draws his revolver. He rolls to the window and looks out into the street, but whoever fired the shot has melted into the crowd.

Carstairs is on his knees, words escape his mouth in panting jerky breaths.

"Oh my God... oh my God... they found him... he's dead."

Leighton replaces the gun; his hands are shaking. A woman is screaming somewhere nearby. The owner of the teahouse is trying to speak with them, shouting, gesticulating – terrified. Leighton does not understand what he is saying. Carstairs responds with monosyllabic answers as the sound of the call to prayer dies away in the distance.

Top Left: Sir Oswald Mosley; Prime Minister of Britain, 1932 to 1938 (Alamay). Top Right: Sir Archibald Sinclair; Prime Minister of Britain, 1941 to 1952 (National Portrait Gallery). Bottom Left: Wendell Willkie, 33rd President of the United States; in office from March 1941 until his death in October 1944 (Library of Congress). Bottom Right: Huey Long; Senator from Louisiana, 1931 to 1938; National Party candidate in the 1940 United States Presidential election (Library of Congress).

Above Left: HMS *Courageous* during the Battle of Lofoten. She took part in the first naval action where the opposing fleets did not catch sight of each other. Her aircraft are credited with sinking the German aircraft carrier *Graf Zeppelin* (US Navy). Above Right: Clement Attlee, Britain's Foreign Minister, with King George VI on the morning of 18th November 1940, shortly after Attlee had signed the Treaty of Leamouth. Both men look uncomfortable. Attlee later described it as 'A disagreeable business.' While he certainly regretted signing the peace treaty with Germany, he had little option (IWM HU 59486).

Above: A Column of German tanks in the Soviet Caucasus. The advance of the Axis forces from Ochamchire to Baku in the summer of 1942 was the decisive campaign of the Axis – Soviet War. Once the oil bearing region had come under Hitler's control, the collapse of the Soviet Union was inevitable (Bundesarchiv).

Above: German Alpenkorps soldiers rest during Operation Tannenbaum, the invasion of Switzerland, 22nd August 1943 (Bundesarchiv).

Above: Hitler declaring war on the United States at the German Reichstag, 8th May 1945. His recovery from illness, courtesy of the American pharmaceutical industry, meant his return to absolute control of the Third Reich (Bundesarchiv).

Above: A Messerschmitt Me 364 bomber above New York City, 23rd June 1945
(EN-Archive/Associated Press).

CHAPTER 21: DISCORD AND DISARRAY –

THE UNITED STATES AND THE BRITISH

COMMONWEALTH IN THE

INTERBELLUM

From 'The Presidency of Wendell Willkie' by Siobhan McCormick, Pelham House, 2004

The question of the rising power of Germany caused consensus in one aspect of US politics, that of foreign policy. President Wendell Willkie was finally able to convince his fellow Republicans that though the party might be determined to remain isolationist, it must be a well-armed isolation. Unfortunately, his term as President of the United States was characterised by a decline in foreign trade and economic opportunity. With Nazi domination of Europe and Japanese expansion in the Far East, the United States trading position deteriorated. The brief boom caused by the cessation of hostilities in 1942 was soon over and the world's economy slowed once again. As the downturn began to bite, world trade decreased and US exporters began to find increasing difficulty in penetrating the two Eurocentric trading blocs led by the British Commonwealth and Germany. The development of trading blocks and other impediments to free trade was a matter beyond Willkie's control, but attempts to negotiate an agreement on commercial policy with the British Empire were partially successful.

The British difficulty was the American desire for the elimination of preferences (which were characteristically British) but only for a reduction in tariffs (which were characteristically American). At the Anglo-American summit on economic affairs held in Quebec City in 1941, the American negotiators adopted a 'holier than thou' attitude from the start. The only justification for this appeared to be that whereas the British had put on duties in the 1930s, the Cordell Hull tariff reduction programme had at that time been making very small (bilateral) reductions in the intimidating American tariff. This tariff had exacerbated the difficulties of repaying war debts in the nineteen twenties and had made more intractable the dollar earning problems of the Sterling area after 1940. In consequence, no general agreement in favour of a multilateral international convention to limit protective measures and to outlaw discriminatory practices was reached. [89] However, a complicated bi-lateral agreement that eased trade between the Sterling and dollar areas was brokered by the Canadians who were caught between the two powers and were desperate for a trade accord.

From 1943 onward, economic help for both the US and the UK came from a surprising quarter – China – though the British saw the lion's share of the profits. The incursions of former Soviet and Japanese armies on to Chinese soil caused very little shift in attitudes among the competing war lords and the Nationalist-Communist feud continued unchecked. The Nationalists, however, began to purchase munitions from both the United States and Britain. One of Chiang Kai Shek's most immediate concerns was the inability of China to produce advanced manufactured goods. Initially the Chinese placed orders for Russian planes, but with the collapse of the USSR and the consequent interruption to deliveries, they sought other sources of supply instead. The reduction in exports from Europe after 1940 served to further assist the American export trade, though the full benefits of this were not immediately apparent because of competition from inexpensive war surplus British military supplies from 1941 onwards. There was increasing competition from Japanese goods also. On balance, increased trade with China was no substitute for the loss of European markets, while competition with the British for South American markets was fierce.

A weak pound sterling and a surplus of many types of weaponry after the War of 1940 meant that British made goods

---

[89] This is essentially how the arguments went before the Bretton Woods agreement in OTL, but in OTL the poverty-smitten British had no choice but to accede to American pressure.

were substantially cheaper than US ones and, in many cases, better quality. Consequently US weaponry failed to make inroads into the Chinese market until 1943, and then it was chiefly armoured fighting vehicles that were purchased.

Willkie was certainly a decent man and as charismatic as his predecessor, Franklin Roosevelt. His stance on racial equality alienated much of his party, though today he is seen as one of the earliest heroes of the civil rights movement. His Administration also oversaw the early independence of the Philippines. His dismantling of many of the measures of the New Deal caused much anguish to many ordinary Americans but put the country on a sound economic footing, placing the American economy in a position to take advantage of the upturn when it finally arrived.

The chief failing of the Willkie administration in its early days was that the White House functioned with too little unity, co-ordination and effectiveness. Willkie was a stubborn man and didn't work well with Congress. His relationship with his fellow Republicans sometimes verged on the disastrous and some publicly denounced him. He lacked the political skills to build consensus, at a time when America needed consensus. The failure of the bill to pass Congress for renewal of the draft in the fall of 1941 [90] delayed American military expansion. It was eventually passed two years later. He was also quite unable to inspire the American people with the idea of a mission to curtail Japanese aggression in China. He was a defender of civil liberties and an interventionist in international affairs, though in this he was at odds with both Republican Party policy and also his own election promises. What unified his Administration, and in some ways defined it, was the 'Ware Wolves' scandal, which came to a head in the late summer of 1941.

J. Edgar Hoover, the formidable head of the Federal Bureau of Investigation and a member of the Republican Party, had been investigating links between individuals in the Roosevelt Administration and the Soviet Union since 1934 when Michael Whitney Straight, an American who had become embroiled in

---

[90] It almost failed in OTL under Roosevelt.

the Apostles scandal at Britain's Cambridge University returned home in disgrace. [91] Whitney Straight became the subject of FBI surveillance and the investigation widened until it revealed an unsettling picture of the extent to which the Roosevelt Administration had been infiltrated by Communist agents, sympathisers and 'fellow-travellers'.

It showed that a large number of people employed in the Administration were Communists and it showed that these people worked constantly to advance the cause of the Soviet Union and destroy the foundations of American government. It was apparent that almost every department and agency of the Government was compromised to varying degrees including State, Treasury, the Foreign Economic Administration and the Office of Strategic Services. The infiltration was concentrated in the departments which made policy, particularly international policy. The FBI discovered that so extensive was this infiltration that it was no exaggeration to say that American government, particularly with regards to its foreign policy, was deeply compromised by the GRU (Glavnoye Razvedyvatel'noye Upravleniye), the Soviet's Main Intelligence Directorate, during the Roosevelt presidency.

Hoover was deeply disturbed by the results of the investigation, but could gain no traction against the conspiracy in the Roosevelt era. However, once the Republican Willkie Administration was in power, he found that it was very willing to listen to the concerns that he raised and also that his agency was able to act with much greater freedom in its investigation. The three factors principally responsible for breaking up the Soviet spy rings in the United States were the testimonies of Whitaker Chambers and Elizabeth Bentley as well as the Venona decrypts.

Venona was the code name given to the highly successful anti-Soviet code breaking effort of American Intelligence. [92] The

---

[91] In OTL he did not return until 1937 and was not in disgrace when he did.

[92] As it was in OTL, but in OTL the Democratic party machine hindered the investigation and refused to act on the evidence to protect its members.

transcripts implicated a substantial number of people and revealed that Roosevelt's New Deal policies had inadvertently aided the infiltration of the American Government by Soviet agents because so many people with left-wing views had been hired by the Democratic Administration to administer it. Many of these were not merely left-leaning but were actual Marxists or Communists and they held a deep affinity with, and sympathy for, the Soviet Union.

Whitaker Chambers was one such left-leaning individual who was in contact with many in the American Government who shared his outlook. In 1925, Chambers had joined the Communist Party of the United States (CPUSA), then known as the Workers Party of America. He also wrote for and edited several Communist publications, including The Daily Worker newspaper and The New Masses magazine. He began his career as a spy, working for a GRU cell led by Alexander Ulanovsky. Soon after he joined, his main controller in this group became Josef Peters who introduced him to Harold Ware.

During the early 1930s Chambers became a member of the so-called 'Ware Group,' another cabal of spies within the American Government who aided Soviet intelligence agents. Ware was an American Marxist and a senior Soviet agent, Chambers continued his work in Washington as an organizer among Communists in the city and as a courier between Washington and New York transporting stolen US Government documents which he delivered to Boris Bykov, the GRU's New York station chief.

However, in 1939 Chambers was so shocked and appalled by the Nazi-Soviet pact that he decided to betray the Russian espionage operation to the American authorities. In September, shortly after the joint invasion of Poland by Nazi Germany and the Soviet Union, he went to Assistant Secretary of State Adolf Berle and revealed the conspiracy, but Berle did not act on the information Chambers gave him. [93]

By March 1941, the new Administration had taken over and the information gathered by the FBI was made available to the

---

[93] In OTL Chambers did not come forward until 1946.

Willkie White House. It gave a startling picture of the Communist penetration that had taken place in the Roosevelt years. The evidence presented by Hoover was sufficiently compelling to cause Willkie to order the FBI to take the investigation public. Once the investigation was announced, Chambers did not hesitate to come forward again, this time presenting his testimony directly to the FBI. This was enough to move the investigation forward and it proceeded under the aegis of an investigative committee of the House of Representatives. This was the House Un-American Activities Committee which had convened on 26th May 1938 and had been established to investigate allegations of subversive and treasonous activities on the part of private citizens, public employees and organizations suspected of having ties to Communist or fascist organisations. It was chaired by Fiorello LaGuardia, the energetic and focussed Republican Mayor of New York City. [94]

When the scandal broke in the newspapers, an editorial writer for the Houston Informer coined the colourful phrase 'Ware Wolves' to describe not only the members of the Ware Cell but all those implicated in the scandal. However, the publicity also bought forth a new witness. Elizabeth Bentley came forward when the investigation was at its height in the autumn of 1941.[95] The majority of Bentley's contacts were in the 'Silvermaster group', a network of spies who reported to Nathan Silvermaster. This network had become one of the most important Soviet spying operations in America. Silvermaster worked with the Resettlement Administration, he had little

---

[94] In OTL, Chambers was marginalised to the extent that in the 1948 investigation that revealed the level of Communist penetration of the Democrat Government, he was never called before the grand jury. When finally he appeared before the House Committee in August of the same year, his testimony against Alger Hiss shook America. Also the chairman of the House Committee in TTL is a Republican, in OTL it was a Democrat (Martin Dies) who had a vested interest in limiting the possible damage to his own party.

[95] In OTL Bentley did not come forward until 1945, otherwise the way the investigation unfolds is similar to OTL except in TTL the administration has a vested interest in its success as it will lower the prestige of the Democratic Party.

access to sensitive information himself, but he knew a number of Communist Party members and Soviet sympathizers within the government who passed information to him. He then gave it to Elizabeth Bentley who sent it to Moscow. Bentley's testimony increased the list of names of Soviet agents to over one hundred. The list now included such apparent pillars of the American establishment as Alger Hiss, who had worked closely with Cordell Hull at the State Department; Laughlin Currie, who was President Roosevelt's economic adviser and Harry Dexter White who had worked closely with Henry Morganthau the Secretary of the Treasury.

At first the investigation struggled to overcome scepticism and disbelief at every level of society, but Bentley's testimony, taken with that of Chambers and the Venona decrypts provided overwhelming evidence. Thomas Dewey, Willkie's Secretary of State, backed Hoover when he ordered the arrest of several of those implicated on a range of charges including treason. The trials began in mid-1942 and highlighted the ability of sophisticated Soviet agents to insinuate themselves in to the confidence of credulous government officials.

Many of the suspects were convicted. Some, like Hiss, Currie and White were executed. The Democrats were left reeling in the wake of the Ware Wolves scandal. As the trials ground on they appeared more and more ridiculous and at the Democratic Party Convention held in Chicago in July 1944 the delegates were subdued and spirits were low. In contrast to this the Republican National Convention assembled in Philadelphia was jubilant and they voted to nominate the incumbent President as their candidate.

Fate, however, was to intervene. Wendell Willkie died in office of a heart attack on the October 8th, 1944. The Vice President, Charles McNary, [96] had pre-deceased Willkie in February of that year and at that time there was no 25th Amendment allowing a new vice-president to be installed in office. The Constitution allowed for the Secretary of State to become President and in this case it was Thomas Dewey who

---

[96] Willkie's running mate in the 1940 election.

also became the Republican candidate in the 1944 Presidential election.

The Democrat candidates for the Presidential nomination were Harry S. Truman, Strom Thurmond and Henry Wallace. One of the central issues at the convention was civil rights and to the dismay of many, thirty-six Southern delegates, led by Strom Thurmond, walked out in response to an announcement by Truman (the front runner) that if nominated his platform would not include any attack on the passage of civil rights laws by the incumbent administration. [97] These formed a spin-off party, which they named the States Rights Democratic Party. More commonly known as the "Dixiecrats", the party's main goal was continuing racial segregation and the Jim Crow laws that sustained it. Strom Thurmond became the Dixiecrats presidential nominee.

Truman defeated Wallace in a close race but partly because of a need to present a united front to the voters after the split by the Dixiecrats, Wallace became Truman's running mate. Thurmond's States Rights Party took away much of the Democrats traditional base in the South, but did not spark the wholesale revolt that had been predicted and he carried only four states.

Truman's campaign was intense and personal, much of it was conducted in a folksy rural style, he had the gift of being able to get on with almost anyone and in his appeal to the New Deal interest groups, he established a modus operandi that was extremely effective. He presented himself as a fighting underdog, one of the people, a champion of the common man. He was also instrumental in restoring confidence in the Democratic Party after a clean out of Soviet sympathisers

By contrast, Dewey did his best to distance himself from Willkie's policies but, unlike Willkie, his campaign ran smoothly and was well organised. A Dewey win was widely predicted, but in campaigning he failed to take any risks, spoke in empty platitudes and made the mistake of not shaving his moustache.

---

[97] In OTL Thurmond did this in 1948. In TTL the issue of race has been bought to the fore by Willkie's policies.

Many women voters were impressed by Dewey's intelligence and integrity, but disliked his facial hair. To many women Dewey's moustache was repugnant. Edith Efron, writing on the subject of Dewey's moustache in the August 1944 edition of the New York Times Sunday Magazine said that Dewey:

"...may be elected to office, but it will be in spite of his 'manly attributes' – not because of them. His Moustache plays many roles today, it is Chaplin-pathetic, Hitler-psychopathic, Gable-debonnair, Lou Lehr-wacky. It perplexes. It fascinates. It amuses. And it repels."

Dewey had reason to be confident of victory but American voters, dismayed by the dismantling of the New Deal, the continuing sluggishness of the American economy and it seems, the Republican candidates facial hair, delivered a victory for Truman.

*

What became known as the Willkie Doctrine; which was that the Soviets were as bad as the Nazis, was one of the defining pillars of American foreign policy for the next five decades. In addition to this and his contribution to the cause of Civil Rights, Wendell Willkie's other great legacy was continuing the build-up of the American forces begun by Roosevelt in the teeth of Congressional opposition and in spite of faltering economic growth. Had he not been hampered by the slowness of the world economy, America might have been far better prepared for the war when it came. As it was, he wisely chose to emphasise the naval build-up, though both the Army and the Army Air Corps also underwent significant growth.

His insistence that black soldiers be treated exactly the same as white, be paid the same, receive the same respect from the Army and undergo the same dangers in combat, was political dynamite in what was then still a surprisingly racist country. His policy was continued by subsequent administrations despite entrenched opposition.

*From 'British Politics after the War of 1940' by Brian Garret,
Gloucester University Press, 2001*

The 1941 election was one of the most tumultuous in Britain's
history. It saw the political destruction of the Labour Party and a
huge and unexpected revival in the fortunes of the Liberals.
Politically, Britain was badly rattled after the signing of the
Treaty of Leamouth and the dissolution of the National
Government which had been formed in September 1939. At the
close of 1940 the Labour Party still possessed a very slim overall
majority in the House of Commons, but the government had
barely survived a vote of no confidence, where only the frantic
activities of the whips and support from minor parties in the
House prevented the vote from being passed.

Militarily Britain was also shaken; she had proved unable to
support an ally successfully, keep another in the war or restrain
an aggressor and had often seemed almost wholly ineffective in
the field. The decisive and very sudden end to the Battle of
Britain and the apparently generous terms of The Treaty of
Leamouth allowed the Government to present the public with
the impression that the war had been bought to a successful
conclusion. It was not long before this deceit was being reviled
as a canard. The other political parties and their supporters
seized on the issue and would not let it go. The Labour party
were branded, often unfairly, as cowards and traitors and the
results obtained by them in subsequent by-elections were cause
for alarm among the leadership.

The confusion in British politics which characterised the
period following Oswald Mosley's resignation from the office of
Prime Minister had continued until the shock of May 1940 and
the surrender of November. The story of the Labour Party from
Prime Minister Clement Attlee's resignation on 10th May 1940
until the election of February 1941 is one of chaos, uncertainty
and warring factions tearing the party to pieces, yet the fault
lines that became so apparent in the wake of Dunkirk had
actually existed for many years.

Oswald Mosley had moved Labour decisively to the right in
political terms which enraged many in the party, most notably
Aneurin Bevan. Bevan, like the other disgruntled members was

only persuaded to stay with Labour by Mosley's charm and by his unarguable success. With Mosley's fall from grace in 1938, Bevan had joined the race to become leader of the party and while he subsequently lost to Attlee, his ambition was certainly not sated. Mosley's deputies, Robert Forgan and Harold Nicholson also ran for the leadership but garnered few votes and eventually followed Mosley into his New Party. Attlee was seen as the compromise candidate, the steady hand who would guide the party, resolve the internal conflicts caused by Mosley's de-facto reorientation of the party's philosophy and guide Labour forward to continued electoral success. There were many however, who found the elevation of Attlee cause for great concern.

Throughout the twenties and until Mosley took over, the Labour Party's stated policy had been to oppose rearmament. It sought security in internationalism and believed that collective safety overseen and mediated by the League of Nations was the way to ensure peace. This appeared on the surface to be similar to Mosley's conception of international security, but the resemblance was only superficial. At the Labour Party Conference in 1934, Attlee, then serving as Home Secretary, gave a speech in which he said that "We have absolutely abandoned any idea of nationalist loyalty. We are deliberately putting a world order before our loyalty to our own country. We say we want to see put on the statute book something which will make our people citizens of the world before they are citizens of this country".

This had bought a sharp rebuke from Mosley, but during a debate on defence in The House of Commons less than a year later, Attlee stated: "We are told (in the White Paper) that there is danger against which we have to guard ourselves. We do not think you can do it by national defence. We think you can only do it by moving forward to a new world. A world of law, the abolition of national armaments with a world force and a world economic system."

Shortly after this, Adolf Hitler announced that German rearmament was not designed to threaten world peace. Attlee responded in a speech in the commons the following day saying that Hitler's speech meant that there was "A chance to call a halt in the armaments race..." and "We do not think that our answer to Herr Hitler should be just rearmament. We are in an age of rearmaments, but we on this side cannot accept that position."

In saying this he was certainly consolidating his own support on the left of the party (opposition to Mosley within Labour hardened as time went on) and this again bought rebuke from the party leadership, but in April 1936 when the Chancellor of the Exchequer, Hugh Dalton, presented his Budget, one which increased the amount spent on the armed forces from 4% of GNP to 6% of GNP, Attlee opposed it in the house, saying the budget meant "... hardly any increase allowed for the services which went to build up the life of the people, education and health. Everything is devoted to piling up the instruments of death." [98] The Chancellor expressed considerable regret that it was necessary to spend so much on weapons, but pointed out that it was advisable because of the actions of other nations.

Nevertheless Attlee, once he became leader, continued Mosley's 'Accommodation' policy with regards to the dictators and he also continued to keep Britain's armaments spending advancing as Mosley had done. [99] It is certain that his attitudes were challenged and then modified as the Nazi threat became more obvious. His logic, like Mosley's, was one of deterrence; that a well-armed Britain would present too formidable an opponent to attack. The failure of this policy and Attlee's internationalist stance were to haunt him and his party in the wake of military defeat.

In the beginning of 1939 however Attlee began to take a tougher diplomatic line towards Germany. On 17 March when the Germans occupied Czechoslovakia he attacked Hitler for breaking the bond of trust that he believed had been established between the German and British Governments and made it clear that Britain would oppose German domination of Europe. This

---

[98] In OTL the increase in defence spending was far less, the Chancellor was Neville Chamberlain and the sentiments were expressed by Attlee in a radio broadcast.

[99] See Annex 8.

seemed starkly different from Mosley's policy. When at the end of March it became apparent that Hitler's next victim would be Poland, Attlee responded by announcing that Britain had agreed unconditionally to come to Poland's aid in the event of its being attacked. Coming from Attlee, who had avoided any binding commitment to the Czechs, the news was a shock. Britain was left asking how precisely the Prime Minister planned to back this change of policy.

*

Clement Attlee resigned as Britain's Prime Minister on Friday the 10th May 1940 because his party had lost confidence in his ability to lead the country through the war. The candidates to replace him were the Chancellor, Hugh Dalton, Stafford Cripps, Herbert Morrison and Aneurin Bevan. Bevan and Cripps were perceived as too left-wing, Morrison was tainted by his conscientious objection and the fact that he had never held any senior government post. Hugh Dalton was an economist and had served as Chancellor of the Exchequer from 1932. [100] He had helped shape Labour Party foreign-policy in the 1930s, opposed pacifism, promoted rearmament against the German threat and it was known within the party that he had quietly opposed the Accommodation strategy of both Prime Ministers Mosley and Attlee while following their policy faithfully and maintaining a loyal silence on the issue in public for the good of the party. It was Dalton who became Britain's Prime Minister as the German campaign against the west was unleashed.

Despite having a new man at the helm, the defeat of 1940 had left Government policy in tatters and Labour clinging to vastly reduced credibility and a miniscule majority. Part of the problem was the way in which Mosley had run the party. The whips under Mosley carried enormous power and were extremely aggressive. [101] The rank and file were certainly cowed,

---

[100] In OTL Dalton was Chancellor from 1945 to 1947.

[101] This was essentially how Tony Blair ran the Labour Party in the OTL 1990s.

but with Mosley's resignation, the restraints that had held it together were removed causing a storm of dissent. Attlee reduced the power of the whips hoping the party would return to its more consensual pre-Mosley character. He was completely wrong.

In desperation, even the right of the Labour Party embraced the proposals of the Beveridge report which was published in November 1940. The report had been initiated by the government in June 1939 [102] as part of its efforts to find a new post-Mosley direction. The report was seen as a way to return Labour to its roots and draw it away from what many in the party felt had become too right-wing a stance. It was hoped that with the promise of across the board increases in all types of benefits, medical and dental care and enhanced pensions and social services the British public would be persuaded to grant Labour a third term in office.

*

None of the parties could face the 1941 election with any confidence. The political situation in the United Kingdom after the Treaty of Leamouth was highly charged. The opposition Conservative Party also suffered schisms with a pro-peace faction forming around Lord Halifax (who was sixty), the shadow foreign secretary. Halifax won the leadership in June 1940 after Neville Chamberlain was forced to step down because of illness. His only opponent for the leadership was Sir Samuel Hoare (who was sixty-one). There was an air of 'Buggins turn' about the appointment of Halifax and the more unkind commentators made the cruel but fair observation that the party leadership consisted solely of out of touch old men.

The Labour government's willingness to embrace the tenets of the Beveridge report had caught the Conservatives on the back foot. At a stroke what appeared to be a lame duck party, ravaged by leadership crises and tarnished by Britain's

---

[102] Two years earlier than it was in OTL when it was initiated by Arthur Greenwood, the Labour MP and Minister without Portfolio on 10th June 1941.

performance in the war, had seized the political initiative. Although the Liberals and Conservatives loudly warned that the Labour Party's plans were financially unworkable they had difficulty inspiring the voting public with their own platforms, Labour's promises, questionable though they might be, proved far more seductive to the working class.

However, both the Tories and Liberals knew that an election was imminent and the opinion polls showed that the Beveridge Report's proposals had across the board support throughout Britain and if that support were reflected in the ballot it would mean defeat. Consequently when the election date was announced the Conservatives published their manifesto which included a commitment to enhanced social services, welfare and health spending that was almost as comprehensive as those put forward by the Liberals though fell well short of Labour. The crucial difference, the manifesto argued, was that the Conservative proposals were affordable whereas the other parties' were not.

*

Labour's majority had been too small in September 1939 to avoid the formation of a National coalition government, but the only member of the Liberal Party given a post in the cabinet was its leader, Sir Archibald Sinclair. His first major political speech as a cabinet member came on 24th February 1940, he used it to remind the country that the Liberals had warned of the dangers of both economic nationalism and Fascism. Though warnings had been sounded by individuals in many parties, it was the Liberal Party alone that had both opposed the folly of appeasement and had supported measures to rearm as party policy. Sinclair also took the opportunity to re-emphasise what he saw as the basic liberal values of British civilization. These were; liberty, justice, mercy, tolerance, the search for truth, the sanctity of contract, the rule of law and the brotherhood of man. He went on; "For make no doubt about it – it is those ideals which Herr Hitler is determined to destroy. He hates and despises them all." Sinclair had to admit that "...the old Liberal truths have become platitudes" but insisted that they "still remain truths". They needed to be given prominence precisely because they had been side-lined for almost twenty years (the last non coalition Liberal government had left office in 1922). Sinclair emphasised that the war highlighted the fact that the Liberals had been right, whereas the other parties had been wrong, but he realised that the British people did not want high ideals or sanctimonious artificiality. They wanted a workable plan for Britain once the war was over.

Sinclair was respected on all sides of the House. He was an excellent speaker and regarded by those who worked with him as thoroughly competent, devoted to duty and a consummate gentleman. He delivered several speeches in the House of Commons during the summer of 1940 that were widely broadcast and seemed to embody Britain's defiance of the Axis threat. None of the other party's leaders were able to summarize the reasons for Britain's resistance to the Germans or inspire it so eloquently. Because of his history of Appeasement (or 'Accommodation' as he preferred to call it), even Mosley, who could be a mesmerising speaker, failed to inspire the people of Britain as thoroughly as Sinclair, nor were Mosley's speeches broadcast as widely.

In a speech Sinclair gave to the Liberal Assembly in January 1941 [103] about the improvements in Social Services advocated by the Liberal parliamentary party, he specifically praised the Beveridge report and was able to present the country with the coup that William Beveridge himself had joined the Liberal Party. [104] Thus gilded by association, the Liberal party emphasised that it wanted to establish a basic minimum standard of living for every citizen in Britain. Sinclair guaranteed the country that "The many and varied problems, social, financial and economic, at home as well as those of world reconstruction abroad, are already being closely studied by

---

[103] Extracts from this speech are actually from one given on 19 July 1941 OTL.

[104] In OTL the Beveridge Report had its nascence in June 1941, Beveridge joined the Liberals in September 1944 and won Berwick for them in the 1945 election.

groups of Liberals." But he also inserted a note of caution: "The conditions of their study are hard because it is so difficult to forecast the limits of what will be practicable..."

Sinclair could not ignore the public outcry for 'New Jerusalem' as it came to be known, but tackled it in terms consistent with Liberal doctrine and economic realism. He was at pains to emphasise that a growing welfare state must not hamper "...that private enterprise and initiative which is the mainspring of the economic life of the country and which gives to industry and commerce much of its adaptability and virility." It was vital to "respect and preserve the dignity of man."

In contrast with Labour, the Liberal Party's new stance did not support nationalisation, and perhaps the weak point in the party's platform was its vagueness about how the new measures would be paid for. Labour wanted nationalisation of public utilities, a measure that was unacceptable to both the Liberals and the Tories. But the Liberal position proved to be nearer to what the British people really wanted than were the agendas of either of the two main parties.

While the link between the Liberal Party and the Beveridge Report was firmly established, Beveridge's membership also brought disadvantages. He was not a committed party member, had no interest in party politics and expected to become the party's leader. At the very least he expected a ministry from which to supervise the execution of the tenets of his report.

What the Liberal Party and the country urgently required was deft and inspiring leadership. The situation called for a leader with moral power and diplomatic skill, respected by all sides of British politics, one who could bring the discord in the Liberal Party under control while simultaneously harnessing the energy it created. Sinclair's long stated opposition to appeasement stood in sharp contrast with either of the other two parties. His basic philosophy was that: "The Liberal Party is the people's party, for it represents the life and liberty of the individual and his family. It will always support measures which aim at an improved standard of life for all." He spoke of the need to eradicate the evils identified in the Beveridge Report, those of 'ignorance, squalor, idleness and want'. He gave support to a raft of programmes to enhance the wellbeing of the people and he was careful to ascribe an international aspect to the reforms. By broadening its perspective, he narrowed its focus and was careful to emphasise that reform at home would be constrained by the imperative of managing Britain's engagement with the outside world in terms of diplomacy and defence. He was careful to point out that the British could not hope for more than was realistic.

Sinclair was also able to show that he could lead the party without crushing its impetuous soul. He was unquestionably patrician, but his politics were not authoritarian. He argued that the politics of class was a dead end and believed that social improvement was essential. He was able to argue persuasively that radical Liberalism, not Labourite Socialism, was the best method of realising that goal. Free trade was his ideal, but he understood that there were now many practical obstacles to making it a reality. The challenge was to present to the country a philosophy that was essentially liberal, one that united the nation. Archibald Sinclair rose to that challenge.

Victory would go to the party that could persuade the electorate of its ability to put into action the recommendations of the report. Doubts about the Conservative commitment were strong. The Tories were unfairly identified with resistance to Beveridge. The Liberals were ideally placed to benefit from the situation; the report was in every way a Liberal document and built on the foundation of the Edwardian welfare reform that the Liberals had championed. [105]

---

[105] In OTL, Sinclair served in Churchill's WW2 cabinet as Secretary of State for Air. Unlike some of the other politicians charged with administering the supply of weapons and materiel to the armed services, he did not interfere unduly with the work of senior military officers, seeing his role as an organiser and co-ordinator. He sacrificed political advantage to the urgent work of winning the war. He held the post of Secretary of State for Air from the day after Churchill took office until VE day. Sinclair worked without ceasing, putting aside party politics or the business of political manoeuvring to devote all his energies to the service of the country. He did not look after himself which was typical of his idealism, but overwork in the war years contributed to the strokes he suffered after 1952. Gerald J. De Groot writes of Sinclair 'His failure to answer this need, no matter how noble his motives, did cause serious damage. The disintegration of his party was a measure of his loyalty to the country.'

Inspired by Sinclair's leadership, the Liberal Nationals began to embrace the idea of rejoining the Liberals. Leadership of the group had passed from the discredited and detested John Simon to the insipid Ernest Brown. The group had little purpose and a weak leader. A number of defections and the general uncertainty of British politics in late 1940 convinced Brown to approach Sinclair in December about the prospect of reunion.

Despite these positive developments, there were obstacles. Sinclair himself was somewhat out of touch with modern British life. A high Victorian in outlook, he usually wore a wing collar. He was a principled man, his reasoning was subtle and academic in an age that was impressed by the glib. But most damaging of all to the Liberal's prospects was their penury.

The Liberal Party in the 1920s and 30s was not well off and had therefore been hostage to the whims of its wealthiest member, former Prime Minister, David Lloyd George. In January 1941, this formidable and mercurial politician was 77 and believed strongly that he should again lead the Liberal Party and the country. Sinclair's success and popularity did nothing to endear him to the wily Welshman but fortunately the Liberals found the support of a new and very powerful friend.

Lord Beaverbrook, the Canadian owner of the Express Newspapers empire, had been dismayed by the chaos and weakness that characterised the British political scene after May 1940. Unimpressed by the leaders of the other parties, he saw Sinclair not only as the anti-appeaser, but the man who carried the torch of much-needed reform without blinkered Socialism. At this time, newspapers held a firm grip on the news agenda, few people had radios and only a handful of televisions existed in private homes.

The Express appealed to all classes and in the 1930s became the first newspaper to garner a circulation of two million copies. From June 1940 Beaverbrook and Express newspapers supported Sinclair both politically and financially. Beaverbrook freely admitted that his newspapers promoted his political agenda and his support for Sinclair, was extremely welcome. Surprisingly, it came with few strings. Like Sinclair, Beaverbrook believed in fundamental Liberal principles, but more importantly, he saw him as the best man to lead the country.

In January 1941 Beveridge, who had been made Chairman of the Liberal's campaign committee, vowed that "If the people of Britain . . . want to have a Liberal government with a radical programme, they will be able to secure it. The party will put up enough candidates to make that possible." He was only able to do this because of Beaverbrook's support for the party.

*

The formation of a coalition National government in September 1939 was all that saved the Labour Party from being forced to call an immediate election. Although the separate Independent Labour Party led by James Maxton could usually be relied on to vote with the government; Labour's majority, as the German and Russian tanks rolled across Poland, amounted to a single seat in the House of Commons. By the time the Treaty of Leamouth was signed and the National government dissolved at the end of 1940, the results of six by-elections had left no single party with an overall majority. The position in the House was as follows:

Labour: 304
Conservative: 256
Liberal: 32
National Liberal: 8
Independent Labour: 3
Others: 12

Dalton frantically cobbled together a coalition with Independent Labour and a rag-bag of independents and in so doing staved off an immediate election. This did little other than buy the Labour party time to try and rescue its severely tarnished image in the eyes of the electorate but Dalton's Government might have soldiered on had it not been for the ego of Oswald Mosley. Dissatisfied with his reduced role in British politics and buoyed by the recent notoriety of the report on the British Empire that bore his name, Mosley orchestrated a backbench revolt of 12 disgruntled Labour MPs in late January. With them, he formed a new political faction which he named the New

Party [106] and he led them across the floor of the House of Commons to sit on the opposition benches to thunderous applause from the Conservatives and Liberals who realised that this precipitous action left the Government with no option but to call an election. As one political observer noted of the revolt; "This was typical Mosley – the action of a man hungry for power and innocent of principals."

Dalton was thunderstruck and had no option but to see the King and request the dissolution of Parliament. He considered hanging on, but it seems that in the end he realised that the political tide had turned against him and did not want to face the humiliation of losing a vote of no-confidence. The election was called for Thursday 20th February 1941 but the MPs who joined in Mosley's revolt did not do well, only one of them, apart from Mosley himself, retained his seat.

*

In spite of the February weather, the 1941 general election saw a very large turnout. Dissatisfaction was palpable in a country riven by political turmoil and the agony of defeat. Not one of the political parties could look forward to the results with confidence. Campaigning was robust and at times vicious, attacks by one party upon another were frequent. There were three great surprises, firstly the scale of the Liberal revival, secondly that no party had an overall majority and thirdly that Oswald Mosley, the disgraced former Prime Minister, retained his seat.

Labour were routed, losing 163 seats. The party's flip-flopping on policy between Mosley and Attlee, the defeat in the war and the legacy of the Mosleyite policy of 'Accommodation' all proved fatal to their prospects. Their adherence to a doctrine of widening socialism also worked against them. The left of the party demanded ever more concessions and their uncritical

---

[106] In OTL Mosley founded the 'New Party' in 1931 because of the Labour Party's narrow rejection of the 'Mosley Memorandum' – his interventionist blueprint for economic recovery.

support for Stalin contrasted starkly with the view propagated by most of the newspapers that he was quite as dangerous a threat to world peace as Hitler. The newspapers also kept the question of the financial viability of Labour's plans very much at the forefront of the debate.

Although they lost fewer seats than the Labour Party did, the Tories also suffered from their association with the policy of Appeasement. The choice of Lord Halifax as leader was very damaging. A man perceived by the British public as yet another old, distant, out of touch British aristocrat was a calamitously poor decision.

In the first decade of the 20th Century, the Conservative Party was torn apart by the issue of Empire. That led to the Liberals winning their huge majority of 1906. In the fifth decade of the century the Labour Party was torn apart by the issue of Appeasement; again, the Liberals were the party to profit. The full results of the election were as follows:

Liberal: 226 (+194)
Conservative: 209 (−47)
Labour: 141 (−163)
National Liberal: 3 (−5)
The New Party: 2 (−10)
Others: 34 (+22)

When it became clear that the results would be close and a hung parliament was likely, both the Liberals and the Tories tried to woo the minor parties to support them in forming a government. Before all the results were known, but after it had become apparent that the Liberals had massively increased their share of the vote, Sir Archibald Sinclair, the Liberal Party leader, initially ruled out a Coalition with either of the two largest parties. This was because Labour had been utterly discredited and Halifax of the Conservatives was an Appeaser. It was a typically principled stand from a highly principled man, but when it became apparent that Halifax would stand down immediately and that the Tories, whose confidence was badly shaken, would not contemplate a coalition with Labour but were open to being the lesser partners in a Coalition with the

Liberals, the Liberal-Conservative Alliance was formed and Sinclair was asked by the King to form a government.

Three days after the election results were counted, a Napier-Heston Racer aircraft recaptured the world airspeed record from the Germans at a speed of 479.36 mph, 10.14 mph faster than the previous record held by a Messerschmitt 209 VI.

From 'The Indian Independence Movement and the Imperial Audit of 1941' by Eugene Goldblum, Stevens and Samuel 1973

"...one of the most idle and ill contrived systems that ever disgraced a nation." John Arthur Roebuck, describing the British Empire in a House of Commons debate, 24th May 1849

In attempting to deal with the Indian independence movement, British policy fell between two stools. On the one hand, the British colonial government in India pursued the time-honoured and previously effective method of asserting its moral right with brute force. It is important to note here that there was little difference in the way the British maintained control of India and the way in which any of the previous regimes including the Moguls, the Muryahs, the Guptas or the Marathas had accomplished it. In the traditional Indian system opposition to the rule of the Government was a crime far worse than banditry and was generally met with violent reprisal. The British merely continued that policy, they did not invent it. It had the benefit of being understood and accepted as a normal function of government by the Indian people. Elected Indian governments post British colonial rule have also been compelled to utilise force to keep order in the country.

What had changed was the outlook of the governing class of the United Kingdom, who were of course the overseers of the colonial government of India. Their view of the British Empire had gone from regarding it in purely commercial terms – those of asset or liability, profit and loss – to an emphasis on what Kipling called 'the high and holy work' of Britain's 'civilising mission'. India, indeed the entirety of the British Empire was no longer a market to be exploited, it was now a ward that needed (in another of Kipling's memorable phrases) to be '...humoured (Ah slowly!) towards the light.'

One of the British conceits regarding the Empire was that its peoples would be, or could be made to be, willing participants in the process of 'civilising' them. This is hardly surprising given the marked differences in scientific and social development between Europe and much of the rest of the world. However, it does not seem to have occurred to the British that the native peoples of their empire might be oblivious to this subtlety, or misinterpret its implementation. While modern approaches to medicine, agriculture and commerce benefitted many Indians; others, particularly the poor, saw little of that benefit and consequently had little use for these advances. The relaxation of the general firmness of British rule; the toleration of such organisations as the Indian Congress Party (which was founded in Britain by a Scot) and the encouragement of the Indian independence movement in British universities were seen by Indians of all classes and castes as signs, not of helpful coaching in a spirit of brotherly love and co-operation; but of weakness.

It is important to note here the genius and potential limitations of Gandhi's non-violent protest movement. In initiating it, he clearly identified the main weakness in British policy and the ideal way in which to exploit it. At that time, the non-violent movement could only have worked in a British colony. Imagine Gandhi attempting to disseminate the notion of non-violent resistance in German Tanganyika, the Belgian Congo, the Dutch East Indies or Portuguese Mozambique. In these places too there was protest and opposition to the colonial government; it came to a rapid and bloody end. Fortunately for the Mahatma, this was not the British way and he suffered no more than imprisonment.

It is also important to note that generally speaking (and the urging of Gandhi notwithstanding) the Indian independence movement was far from being non-violent. A mythology has grown up in our own age that only peaceful forms of protest were used to achieve the goal of Indian independence, this is quite false.

*

The outline of the debate on India and indeed the debate on the direction that the Empire should take can be clarified by Sir John Seely's question in 1883 as to whether the Empire was capable of further development (and if so, what kind of development) or whether it was 'a mischievous encumbrance' to be got rid of as quickly as possible. He further asked; '…whether the possession of India does now, or ever can, increase our power and our security while there is no doubt it vastly increases our dangers and responsibilities.'

The Montagu – Chelmsford Report on India and constitutional reforms of 1918 pointed out that India depended for both internal and external security upon the Armed Forces of the United Kingdom, an assessment echoed by the Simon commission in 1930. One third of the British Army was stationed in India, possession of India forced upon Britain extensive commitments in the Middle East and southern Asia.

The British attachment to India was essentially romantic. Since the displacement in British government in the late 19th century of the commercial middle-class by the academic middle-class, British rule in India had very little focus on economic development. Although hailed as the 'Jewel in the Crown' of Empire it appeared that the British had almost no idea what to do with India other than to hang onto it. While the British recognised that India was in many ways a burden, they also felt that it was somehow the proof of Britain's status as a world power. Describing this as policy would be essentially incorrect. It was a negation of policy, a continuation of the status quo for reasons no one had really thought out. But it is also true to say that without the British, India would never have been a single united country.

The debate in Parliament over India during the early 1930s was at times fierce; however the death of Winston Churchill in December 1931 meant that the diehard opponents of Indian self–government lost their eloquent and politically adept leader. Shortly after coming to power as Britain's Prime Minister in the summer of 1932, Oswald Mosley sought to toughen policy with regards to dissent throughout the Empire. This bought him into conflict with the Viceroy of India, the Earl of Willingdon. Willingdon did not shrink from the use of force in governing

India, though his use of force was certainly limited compared to previous regimes, and he resisted Mosley's insistence that he be more forceful still. Mosley wanted him dismissed, but Governor's General were appointed not by the Prime Minister, but by the Privy Council.

The instinctive feeling within the Labour Party, both pre- and post-Mosley, was to grant independence or dominion status to every territory under the Crown as quickly as possible, providing that the rapid transfer of government did not cause chaos in the territory concerned. In the turmoil and climate of harsh national self-appraisal that swept the British government after the debacle of May 1940, it was decided to undertake a survey of the British Empire. This was to appraise the relative strengths and weaknesses, in strategic and economic terms, of each of the Empire's territories. Only then could a calculation of each colony's viability as an independent state be made, and a schedule whereby it might become independent, drawn up.

The Idea of an Imperial Audit had first been put forward in 1938 by Oswald Mosley. Under Mosley, British policy had changed sharply with regard to its attitude to the rest of the world. Before he had taken office British Governments were increasingly inclined towards the view that the world was one unitary society that was naturally harmonious and armed conflict was a breakdown in that natural harmony. This of course was very different from Britain's 19th-century view of the world as characterised and codified by Palmerston. To 19th century Britain, the world was an arena where nation states competed for advantage. One where national interests – though they might sometimes conflict with the interests of others and sometimes coincide – were always paramount, and where relations between states were governed not by legal or moral principle but by power and ambition. It was a place of perpetual struggle, and the possession of empire was not immoral or wicked, but simply a natural function of the pursuit of national interest.

Mosley's view was much closer to that of Palmerston than to that of the majority of Britain's governing class. All parties were split on the issue of the Empire but many MPs on both sides of the house were convinced that the Audit would reveal that the Empire was a pillar of strength that supported the mother country, only a few realised that it would reveal a very different picture.

The obvious choice for the chair of the committee was Mosley himself. Mosley was very much an Empire-centric figure, and the Empire was central to his idea of Britain as a Great Power. After his resignation from the office of Prime Minister, Mosley had taken up an appointment as British Ambassador to the League of Nations. The new leadership of the Labour Party were keen to have Mosley out of the way – it would hardly have been comfortable for men like Clement Attlee and Hugh Dalton to have the former Prime Minister looking over their shoulders from the back benches. Always a strong advocate of the League, Mosley quickly became frustrated with the glacial slowness of its workings and its general ineffectiveness and resigned the post in early 1940. This left him without a task that might keep him at a safe distance from the British Parliament.

Mosley was enthusiastic about the appointment from the first and bought all of his customary energy and powers of observation to the work. It must be noted that the committee had no mandate to take into account the world geo-political situation, it was meant to be only an analysis of the internal conditions and external trade prospects of the territories it covered. Mosley however, could not resist the temptation to suggest policy changes with strategic realities (as he perceived them) firmly in view. He produced an unflinching and thorough investigation of the economic and strategic issues concerning the British Empire, one that surprised even him.

Known as the Mosley Committee it convened in early 1940 and reported in January 1941. In sharp contrast to its initial brief, it could be read as a commercial and strategic audit of the Empire to establish which parts were assets or had the potential to be assets, and which parts were liabilities. Its findings therefore, were strongly indicative of which of the many British territories were in reality worth keeping.

The report's findings burst upon Parliament like a bombshell. It clearly and unequivocally drew the surprising conclusions that:

1.) Instead of being a powerful alliance, the Empire was a ramshackle collection of mismatched lands with little in common.

2.) That far from being any sort of asset to the UK, the Empire was a collective liability.

3.) The best way to limit that liability was by either investing heavily in the Empire to stimulate economic development or by releasing most of its unprofitable and indefensible territories from the Imperial yoke and giving them independence immediately.

In recommending a way to proceed, the report noted that although Imperial Preference had caused an improvement in the Empire's general trading position, the fundamental problem, which was the poverty of most of the Empire's territories, could only be addressed by development. However, it also observed that the kind of capital outlay required to stimulate such changes was unlikely to be forthcoming in the climate of financial reticence and high defence spending following the War of 1940. It also addressed the argument that release from the Empire would inevitably mean the loss of the market presented by the territory concerned to British goods by arguing that:

1.) Political independence from Westminster did not mean exclusion from the sterling zone.

2.) Many countries and territories not part of the British Empire were far more profitable markets for British goods than those within it.

3.) Many British territories were dollar countries but were still profitable markets.

In addressing Imperial defence, the report forcefully made the point that the Empire was extremely vulnerable if attacked simultaneously by a coalition of two or more hostile great powers and would have some difficulty in supporting widely separated campaigns. This had been recently underlined by British losses to Italian opportunism in the War of 1940. While admitting that the Dominions of Australia, Canada and New Zealand had raised substantial forces to fight alongside the British in The Great War, it also noted that many of Britain's territories had provided only a paltry contribution to Empire defence while remaining wholly reliant on Britain for their own safety. The same pattern had been repeated in the War of 1940.

The Mosley Report was particularly scathing about India, noting that "… in no other part of the Empire has the transition from commerce to charity been so marked." India was unprofitable. It could be made profitable, but the independence movement was clamorous and its activities would almost certainly be bad for business. Worst of all, India's British educated middle-class were politicised, strident and disinclined to undertake commercial endeavour. (In this respect it closely resembled its British academic middle-class teachers!) The report noted also that; "Mohandas K. Gandhi is a consummate politician" and; "…a shrewd political operator, pretending to be an innocent." it further noted that; "Gandhi has no grasp of economic realities, his blueprint for the future of India, in so far as he has considered India's economic future at all, will cause regression rather than advancement."

The failure to initiate wide development or even adequately survey almost all of the territories of the British Empire was also noted. This observation was particularly acute in the case of India, part of the report read:

"If India had been exploited with even half the ruthless vigour that it is commonly supposed that the British Empire exploits its subject territories; India would, by now, possess one of the largest and strongest economies in the world."

By the time the report was ready to be printed however, India was too far along the road to dominion status for any brake to be applied. It is certainly true that the British failure to stimulate the Indian economy into industrial and commercial growth was one of the reasons that India remained an economic backwater for the rest of the 20th century.

In conclusion, the only territories which the report recommended that Britain should retain were those that were, or might swiftly become, profitable. Those that were worth retaining for strategic reasons and those whose defence and upkeep presented little prospect of difficulty as well as minimal expenditure.

There was a secret appendix to the report that was not widely circulated outside the British Parliament. This pointed out that in almost all of Britain's possessions and territories overseas there was some form of opposition to colonial rule and the arguments presented by those who sought independence from Britain could be effectively used to permit Britain to wash its hands of unprofitable territories and leave them to make their own way in the world. A minority report to the secret appendix opined that this would amount to a dereliction of Britain's duty to safeguard the peoples of the Empire and held that most of the territories to which such ruthless treatment might apply were quite incapable of political or economic independence.

In sum, the Mosley Report recommended the setting down what Kipling described as 'The White Man's Burden' post haste. In that respect, it was quite shocking to the widely-held, over-romanticised opinion of the day. The government certainly did not contemplate a disorderly withdrawal from Empire, in part to ensure that former British territories did not fail as independent nations to the embarrassment of Britain, or fall into the hands of Britain's rivals. It was noted that the mere act of leaving a territory might not mean that Britain could remain uninvolved in its future development. In any case, the government considered that most of the findings of the report could not be implemented immediately due to the world situation and the necessity of maintaining the most advantageous strategic position possible.

It was noted by the Government that the Mosley Report took very little account of invisible trade such as shipping and banking and the effect the report's recommendations might have on that sector. It was also noted that after the War of 1940, India had become a net creditor to Britain – previously she had always been a debtor. Nevertheless, the report eventually served as a guiding light to the Empire's future progress and development. The British Commonwealth and The Third British Empire would have developed very differently without it.

[107] India attained dominion status at midnight on Saturday 15th August 1942. [108]

---

[107] See Annex 5 for a fuller account of the Mosley Report.

[108] In OTL this did not happen until 1947. It would be a united India at least at the outset, not India, West Pakistan and East Pakistan. See Annex 6 for a detailed picture of Indian independence and partition in TTL.

CHAPTER 22: 9th JULY 1967

The following is composed of extracts from the text of a series of interviews conducted by Dominic Walton Hartnell with President Harry S. Truman, President of the United States from 1945 to 1952. They were originally broadcast on 'Voice of America Radio' on the 23rd of October 1967.

DWH: What was your first concern when you were sworn in to office in January 1945?

HST: To put it simply, the Germans and the Japanese. Wendell Willkie's Administration confirmed what Roosevelt already realised, which was that Germany and Japan were the principal threats to the United States. He had been reluctant to really force the issue of oil supplies to Japan from the Netherlands East Indies, but I wanted to make a foreign policy statement right off the bat. The Japanese were still digesting their conquests in Far Eastern Russia; Amur, Southern Khabarovsk, Sakhalin and Primorsky. It was important to show them right away that we weren't going to be trifled with. I simply wasn't willing to let the oil issue go. Almost weekly there were new stories of atrocities coming out of China, out of Far Eastern Russia. I was determined to take a strong line with both Germany and Japan.

I was very concerned by the expansion of the Japanese, Italian, Spanish and German Navies, and of course the Argentine-Chilean war that started in '43. It bought the issues into sharp focus as far as I was concerned. It's no secret that I saw the German supply of arms to Argentina as a direct violation of the Monroe Doctrine.

Germany was a nation that seemed to have lost its mind. The way they were treating Jews, of course we didn't realise then just how completely evil it was, but we did notice the weird Aryan race cult they were starting. They believed the concept of race was something to worship. They were building temples, inventing rituals and they even named some warships after the old Norse gods for heaven sakes! I know the British had a habit of naming some of their warships after Roman gods but this was something much deeper, much more disturbing.

The Russians too seemed to have got religion in a big way, they had turned back to Orthodoxy and even as they fought to put their country back together their leaders didn't try to re–impose the atheistic aspects of communism.

DWH: Your Administration was instrumental in negotiating an end to the Argentine-Chilean War which was also one of your first foreign policy concerns.

HST: Well, I'm inclined to say that common-sense broke out, but we did have to crack some heads. It was an absurd squabble over three tiny pieces of rock in the Beagle Channel [109] started by some sealers and whalers and Latin American machismo did the rest.

DWH: Both regimes were quasi-fascist though, and very much a part of the Sterling trading bloc.

HST: Nevertheless, the Monroe Doctrine applied, which is why we needed to crack heads. We were very concerned about the way the Germans were trying to cuddle up to Argentina. Brazil also had a fairly questionable regime in power but we were able to keep them on side.

*

DWH: It's been said that as a young man you were 'a typical rural bigot'. How would you respond to that?

HST: Well, I don't know as I should even dignify it. We all make mistakes when we're young, I think my record on advancing the civil rights movement speaks for itself.

---

[109] In OTL the Beagle Channel dispute over the possession of the Picton, Lennox and Nueva Islands had festered since 1881. It almost bought Argentina and Chile to war in 1978 and was not finally resolved until 1984.

DWH: You ran into a lot of opposition for your policy on completely desegregating the army.

HST; Yes I did, but it was the right decision on every level. That process was started under Wendell Willkie's administration but we saw it through. Black regiments have fought in American armies since as far back as the Civil War. It makes no sense to exclude a man from the duties and responsibilities of citizenship based on his colour. The armed services should represent the whole country and the integration of the military was a top priority. Besides, all that segregation was inefficient.

HST: Which of the services did you have the most difficulty with?

DWH: The Army without a doubt. Not the Army Air Force so much as the regular soldier's Army. The Navy and Marine Corps didn't give me nearly as much trouble, but the Army tried to evade both the letter and the spirit of my programme. It was really the war and the need for manpower that put a stop to all that.

*

DWH: Mr President, you have been criticised for basing the Fair Deal policies you espoused in the presidential election campaign of 1944 too closely on those of Franklin Roosevelt's New Deal. How would you respond to that?

HST: Economic recovery was the central aim of both policies, but the New Deal didn't really work. It didn't generate prosperity in part because it was regarded with hostility by the Supreme Court, by Congress, by big business and by the wealthy. I believe that trying to imitate or update the New Deal would have failed, so what we were going to try to do was avoid the confrontation and stalemate that characterised the New Deal years.

DWH: Despite that, your relations with the business community weren't always good.

HST: That's true, but on the whole, the emphasis of my Administration was less confrontational than that of FDR's. I guess the FDR years kind of hung over us, we did everything we could to try and avoid the imagery of capital and labour locked in a permanent struggle over the distribution of wealth. In that sense we were mediators rather than reformers. Unlike FDR and his people, we weren't trying to change the existing structure of the economy and we were willing to concede economic leadership to the corporate sector, but we weren't as 'hands-off' regarding business as the Republicans certainly.

DWH: So the 'Fair Deal' was a continuation of your predecessor President Willkie's policies?

HST: We certainly rounded out a process that he started. I've got to hand it to Wendell and his advisers, they got the economic basics right. It's a shame that he didn't live to see the economy come out of the recession the way it did. Where we parted ways with the general outlook of the Willkie Administration was that we tried to take more care of the American people; at times the Republicans almost seem to be saying 'Devil take the hind most.'

DWH: During your presidency you were often in conflict with your generals.

HST: Well, not all of them. I got on very well with Bradley and with Eisenhower but you must remember that I served as an officer in the artillery in the Great War and I came away from that with a very low opinion of high military office. Eisenhower and Bradley did a lot to change my opinion. They were good soldiers and loyal servants of this country and its people.

DWH: You've been accused of trying to be all things to all men, it's been said that as president you were a political pacifier. Is that fair?

227

HST: The point is that the world is neither perfect nor perfectible. We live in it and we do what we can to preserve our own sense of honour, but human nature is mixed. There's nothing we can do about that and it's always easier to work with people than against them. Compromise is essential in politics. I was reared as a moral absolutist; but politics in America, especially in the 1930s and 40s, was an arena where if you wanted to be successful you had to learn to function in the shadow world in which honest public service coexisted with graft, organised crime, electoral dishonesty and all kinds of vice. Compromise was the only way to keep the Democratic Party together.

Under both FDR and Wendell Willkie, the patterns of jurisdiction that characterised the administration were quite chaotic. There were few clear lines of authority, very little issue jurisdiction, it was messy, piecemeal. American government is decentralised by design, and I believe that's a good thing; but what I tried to do was to introduce some structure. I tried to get rid of the disorderliness of the executive branch. For instance, where FDR had relied on a network of unofficial advisers I tried to introduce more responsible cabinet government as well as bring the Washington bureaucracy under some sort of control. One of the reasons for FDR's failure was that he never did that. Any legislation the executive branch passed would be modified on its way down through the administrative layers of government, sometimes to the point where it became unrecognisable .

DWH: Do you see yourself as a manager rather than a leader?

HST: Yes I think that's a fair comment on my style, but a good manager *is* a leader. Both know when to delegate authority and both should back up their subordinates.

DWH: What formed your foreign policy?

HST: I believe that America has a mission in the world, a mission to make it a better place and I believe that totalitarianism, whether its origins are from the left or from the right, is a threat to world peace, to the American way of life and therefore had to be opposed.

*

DWH: I'd like to ask you about relations with the British at this time, which of course were absolutely crucial during that period of history.

HST: That's about right, though I have to say the relationship was pretty fractious at times it was generally a close one.

DWH: What was the cause of the disputes?

HST: The British had this idea that we Americans were ruthlessly hard-nosed negotiators and inclined to sharp practice. They felt that our business methods were predatory and so I think they were trying to outdo us at our own game. The British had a bit of a problem at the time, most of their Governments during the 1920s and early 1930s were quite utopian in their outlook. When I say utopian, I mean in the sense that they seemed to think that the world was a nice place where everyone could be friendly and reasonable. When Oswald Mosley came along that changed. He had a much more realistic view of the world; that it was an arena of contest, a place of struggle. He was quite comfortable with the notion of business being about competition, but this didn't sit well with much of Britain's governing class who regarded commerce as something sordid, something whose chief function was to provide jobs for the British working class. So the British working class wouldn't do away with them the way they did in Russia. I think their confrontational attitude was because they were overcompensating for what happened in 1940.

DWH: Could you expand on that?

HST: My perception of it is that over the course of the 19th century, Britain's governing class was composed mostly of pragmatic realists, businessman, soldiers and the like. But it went to being composed mostly of liberal romantics; academics, intellectuals, what have you. That's a good part of the reason for Britain's industrial decline from about 1870 up to about 1935. As I say, Mosley did a lot to reverse this, but when he crashed out of British politics in 1938 and Clement Attlee took over, Britain again went back to having the romantics in charge rather than the realists. Sinclair was a realist with romantic leanings.

DWH: What did you think of Britain's Prime Ministers at this time?

HST: I thought Attlee was patronising and naïve; Dalton was a decent man and good technically but couldn't inspire people. I found Sinclair easier to deal with, though he could be pompous.

DWH: It was under Sinclair's administration that the Tizard mission came to Washington.

HST. Yes, it was around Christmas of '45 and as I hardly need say we were right on the back foot at that time.

DWH: What was the American attitude to the British?

HST: We were looking for their help quite frankly but we were also disappointed that they threw in the towel in 1940. That rankled with me personally, because it made Joe Kennedy look like a prophet, which he wasn't. So there was a real question mark over how much spine they had, over whether they really had the stomach to get back into the fight and worse than that, they seemed intent on blaming us for them giving up in 1940.

DWH: Is that fair comment?

HST: Well if Franklin Roosevelt had won the 1940 election he would have found some way to help the British out. We didn't know it at the time but money was their principal problem, they were just about broke. They were telling us that, but we didn't believe them. You see, that's another example of the difference between a country governed by a romantic class and one governed by a realist class. The British were just being honest with us when they said they were out of money, but honesty, complete honesty, is as rare as hen's teeth in international diplomacy. Not least because international diplomacy is a cutthroat game and honesty can be the mark of a fool. Mark Twain said that "...the surest way to convey misinformation is to tell the strictest truth.", so we didn't believe them because it looked suspiciously like they wanted to find a way to get us to pay for their war again. We looked at them as any businessman would look at a competitor. But overall, no it's not a fair comment, if you have to ascribe blame on that issue it has to go to the British themselves, they underestimated the Germans plain and simple.

DWH: Was bringing the British Empire to an end a policy goal of the Roosevelt Administration?

HST: Well, bringing down the British Empire wasn't something they were going to pursue actively, but it also wasn't something they were going to make an effort to stop, let's put it that way. There were many individuals within the Roosevelt administration who would have liked that, the under-cover Communists and such like, but it wasn't policy. Willkie had a more pragmatic approach, he grasped the fact that the British did an awful lot behind the scenes in the world. The Royal Navy policed the seas, British diplomacy oiled the wheels of international relations, many of the territories they controlled weren't capable of self-government and some of them were in our backyard. So they would have become our responsibility if we didn't want to see them sliding into chaos.

Oswald Mosley was given some busy work by Attlee after he was forced out as Prime Minister. Attlee didn't want him around so he sent him off to do an audit of the Empire. That was an eye opener for our State Department. It was the first time we had looked seriously at what a British Imperial retreat would have meant to us and it wasn't pretty. That drove a tolerant approach to the British Empire.

DWH: A tolerant approach?

HST: Yes, we decided to mind our own business basically.

DWH: What was your attitude to Russia?

HST: Well, there was a lot of resentment over their spying activities in our country. I mean a lot. As you know the Soviet Union came apart over the winter of 1942 to 43, the place was chaos for a while, and then Kaganovitch took over what was left and started trying to put it back together again.

By the time I took office, the British were beginning to supply the Russians with food, medicines, fuel and some weaponry through eastern Iran. From late '45 we started to send supplies that way too. We really started pouring food, fuel, raw materials and munitions in there.

At that time, Reza Shah wouldn't let us put a lot of troops on the ground in Iran, he wanted to stay neutral so he was hedging his bets, but he was fine with letting us transport supplies through there. Because of that the Russians were able to start planning for real military operations against the Germans rather than the partisan/guerrilla style stuff they had been doing up to that time. We knew we were going to need their help fighting Germany. Most of their industrial infrastructure had survived the Axis-Soviet War, they moved it all away from the front line in '41 and '42.

DWH: Going back to the Tizard mission; was it actually very significant in terms of our armed forces and our military build-up?

HST: Yes it was, Tizard came over here with quite a bag of tricks. The most important were aircraft engines and the work the British had done on developing an atomic bomb, but there was all sorts of other stuff as well.

DWH: Rolls-Royce were building military aircraft engines in Indiana at this time, weren't they?

HST: Yes that's correct, in Auburn, at the old Auburn – Cord – Duesenberg factory. Michigan too, at the Packard factory in Detroit.

DWH: How did that come about?

HST: When the Auburn automobile company closed their doors in 1937, they were bought by Rolls-Royce using a loan from the British government. The British were worried about their manufacturing capacity and they were exploring the possibilities of using American and Canadian factories to build stuff for them. The American aero-engine companies were pretty unhappy about that and got Franklin Roosevelt's Administration to ensure that none of the engines built at Auburn would come onto the American market, they would all just go straight to the UK.

DWH: Why didn't the British just buy American engines?

HST: They didn't think they were good enough, not the liquid-cooled in-line engines anyway, they liked our air-cooled radials better. They were telling the Air Force that our fighter aircraft weren't as good as theirs and we even tested a few of their types and found that they were right. They were really giving our manufacturers a hiding in the international market for military aircraft. Sterling was weak against the dollar, and because of the abrupt end of the War of 1940 they had a surplus of warplanes. The loss of orders for aircraft from Turkey, China, Thailand and Chile really hurt our industry. But none of our manufacturers wanted to build British planes let alone pay the licence fees.

The Argentine-Chilean war – that's what really bought the message home, the Argentine air force was mostly equipped with German aircraft, Focke-Wulf fighters and so on, while the Chileans used American airplanes. Our bombers were as good as or better than theirs, but our fighters, P38s, P39s and P40s were at a real disadvantage to the best European types, the P39 just wasn't much good at altitude, the P38 was too hard to fly in combat, and the P40 was just about at the end of its development.

DWH: The Chileans bought British fighters eventually.

HST: Yeah, Spitfire fives I think it was. They still weren't as good as the German fighters, but they were much better than ours, and because they were surplus to British requirements they were much cheaper too. The same thing happened with the Turks and the Chinese. Once the aircraft industry began to appreciate this, it wasn't long before they decided to try a British engine in one of our fighters.

DWH: These were built by Packard though.

HST: Yes, that's right. The British had got Packard all tooled up to build engines on the same basis as Auburn, but when the war of 1940 came to an end, Packard were left hanging in the breeze. Anyway, they got it together with the North American aircraft company to swap out the Allison engine from one of their A36 planes for a Rolls-Royce engine and they came up with the P51. Our airplane engine manufacturers were as mad as hell about it, but I backed the Air Force's decision. We had to get our boys the best weapons we could and if that meant paying royalties on non-American engines then so be it. Their jet engines were well ahead of ours too.

DWH: What did the British do for the Manhattan Project?

HST: As you know, Franklin Roosevelt started our atomic bomb programme in 1940. He had received a letter from Albert Einstein warning him that the Germans might be developing atomic weapons so he got the ball rolling. Under Wendell Willkie's administration things moved forward but not as fast as they might have done. The problem was the whole project was just so darned expensive, Willkie's administration understood the importance of the thing but they had to surround it with secrecy and one way to keep it as quiet as possible was to limit the amount of money that it got. If items turned up in the budget with huge dollar figures in front of them people tended to ask questions, people in Congress and the Senate. So Wendell had to disguise spending on the bomb as much as possible.

The British were already ahead of us and their government isn't nearly as open and accessible as ours is. In consequence it was much easier for the British to hide what it was costing. The Tizard mission showed us how far they had got. I got Oppenheimer and Groves to come and look at the documents Tizard had bought with him and they confirmed that the British were well ahead. Now we knew that we would be able to catch them up, but the problem was time. We had no idea how far ahead the Germans were, no idea at all, and frankly a lot of people were very scared about what would happen if they got the bomb first. We were getting warnings through the Danish resistance from a guy named Niels Bohr, a Danish atomic physicist, one of the best in the world. He kept getting German atomic physicists coming and asking him questions, stuff that could only be related to atomic weapons. He did what he could to mislead them but of course there was only so much he could do, and he was really worried about where the Germans were with their bomb development.

Oppenheimer and Groves both agreed with me that any shortcut would help us out. As I say, we were really on the back foot at that time and it was imperative that we get a working atomic bomb as quickly as possible. It was no time to stand on national pride.

DWH: The British drove a hard bargain though didn't they?

HST: Yes but I respected them for it. There were big changes between the way Attlee's Administration approached us and the way Sinclair's did. Dealing with Attlee's people was like dealing with a bunch of beggars, dealing with Sinclair's was more like doing business. Their chief negotiator was Louis Mountbatten, and a real charming British aristocrat he is too. He really knew how to get around people. But in the end I think we got a good deal. We agreed to bear three quarters of the cost of the programme and the British agreed to give us 50% access to the Canadian uranium ore, we agreed to complete disclosure between the laboratories, ours at Los Alamos and theirs at Chalk River in Ontario, which meant less wasteful duplication of effort.

DWH: This wasn't just another example of the British getting us to fight their wars for them, or more specifically, getting us to pay for their wars for them?

HST: No, no, not at all. We could tell from the way they had cut their naval programme back in July of '43 and the limits they put on expanding their army that they were strapped for cash.

DWH: How much time in developing the bomb did the deal save us?

HST: I believe it may have saved us two to three years.

CHAPTER 23: NO CALM BEFORE THE STORM

From 'Germany and the Conquered Territories' by Heinz Lang, Macallister 1997

There were seven versions of the Generalplan Ost, the Nazi's plan for Eastern Europe. The final version was set down in a document of 374 pages dated 28th January 1943. [110] As well as the 'Germanisation' of the annexed Polish territories, it recommended the creation of four 'borderlands' (Marken), Ostland, Ukraine, Caucasus and Gotengau (Crimea and Kherson province) and one Verteidigungzone (a defensive area under military jurisdiction) – Muskovy. There were no proposals for German settlement in most of the Russian heartland. Certainly there was the intention of long-term German domination, but there does not appear to have been any plan for Russia comparable to the other settlement plans which focused on Ukraine and Belorussia. The timescale over which the plan was to be implemented was twenty-five to thirty years, the greater part of the cost was to be raised by borrowing.

In addition to their plans for the east, there were also detailed plans for regions closer to the 1939 borders of Germany. The plan defined a Volksraum (People's Room) with seven settlement areas: Belgium, Luxemburg, Elass-Lothringen (Alsace-Lorraine), Upper Carinthia, Lower Styria, Bohemia-Moravia and the Incorporated Eastern Territories annexed from Poland. All of these were subsumed by decree into Germany proper between 1942 and 1944. Switzerland was annexed in 1943 following the German conquest when it was re-named

---

[110] In OTL there was no final draft of Generalplan Ost, the last known preliminary draft, the sixth, is dated 23rd December 1942, and was written by Greifelt. Much has been made of Hitler's rambling and self contradictory soliloquies on the subject, this version is speculative and is simplified from several accounts and criticisms of his incomprehensible rantings.

'Schweizmark'. It does not seem to have figured in the 'Volksraum' plans, perhaps because most of the population were already ethnic Germans.

The plan proposed a future population of 30 million people in the settlement areas of the Volksraum, consisting of an existing ethnic German population of 5.6 million, a residual Germanised native population of 7.4 million, and 17 million German immigrants. As the existing population was 36.3 million, of which 5.6 million were already German (German citizens, ethnic Germans etc) and 5.4 million were defined as 'Germanisable' natives; the plan implied, but did not explicitly mention, the expulsion of around 25 million people.

For the Ostland area, out of a population of 7.2 million, of which few were considered German, 2.1 million were considered Germanisable while the remaining 5.1 million would be required to disappear. 3.1 million German settlers would have been needed to bring the population back up to 5.2 million.

In total, the disappearance of around 30 million non-Germans out of the settlement areas of the Volksraum, the Marken and the Verteidigungzone was implied in the plan, but this mass movement of peoples across Europe was hardly even begun by 1945. Generalplan Ost was wholly divorced from socio-economic realities and completely unworkable. More than one German observer dismissed it as "Realitätsferne Hirngespinste" (pipedreams divorced from reality) and the entire process of planning for Germany's eastern conquests, has an air of delusion, unreality and disorganisation.

Hitler set only vague policy guidelines, which were based on Nazi ideology, itself a fundamentally confused system of ideas. His underlings devised models that were based on their own interpretation of this mish-mash of half-baked thinking and then attempted to obtain Hitler's endorsement. In many cases there were direct conflicts between the conceptions advanced by different subordinates and Hitler would not give clear approval of one idea over a competing one, leading to uncertainty and confusion in the administration of the conquered territories.

A number of cities in the east were renamed by the Nazis. Moscow became Liststadt after Guido von List, while Leningrad was officially renamed Landsberg, though Lanzberg and Petersberg were also commonly used. Hitler's fixation with Ulrich von Hutten manifested itself in the renaming of Minsk as Huttenberg and Kiev became Amalia, after the quasi-fictional capital of the Goths on the Dnieper. Sevastopol became Goetheberg for Johann Wolfgang von Goethe and Tbilisi was renamed Schönerer for Georg von Schönerer (an Austrian, with nothing to recommend him, other than his rabid anti Semitism).

Europe 1943.

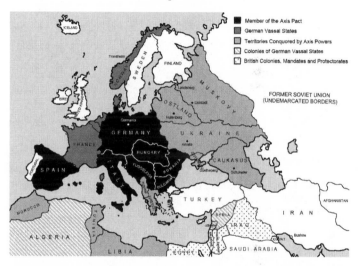

Generalplan Ost was a failure. The fundamental problem was that millions of Germans did not suddenly volunteer to become settlers since the post-war economic boom in Germany absorbed all available German manpower and even drew in foreign labour. Furthermore, the inhabitants of a prosperous developed country such as Germany could not be induced to leave for a hazardous, uncomfortable life in the undeveloped East.

Ostland, Ukraine, Gottengau and Caukasus continued as military occupation zones tying down large numbers of German troops. There was sporadic partisan activity and the Germans committed many atrocities in response. Economic activity was greatly subdued and the Germans even found difficulty in inducing the people of the region to plant grain.

Finally, there was the question of the territories of Holland, Denmark, the Danish colonies and Norway. The people of these countries were regarded by the Nazis as Aryans and they were therefore eligible to be Germanised. Norway, largely because of Norse mythology which had been adopted by the Nazis, was an obvious choice. Denmark followed on as a kind of stepping stone to Norway and though annexation had been planned for 1950 this was bought forward and both were officially annexed in January 1945. Holland presented a slightly different case but was also annexed in the spring of 1945.

After the occupation of Denmark, the Nazis made no move to annex Iceland and Greenland. Although theoretically independent since 1874, Iceland's foreign affairs were handled by Denmark and consequently the Parliament of Iceland, the Althing, decided to take control of external dealings and elected a provisional governor. The Althing also resolved to strictly enforce a position of neutrality and sought the assistance of the United States which warned the German government that any attempt to occupy or coerce Iceland or Greenland would be dimly viewed in Washington. Involved as they were with their plans for Europe the status of Iceland and Greenland were not matters the Germans desired to pursue at that time.

Following a referendum, Iceland formally became an independent republic on 17th June, 1944, while Denmark was still under German occupation. Despite this, Christian X, the deposed and exiled Danish King, sent a message of congratulations to the Icelandic people. Greenland, though still theoretically a Danish colony came under the administration of Reykjavik though some assistance with practicalities was rendered by Canada and the United States.

From 'British Politics after the War of 1940' by Brian Garret, Gloucester University Press, 2001

With their disappointing showing in the election of 1941, the Conservative Party quickly realised that the choice of Lord Halifax was a mistake and he stepped down before the final results were tallied. The new leadership race saw the selection of

Anthony Eden who had previously been the Shadow Foreign Secretary instead. The choice of Eden as party leader was not without controversy, there was concern about his youth and comparative inexperience. Appointed at the age of 42, the party saw in him a figure that would modernise and revitalise it, in essence he was the Conservative's answer to Oswald Mosley though as one of the Conservative 'Grandees' put it "Unlike Mosley, the man is not an utter blaggard." [111]

As part of the Liberal-Conservative Coalition government, Eden was given the deputy Prime Ministership but held the portfolio of Foreign Secretary. His good looks, obvious intelligence and relaxed style had great appeal both in the House and for the voters, especially when contrasted with what had gone before. The alliance had first to resolve the issue of free trade which was traditionally one of the chief points of difference between the two parties, but with a world rapidly dividing into trading blocs, the point was rendered moot. While hoping for a return to free trade, the Liberals in the Coalition were forced to confirm the status quo of Imperial Preference for the time being and thus support the Sterling Bloc against the rapidly developing dollar and Reichmark blocs. This was one of the issues which permitted the National Liberals to return to the Liberal fold and the decade-long schism in the Liberal Party was healed.

In the wake of the 1941 election, the uproar in the Labour Party showed no signs of ceasing. Hugh Dalton resigned and the new leader, Stafford Cripps, could barely contain a fractious and demoralised group of MPs. Labour had been disconcerted by the Alvarez Affair, thrown into disarray by the armistice of 1940 and the subsequent Treaty of Leamouth, and had lost massively in the election. Yet the divisions caused by Oswald Mosley's intemperate appetites, Britain's exit from the war and political defeat, were as nothing in comparison with the split caused by the news in June 1941 of the start of Operation Barbarossa. In some ways this was surprising as the German invasion of the

---

[111] Not a genuine quote.

Balkans in April had not excited nearly as much controversy on the left of British politics as it did on the right. [112]

A group on the left of the party, led by Aneurin Bevan, wanted a commitment from the government for direct support of the Soviet Union while the centrists united behind Cripps who preferred a more indirect approach. The pro-Conservative press was able to present Labour as not only split on policy, but both appeasers of Nazism and supporters of Communism!

Bevan's rages became worse as the unlikelihood of either intervening in Russia abroad, or persuading the country that Labour's wildly ambitious social programmes at home could be financed, became apparent. It was politically impossible for the government of the day to raise taxes which had not yet returned to their pre-war levels. Furthermore, the Alliance's own proposals for expanded social spending and the National Health Service were demonstrably less costly than those the Labour Party was demanding. Crucially, they could be funded through greater utilisation of the resources of the Empire. It rubbed salt into the wound that the Alliance used the Mosley report to back their claims. Bevan on the other hand, wanted Labour to commit to giving the territories of the Empire independence as soon as was practicable and advocated borrowing money on the world markets to finance Labour's plans. However, as these were somewhat depressed due to the recession, and British finances were at a low ebb after the war, this was unlikely to meet with success.

The Alliance renewed the attack on what they branded Labour's 'unrealistic and irresponsible' spending plans with regards to health and social services and also showed why there could be no large-scale attempt to prop up the USSR. Bevan, who was now shadow Home Secretary was easily needled by trenchant attacks on both subjects in the House of Commons

---

[112] This would be somewhat different from the OTL Balkan invasion, without the British encouraging opposition to the Germans, Prince Paul is not deposed after joining the Axis Pact in March 1941. Yugoslavia would then not oppose the passage of German troops through the country on their way to attack Greece. In TTL the attack would start in April and conclude two weeks later.

most notably from Randolph Churchill who, at the age of thirty, had much of his father's penetrating intellect, acerbic wit and ability as a speaker. [113]

Unsupported by his party and marginalised in the House, Bevan organised a back-bench revolt and with twenty-seven other disgruntled Labour MPs (all from the left or far-left of the party) resigned the Labour whip and formed a new group in the House of Commons known as the Democratic Labour Party. Soon after this, two other labour MPs defected to the Liberals. After the dust had settled in June 1941 the House of Commons looked like this,

Liberals 231
Conservatives 209
Labour 112
Democratic Labour 27
Others 36

*

The Commonwealth conference of early 1942 was a difficult one. Held in London, the atmosphere was strained by the attitude of the dominions to the UK after the debacle of 1940 and the question mark placed over the Empire by the report of the Mosley Commission. Although trade with Germany and the rest of Europe was beginning to pick up, the mismanagement of the German economy and the decline in the sizes of the other European economies under Nazi control meant that the British economy, like that of the entire globe, languished in the doldrums. The brief recession that followed the war of 1940, made promises of a 'New Jerusalem' financially questionable at

---

[113] In OTL, during WW2, Bevan constantly needled Randolph's father on every aspect of government policy. Winston Churchill once angrily derided Bevan as 'a squalid nuisance' and A. A. Milne (author of Winnie the Pooh) penned the ditty. *Goebbels, though not religious, must thank Heaven, for dropping in his lap, Aneurin Bevan.*

best, particularly as comparatively high armaments expenditure was seen as essential to the maintenance of British security.

American competition in the export trade was stiff but 'Imperial Preference' provided a platform on which to rebuild Britain's exports and the much-reduced volume of export goods leaving continental Europe opened new markets. Because of this, Britain suffered much less from the recession of 1941/42 than might otherwise have been the case.

When the new government of Sir Archibald Sinclair turned to foreign policy there was a very clear break with that pursued by the previous administration and this was noted by the governments of the Dominions. The Australian Prime Minister, Robert Menzies said, "You could tell right away, there was a new attitude about the British government, we knew then that there would be a reckoning with Germany and Italy." [114]

The British harboured grave concerns about the Indian Ocean littoral and the plans of the Japanese and Italians. If a coalition of the two gained control of the Indian Ocean, then the Far and Middle East would be directly cut off from Britain. The geopolitical consequences would be immense. With regards to Italy it was decided to pursue a strategy of containment until Mussolini could be brought to account and Italian forces ejected from Egypt and the Horn of Africa. As Antony Eden said, "We cannot allow a man with Il Duce's record to have his thumb on our windpipe." [115]

The Middle East was the key to several parts of both the new British government's domestic and foreign policies. Britain's territories in the region were the Crown Colonies of Aden and Bushire, the protectorates of Bahrain, Kuwait, Oman, Qatar and Trucial Oman as well as the mandated territories of Iraq and Trans-Jordan. The Iraqi revolt of May 1941, although haphazard and quickly put down, was an unpleasant shock to

---

[114] Not a genuine quote. In OTL Menzies was ousted as the United Australia Party leader after spending much of 1941 in Britain discussing Imperial policy. In TTL he stays at home and ensures his support base.

[115] Sorry, I just can't resist it…

British interests in the area and the German thrust into the Caucasus in the autumn of 1942 was the spur for action. [116]

The British quickly moved substantial forces into the region, greatly strengthening their hold on Iraq. It was fortunate that many British civil servants were leaving India as independence drew closer. The British Raj had built up substantial skills in dealing with minor potentates as the British had often used Indian princes to govern India by proxy. The work was a mixture of diplomacy, flattery and cajolery and was not for the politically squeamish, but the men who had so skilfully implemented this policy now found employment in the Middle East. Some of the more imaginative newspapers saw the movement of British civil servants and troops into the region as the founding of an 'Arabian Raj'.

Iran was an independent country, though it now found itself wooed by both Britain and Germany. Shah Reza had been installed on his throne by the British, but felt no gratitude to them and had bought Iran much closer to Germany. He even kept a signed photograph of Adolf Hitler by his bed. The British, understandably, found this irritating. It was a serious concern to the Government in London, who feared that the Abadan Oil Refinery might fall into either German or renegade Soviet hands. The refinery had produced eight million tons of oil in 1940 and was thus a crucial component of British economic life. For the Russians, Iran had always been a country of extreme strategic importance and an occupation of part or all of the country by Soviet troops, either acting on behalf of the Soviet Union or independently if the Soviet Union had ceased to exist, raised the spectre of the Germans having a pretext to invade.

The Shah was canny enough to realise that although the Nazis regarded the Persians as Aryan, they saw him and his people as third-rate Aryans, debased by breeding with what the Nazis considered to be lesser peoples. The British Ambassador

---

[116] In OTL the revolt was supported by the Germans and Italians with direct military aid including the sending of small numbers of aircraft. Axis support in TTL would be limited to the political and diplomatic.

to Iran, Sir Reader Bullard, was happy to give the Shah copies of the writings of the Nazi racial theorist Hans F. K. Günther translated into Persian to confirm this. Above all, Reza Shah wanted to keep his country as independent as possible and the British seemed the lesser of two evils. He tried to keep up a delicate balancing act between the two powers and Tehran was, for a while, a hotbed of intrigue. However, after the armistice of 1940, German interest in Iran lessened considerably. Shah Reza was forced to the conclusion that it had only been because of Germany's conflict with the UK and with that danger apparently eliminated, the Germans had no more use for him. Certainly Hitler's attention was now elsewhere. [117]

Anglo-Iranian Oil had discovered several new deposits of oil in the country at Lali, Naft Safid, Gach Saran and Agha Jari, all of which were producing by 1944. [118] Demand was buoyant from Europe, and the inflow of money to the Iranian treasury was most welcome to what was essentially a self-absorbed and venal man.

The notion of an 'Arabian Raj' was not as far from the truth as might at first be suspected. The new British government fully intended to finance the ambitious social policies that the Liberals had promised in the election by the annexation and exploitation of as much of the region's oil wealth as they could retain. It would have been political suicide to announce a repeal of the measures taken in the wake of the Beveridge report, but unless a source of wealth could be harnessed, then taxes would have to be increased to levels that would be destructive to Britain's economic life. The policy was vigorously pursued by Anthony Eden to whom Sinclair was happy to delegate. Eden was an Arabist scholar, fluent in the Arabic language, considered to be a deft hand at foreign policy and justly regarded as an expert on the Middle East.

---

[117] In OTL Reza Shah had to be bought sharply to heel by the British/Soviet invasion of 1941. In TTL he is uncharacteristically shrewd.

[118] These deposits were known about but went untapped until after WW2 in OTL.

At this time the Arab nationalist movement was little more than an amorphous and disjointed counter-position to British imperialism. It had little local or international appeal and was essentially a European import to the Arab world sponsored by Berlin. In the case of Iraq and many of the other territories of the Middle East, it was completely incompatible with a highly stratified social order. It was also true that the territories which the British believed they could retain in the long-term; namely the protectorate's of Bahrain, Kuwait, Qatar and Trucial Oman had an area roughly comparable to that of Scotland but between them an entire population of less than 300,000 people. There was a definite policy to persuade as many of them to become Crown Colonies as was possible. Bad government was endemic, revolts were frequent and as one British diplomat put it; " The region was beset by incompetent rulers and disgruntled peoples, if ever a place was ripe for change of the more positive sort, it was the British protectorates of the Trucial coast."

There was no plan for long-term inclusion of Iran into the British Empire. The British reinforcement of the region was merely a response to the German move into the Caucasus; however, the Crown Colony of Bushire housed a British Residency and guarded the oil refinery at Abadan which was controlled by the Anglo-Iranian Oil Company. It was decided very early that Iraq and Jordan would become independent as soon as the international situation allowed and there was also a plan to use the threat of the removal of British restraint upon Iran and Iraq to frighten the minor nations into acquiescence.

The British were also extremely concerned at the prospect of the collapse of the Soviet Union causing a massive and potentially destabilising influx of refugees into Iran. In late 1942, large numbers of armed Soviet troops retreating before the German onslaught entered the north west of the country and camped near Ardabil. These were a remnant of the South Front under General Malinovski and numbered no more than seven or eight thousand men. They had lost most of their equipment and had little food remaining.

Reza Shah had been building up his armed forces since 1932 and now had some 50,000 men at his command. He ordered a large proportion of this force northward to Tabriz and it seemed a dangerous confrontation was imminent. [119]

The British Foreign Office had been prescient enough to see that if the Germans took the oilfields of the Caucasus, then the end of the Soviet Union would ensue and it was critical to forestall a possible German invasion and to safeguard British oil interests in the region. While the prospect of occupying a neutral country put the British in a severe moral dilemma, the loss of British controlled oilfields could rapidly have led to the collapse of Britain itself and in that sense the situation was desperate and required extreme measures. [120] On 15th October 1942, the same day Adolf Hitler announced the end of major operations on the eastern front, the oil installations at Abadan were secured by two battalions of the Gloucestershire Regiment who made an amphibious crossing of the Shatt al-Arab waterway from Basra. Another force was landed at Bandar-e-Shahpur to secure the port and oil terminal there and a force was landed at Bushire to safeguard the British Residency.

The Shah was understandably alarmed; his previous policy of playing the British and Germans off against each other now seemed little more than foolish hubris. His confidence evaporated. It was one thing to consider the Germans to be friendly while they were issuing honeyed words through diplomats in Tehran, quite another to have a renegade force of Soviet soldiers on your territory and a panzer division on your border. He quickly invited the British in to broker an agreement that would see the Russians left as quickly as possible.

Major-General William Slim, the commanding officer of British forces in Iraq, immediately made contact with the commander of the Russian troops occupying the area around Ardabil. He promised Malinovski that they would be repatriated via Ashkhabat if they offered no resistance. Malinovski agreed and the troops were transported by sealed train from Tabriz to Shirvan and marched the last thirty miles to the border.

---

[119] In OTL his forces were much smaller.

[120] In OTL, Soviet and British forces occupied Iran in September 1941.

At that time, Hitler had no designs on Iran and was content to let it remain in the British sphere of influence. The kerfuffle on Iran's north-west border was hardly noticed in Germany amid the general rejoicing at the victory over the Soviet Union. Reza Shah was shaken by these events, dismayed by Hitler's ambivalence and compelled to the realisation that the British had used the crisis to bind his country closer to their Empire. All he could do was bide his time and continue the build-up of his armed forces.

From 'Anglo-American Relations – A Study in Competitive Cooperation' by Alan Drexel writing in the Economic History Chronicle *volume 3 1978*

"America is potentially our ally. America is not our friend." [121] With this simple yet penetrating statement uttered in a cabinet meeting in early 1941, Prime Minister Sir Archibald Sinclair exposed a fallacy at the heart of British foreign policy and furthermore suggested a way to proceed in Anglo-American relations.

Since before the war of 1940, Britain had wooed America as a potential partner in the struggle with the dictatorships, but had found that American assistance always came at a high price. Successive British governments had confused the relations of Britain and the United States with the relations of Britain and the Dominions. In consequence, it was assumed by the British Government that a partnership existed between Britain and America. The Americans however, simply did not see it this way. To them, Britain was just another state; one with shared antecedents and a similar outlook certainly, but essentially no more of a potential partner or opponent than any other strong democratic nation.

In some ways America had good reason to be suspicious of Britain. Partly due to American perceptions of the two countries shared history, the United States was an opponent of

---

[121] Not a genuine quote.

imperialism generally and it was certainly true that the British Empire was one of America's chief rivals in all aspects of world trade.

Despite the general climate of optimism that prevailed in Whitehall with regards to relations with the United States, warnings were sounded. Rab Butler, a pillar of the Tory party wrote in 1938 that: "In my political life, I have always been convinced that we can no more count on America than Brazil."

As Britain's strategic position collapsed in the summer of 1940, the only hope of continuing the struggle was to turn to America for money. In May of that year, the Chiefs of Staff recommended that Britain's position in the Far East could be immeasurably strengthened if the United States Navy was to deploy to Singapore as a clear signal of a willingness to defend Imperial interests in the area as a warning to Japan. Despite the general American opposition to Japanese expansion however, the United States Government would commit to no such thing. Their failure to respond left the British alone to counter Japanese diplomatic pressure, which of course was always backed up by the threat of military force. This severely complicated Britain's strategic position.

At the end of June 1940, the Japanese, knowing that the British were at full stretch with the war in Europe, demanded the withdrawal of all British military assets from the Japanese controlled areas of China; the cessation of supplies to the Chinese via Hong Kong, and the closure of the Burma Road which was the main supply route to Chiang Kai-shek's Nationalist Chinese forces. The British fear of a German invasion of southern England meant that most of the fleet in the Far East had been withdrawn to home waters leaving Britain desperately vulnerable in the region. Try as they might, the British could not wrest a firmer policy from the Americans. The Dalton Government saw no option other than to try and mollify Japan. There was even talk of a revival of the Anglo-Japanese alliance but this was both politically and morally unacceptable.

There was one area in which the British and the Americans were in complete agreement. This was in supporting and developing functioning governments behind the Ural Mountains and in China that might someday be sufficiently strong to assist in the destruction of the Fascist regimes.

From 'The Presidency of Wendell Willkie' by Siobhan McCormick, Pelham House, 2004

With the collapse of the USSR and the resulting chaos within the former borders of that country, the United States stood alone as the only functioning democracy not constrained by a peace treaty with the Nazis (like Britain) or too close to Nazi Germany and too weak to be anything other than co-operative (like Sweden). The Americans knew that it was not in their interests to have a single power dominating Europe. Public opinion was firmly anti-Nazi; but, after the Ware Wolves scandal, also anti-Soviet. Willkie's administration could not be seen to be actively supporting the new Soviet Government formed in early 1943 after Stalin and Molotov were assassinated. This was done by a cabal consisting of Larentiy Beria, chief of the NKVD; Lazar Kaganovitch, Commissar for Turkestan [122] and Nikolai Bulganin, one of the members of the State Defence Committee who then took control of what remained of the USSR.

The Germans now occupied some 95% of the former Soviet Union's coal and oil producing areas, but during 1941 and 42 much of the surviving production plant had been moved from its bases in the west of the country to new locations east of the Ural Mountains. These factories were all still extant and largely undamaged, but the scarcity of fuel and the attendant shortages of electricity meant that they were mostly idle.

The new Soviet leader's first task was to reunite the country. In the economic and social collapse that occurred in the winter of 1942 to 43, several new polities had sprung up within the former borders of the Soviet Union. Some were nationalist movements in the Turkic-speaking Soviets of the southern USSR, some were just ad-hoc alignments of groups of former soldiers. All were ruthlessly crushed between 1943 and 1947 and

---

[122] In OTL he was Commissar of the Caucasian and Trans Caucasian Regions.

in this, the Red Army was assisted by imports of oil and other supplies through Iran's north eastern border.

To facilitate this supply, a spur was built off the Garmshar to Masshad railway from Shirvan to Ashkhabad. Once at Ashkhabad, these exports were on the Russian rail network and able to reach the temporary capital at Sverdlovsk within three days. The Shirvan to Ashkhabad line opened in 1944. Shah Reza was not happy about selling oil to the rump Soviet Union, but his British sponsors forced him to do it, worsening their relations. By 1943, the Shah was a sick man and quite susceptible to the threat that if he did not do as the British asked, his son would not be permitted to inherit the throne.

The imports of oil went unnoticed by the Germans. Like its counterparts in the UK and elsewhere, the German spy network in Iran was deeply compromised by British Intelligence. Most German spies in Iran were in the pay of MI5. A few reports did get through to Germany, but the head of the Abwher (Wilhelm Canaris) failed to pass them on. The Germans sent regular reconnaissance flights over the unconquered areas of the Soviet Union and most of these were undertaken by Focke-Wulf FW 189 aircraft operating from bases at Baku and Geryev. However, these aircraft had a maximum radius of action of only 800 kilometres with extra fuel carried in drop tanks. This meant that only the rail head at Ashkhabad and the section of line between Aralsk and Orsk could be covered by them. In this respect German efficiency worked against them, the reconnaissance flights were performed at regular intervals and were predictable. The trains on the 'visible' section of the line ran only at night, in bad weather, or when German reconnaissance aircraft could be relied on not to be present.

Shah Reza died on 26th July 1944 and was succeeded by his son Shah Mohamed Reza. He was only 27 and more easily manipulated by the British Foreign Office than his father. The trade with the Soviet Union was good for Iran. The Soviets paid for the oil and goods they received with gold mined from the vast deposits at Muruntau in the Uzbeck Soviet Socialist Republic. These had been discovered in 1938 when Stalin had ordered a search for more deposits of precious stones and metals with a view to exporting them to improve the Soviet Union's trade balance. The Muruntau area had been a source of turquoise since the days of the Silk Road. However, until the late 30s the area had not been systematically explored. Mining had commenced in 1942. [123]

As well as oil, the trains were soon carrying many types of goods that were aid from Britain and the United States. Food and raw materials were transported into Soviet territory in this way and while the amounts were small, the assistance was put to good use. Still, the build-up was slow. Although partisan activity was constant, the Red Army did not begin major operations against German forces until 1947. By this time most of the renegade post-Soviet polities had been once more bought under the control of the rump USSR and the trickle of goods coming over the Iranian border had become a flood. From 1944 onwards, with the growing influx of oil, the idle Soviet factories began once more to produce munitions though in volume the amount produced was limited compared to the country's productive capacity before November 1942.

*

The German invasion of Switzerland in August 1943 ran concurrently with a raubzug (raid) into the territories of what had been the USSR. Objectives were limited, although some twenty divisions were involved. The operation was named 'Hedda' and the advance used the axes of the Kazan-Sverdlovsk and the Kuiybishev-Chelyabinsk railway lines. The operation was not designed to hold new territory but to raze villages and spoil crops in a 200 km wide 'buffer zone' between German-controlled areas and partisan-controlled areas. The operation was a complete success and met only limited resistance.

In the summer of 1944, a second Raubzug Ost, christened Operation 'Emmeline' and designed to bring Chaklov and the entirety of the North-West Caspian coal-mining region under German control took place. It went ahead in conjunction with Operation 'Magda' which was hurled against Kotlas. The

---

[123] In OTL the Muruntau gold deposit was not discovered until 1958.

Germans met a surprising amount of resistance from irregular forces before returning to their start lines.

A large operation in southern and central Russia planned before the declaration of war on the United States took place in July and August 1945 and was designed to provide useful experience for some of the newer German formations. This was named 'Adelheid' and pushed 450 km into southern and central Russia, again destroying villages and burning crops. Once more, while the operation was a success, there was great surprise at the amount of resistance encountered. This included attacks by armoured formations in Company strength.

Discussion in the German High Command about what the hardening of Soviet resistance might mean was biased by underlying assumptions about the nature of 'The Slavs'. The Germans found difficulty accepting that their belief that the Soviet Union must have utterly collapsed, leaving a mish-mash of unconnected and essentially tribal polities behind, did not die easily. The Luftwaffe's failure to provide adequate reconnaissance of the rump Soviet Union, also premised on the assumption of collapse, meant that the Germans were essentially blind to the recovery that was gathering strength on the Reich's eastern border.

In fact, the Soviet Union was once again stirring. Lazar Kaganovitch had taken over Stalin's role, was supported by Bulganin (Beria had been assassinated in late 1943 on Kaganovitch's orders), and was consolidating his power from the de-facto capital at Sverdlovsk.

From 'The Path to War in Asia' by Michael Stravinski, Halifax University Press, 2001

Although they had fought sporadically since 1931, total war between China and Japan began in earnest in 1937. Before this, the war consisted of small, localized engagements, which were referred to as "incidents". For the Chinese however, the war began almost a decade before it did for the Americans.

In 1939 the war entered a new phase with the defeat of the Japanese at Changsha and in Guangxi. Encouraged by their success, the NRA (National Revolutionary Army, the military branch of the Kuomintang) launched their first major counter-offensive against the Japanese in early 1940. However, the operation was poorly planned, poorly executed and under-resourced and defeat was perhaps inevitable. Afterwards Chiang Kai Shek did not risk any more all-out offensive campaigns until after 1945, opting for a defensive strategy, but opposition to his leadership both within the KMT (Kuomintang) and in China in general saw a sharp upturn.

By 1941, Japan had occupied much of north and coastal China, as well as the coastal areas of Indochina. The Kuomintang had withdrawn to the western interior making their capital at Chungking, while the Chinese Communists remained in control of the rural areas of Shaanxi. In the occupied districts, Japanese control was limited to major cities and the railways, but they simply lacked the manpower to subdue the Chinese countryside, which was a hotbed of partisan activity most of it sponsored by warlords of one sort or another.

Chinese troops administered another resounding defeat to the Japanese in the Second Battle of Changsha in January 1942. In the wake of this, Chiang Kai Shek felt secure enough to go on a tour of Germany, the UK and the USA in March and April, hoping to drum up support for the KMT. He took Madame Chiang (Soong Mai Ling) with him, a decision that was to have significant diplomatic repercussions.

Germany had provided the KMT with assistance in the 1930s, but was a member of the Axis pact along with Japan and ambivalent to the progress of the Sino-Japanese War. Chiang was not well received there, being granted meetings with only low ranking officials. Humiliated, he cut short his visit but got a better welcome from the British who were mindful of the threat posed by Japan to their far eastern possessions and realised that China might be an ally in any future war. Chiang was able to get a promise from the British that the Burma Road – the only supply route into areas of China controlled by the Nationalists – would not be closed and was delighted to learn that the rail line was being extended 100km from Lashio to Muse on the Yunnan border.

Better yet, the British had stocks of surplus military equipment left over from the leap in production during 1940 which they were willing to sell at fair prices and for reasonable credit terms. Payment for these weapons would come from the Nationalist-controlled gold mines in Sichuan, Hunan and Hubei.

By far the most successful part of the Chiang's tour of Europe and America was in the United States. They were feted in Washington where President Willkie, a profoundly humanitarian man who was sickened and appalled by Japanese atrocities, was determined to support the Chinese in their struggle. Willkie promised both financial and diplomatic support and while it must be said that the disorganised Willkie administration failed to provide very much of either, his successor, President Truman, continued the policy with significantly more success. By 1945, the flow of American military equipment to the KMT had greatly increased.

One bizarre aspect of the visit was that the President had a brief affair with Madame Chiang. This was much to the annoyance of her husband and some have speculated that this was the main reason for Willkie's support of the Nationalists! [124]

The only major Japanese operation undertaken in China in 1942 was the Zhejiang-Jiangxi Campaign which ran from May to September and was an attempt to subdue the countryside in the two provinces. This was unopposed by the NRA proper whose base of operations was too far to the west for them to intervene, but it was sporadically opposed by various warlord factions which took over once more as soon as the Japanese

---

[124] Gardner Cowles, an American publisher who accompanied Wendell Willkie's visit to China in 1942 OTL when he was acting as an emissary for Franklin Roosevelt, alleges that Soong May Ling, the wife of Chinese leader Chiang Kai Shek seduced Willkie. He further alleges that Madame Chiang had a plan to use China's wealth to support a Willkie Presidential campaign in 1944. Cowles' main evidence is that Willkie and Soong suddenly went missing during a dinner party. Cowles claims that Soong later said, "If Wendell could be elected, then he and I would rule the world. I would rule the Orient and Wendell would rule the western world." – Peter Carlson, 'Wendell Willkie Romances Madame Chiang Kai-shek' American History, Aug 2010, Vol. 45 Issue 3, pp 20–21)

withdrew their armies. This was typical of the entire course of the Second Sino-Japanese war until the battles of Huaning and Quijing in 1944. Japanese attacks were often successful, but as soon as the forces involved withdrew, all the ground gained tended to revert to control of the Chinese. [125]

This frustrating situation for the Imperial Japanese Army was partially masked by Japanese success against the Soviets in 1942 but, unbeknown to them, the KMT were now building up their forces with the help of surplus British war equipment supplied via the Burma Road or flown over the Eastern Himalayas. This included medicines, food, trucks, artillery, small arms, gas masks, Valentine tanks (transported in pieces), Hurricane fighters and even a few Wellington bombers. [126]

The KMT was a corrupt and dishonest organisation, and at least half of the equipment and particularly the medicines and food were lost through theft and found their way onto the black market. Some items even ending up being sold to the Japanese! Wei Lihuang, who commanded the Nationalist Chinese XI Group Army based in Yunnan, was one of the less corrupt Chinese Army officers, but still managed to hoard large quantities of war materiel and provisions (sometimes by ignoring direct orders to send them elsewhere). This had the effect of making Chinese forces in Yunnan better equipped than the rest of the NRA. [127]

---

[125] The OTL Zhejiang-Jiangxi Campaign was launched to capture Doolittle raid airmen and deny the area to US air bases.

[126] In OTL between the closing of the Burma Road in 1942 and its re-opening as the Ledo Road in 1945, foreign aid was largely limited to what could be flown in over 'The Hump', i.e. The Himalayas.

[127] Wei Lihuang became one of China's most successful military leaders. He joined the KMT in the 1920s, and became a general after a two year campaign to unify China. His success during the Bandit (Communist) Suppression Campaigns of 1930 to 1934 earned him the nickname "Hundred Victories Wei". In OTL during the Second Sino-Japanese War, he commanded the First War Area and later the Nationalist Chinese XI Group Army. unlike most of his contemporaries, he was able to work effectively with the Americans.

By 1942, China was increasingly becoming a thorn in Japan's side. The inability to finally destroy all Chinese resistance was an embarrassment. The Imperial Japanese Army tended to become less and less effective the further it moved from China's limited railway net. Despite the stalemate, a decisive victory did not seem impossible to the Japanese. In fact it concentrated Japanese attention away from The Southern Resources Zone (Malaya, Borneo and The Dutch East Indies) and towards China.

From 'Thai Diplomacy 1940-45' by Sombat Retanurang writing in the Historical Review *Volume 1, 1981*

To ensure the success of the invasion of Malaya and Burma, the Japanese needed Thai ports, railways and airfields, and while the Japanese had no compunction about invading Thailand, the Thai army was comparatively well-equipped, well-led and well-trained. If delay in attacking the British was to be avoided, it was imperative that Thailand should be willing to permit the passage of Japanese forces through its territory unopposed.

The Japanese opened secret negotiations with the Thai government in October 1940 directly after they annexed Vietnam, Cambodia and Laos – formerly French Indochina. The Thai Prime Minister, Field Marshal Plaek Phibun Songkhram, who headed a military dictatorship, verbally gave his assent to the Japanese plan to use Thailand as a stepping stone to the invasions of Malaya and Burma. In return for this, the Japanese guaranteed to give back Thai provinces in Malaya which were ceded to the British in 1909 and Thai provinces in Cambodia ceded to the French in 1907. In addition they promised to give Thailand Burma's Shan State. [128]

However, Phibun realised that Thailand was in an extremely difficult position. The country had remained independent

---

[128] The Malay territories were the sultanates of Kelantan, Terengganu, Perlis and Saiburi (Kedah). The Cambodian territories were Siam Rat (Siem Reap and Oddar Meanchey) and Phra Tabong (Battambang, Pailin and Bantay Meanchy). The Shan State of Burma had never been a part of Thailand.

despite being entirely surrounded by British and French territory, but the Japanese takeover of French Indochina placed a dangerous, acquisitive and ruthless state in alarmingly close proximity to his country.

Having bought time by telling the Japanese what they wanted to hear, he then contacted both the British and Americans in January 1941 looking for guarantees of effective support if Thailand were invaded by Japan. The Willkie administration did not respond and the British seemed willing only to give assurances of limited support, including giving a public warning to Japan that an invasion of the South East Asian kingdom could result in a British declaration of war.

Phibun was by no means satisfied at this and in late 1942, as the world situation worsened. With a new British Government in power, he decided to try again. The response he now got was somewhat different. At this time the ongoing plan for British defence in South East Asia was called Operation Matador which included the placing of British troops on Thai territory in the event of an attack on Malaya by Japan. While the British did not trust Phibun sufficiently to acquaint him with details of the plan, they did furnish him with a secret guarantee of direct British military support in the event of a Japanese invasion of Thailand.

This promise caused Phibun to take a much firmer line with the Japanese and the sharp curtailment of co-operation was noted by the Japanese planners as they unsuccessfully tried to iron out the details of the passage of their forces through Thai territory. Suspecting that some arrangement had been made with the British (and possibly the Americans as well) General Count Terauchi, who was in charge of the planning of the invasion of South East Asia, took the decision for Japanese forces to enter Thailand at the start of any hostilities with or without permission.

The British however demanded something in return from Thailand. Oil from the Dutch East Indies was reaching Japan through Thai middlemen. Oil would be bought by Thai businesses, transported to Thailand, then sold to the Japanese for transport to the home islands by tanker or to Japanese forces in French Indo China by train and pipeline. The British insisted that Phibun put an end to this trade. Although he moved slowly in bringing it to an end, by early 1945 the supply of oil from the Dutch East Indies to Japan had at last been stopped.

From 'A Concise History of China' by Stephen Malthus, Pelham House, 1989

Whether the allegations that Wendell Willkie had an affair with Madame Chiang are true or not, the strategic situation of 1942-43 meant that it was in American interests for China to begin to more effectively resist the ongoing Japanese invasion. However, the incompetence and corruption of the Nationalists under Chiang Kai-shek caused despair in the American State Department.

Like that of the British, American aid was not limited to moral support but included shipments of food and obsolete or obsolescent American weapons. This, of course, enraged the Japanese Government whose relations with both Britain and the United States continued to deteriorate. The Americans gave the Japanese protests short shrift, declaring that the United States was entitled to sell whatever it liked to whomever it liked at whatever price it cared to charge. This response was in no way satisfactory to the Japanese who pointed out that the US was attempting diplomatically (though admittedly unsuccessfully) to inhibit imports of oil to Japan from the Netherlands East Indies.

By 1943, China had already endured seven years of warfare with the Japanese. The country was ravaged and the people starving and weary. In spite of all this, Chiang Kai-shek had evolved a strategy to fight the Japanese that was perfectly suited to the ill-equipped but numerous Chinese armies.

The Japanese had many critical advantages: their control of the tactical air space over the battlefields; their ability to mount air raids deep inside Chinese territory and their overall superiority in artillery, logistics, communications and armour were all significant. But in sspite of this, the Chinese would not give up. They were even able to mount major counter-attacks which frequently achieved localised success; though generally, the Kuomintang was forced to concede ground and the front tended to stabilise at the point where Japanese logistics reached the limits of their reach.

Much to the annoyance of the Japanese, the British temporised when they received their request to cut off supplies to the Chinese along the Burma Road. In fact the British were undertaking a programme of extending the railhead from Mandalay to Muse and improving the road on the Chinese side as well as the storage facilities in Rangoon and the riverine ports that fed them. The amount of material that could be delivered along the route was quite small, averaging only 3,500 tonnes a month. It was hoped to raise this to 5,000 tons and eventually the volume of goods transported far exceeded even that.

This had the added, unforeseen effect, of making the Japanese reluctant to commit all their forces to China, regarding war with Britain and the United States as increasingly likely due to what was perceived in Tokyo as Anglo-American diplomatic intransigence. Another major supply route, the Haiphong-Kunming rail line, had been cut in 1940 by the Japanese occupation of French Indochina. In 1941, in another blow to the KMT, Japanese landings in the Pearl River delta took Canton and surrounded the British colony of Hong Kong, cutting off riverine communications to the interior of China.

The British, preoccupied with the German threat, had no reason to antagonise Japan at that time and indeed wished to avoid conflict with them until they were better prepared. However, this policy proceeded concurrently with a growing understanding in London that renewed conflict with the entirety of the Axis was inevitable.

*

By mid-1943, the Imperial Japanese Army was heavily extended in China. 1942 had seen only limited operations on the Chinese mainland due to the Japanese attack on the Russian Far East. The Chinese had used the time to enlarge, re-train and re-equip their forces. The Japanese were planning new offensives, but one of their major problems was the lack of Chinese infrastructure. Their advances tended to be successful along the axes of the

Chinese railway lines, but usually petered out the further from the railheads the Japanese army went.

War with the British and the Americans was put off; in 1942 by the need to consolidate Japan's gains in far eastern Russia; then in 1943 by the Japanese offensives in Changde and Hubei and in 1944 by operation Ichi-Go. This was the Japanese offensive designed to open a land route from Kwangsi to Indochina and bring all of Eastern China under Japanese over-lordship.

For Operation Ichi-Go, the IJA mobilized over 550,000 men, [129] their largest offensive to date. The first part (Operation Ko-Go) was launched in April and May 1944 to consolidate their hold on Hunan and Hupeh. The second, third and fourth parts (Operations To-Go 1, 2 and 3) struck south into Hunan, Kwangsi and Kwangtung during July, August and September, taking Guilin for the first time. The fifth part (To-Go 4) was a pincer movement into Kweichow and Yunnan begun in October using the axis of the Chinese railway for the push towards Kweiyang and that of the Hanoi-Kunming Railway from Indochina for the advance on Kunming which was a vital strategic nexus for the Chinese nationalists as it was the terminus of the Burma road. [130]

Operations Ko-Go and To-Go 1, 2 and 3 were highly successful, but To-Go 4 turned into a disaster. The Japanese were overconfident and were drawn into a trap. In contrast to the usual situation, the Chinese forces opposing them were well-trained, well-rested and well-equipped.

Initially resistance was light, but on 8th October, day five of the operation, forward units of the Japanese 23rd Army advancing toward Kunming encountered Lieutenant General Sun Li-Jen's New 38th Division at the town of Huaning, some seventy kilometres short of their objective. This unit had been German-trained in the late 1930s and was equipped with a

---

[129] In OTL it was 400,000

[130] This is essentially the same as the OTL Operation Ichi-Go but in OTL it had no To-Go 4 component.

mixture of British Valentine and American M3 Lee tanks, which, while they were obsolescent, were far superior to the Type 97 Chi-Ha, Type 1 Chi-He and Type 2 Ki-To tanks with which the Japanese were equipped. [131]

For two days Sun's forces repulsed Japanese attacks inflicting heavy losses. Then on 10th October, 'Double Ten Day' (a day of national celebration in the Republic of China which commemorates the start of the Wuchang Uprising of 10th October 1911, which led to the overthrow of the Quing Dynasty), Lieutenant General Du Yu-ming's Chinese 5th Corps attacked from positions west of the Japanese axis of advance retaking the town of Honghe and cutting off the Japanese 104th and 129th Infantry Divisions which were subsequently destroyed. [132]

On 20th October, a Japanese column from 11th Army under General Isamu Yokoyama began an advance from Kweiyang (which had fallen to the Japanese on October 13th) towards Kunming, an eventuality that had been foreseen by General Wei Lihuang whose XI Group Army based in Yunnan was headquartered at Kunming. He had resisted the temptation to follow the retreating remnants of 23rd Army back to Vietnam

---

[131] Born in 1900, Sun Li-jen in OTL displayed exemplary courage and leadership and earned the nickname 'The Rommel of the East'. He studied at Purdue University in Indiana and led the Chinese basketball team to an upset victory over the Philippines, in the Far Eastern Championship Games of 1921, China's first gold medal in international basketball. As a colonel, he was wounded during the Battle of Shanghai in 1937 and was later given command of the New 38th Division which in OTL was part of the force Chiang Kai-shek sent into Burma to protect the Burma Road in 1942. There, he gained the respect of General William Slim, the Commander of the British 14th Army for his competence. Later New 38th division spearheaded Joseph Stilwell's 1943 drive to re-conquer North Burma and re-establish the land route to China by the Ledo Road.

[132] In OTL Du Yuming commanded the Nationalist Army's 5th Corps in the First Changsha Campaign and the Battle of South Kwangsi (Guangxi). The corps later became the Nationalist Fifth Army. For most of the Chinese Civil War, he served as a field commander in Manchuria and Eastern China but was captured during the Huai Hai Campaign and held in Communist prisons until his pardon in 1959.

but withdrawn his forces to defensive positions around Quijing, 100 km east of Kunming.

The battle of Quijing took place on 2nd November and was another sharp defeat for the Japanese who retreated back to Kweiyang after suffering heavy casualties. Wei was unable to pursue them because of logistical issues but the Battles of Huaning and Quijing were significant Chinese victories.

General Wei Lihuang and Lieutenant Generals Sun Li-Jen and Du Yu-ming had all distinguished themselves in the action and were all personally loyal to Chiang Kai Shek. The forces under their command were now the most powerful in Yunnan, and consequently Chiang ordered them to depose Long Yung who was both Nationalist Governor of Yunnan as well as the local warlord and install a more loyal governor.

The Battles of Huaning and Quijing and the removal of Long Yung meant that Chiang was now in complete unopposed control of Yunnan and Sichuan and was being supplied with Anglo-American war materiel. This was in many ways the best position he had been in since 1937. In the second half of 1942, the Kuomintang looked to be a spent force on the verge of annihilation and Chiang himself seemed about to lose power. The events of 1944 prevented internal collapse and laid the foundation of future success. Its significance went beyond the Sino-Japanese conflict however, as it showed both Washington and London that the Chinese, even though under-equipped, under-resourced and lacking in training, were quite capable of defeating the Japanese and very willing to continue the fight.

From 'New Air Speed Record Set by Germans' by Phillip Bell writing in Aviation, *No. 1777 Vol XLIII, January 14th, 1943*

Reports have been confirmed that a specially modified Heinkel He 280 aircraft has set a new world speed record of 508.06 mph, beating the previous record of 479.76 mph set by a Napier Heston racer in 1941. The He 280 is of interest to those of us who follow aeronautical developments because it is powered by twin jet engines.

CHAPTER 24: SUNDAY 23rd JUNE 1945

Downtown Manhattan does not feel like the heart of a city at war. The morning sun shines on bustling streets and the scent of newly mown grass drifts along the lanes and pathways in Central Park. Captain Mike Brevard has a week's leave. His ship, the carrier USS *Alliance,* is under refit at Norfolk Naval Yard after her shakedown cruise and he has taken the train northward to visit his family who live in upstate New York.

When Captain Richards had told him that he was being given a command of his own he had done so with typically brusque humour. "Well Brevard, I've got good news and bad news for you, the good news is they've given you a cruiser. The bad news is that it's an aviation cruiser." He had been so surprised he had hardly known what to say and although he has been *Alliance's* captain for more than a year he is still very conscious of the silver eagles of his new rank on the collar of his shirt.

He has four hours to kill between trains and after treating himself to a good breakfast at the restaurant in Grand Central Station he walks a couple of blocks and wanders into a drugstore near Times Square. He buys a Coke and a newspaper, places his hat on the countertop and prepares to while away the time.

The windows of the drugstore are open and the sounds of cars, the shouts of newspaper boys and snatches of a thousand conversations drift in. The headlines in the paper are all concerned with the war. A small column at the bottom of the second page says;

MIAMI'S LIGHTS TURNED OFF

The city of Miami has finally fallen into line with the other cities of the East Coast by enforcing a blackout from sunset to sunrise.

Brevard shakes his head and says under his breath 'One little victory'. Since the declaration of war on May 7th, 1945 German submarines had begun attacking American merchant ships plying their trade on the eastern seaboard. The brilliantly lit cities along the coast had made the task of the U-boats easy. At night they had no difficulty in picking out the silhouettes of ships against the shoreline and most of the cities on the east coast had begun to enforce a blackout. But Miami for some reason took more persuading than the rest and the lights had burned all night while out to sea American sailors had died within sight of those lights.

There is a girl sitting at the counter, she looks over at him and says; "You in the Navy?" Brevard smiles, he is dressed in Navy khakis, he lowers the newspaper and replies;

"Yes ma'am, what was that gave it away?" She laughs.

"What do you do?"

"Well I'm an officer on a warship ma'am." She is a little plump and looks tired but she has a nice smile and seems impressed at any rate.

"What kind of ship?"

"An aircraft carrier actually, the navy has made me the captain of a carrier. What do you do?"

"I just got a job in a factory, it's not much of a job but it pays the bills."

"What does the factory make?"

"Trucks for the Army, I'm on the night shift, I just got off work 'couple hours ago. I hate it, it's so hard to sleep in the day. You got a cigarette?" He reaches into his pocket and finds a pack of Chesterfields. He lights two and gives her one of them. She inhales deeply and says;

"Thanks." she pauses for a moment "So who's going to win the war?" She smiles as she says it, but Brevard doesn't smile back. He is just deciding to ask her name when he feels the ground shake. A short, sudden jolt, followed by another. As he looks up he realises that the sounds from the street have changed. There is a noise underlying the other noises, a growling mechanical snarl, rising in pitch and intensity, a throbbing hum like the sound of a swarm of wasps only lower in tone and more urgent.

Aircraft. Many aircraft.

He throws the newspaper down onto the counter and jumps off the stool but before he can reach the door he is knocked off his feet as the building is jolted by a massive impact. The girl screams, the lights go off and showers of choking dust fill the air. He picks himself up and runs outside.

In Times Square people are standing in dazed groups looking up at the sky. There is shock and terror in their eyes and the noise, the throbbing hum, has grown to a crescendo, obliterating all other sound except the jarring crump of explosions.

Brevard cannot believe what he is seeing. New York City is under attack. There, above them in the lambent summer sky, the black cross shapes of warplanes, perhaps a hundred, with bombs spilling from their gaping bellies. A stick of them lands nearby and they are engulfed in the terrible sounds of breaking glass and falling masonry, the crowd scatters in panic, bumping into one another in their haste to escape while the screaming of a child is for a moment the loudest sound he can hear.

One of the bombers is on fire, flames spilling from its wing and a black trail of smoke curls out behind it. He realises that there are smaller aircraft darting between them – fighters! As he watches the burning bomber rolls onto its back and spirals earthwards, a parachute opens, another, then it explodes sending flaming wreckage tumbling through the sky. There is an urgent tugging at his arm, the girl from the drugstore, she is shouting.

"Jesus, don't just stand there…" He looks at her for a moment but his mind is so engulfed in inchoate rage that he has no words and he pulls his arm from her hand and looks again at the sky. She stares uncomprehending at him, barely able to recognise the affable man she had just been speaking to. He stands like a statue, face turned upwards, his fists clenching and unclenching, fury in his eyes. As the bubbling wail of an air raid siren begins its mournful call she turns and runs for shelter.

CHAPTER 25: THE BREAKING

OF THE PEACE

From 'Studies in the Psychology of Institutional Incompetence' by Christopher Melancamp, Halder and Stratton 1976

It has been noted that just because a plan might be obviously absurd, delusional or insane; that this did not necessarily disqualify it from pursuit by the Nazis. Operation Sealion, as it was constituted in 1940, the Madagascar Plan and the various iterations of Generalplan Ost all fall in to this category, but perhaps the most ridiculous example of the Nazis hubris and limitless self-belief was Betriebsplan drei (Operational Plan Three).

Given the events of September 1939 to December 1942, Nazi overconfidence is perhaps understandable. Every nation that had stood against Germany had been defeated. This both confirmed and enhanced the Nazis conviction that they were invincible and that it was their destiny to rule the world. In considering the United States, they perceived a wealthy, pampered, decadent society that was racially impure and controlled by Jewish interests; one that would be hard put to effectively oppose the 'Master Race'. Hitler is reported to have actually repeated the very words he used to describe the state of the USSR before the German attack in 1941; "With one good kick in the door, the whole rotten edifice will come tumbling down."

German plans for an invasion of the Americas did not begin with the Nazis. Naval planners first considered an attack upon the continental USA in 1897 during that year's Winterarbeiten. These were theoretical studies and war games intended to examine various potential conflict scenarios and served as the basis for actual war plans. Previously German naval planning had concerned itself principally with operations against the Royal Navy and the United Kingdom. The 1899 Winterarbeiten included detailed studies of the forts protecting the entrance to New York harbour, Fort Hamilton and Fort Tomkins. New

York was considered as the primary target and the plan included the shelling of Manhattan by German naval units. This was at a time when, generally speaking, armed forces did not make war upon civilians. The main assault would involve a landing of German troops on Long Island, and an assault on New York City itself the following day.

In early 1942, well before Hitler had declared victory on the eastern front, he ordered the preparation of detailed plans for an attack upon America. One important modification of the previous studies was the plan to take Puerto Rico as a preliminary to the main assault. The idea was to use the island as a staging post in the attack, but also as bait to draw the American fleet into a decisive battle. With the conclusion of operations in Europe and the subjugation of France and the Netherlands, as well as the passive strategic position in which Axis domination of the continent placed Portugal, this plan changed again with the inclusion of staging posts in Dutch Guyana (Suriname), Dakar in Senegal and the Azores.

Use of the Azores first appears in German planning documents dating to 1940. On the 24th of August, Hitler approved the preparation of a draft plan drawn up by Admiral Eric Raider to be named operation Felix. In its first incarnation, Felix was a joint attack on the Azores, the Cape Verde and the Canary Islands as well as Gibraltar and was designed to close the western end of the Mediterranean to Allied shipping. With the inclusion of Spain within the Axis and the Treaty of Leamouth, which had apparently neutralised the threat from Britain, Portugal was in no position to oppose Hitler. President, António Salazar was in some ways sympathetic to the Axis cause. In consequence the plan was changed to encompassing only an annexation of the Azores by Spain.

In November 1940, even as operation Barbarossa was being planned, Hitler also demanded an immediate inquiry into the possibility of mounting air attacks against the east coast cities of the United States using German bombers based in the Azores. [133] An attack on Iceland during the early part of hostilities to

---

[133] With a few modifications for TTL, most of this is very much based on actual German plans in OTL.

secure Germany's northern flank from a possible American counter thrust was also contemplated.

From 'Britain Takes Back Air Speed Record From Germans' by Horace Shaw writing in Aviation, *No. 1846 Vol XLV, May 11th, 1944*

The world air speed record was regained by Britain on Thursday last, when a Napier Heston Racer Mk III powered by a specially modified Napier Sabre VIII sprint engine developing 'in excess of 4000 hp' flew to a speed of 512.41 mph after a brief flight from Heston aerodrome. The aircraft was flown by Wing Commander G.L.G. Richmond who set a record of over 479 mph in 1941. Lord Nuffield, who has sponsored the project was said to be 'very pleased'.

From 'The Hitlerian Wars' by Jason Corell, Tormeline 1973

By the autumn of 1942 with the collapse of the Soviet Union already underway and the conclusion of operation Barbarossa in sight, the construction of the new German naval base at Trondheim in Norway was begun. As well as this, construction commenced on the Hamburg-Trondheim autobahn, with its ambitious plans for bridging the Danish belts and the sound between Copenhagen and Malmö in Sweden. In addition to these projects, the French colonial authorities in Dakar, acting under German orders, began improvements to the military facilities there. The aerodrome at Lajes Field in the Azores was enlarged with extended runways and large new hangers and workshops. The flying boat facilities at Horta were also upgraded. The work was financed by Lufthansa who apparently required enhanced facilities for their North and South American routes.

Plans for rapid growth in the size and capabilities of the Kreigsmarine were well in hand by the time Hitler declared the end of major operations on the eastern front. By the close of 1942 the German army had grown to a size of 284 divisions but with the end of hostilities and the return of many conscripted men to civilian life it underwent rapid shrinkage. The Luftwaffe was also reduced in size but by contrast the German Navy was set for a massive escalation in the numbers of major warships it possessed.

In early 1943, the Kreigsmarine possessed ten battleships and battle cruisers, though two were not yet fully worked up and two more were not yet complete. Two of these were war prizes from the French navy. There were also three aircraft carriers with three more completing, nine cruisers, with eight more completing, 47 destroyers and torpedo boats, with 11 more completing and 126 submarines with 17 more completing. In addition to this, eight more very large battleships, two more battle cruisers, three aircraft carriers, 18 cruisers, 91 destroyers and torpedo boats and 114 submarines were planned. (See Appendices)

The shrinkage in the size of the German army and air force as well as the expansion in the size of the Navy were symptoms of Hitler's desire to attack America. But it is also intriguing to note (and this was typical of the way German military planning was always concerned with 'the war after next') is the fact that even as Hitler planned joint operations with the Japanese against the United States, the German armed forces had begun considering the possibility of war with Japan after America had been subjugated.

From 'The Path to War in Asia' by Michael Stravinski, Halifax University Press, 2001

Although generally the Germans did not hold their Japanese allies in high regard, Lieutenant General Hiroshi Oshima, the Japanese Ambassador to Germany, was an exception. The leaders of the Third Reich confided in him to an unprecedented degree. His knowledge of German plans and the status of German operations was very detailed and he faithfully reported all that he knew about them to Tokyo. Unbeknown to either Oshima or the German high command, the Americans had broken the Japanese diplomatic PURPLE code in 1940 while the British had later broken the German Enigma codes. Consequently, many things the Germans and the Japanese believed to be secret were in fact well-known by both the British and the Americans whose intelligence services engaged in a high degree of co-operation even then.

By the autumn of 1943, Japanese plans for an attack south and eastwards from the home islands against the territories of Britain, the Netherlands and the United States had reached an advanced stage. This was in part driven by the need to resolve the war in China. In June 1940 the Japanese had estimated that of the outside supplies reaching Chinese forces: 41% came from Indochina; 31% via the Burma Road; 19% through coastal waters and 2% from the USSR. The Japanese were surprised and dismayed that the collapse of the USSR and the occupation of Indochina did not seem to have had much effect on their campaign in China. It was assumed (correctly) that the Burma Road was now the principal route by which supplies were reaching their opponents.

In 1943 the Japanese did not want to start a full scale war with the British. They were still consolidating their position in Far Eastern Russia and eastern Mongolia where, now that the Soviet Union had collapsed, they had finally taken the site of their defeat at Khalkin Gol. However, Colonel Keiji Suzuki, an intelligence officer in the Japanese Army, had founded a group called the Burma Independence Army (BIA) in 1941. He had been in Bangkok since the 1930s recruiting Burmese dissidents including Aung San, Ne Win and Bo Let Ya. The organisation was decidedly amateurish. As well as giving the dissidents some limited military training, Suzuki told them he was descended from Burmese royalty and had them engage in bizarre ceremonies where they pledged allegiance to Burma and drank each other's blood. In 1942 Suzuki was recalled to Japan and the BIA was ordered to carry out guerrilla operations against the Burma Road. It was placed under the direction of Aung San.

When the BIA entered Burma in January 1943 it was made up of roughly 2,000 men. They crossed the Mekong into Burma's Shan province which bordered western Laos. Many fell sick on the journey but the BIA found support from the civilian population and were bolstered by many Burmese volunteers which caused their numbers to grow to about 5,000. Many of the 'volunteers' however were simply criminal gangs who took to calling themselves BIA to advance their own agendas. The Japanese had provided few weapons, so the volunteers had to arm themselves with what they could. A large number of pointless attacks were made on the tribal peoples of the area, particularly the Karen. Many Karen villages were destroyed by the BIA and as many as 1,500 Karen people may have been murdered by Aung San's Army.

Their first major attack on the Burma Road came on 19th March when they mounted an assault on Wan Ling. Other operations followed until 13th May when an attack on a fuel dump on the road outside Lashio by 1000 men was met by two companies of the Cheshire Regiment. A pitched battle ensued, but the half trained and poorly equipped BIA suffered heavy casualties; 120 killed, 300 wounded, 60 captured and 350 missing (all of whom had deserted). Bo Let Ya and Ne Win were both killed. The Cheshire's suffered 11 dead and 16 wounded.

Once the BIA made its presence known with attacks on the road, the British had sent a few loyal Burmese to infiltrate it. Now, every attack they made was met by British troops. Aung San dismissed most of the recruits the BIA had gained in Burma but their campaign had run out of steam. Minimal Japanese assistance, British infiltration, a lack of genuine commitment from most of the recruits and mounting casualties had doomed it.

By 1944 the Japanese had to accept that the BIA campaign had utterly failed, but it was still imperative for them to cut the Burma Road. Now, closing the supply route was seen in the context of ejecting the British from South East Asia entirely. The only problem with this was that any attempt to attack Malaya, Borneo and the Dutch East Indies meant war with America, so subduing the Philippines first was also a priority. This was a tall order even for a state with as much self-belief as Japan.

A Japanese delegation met with Hitler, Ribbentrop and various members of the German high command in Berlin on the 17th November 1943. At this meeting the Germans urged restraint upon the Japanese, putting forward the prospect of joint action by the entire Axis against the United States in the future.

Japanese-German relations were at that time slightly soured by the dismissal of a lawsuit brought by the German armaments maker Krupp in Japan. These was against various Japanese engineering firms who had reverse engineered German products captured in China and were producing unlicensed copies. These included 88mm anti-aircraft guns which were a product of Krupp, the German armaments firm. The main upshot of this was a reluctance to share technology between the two primary Axis partners.

The Japanese decision in 1943 to postpone an attack on the British, Dutch and American territories in South East Asia was made easier by the strategic situation. Oil and raw materials supplies were stable and large stockpiles were developing. This was in part because Japan had secured imports of oil from the DEI via Thailand, and in part because at that time it appeared that the transfer of German synthetic fuel technology to Japan would improve the situation still further.

*

German proxy control over the Dutch East Indies was no more than theoretical while the Americans were reluctant to take on a new colonial responsibility. This left the status of the NEI and the authority of the Dutch Government-in-Exile somewhat unclear, but because of their distance from Europe it was not an issue the Germans felt should be forced to a point of crisis. They were certain a new war was coming in which they were happy for the Japanese to take over the NEI.

Queen Wilhelmina was acutely aware that the Netherlands' only hope for liberation was The United States. She had dismissed the sitting Dutch Prime Minister, Dirk Jan De Geer, in September 1940 and replaced him with Pieter Sjoerds Gerbrandy, but the first concern of all members of the Dutch Government was the welfare of the people of Holland. This impelled their reluctance to support calls for a total oil embargo to Japan which seemed almost certain to lead to reprisals on them.

274

The Queen seriously considered returning to the Netherlands to be with her people and share their suffering; however it was felt by her advisors and by the US State Department, that by so doing, she might confer legitimacy on the puppet regime the Nazis had installed and they urged her not to. One of the Dutch Government-in-Exile's chief claims to legitimacy was that it was appointed by the Sovereign of the Netherlands. Queen Wilhelmina eventually realised that the gesture of returning would be a serious mistake.

At this time the Germans were planning for a war with the United States in 1946 or 1947 at the latest and the Japanese were persuaded to wait for at least a little while. These plans were also made known to Benito Mussolini who viewed them with some disquiet. Unlike Hitler, the Italian dictator was not convinced that the British Empire was a spent force. In fact, Italy's strategic position in Africa looked particularly vulnerable to the British should they choose to attack it.

Mussolini's great hope was that a resumption in hostilities with Britain in concert with Germany would quickly lead to the destruction of the British Empire and the realisation of his 'New Roman Empire'. His great fear was that Italy's entanglement with the Axis would inevitably lead to Italy becoming embroiled in war with America. Even then he realised that it would be very difficult to deflect German requests for the participation of the Italian fleet in an attack on the United States.

From 'Mussolini and Franco; Their Plans for Empire in Africa, Asia and the Americas' by Umberto Scilacci writing in The Historical Society Record *volume 236 issue 11*

Il Duce's ambitions in Africa and Arabia were extensive. Initial plans involved the acquisition of a vast area stretching from the Horn of Africa to the Mediterranean and the Gulf of Guinea. Under this plan Ghana, Togo, Dahomey, Nigeria, Niger, Chad, Libya, half of Algeria, the Sudan, Ethiopia, Somalia, Uganda, and Kenya as well as Sierra Leone and the islands of the western Indian Ocean would all be under Italian rule. [134]

At the time this first plan was drawn up it was also believed that a vast swathe of territory across the centre of Africa would be subjugated by the Third Reich. However, it became apparent that Hitler had little interest in reacquiring the African colonies of Willhelmine Germany, let alone new territories in Africa and this, along with the terms of the Treaty of Leamouth, seems to have acted to cause a reappraisal in the plan and the setting of more modest goals.

Still, the modified plan was not un-ambitious and now included a third of Algeria, half of Niger, and all of Chad, Sudan, Ethiopia and Somalia as well as Kenya and Uganda. The dictated peace with France enabled Mussolini to realise his territorial goals at the expense of the French, but not all of those he planned at the expense of the British. This was partly because of a lack of support from the Germans and in consequence Kenya, Uganda and the Sudan remained under British administration.

In Arabia, Mussolini's plans were also extensive. Aden, Kuwait, the Sinai and the island of Socotra were all British territories of one sort or another, and he wished to turn all of them into Italian colonies. Oman, Qatar and the Sheikhdoms of the Trucial Coast, as well as the eastern half of the Rub al Khali of Saudi Arabia were to become Italian protectorates.

It was readily apparent to the dictator of Italy that the main obstacle to the realisation of his territorial ambitions was the United Kingdom and its Commonwealth but, unlike Hitler, Il Duce did not consider the British Empire to be neutralised. He made the logical and prescient calculation that German plans to attack America must certainly result in drawing the British into the conflict. This was not something that Hitler was able to

---

[134] This is based on two files of documents discovered in the Italian archives (Ufficio Storico Marina Militare) by Davide Pastorre and posted at comandosupremo.com. They are labelled Ministero dell'Africa Italiana - Relazione per Commissione Trattati di Pace. (Ministry of Italian Africa - Report for the Peace Treaties Commission.)

grasp, and while many others in the Nazi hierarchy certainly saw the danger, their voices went unheard or were ignored.

Mussolini was uncertain as to whether the coming war would result in America's total defeat, but it seems that he was willing to commit the Regia Marina (Italian Navy) in pursuit of Hitler's aims because he believed that German assistance must certainly result in Italian triumph over Britain. However, his increasing support of Hitler bought him into conflict with King Victor Emanuel III. The King had become distrustful of the Nazi regime, particularly after the dismissal of his son-in-law Philipp of Hesse, the Landgrave of Hesse-Kassel. [135] The King was concerned that Italy would once again be drawn into war – a prospect he found alarming, but he knew that Mussolini was extremely popular with the armed forces after Italy's territorial gains in 1940 and 41. He rightly supposed that in any power struggle between the crown and Il Duce, he would be the loser.

Some of Mussolini's enthusiasm rubbed off on Franco. Spain's economic condition in 1944, even five years after the conclusion of the civil war, was not good and the Spanish annexation of French Morocco – while helpful – did not do enough to alleviate the situation. Against this backdrop it was easy for him to be tempted by the prospect of reacquiring some, or all, of Spain's former colonies in the Americas. Franco, up to this point, had been a steely realist; but the temptation of reviving the days of Spanish glory and the seeming invincibility of Germany was too much even for him to dismiss out of hand.

Franco's acceptance of substantial loans from the Third Reich to enlarge and modernise the Spanish armed forces also served to compromise his independence of action. It was not just

---

[135] In OTL May 1943 Hitler issued the "Decree Concerning Internationally Connected Men" declaring that princes could not hold positions in the party, state, or armed forces. This made Philipp of Hesse's position quite difficult though he was not relieved of his positions and arrested until September after his father-in-law, King Victor Emmanuel III of Italy, dismissed Mussolini. His wife Princess Mafalda, Victor Emmanuel's daughter, was arrested in Italy on the German takeover and died in a concentration camp. In TTL Hitler has issued the decree but Philipp has not been dethroned or arrested. However Victor Emmanuel would still see it as an insult.

that Franco had accepted German bribes however; other factors standing in the way of closer co-operation between Spain and Germany were also in abeyance. Admiral Canaris, the head of the Abwehr had previously been quick to warn Franco against joining the Axis and, even after Spain did join, had still continued to advise him against too close involvement in Hitler's more ambitious schemes. However, Canaris had been impelled into the 1943 infighting in the Nazi hierarchy and his backing of Bormann had largely been a product of the suspicions about his motives and loyalty harboured by Himmler, Goebbels and Heydrich. The deaths of these three certainly alleviated what was becoming a very difficult position for Canaris, but afterwards he was much more circumspect in his dealings with Franco and the admonitory tone of his advice was gone entirely. Instead, Canaris began to warn Franco of the threat posed to his leadership by General Augustin Muñoz Grandes.

The Spanish Army's most prominent leader, General Muñoz Grandes, was a firm supporter of the Nazis and a true believer in the invincibility of the Third Reich. Muñoz Grandes had led the Spanish Blue Division in Russia and was a popular figure. As a young officer, he had served with distinction in Morocco and had held key positions in government. During the Civil War he had been a competent leader. With his military background, experience as Secretary General of the Falange, popularity and proven battlefield leadership, he became the focus of an impressive amount of attention. His speeches were even broadcast over Spanish radio. They tended toward the histrionic.

"Hard is the enemy, and harder still is the Russian winter. But it does not matter: even harder is my race, supported by reason and the courage of its sons who, embracing their heroic German comrades, will in the end achieve the victory, towards which we fight without ceasing."

Muñoz Grandes had also been noticed by Hitler, who saw in him a potential replacement for Franco. The Fuhrer met many times with the Spanish general, gave him high decorations and encouraged him to become more involved in politics. Franco became alarmed by this, and wanted to replace Muñoz Grandes as commander of the Blue Division but as the formation was nominally a part of the German Army his replacement was refused. Hitler thus ensured that the Blue Division's commander gained sufficient recognition to become even more popular in Spain.

Upon his return in January 1943, to a hero's welcome, Franco promoted Muñoz Grandes to the rank of Lieutenant General and appointed him to the General staff. It was a case of 'keep your friends close and your enemies' closer', because Franco now realised that because of his previous reluctance to join in the attack on America, Hitler had lined up his successor. Despite an outward appearance of unity, the Spanish regime was split by hostile factions, undermined by incompetence and tended to a vague authoritarianism that reflected the schisms within it. Muñoz Grandes represented a real threat. It was hard for a proud man like Franco to realise that his leadership of Spain now rested only on the good offices of the Germans, but accept it he had to. All of this very much cleared the way for Spain to be drawn closely into Hitler's scheme to attack America.

From 'Hitler's Health' by Doctor Irene Kerr writing in The Medical Journal of Britain *Volume 291 Issue 562*

Healthcare in Nazi Germany became an increasingly haphazard affair. The man whom Hitler made Führer of National Socialist Health in 1934, Dr. Gerhard Wagner, licensed naturopaths, faith-healers and all manner of quacks. He was jointly responsible for the policies of euthanasia and sterilization carried out against Jews and the handicapped, and was a staunch proponent of Nazi Germany's racial policies. He died in 1939 at the age of 51.

His successor was a paediatrician named Leonardo Conti, the son of Hitler's "Führerin of Midwives." In 1940 Conti distributed to American doctors a range of statistics on German health that purported to show the advances made in healthcare in Germany. However, in Heil Hunger! by Dr. Martin Gumpert published in the United States by Alliance Books in the same year, these were analysed and found to show not an advance in German healthcare but its rapid deterioration. [136]

Even the Fuhrer himself could not obtain good medical treatment. By January 1945, Adolf Hitler was a very sick man in the throes of tertiary-stage syphilis and was becoming increasingly erratic and delusional. He appears to have suffered from a range of ailments and his physician, Dr Theodor Morell, was inclined to overprescribe medication, some of which would be viewed as dangerous today and certainly made Hitler's mental condition worse. [137]

By late 1944, the Fuhrer had become dependent on methamphetamines that Morell supplied to him daily, along with other medicines including Nux Vomica (which contains strychnine) and cocaine which Morell administered via eye drops. During the 1920s, 30s and 40s in Germany, both cocaine and methamphetamines were routinely prescribed for many ailments. In combination with Hitler's deteriorating mental condition the ingestion of narcotics can hardly have had other than a ruinous effect.

The result of the Fuhrer's increasing instability was that more and more responsibility fell on the shoulders of Martin Bormann, a man who, although most adept at Nazi Germany's brutal domestic politics, lacked any of the subtlety and

---

[136] The book Heil Hunger! can be found quite easily through second hand book dealers.

[137] This was very much the OTL situation also. There is no direct evidence that the Nazi leader had advanced syphilis, but it is certainly true that there is a preponderance of circumstantial evidence that strongly suggests that he did. Hitler had a bizarre fixation with syphilis, which he considered a "Jewish disease". Firstly there is a 14-page diatribe in Mein Kampf on the subject, there is also his fascination with Ulrich von Hutten, the 16th Century German scholar, poet and reformer who wrote one of the first patient narratives of his own struggle with the disease. But Hitler also had many of the symptoms of the advanced stages such as an irregular heartbeat, tremors, chest pain, a shuffling walk, mania, paranoid rages and other forms of mental disturbance. He is known to have taken iodide salts – a common treatment for late-stage, or tertiary syphilis and even his choice of doctor might have been because of Morell's claim (made in the 1930s) to be a specialist in venereology.

understanding required of international diplomacy. Bormann's greatest oversight was unquestionably his mis-estimation of the intentions of Britain, though it must be noted that he did not receive good intelligence from Canaris or good advice from either the disgruntled Keitel or the increasingly disengaged Goering. It is also true that he was faithfully following Hitler's flawed policy.

Although Bormann wished to be Hitler's instrument, he was an instrument that was out of tune and played by a sick and progressively more delusional musician. We can speculate that if Hitler had not been ill and addled by drugs, he would have proceeded more cautiously with the annexation of Belgium and the Netherlands, might have comprehended more clearly the consequences of failing to rein in his Japanese allies and might have grasped that annexation of the Azores could only be seen in Washington as Casus Belli.

Yet, in one of history's ironies, shortly before the outbreak of war in 1945, there was a marked improvement in Hitler's prognosis, courtesy of the American pharmaceutical industry. At the Pfizer company in Brooklyn, New York, a bio-chemist named Jasper Kane led a team of scientists in the development of the deep-tank fermentation method that was critical to the production of large quantities of pharmaceutical-grade penicillin. Although penicillin had been discovered in 1928, it was not until Pfizer's research in 1941–1944 that it was possible to manufacture it in commercial quantities. Hitler's physician, Dr Theodor Morell, began administering the drug to Hitler shortly after its release in Europe in March 1945. [138]

Before April 1945, Hitler had been seen in public only rarely for more than a year. Speculation as to the state of his health was rife but, thanks to Pfizer, his illness was now in remission and he was once more full of his characteristic ferociousness and ready to take up the reins of the Third Reich once more.

---

[138] The dates and course of events regarding penicillin's introduction are as OTL.

Part of the Treaty of Leamouth included a clause whereby Britain agreed not to harbour any governments in exile. The Polish, Norwegian, Dutch and Belgian governments who had taken refuge at their embassies in London were compelled to decamp to Washington providing a further reason for diplomatic conflict between Germany and the United States. Brazilian forces, with American approval, had occupied French and Dutch Guyana in 1941, however President Willkie warned the Brazilians off any attempt to annex either territory.

The Chilean-Argentine war, coming so soon on the heels of the Peruvian-Ecuadorian war, was something of an annoyance to the Willkie administration which was embarrassed by the squabbling in America's back yard. The conflict flared up over the Beagle Channel dispute which had been festering since the 19th century. Argentina, with some encouragement from Germany, had been involved in several diplomatic conflicts with its neighbours. Threats against both Uruguay and Paraguay had caused disquiet in Brazil as well as Washington.

Ramón Castillo, the president of Argentina from June 1942 until June 1943 leaned towards the Axis powers and, although he was deposed in a military coup, his successors Generals Rawson, Ramírez and Farrell (who was president until the elections in 1946) were also supporters of the fascist alliance.

*

In understanding the events that led to the resumption of hostilities, it must be realised that the League of Nations after the war of 1940 was completely marginalised, seen by the major powers as an irrelevance and therefore unable to fulfil its brief. The world temporarily returned to the style of diplomacy that had pertained before the First World War.

The German annexation of Holland, Belgium, Denmark and Norway in 1944 and 1945 raised the question of the Dutch and Belgian colonies. Germany claimed sovereignty over the Congo, Suriname and the Netherlands East Indies, but this claim was rejected by the United States which had recently installed the Dutch Government in Exile in Batavia.

In early March 1945, in one of his first acts as President, Harry S. Truman, in concert with the government of Australia, supported an immediate change in the status of the Dutch East Indies. The Willkie Administration was unwilling to countenance their takeover by the United States. There was no appetite in Washington for the acquisition of a new colony by America. Truman however, was determined to take a strong line against the Axis powers and in a flurry of diplomatic correspondence between Washington, Canberra, London and Batavia it was decided that the United States would support the continuance of Dutch rule over the territory of the Netherlands East Indies. What this meant in practice was that it was to be ruled by the Dutch Government in Exile rather than the colonial administrators who had simply carried on after the German victory in 1940. At this point, the new administration was little more than an American puppet.

This was immediately opposed politically by both Germany and Japan supported only slightly less vocally by the other Axis powers. The Dutch Government in Exile was not entirely happy at this turn of events. They saw direct American support, quite correctly, as a probable point of conflict with Japan, as well as a factor that would undermine what little authority they still possessed. On the other hand, indirect American support was believed to be the best way of maintaining the status quo and avoiding war. The Dutch were particularly alarmed by the American assertion that part of the reason for its backing, was that it would bring the goal of Indonesian independence closer. Eventually however, strong American diplomatic pressure, plus the fact of Holland's diplomatic and military impotence bought acceptance of the new arrangement.

An immediate result of this was that within a month, exports of strategic materials to Japan from the DEI, Malaya and north Borneo had ceased entirely although this did not prevent all supplies from getting through. The fact that the volume of materials reaching Japan from South East Asia was now greatly reduced combined with Japan's inability to master the technologies involved with the creation of a synthetic fuel industry, meant the problem of fuel supply became critical. (See Appendices)

Even if Japan's immediate need for fuel could be ameliorated by their considerable strategic stockpiles of oil (at that time it stood at 80 million barrels [139]), they now saw the situation as presenting even more reason for aggressive military action. The natural resources of the DEI, British North Borneo, Malaya and the Philippines included petroleum, tin, nickel, timber, bauxite, iron ore, copper, cobalt, coal and even precious metals. An increasingly mechanised army, a growing and fuel-hungry navy and air force; operating ever more fuel-thirsty equipment meant that the securing of 'The Southern Resources Zone' was now of particular importance.

An unspoken assumption by the Germans and Japanese was that they would act in concert against America. Each hoped that the other would divert a large portion of America's strength. The news that the Germans were bringing forward the first phase of Betriebsplan drei (the annexation of the Azores), caused great satisfaction in Japan. It is important to note, that it was seen by the Germans as a preliminary operation, but the Japanese took it as signalling that war was imminent.

Because access to the Fuhrer was controlled through Bormann, who was not an adept at international affairs, and because the Nazi hierarchy now consisted almost solely of sycophants whom Bormann trusted, no credible voice was raised against the plan. Both Keitel and Carls were prevented from seeing the Fuhrer and Goering, to whom Hitler might have listened, was becoming more withdrawn and disengaged from policy. His health problems and addiction to morphine meant that the Reichsmarschall was concerned less and less with Germany's international position and more and more with spending time on his estate hunting deer. [140]

Although Franco harboured serious reservations, Hitler was quite convinced that possession of the islands, while vastly

---

[139] In OTL they had 60 million barrels in 1941 – see Appendices.

[140] This was true OTL also, by late 1944/early 1945.

improving the Axis' strategic position, would not lead directly to war with the United States. He was in fact surprised when he received the American ultimatum on 5th May but nevertheless rejected it out of hand.

The plan had been in process for a long time and required only the finishing touches. On Friday 4th May 1945, three battalions of German paratroopers dropped on Ponta Delgada, Angra and Horta while 10,000 Spanish troops were landed from requisitioned passenger liners at the major ports. The Government of Portugal, informed only one hour previously, ordered its forces not to oppose the landings, and though some sporadic and desultory fighting occurred, resistance quickly ceased.

President Truman's address to the 79th Congress of the United States; 7th May 1945

"It is my duty to tell you today that I have received no satisfactory response from the German and Spanish governments to the ultimatum which we presented them two days ago; that if they did not immediately begin the withdrawal of their forces from the Portuguese territory of the Azores Islands that a state of war would exist between this country and theirs.

The occupation of the Azores Islands cannot be interpreted in any other way than as an action designed to directly menace the continental United States. As Commander-in-Chief of the Army and Navy, I have directed that all measures be taken for our defence. To pre-empt any other such action, I have today signed legislation to authorise the occupation of Iceland, Greenland and the Faroe Islands by forces of the United States Navy and Marine Corps.

"It is no small thing to seek war with the United States, so let the leaders of Spain and Germany be in no doubt that we will take whatever measures we deem necessary to defend our shores from aggression and let the other members of the Axis Pact be aware, that the United States will not shrink from opening hostilities against any nation that chooses to threaten it.

"I ask that the Congress declare today, that the United States is now in a state of war with Nazi Germany and the Republic of Spain."

Adolf Hitler's address to the Reichsenat 8th May 1945

"Germany does not wish for war, the German people desire only peace – but I tell you also that we shall not shrink before American aggression; that we shall not be dictated to by America or any other power. If they choose to attack us, then our fury will descend upon them until they know the taste of total defeat!

"It is the destiny of our race to dominate the world, those who stand against us will be utterly smashed! Obliterated as if they had never existed! The Americans are weak! Prosperity has made them soft! Their country is riddled with Jews! I tell you that they cannot stand against the might of our forces! Total victory shall be ours, America will rue the day it chose to threaten the German Reich!"

Annexes

ANNEX 1: LOSSES OF GERMAN CAPITAL

SHIPS AT THE BATTLE OF JUTLAND

From 'The Rule of the Waves' by Michael Fanshaw, Twelvemonth 1963

Moltke

Moltke was the fourth ship in the 1st Scouting Group line. She was being fired on by *Tiger*, *Australia* and *New Zealand* during the run to the south and received an underwater hit on her starboard side, in the forward part of the hull from *Tiger* at 16:02 at approximately the same time that *Indefatigable* blew up. The result of this hit is unknown, but was probably limited to structural damage and flooding. From 16:08, the 1st Scouting Group also came under fire from the British 5th Battle Squadron and *Moltke* was hit at 16:16 by either *Barham* or *Valiant* below her starboard number 5 casemate and exploded. [141] *Von Der Tann*, the next ship in line, had to swerve violently to avoid the smoke cloud. Eyewitness reports from members of *Von*

---

[141] In OTL, British shells at Jutland did not work properly. The results of shell hits given here are the product of analysis of three resources. N. J. M. Campbell's *Jutland: An Analysis of the Fighting* and Arthur Marder's *From the Dreadnought to Scapa Flow* Volume III to establish where and at what angle British shells landed on German ships; As well as Stephen Lorenz, Robert McCoy and Nathan Okun's NAaB (Naval Armour and Ballistics) computer program which was used to calculate the probable results of hits obtained on the German ships if British shells had worked properly. In OTL *Moltke* was hit by a 15 inch shell on the 8 inch part of her belt armour at 18,000 yards. The angle of obliquity was roughly 35°. The shell burst on the belt. If the shell had been working properly it would have achieved complete penetration of the belt with sufficient remaining energy to pierce both the 2 inch part of the sloped deck armour and the 2 inch torpedo bulkhead. The naval armour and ballistics program suggests complete penetration all the way to the magazines, but it should be noted that due to the German habit of storing shells with their nose caps out ward (i.e. towards the exterior of the ship) then even partial penetration by splinters had the potential to cause a magazine explosion.

Der Tann's crew described an enormous deflagration amidships. Only seven members of her crew were saved.

Seydlitz

The first hit scored on *Seydlitz* was at 15:55 by a 1400lb 13.5 inch shell from the *Queen Mary*. It struck her starboard side above the battery deck forward of the foremast and caused substantial damage but did not reduce the ships fighting efficiency. Two minutes later, she was hit by *Queen Mary* again, the shell striking the 9 inch armour of her aft super firing barbette. It penetrated and caused the destruction of the turret but did not otherwise disable the ship.

She was hit by another 13.5 inch shell (again probably from the *Queen Mary*) at 16;05 underwater in the region of the Starboard wing barbette. The shell is believed to have exploded just outside the torpedo bulkhead and splinters penetrated the magazine and adjacent engine room but the resultant flooding rapidly extinguished any fires thereby saving the ship. [142]

A fourth 13.5 inch shell struck the 210mm armour at 16:17 just aft of her starboard rearmost 150mm casemate. It caused heavy damage, disabling the gun, wrecking a large area of the ship and forcing the temporary evacuation of the starboard turbine compartment.

At 16:50 she was hit by a 15 inch shell on the starboard side of the focsle deck above her torpedo flat which exploded well inside the ship and caused major structural damage. [143] Strained by the hit on a weak part of her hull structure and the high-speed at which she was travelling, several bulkheads collapsed and the fore-part of the ship took on large amounts of water. By 16:55 she had slowed noticeably, and when struck by a torpedo from the destroyer *Petard* at 16:57 below and slightly aft of the spot where the shell had hit, she pulled out of line and slowed to four knots. The hull, already strained, was now riven by the

---

[142] In OTL the shell burst in penetrating.

[143] In OTL the shell burst in the water outside the ship.

explosion of the British torpedo and the subsequent explosion of several of her own torpedoes. Splinters penetrated as far back as her forward boiler rooms which began to flood.

At 15:01, though heavily damaged, listing to starboard and down by the bows, the ship was saveable but unfortunately two British destroyers, *Obdurate* and *Morris* were approaching at 31 knots from the west on a bearing of east-south-east less than 10,000 yards on *Seydlitz'* starboard beam, and seeing her in distress accelerated to 34 knots to attack. They were within firing range in two minutes and fired six of their eight 21 inch torpedoes at the stricken battle cruiser at a range of 8000 yards before turning away. Their approach and the launching of their torpedoes was masked by the smoke from the German 9th Destroyer Flotilla and the light cruiser *Regensberg* which were then steaming past *Seydlitz* to the west (i.e. between her and the British destroyers) steering north-north-east, though both the German destroyers and the cruiser engaged the British ships scoring several hits their intervention came too late to prevent the British launching torpedoes.

The breeze, which was from west-south-west [144] carried the funnel smoke of the German light forces towards the battle cruiser making observation difficult for her lookouts while her masts were clearly visible to the attacking British destroyers above the smoke. The torpedo tracks were not observed by the *Seydlitz* until 15:08 when they were less than 1500 yards away. *Seydlitz* started to turn towards the torpedoes in an attempt to 'comb the tracks' but the slowly moving ship did not answer the helm rapidly enough and four of the six torpedoes found their mark striking at 17:10. One exploded adjacent to the site of the 16:05 hit while two more struck very close together abreast of the aft boiler rooms.

Seydlitz was stopped completely by 17:12 and there was no saving her at this point. Captain von Egidy gave the order to abandon ship at 17:14, she sank by the bows while also rolling to

---

[144] The approach of the British destroyers and the wind direction are both as OTL.

starboard and at 17:26 her stern was clear of the water, it finally disappeared at 17:31. 467 members of her crew were rescued.

Derfflinger

Derfflinger was leading the 1st Scouting Group line when she suffered a magazine explosion at 17:13. The shell was of 15 inch calibre and fired by either *Barham* or *Valiant* at a range of 18,000 yards and an angle of obliquity of approximately 33°. The shell is believed to have struck on the starboard side below the waterline in the region of the forward magazines. [145]

Several historians have noted that had it not been for an incident at approximately 16:02, Hipper's flagship *Lutzow* would have been leading the line. This was a near collision between the flagship and one of the escorting destroyers of the 9th Flotilla. The 1st Scouting Group was executing a manoeuvre whereby they were turning from line abreast to line astern formation while changing course from east-south-east to south-south-east. While this movement was a well-practised one, it is possible that the helmsmen of *Lutzow*, *Derfflinger* and the destroyer *S52* were distracted by the explosion of the *Queen Mary* which had just occurred and the destroyer came too close to the *Lutzow* causing a violent course correction by the flagship and a sudden loss of speed. It seems that the crew of the *Derfflinger* (also possibly distracted by the action) failed to notice the *Lutzow's* turn and sailed past her to port, though *Seydlitz* both slowed down and manoeuvred to follow the *Lutzow* leaving *Derfflinger* slightly ahead of the rest of the squadron.

S52 had exchanged fire with the British destroyers *Morris* and *Obdurate* at around 15:03 and a shell from *Obdurate* had

---

[145] In OTL this was a hit on the *Lutzow*. (As *Derfflinger* and *Lutzow* were sister ships it seems reasonable to assume that if they were to change places, shells aimed at either one would land in the same place.) The shell struck the thin lower edge of the armour belt beneath the waterline abeam of the forward main magazines and exploded without penetrating causing the ship to be violently shaken. The naval armour and ballistics program suggests a good probability of partial penetration of the magazines if the shell had worked properly. Again deficiencies in German shell storage could easily have doomed the ship.

struck her bridge killing many of its occupants and disabling the steering gear. Consequently the ship was being conned from the secondary steering position which had a restricted view. Furthermore the man conning the ship was not a senior rating (as would be normal practice) and the ship was under the command of a junior officer (the senior officers having been killed or injured when the bridge was hit).

Hipper then ordered *Derfflinger* to take up position in the lead of the 1st Scouting Group , possibly because this would bring the ship's back into formation more quickly and with less confusion than if *Derfflinger* had attempted to take up her old place in the line. [146] Hipper preferred to lead his force from the front, Scheer's flagship always took up a position in the middle of the German battle line.

Konig

The exact sequence of events in the loss of *Konig* is unclear, but between 18:15 and 18:35 she suffered many hits from the British battleships. It is believed that the shell that doomed her came from Jellicoe's flagship *Iron Duke* which was credited with her destruction. She was observed to suffer multiple internal detonations which caused severe fires before she rolled over and sank. [147] The ship was lost with all hands.

---

[146] The described manoeuvre at the time of the sinking of the *Queen Mary* is historic, the near-collision incident is not, though the potential for difficulty certainly existed

[147] In OTL a 13.5 inch shell from *Iron Duke*, fired at a range of 12,000 yards and striking at approximately 18° from the normal, struck the lower edge of the armour belt 5 1/2 feet beneath the waterline between the bottom of the armour belt (which was only seven inches thick at this point) and the shelf that supported it. The hit was in line with 'B' barbette and burst on the wing longitudinal bulkhead after travelling only 6 1/2 feet inside the ship. It blew holes in several bulkheads and destroyed the ship's number 14 magazine igniting about 15 charges and arming the fuse on one of the 150 mm shells of her secondary armament. Some shell and torpedo bulkhead fragments even penetrated her main armament magazines. The crew of the *Konig* were incredibly lucky. In TTL a properly working shell penetrates much further into the ship causing multiple explosions and her loss.

Helgoland

In contrast to *Konig*, *Helgoland* was only hit once at 19:15 by a 15 inch armour-piercing shell from *Valiant* at 17,000 yards at an angle of roughly 45°. The shell struck above the torpedo flat on 6 inch vertical armour, but passed right through this to burst inside the ship causing sympathetic explosions of *Helgoland's* own torpedoes. [148] Although the bulkhead forward of the magazine was holed by splinters it held, forward of this bulkhead the ship was open to the sea and many compartments flooded rapidly. Captain von Kameke ordered the ship to slow to a crawl and the rest of the HSF soon left her behind but her forward pumps were inoperable due to shock damage from the explosions in her torpedo flat and, like all German ships of this era, her watertight subdivision was compromised by cable runs, voice pipes and other systems and she began to settle. By 20:09 her focsle was underwater and the sea was now entering the ship through her casemate embrasures. The situation became even worse at 20:24 when one of her remaining pumps failed and she foundered at 22:07.

Lutzow

The flagship of 1st Scouting Group received a tremendous battering throughout the action and by 18:40 her condition was extremely serious. She had endured a total of nineteen heavy-calibre hits, eight 12 inch, seven 13.5 inch and four 15 inch. The ship's upper-works were wrecked, almost 8,000 tons of water were inside the hull and 25% of her boilers were out of action as were most of her guns. In addition, she was down by the bows and listing to port. Yet when at 19:13 Scheer ordered Hipper to charge the British line in a desperate bid to draw the Grand Fleet's fire away from the fleeing van of the High Seas Fleet, *Lutzow* turned towards the hurricane of fire without a moment's hesitation. It is possible that in the confusion Scheer was unaware that the 1st Scouting Group consisted now of only a

---

[148] In OTL the shell broke up on 6 inch armour and failed to explode.

single battle cruiser. Writing after the battle he said of Hipper 'His devotion to duty was exemplary, his courage beyond praise'. *Lutzow* did not last long and the tactical sense, situational awareness and downright good luck that had helped Hipper thumb his nose at the Grand Fleet at Flamborough Head, Dogger Bank and up to this point at Jutland were finally of no avail. Between 19:14 and 19:18, it is estimated that the ship was hit by four 15 inch, five 13.5 inch and nine 12 inch [149] shells before the British shifted their fire from the stopped, smoking wreck and on to the German battleships. The exact sequence of events on board *Lutzow* is unknown but at 19:20 she capsized and sank shortly after. Only 121 members of her crew were rescued, Admiral Hipper was not among them.

Von der Tann

The first hit on *Von der Tann* came at 16:09 from *Barham*. It struck a joint in the belt armour 3 feet above the legend waterline and some 28 feet from the stern, penetrated the armour deck and burst, jamming one of the rudders and bending the number 3 propeller shaft which continued to turn, damaging the shaft gland and flooding the number 3 engine room.

She was hit by *Tiger* at 16:20 and 16:23. The first hit pierced the 200mm armour of A barbette and burst, destroying much of the rotating mechanism, killing or injuring most of the crew and causing the turret to jam. The second pierced the main deck and exploded inside X barbette causing the turret to burn out. Between 17:06 and 17:55 she received five hits from 15 inch shells that destroyed P turret and wrecked the forward part of the ship causing extensive flooding. [150] Combined with the now serious flooding aft from the 16:09 hit it was estimated by the ships damage control officer that some 7,000 tons of water were

---

[149] These hits were divided between the four surviving German battle cruisers in OTL

[150] In OTL these were hits on the *Seydlitz*. I have calculated where the hits would land, assuming the stem of the ship was the aiming point.

inside the hull causing her to settle lower and reducing her speed to 5 knots so that she fell well behind the rest of the German fleet.

Progressive flooding along cable runs and through voice pipes as well as that due to action damage meant that by 20:21 her focsle was awash and her screws were out of the water. The crew struggled for hours to contain the flooding and attempts were made to take her in tow but she foundered at approximately 00:15 on 1st June.

Damage

The battleship *Grosser Karfurst* sustained extremely heavy damage but survived the action. The former suffered twelve heavy hits, six by 15 inch shell, five by 13.5 inch and one twelve inch. Both her forward turrets and her X turret were burned out, her forward superstructure was severely damaged as was her number 2 turbine room. A 13.5 inch shell from the Lion had burst inside the battery armour underneath the bridge causing heavy casualties and badly injuring Captain Goette. Heroic efforts by her crew saved her and when she finally reached the mouth of the Jade in late afternoon on 1 June she could only manage 5 knots and her forward freeboard was down to 4 feet.

The battleship *Westfalen*, leading the High Seas Fleet in its headlong dash for home after Scheer's second battle turnaway, came under fire from Beatty's battle cruisers during the fifth phase of the action at ranges between 13,000 and 19,000 yards. She was hit four times between 20:24 and 20:30, one of the hits at 20:28 was a 13.5 inch from *Princess Royal* that caused heavy but localised damage to and in the vicinity of her number 2 boiler room. The other three hits – two 12 inch from *New Zealand* and another 13.5 inch from *Princess Royal*, struck aft of X turret, the 13.5 inch penetrating the armour, bending one of her shafts and wrecking her steering gear. Prompt action by the chief engineer in stopping the bent shaft meant that her damage was not as serious as that suffered by the *Seydlitz*. Nevertheless, her damage took some 13 hours to repair as it involved sending divers into the flooded stern of the ship and she did not limp home until midnight on 1st June.

The battleship *Kronprinz* suffered a single 15 inch hit from *Royal Oak* at 19:27. It struck the front of Y turret's roof and penetrated, bursting on the right hand breech mechanism. The turret was destroyed.

The battleship *Markgraf* received three 15 inch hits, one 13.5 inch hit and one 12 inch hit. The first two 15 inch hits struck parts of the foremast but the third, at 17:10, penetrated a joint between two pieces of 8 inch armour 71 feet forward of the stern. It glanced off the armour deck and exploded causing flooding and extensive local damage. She was hit again at 18:35 by the 13.5 inch shell which penetrated the 170mm armour of her port number 6 casemate, as well as the 60mm deck and burst in her port aft boiler room destroying it.

The last hit on *Markgraf* was a 14 inch CPC shell from *Agincourt* of the old Lyddite filled type that broke up on her side armour causing little damage. *Agincourt* also hit the battleship *Kaiser* twice, at 19:23 and again at 19:26. Both hits were ineffective, the first bursting outside the ship, the second failing to explode. She was one of the ships of the Grand Fleet that had not been re-equipped with the new pattern 'Greenboy' shell. It is interesting to speculate at this point what the outcome of Jutland might have been had all the British ships been equipped with the defective pattern of shell so recently replaced in most of them. [151]

---

[151] The non OTL late fourth and fifth phase hits (19:21 – 20:30) on *Westfalen*, *Kronprinz* and *Grosser Karfurst* are derived from the OTL hits on *Lutzow*, *Von der Tann*, *Derfflinger*, *Konig* and *Seydlitz* which in TTL are sunk before the shells aimed at them OTL are fired. The three battleships are the most obvious targets for the British at this point. *Grosser Karfurst* will be the *Seydlitz* of this timeline, staggering home despite enormous damage.

Table of Losses of ships at The Battle of Jutland

Ship type	Royal Navy	Kaiserlich Marine
Battleships		*Konig* *Helgoland*
Battle Cruisers	*Indefatigable* *Queen Mary* *Invincible*	*Moltke* *Seydlitz* *Derrflinger* *Lutzow* *Von der Tann*
Pre-Dreadnoughts		*Pommern*
Armoured Cruisers	*Black Prince* *Defence* *Warrior*	
Light Cruisers		*Elbing* *Frauenlob* *Rostock* *Weisbaden*
Destroyers	*Ardent* *Fortune* *Nestor* *Nomad* *Shark* *Sparrowhawk* *Tipperary* *Turbulent*	*S35* *V4* *V27* *V29* *V48*

ANNEX 2: THE WASHINGTON
NAVAL TREATY

At the Washington Conference of 1922 the major powers adopted a plan to govern both the proportionate division of their naval strength and also changes in that strength. The resultant treaty's fundamental principle was a managed building and scrapping programme that would permit the construction of an agreed amount of new warships while overseeing the disposal of obsolete or time expired vessels and maintaining the relative war potential of the navies of the signatory powers. The treaty's term was 10 years.

The main clauses of the treaty were as follows. All ratios are expressed: UK/US/Japan/France/Italy, it is important to note that the following figures refer to what was allowed under the treaty not what was actually built by the contracting powers.

Capital Ships

1. Capital ship tonnage was divided using a ratio of 5/5/3/1.75/1.75 [152]. The treaty was so written that the differential between the displacement tonnage of capital ship hulls finally retained by each of the signatory powers was maintained over the term of the treaty by the agreed commissioning and disposal clauses.

2. The maximum permissible gun calibre was set at 16 inches.

3. The maximum displacement of a capital ship was set at 35,000 tons with allowances as set out below.

4. (a) Upon signature of the treaty the United States was permitted to retain 18 capital ships.

---

[152] In historic reality the ratios was 5/5/3/1.67/1.67.

Name	Tonnage
Maryland	32,600
California	32,300
Tennessee	32,300
Idaho	32,000
New Mexico	32,000
Mississippi	32,000
Arizona	31,400
Pennsylvania	31,400
Oklahoma	27,500
Nevada	27,500
New York	27,000
Texas	27,000
Arkansas	26,000
Wyoming	26,000
Florida	21,825
Utah	21,825
North Dakota	20,000
Delaware	20,000

The total displacement retained by the United States on this date was 500,650 tons. [153]

4. (b) By December 31st 1931 The United States was permitted to retain 20 capital ships. [154]

Name	Tonnage
45,000ton D	48,000
45,000ton C	48,000
45,000ton B	48,000
45,000ton A	48,000

---

[153] Exactly as in OTL.

[154] The tonnage figures here include the 3000 ton allowance for modernisation of capital ships. This was permitted in OTL and is also in TTL.

Georgia	35,600
Colorado	35,600
West Virginia	35,600
Maryland	35,600
California	35,300
Tennessee	35,300
Idaho	35,000
New Mexico	35,000
Mississippi	35,000
Arizona	34,400
Pennsylvania	34,400
Oklahoma	30,500
Nevada	30,500
New York	30,000
Texas	30,000
Arkansas	29,000

The total permissible displacement to be retained by the United States on this date was 729,800 tons.

5. (a) Upon signature of the treaty the British Commonwealth was permitted to retain 22 capital ships.

Name	Tonnage
Hood	41,200
Renown	26,500
Repulse	26,500
Royal Sovereign	25,750
Royal Oak	25,750
Revenge	25,750
Resolution	25,750
Ramilies	25,750
Malaya	27,500
Valiant	27,500
Barham	27,500
QueenElizabeth	27,500
Warspite	27,500
Benbow	25,000

Emperor of India	25,000
Iron Duke	25,000
Marlborough	25,000
Tiger	28,500
Canada	28,000
King George V	23,000
Ajax	23,000
Centurion	23,000

The total tonnage retained by the British Commonwealth on this date was 585,950 tons.

5. (b) By December 31st 1931 the British Commonwealth was permitted to retain 20 capital ships.

Name	Tonnage
45,000ton B	48,000
45,000ton A	48,000
35,000ton D	38,000
35,000ton C	38,000
35,000ton B	38,000
35,000ton A	38,000
Endeavour	48,000
Hood	45,000
Renown	29,500
Repulse	29,500
Royal Sovereign	28,750
Royal Oak	28,750
Revenge	28,750
Resolution	28,750
Ramilies	28,750
Malaya	30,500
Valiant	30,500
Barham	30,500
Queen Elizabeth	30,500
Warspite	30,500

The total permissible tonnage to be retained by the British Commonwealth on this date was 696,250 tons.

6. (a) Upon signature of the treaty, the Empire of Japan was permitted to retain 10 capital ships.

Name	Tonnage (metric tons)
Mutsu	33,800
Nagato	33,800
Hyuga	31,260
Ise	31,260
Yamashiro	30,600
Fuso	30,600
Kirishima	27,500
Haruna	27,500
Hiei	27,500
Kongo	27,500

The total tonnage retained by the Empire of Japan on this date was 301,320 metric tons.

6. (b) By December 31st 1931 the Empire of Japan was permitted to retain 12 capital ships.

Name	Tonnage (metric tons)
45,000ton B	48,768
45,000ton A	48,768
Tosa	43,900
Mutsu	36,800
Nagato	36,800
Hyuga	34,260
Ise	34,260
Yamashiro	33,600
Fuso	33,600
Kirishima	30,500
Haruna	30,500
Kongo	30,500

The total permissible tonnage to be retained by the Empire of Japan on this date was 442,256 metric tons.

7. (a) Upon signature of the treaty the Republic of France was permitted to retain 10 capital ships.

Name	Tonnage (metric tons)
Bretagne	23,500
Lorraine	23,500
Provence	23,500
Paris	23,500
France	23,500
Jean Bart	23,500
Courbet	23,500
Condorect	18,900
Diderot	18,900
Voltaire	18,900

The total tonnage retained by the Republic of France on this date was 221,170 metric tons.

7. (b) By December 31st 1931 the Republic of France was permitted to retain 7 capital ships.

Name	Tonnage (metric tons)
35,000ton D	38,608
35,000ton C	38,608
35,000ton B	38,608
35,000ton A	38,608
Bretagne	28,500
Lorraine	28,500
Provence	28,500

The total permissible tonnage to be retained by the Republic of France on this date was 239,932 metric tons.

8. (a) Upon signature of the treaty the Kingdom of Italy was permitted to retain 10 capital ships.

Name	Tonnage (metric)
Andrea Doria	22,700
Caio Duilio	22,700
Conte Di Cavour	22,500
Giulio Cesare	22,500
Leonardo Da Vinci	22,500
Dante Alighieri	19,500
Roma	12,600
Napoli	12,600
Vittorio Emanuele	12,600
Regina Elena	12,600

The total tonnage retained by the Kingdom of Italy on this date was 182,800 metric tons.

8. (b) By December 31st 1931 the Kingdom of Italy was permitted to retain 7 capital ships.

Name	Tonnage (metric)
35,000ton B	38,608
35,000ton A	38,608
Carracciolo	34,400
Andrea Doria	25,700
Caio Duilio	25,700
Conte Di Cavour	25,500
Giulio Cesare	25,500

The total permissible tonnage to be retained by the Kingdom of Italy on this date was 179,616 metric tons.

Aircraft Carriers

1. Aircraft Carriers were permitted on a ratio of 3/3/3/1/1.

2. Displacement limits were set at 27,500 tons with allowances for certain specific ships (The Americans, British and Japanese were each permitted 2 aircraft carriers of up to 33,000 tons.)

Cruisers

1. Cruisers were permitted on a tonnage ratio of 5/5/3/1.75/1.75.

2. Maximum gun calibre was set at 8 inches for heavy cruisers and six inches for light cruisers.

3. Maximum standard displacement for new cruisers was set at 12,000 tons.

4. The United States was permitted to complete or retain a quantity of cruisers not displacing more than 420,000 tons.

5. The British Commonwealth was permitted to complete or retain a quantity of cruisers not displacing more than 420,000 tons.

6. Japan was permitted to complete or retain a quantity of cruisers not displacing more than 252,000 tons.

7. France was permitted to complete or retain a quantity of cruisers not displacing more than 147,000 tons.

8. Italy was permitted to complete or retain a quantity of cruisers not displacing more than 147,000 tons.

Submarines

1. Submarines were permitted on a tonnage ratio of 5/5/3/1.75/1.75

2. The maximum permissible gun calibre was not to exceed 6.1 inches.

3. The United States was permitted to complete or retain a quantity of submarines not displacing more than 75,000 tons.

4. The British Commonwealth was permitted to complete or retain a quantity of submarines not displacing more than 75,000 tons.

5. Japan was permitted to complete or retain a quantity of submarines not displacing more than 45,000 tons.

6. France was permitted to complete or retain a quantity of submarines not displacing more than 26,250 tons

7. Italy was permitted to complete or retain a quantity of submarines not displacing more than 26,250 tons

Training and Target Ships

1. Training ships, that were former capital ships, were permitted on a ratio of 3/3/1/1/1.

2. Training ships, that were former capital ships, had to have their side armour and at least 25% of their main armament removed.

3. The United States was permitted to retain *Wyoming*, *Florida* and *Utah* as training ships.

4. The British Commonwealth was permitted to complete or retain *Canada*, *New Zealand* and *Emperor of India* as training ships.

5. Japan was permitted to retain *Hiei* as a training ship and *Settsu* as a target ship.

6. France was permitted to retain *Paris* as a training ship.

7. Italy was permitted to retain *Dante Alighieri* as a training ship.

Museum Ships

A special clause was written into the treaty permitting Britain to retain HMS *Iron Duke* as a museum ship, Japan to retain *Mikasa* as a museum ship and Australia to retain HMAS *Australia* as a museum ship. All were to be kept in a demilitarised state and had to have their side armour removed and their machinery rendered inoperable.

Mobile Naval Base Ship

A special clause was written into the treaty permitting Britain to retain *Agincourt* as a mobile naval base. She was to have her side armour and 60% of her armament removed.

The Soviet Union was not a signatory and the strength of the German Navy was set under the Treaty of Versailles. [155]

---

[155] All other types of warship and all other treaty clauses are as set out in the OTL Washington Treaty.

ANNEX 3: THE LONDON
NAVAL DISARMAMENT CONFERENCES

From 'The Naval Disarmament Conferences' by Anthony Radcliffe writing in Man O'War *Volume 5*

In the First London Naval Conference of 1930, the British delegation sought to prevent the start of the construction of new capital ships other than those agreed to in the Washington Treaty until 1936. It was due to expire at the end of 1931. However, despite the recession, agreement was elusive; France and Italy refused to sign and Japan would only agree to extend the treaty until December 1934. This was agreed, but no new treaty was signed and the time limits on clauses regarding other types of warship were not extended.

The Second London Conference was convened in March 1934 at the height of the commotion in naval circles caused by the reconstruction of the Russian battleship *Frunze* and her subsequent reclassification as a battle cruiser. In addition to this, there was the announcement of the construction of two new capital ships in Japan, one of which was subsequently cancelled, and the plans announced in Germany for the construction of a second 'Panzerschiff', much larger than the first. Plans for the new construction of capital ships were also well in hand in France, Italy and Japan. Therefore the British, instead of seeking to reduce the numbers of capital ships, attempted to limit their future size and power.

The opening British position was that a treaty where the maximum size of capital ship was limited to 35,000 tons with no 3000 ton modification clause would be satisfactory. However, their proposal to limit gun calibre to 14 inch was defeated when Japan and France rejected it. The Mosley government was not at all sanguine about the prospects for disarmament and had anticipated the failure of their proposals. The only concrete agreement reached was that the capital ship tonnage limit for new construction should continue to be set at 38,000 tons in

January 1935 and rise to 45,000 tons at the end of December 1937 if Japan did not sign the final treaty.

Japan did not sign, neither did France or Italy and there was much concern as to the plans of the USSR. The Treaty was effectively worthless and though the British stated their intention to produce treaty limited designs in the hope that other navies would follow suite they had no option but to resume new capital ship construction in 1935. The United States was the only other power to produce designs limited by the tenets of the treaty.

It must be noted that the French *Richelieu* class battleship design was of 45,000 tons standard displacement. It is therefore obvious that the French as well as the Japanese and Italians had no intention of accepting a 35,000 ton capital ship tonnage limit from the outset of the conference.

ANNEX 4: THE IMPACT ON TRADE AND INDUSTRY OF THE ECONOMIC POLICIES OF THE LABOUR GOVERNMENT OF 1932 – 1938

From: Industry, Money and Government – Britain's Economy in the First Half of the Twentieth Century, Michael Horvath, Hamish Horton 1997

When the Labour Party entered office in July 1932, they inherited a difficult financial position. Although World War I had ended more than a decade earlier, it had wrecked international trade while the recovery had been slow and fragmentary. The export trade in manufactured goods was seriously damaged as was the invisible trade of the United Kingdom. Both were as affected by the Great War as by the depression which had begun in 1929 and by the protectionism that was the principal feature of the economic landscape of the early 1930s.

In outline, Oswald Mosley's Labour government of 1932 sought to revitalise the British economy with measures that were focused on manufacturing industry and would see significant job creation. Mosley's strategy upon entering office was broadly based on his memorandum of 1931. This was a 'New Deal' style call for government intervention with high tariffs to protect British industries from international competition, nationalisation of industry and a programme of public works to solve unemployment. The government agenda was thrashed out with the chancellor, Hugh Dalton, and followed the advice of John Maynard Keynes in its advocacy of intervention by government in times of financial hardship. Keynes was often consulted by Mosley for his advice and opinion on economic matters. This was a sharp reversal of previous government policy, but was certain to be popular with Labour voters as it was designed to create an increase in employment.

The declining competitiveness of British manufacturing industry was apparent well before the start of the Great War, but the impact of that war and of the Great Depression accelerated decline by closing markets and stimulating import substitution. British exports of goods in the 1920s struggled to approach their pre-war levels in terms of volume. After a decade spent hoping that the pre-1914 situation could be re-established, it became generally accepted by 1932 that the staple industries of provincial Britain would never regain all of their former export success. While, in spite of rapid growth in output, competitive new technology-based industries like aircraft manufacture were unable to do well outside the Sterling area because of protectionism.

The problems of manufacturing industry were amplified by competitive failures in markets which had been vital to British exports before 1914. Invisible exports were also endangered by increased competition. New York proved to be an effective rival source of long-term international finance in the decade before 1929; however, in the 1930s neither London nor New York were able to lend abroad. In spite of the fact that its development was restrained more by limited opportunities than by competition; the City of London remained the locus of the largest commercial and financial bloc in the world – the Sterling area.

The decline in income from invisible exports such as credit and finance was equally severe. In the 1920s, the City of London was performing significantly more poorly than in 1913. Just as industry had become dependent on protection and Imperial markets, so the City too had to settle for dominance within a sterling bloc centred on the Empire. In this sense, the overseas interests of industry and finance converged markedly after 1914 though this was not fully appreciated until the 1930s.

The Labour Party's policy of nationalisation of industry was not as seriously pursued as the left of the party wanted once Mosley gained office. The idea that the industrial engines of the country could be made to exert their strength on behalf of all of the people, rather than a small number of them, was politically seductive and certainly a vote catcher. But nationalisations were limited to the coal, steel and electricity supply industries while the expansion of the Royal Mail into telecommunications was also fostered. This shift in policy can be attributed to Mosley's consultation with John Maynard Keynes, who, while advocating state intervention, had come to the conclusion that intervention itself had to be carefully constrained. [156]

Again, as in so many other areas, Mosley's political philosophy was subservient to his hunger for power

The Reintegration of Finance and Industry

The strong growth the British economy's manufacturing sector saw after 1933 was a direct result of government inspired 'pump priming' – but the financing of this venture was not limited to government money. Instead Hugh Dalton (the Chancellor of the Exchequer), aided (somewhat unwillingly) by Montagu Norman (Governor of the Bank of England), sought to cajole

---

[156] This is somewhat ahistoric in that Keynes did not come to this view until the late 1940's OTL and possibly did so as a result of working with Friedrich von Hayek. Mosley's grasp of economics was weak. His policies were an unworkable blend of free market capitalism and state intervention of the type attempted in the Blair/Brown era and would probably have led to equally poor results. Keynes was the most respected economist in Britain and while he has been presented as an enemy of free market capitalism this view is wrong. He held that both had a place in government policy but because his political views can be seen as being to the left of Hayek's he is sometimes incorrectly presented as holding an opposite view to Hayek when in fact the two economist's work is in broad agreement. Keynes did not disagree with many of Hayek's ideas in the book The Road to Serfdom, a book he had indirectly helped Hayek to write. Both men were liberals with a distrust of authoritarian regimes and Keynes agreed with Hayek that Fascism was just as dangerous as Communism. As an article in The Economist by 'C.R.' published on Mar 14th 2014 puts it: "Keynes rejected the populist interpretation of Hayek's argument – that any increase in state planning is the first step on the way to tyranny — but agreed with the overall view that the bounds of state intervention needed to be clearly defined for liberal democracy to remain safe (and more explicitly than even Hayek himself did in the book). Receiving an early copy of The Road to Serfdom from Hayek personally, Keynes wrote back to him, praising the book. But Keynes thought Hayek should have been more explicit in what sort of red lines would be necessary for increased state intervention not to imperil liberty." The rest of the article can be read at http://www.economist.com/blogs/freeexchange/2014/03/keynes–and–hayek

Britain's banks and financiers to lend at home rather than abroad.

In contrast to the situation in the United States and Germany, relations between finance and industry in the UK were loose. British finance had traditionally found better profits abroad, but the decision in 1926 to 'stay off Gold' meant that lending from sterling assets outside the Sterling area was less profitable and more expensive. Because the pound was now subject to exchange rate fluctuations, the cost of lending and the expectation of profit were now hostage to the changeable value of sterling. In terms of the export of capital, this presented difficulties for both borrower and lender. Gold-backed American dollars were not subject to this problem. This had been the predicament that those who sought to 'get back on gold' had foreseen in 1926. But it also meant that demand for lending from within the Sterling area was now more likely to be met. In terms of the export of manufactured goods, the government were now in a position to manipulate exchange rates to make British manufactures cheaper in world markets.

For the Labour leadership, a way had to be found to invigorate the export industries and by so doing alleviate the heavy unemployment that characterised the northern industrial regions that were the heartland of Labour support. This was the central plank of the manifesto that had seen the party elected to office.

Montagu Norman, who had been Governor of the Bank of England since 1920 had launched a series of initiatives before Labour took office designed to bring the City and provincial industry together. The Bank was aware of the mounting criticism of financial policy in the 1920s. Norman, in particular, was convinced that the failure of the financial sector to actively attempt to resuscitate the industrial sector would inspire politicians (he principally feared Labour politicians) to intervene with deleterious effects on the market system which the Bank oversaw. He was also aware that when opportunities for overseas investment were declining, the banks needed to tap the domestic market for business. As he put it in 1930:

"I believe that the finance which for 100 years has been directed by them abroad can be directed by them into British industry, that a marriage can take place between the industry of the North and the finance of the South."

The Bank of England had urged the clearing banks to use their financial position with industry to impose rationalisation. One of the Bank's goals was the creation of efficient big business. However, it is important not to overemphasise the Bank of England's initiatives in this field. It was opposed to providing much new finance for industry from its own resources and it saw its role as facilitating contacts with lenders and promoting self-help. Many of its schemes were little more than gestures designed to divert criticism from financial policy. The small quantity of help the Bank of England and the Treasury did give before 1932 went to older industries that were ailing. [157]

The Macmillan Committee's verdict of 1930 was that "...in some respects the City is more highly organized to provide capital to foreign countries than to British industry..." The ascent of the Labour Party to power in 1932 can be easily characterised as Montagu Norman's nightmare come true. But Mosley and Dalton, as advised by Keynes, had successfully identified that the two halves of British industrial capitalism – finance and manufacture – had become increasingly disengaged for the preceding half century. It was the new government's policy to reverse that trend.

The new government's initial approach to the problem was commendably subtle. When first elected, Oswald Mosley was widely admired in every strata of the British Establishment and he was able to use his charm and influence as well as an appeal to patriotism to overcome opposition to the new policy. The reduced opportunities available to British investment interests due to the fall in the value of the pound were also used as an argument to strengthen the incentive to invest in UK industry.

---

[157] All this is Montagu Norman OTL, but in OTL the National Government's aim was to compel industry to help itself while pursuing a balanced budget, limited government spending and a strong pound.

When this worked only partially, Mosley raised the spectre of increasing taxation on the activities of the City – a move widely condemned in the City as 'thuggery' and 'cajolery' – but the outcome was a much healthier flow of capital to industry and a reinvigorated union between the two halves of capitalism.

It was certainly not the case that all British finance was now directed towards British industry or that profits from foreign loans were much reduced. Large holdings of loans abroad continued to bring in substantial returns and be one of the principal features of the British financial landscape, but it is the case that in the build up to 1939 and after, capital for industry was much more forthcoming from the City. The irony of the Labour Party seeking to accomplish this by forcing a Hilferdingian union between capital and industry on the City of London hardly needs emphasis. [158]

---

[158] By 1939 OTL, finance and industry had intermingled to a high degree – but it is questionable whether the outcome can be described as 'finance capitalism', in Rudolf Hilferding's sense of the term. The large firms which were the products of mergers that had been financed by the London Stock Exchange still did not make use of it for new capital, which was usually raised internally, while small firms found London too expensive a place to raise finance. Nor did this closer engagement of the banks with industry, lead to fundamental changes in the relationship between the two. Montagu Norman's hope that the banks would use their influence to compel industry into efficiency failed to materialise. The clearing banks did not evolve into industrial banks and they continued to be dependent for their income on investment outlets controlled by the City of London and the money market. Consequently, they remained uncomfortably placed between manufacturing industry and the financial sector and their standing and authority remained restricted so that when profits rose after 1933, their lending to industry actually fell substantially. Even successful industrial mergers often turned out to be no more than an uneasy union of disparate elements which opposed change in managerial organization and method. This disengagement from industry can be explained both as a conscious decision by the banks to pursue their primary goal of maintaining liquidity, or as a negation of enduring association with bank capital by industry. In either case, the result was that in OTL the two halves of capitalism were not committed to each other. Merchant banks and Stock Exchange investors were also wary of industry. The raising of new industrial finance on the Stock Exchange was also restricted in this time period by the growth of the national debt.

A Case Study in the Reintegration of Finance and Industry: Steel

In the later part of 1914, when British industry had gone over to the production of munitions, it was found that it was inadequate to the task. The shell crisis of 1915, and in particular, the problems encountered with naval ordnance as exposed by the Battles of Flamborough Head and Dogger Bank, further underlined the point of the embarrassing backwardness of the British steel industry. It was not that new and better shells could not be designed, tested and made ready for mass production quickly, they were; the problem lay in the process of their manufacture.

Successful munitions provision for the type of total war ushered in by the conflict of 1914 to 1918 is not so much a question of the output of specialised armaments manufacturers, like Krupp or Vickers. It is the ability to convert the multifarious industrial and scientific assets that in peace allow a trading nation to build high quality manufactured goods to war production.

In the 20th century, iron and steel output was one of the key measures of national strength. Before the Great War, Britain produced only half as much steel as Germany, but this quantitative deficiency was not as alarming as the technical backwardness of the industry. After 1914 there was a desperate shortage of high quality steel and it was discovered that supplies of many types of specialised steels had previously been obtained from German manufacturers. The Iron and Steel Industries Committee, which convened in 1917, found that in Britain, modern steelworks were the exception, rather than the rule. The official History of the Ministry of Munitions published after the war put it thus:

'British manufacturers were behind other countries in research, plant and method. Many of the iron and steel firms were working on a small scale. They tended to utilise old systems, outdated practices and uneconomical plant. Consequently, their cost of production was so high that competition with the steel works of the United States and

317

Germany was not merely difficult but rapidly becoming impossible.'

Productivity too was poor, the annual output per man in pig-iron was 380 tons, in the United States it was nearly 600 tons per man. It was only the availability of imported shells and steel from neutral America that permitted the guns of the Western Front and of Britain's capital ships at Jutland to keep firing.

Britain was also sorely lacking in the expertise of the new industries of the second phase of the industrial revolution. (We can identify the second phase as that which occurred after 1870.) There were too few light engineering factories equipped with the modern machine tools required to build sophisticated finished goods like tanks and aeroplanes. There were too few precision industries that could undertake the large scale manufacture of such items as shell and bomb fuses.

Although the problem was formidable, by 1916 Britain had succeeded in creating a light engineering industry practically from scratch. There were certainly difficulties in accomplishing this, not least of which was the dearth of modern machine-tool, electrical equipment and ball bearing manufacturers. The gap was bridged by the import of American, Swiss and Swedish goods.

Such a salutary example might, and perhaps should, have stood as a lesson for all time. Yet, by the mid-1930s, with the continuation of the recession and the generally risk-averse attitude of British management, the steel industry, along with many others, was in danger of slipping back into its old ways. Several factors mitigated against this. The influence exerted by the urgency of re-armament and the consequent oversight of weapons procurement by the armed services, the Admiralty and the Ministry of Supply cannot be understated. The setting up of the Ministry of Supply in 1936 was vitally important, in that it coordinated much of the Country's design and manufacturing effort. However, had it not been for the government induced willingness of British bankers to lend to industry, the War of 1940 might have produced a similar crisis to that of 1915. As it was, Britain was defeated anyway, but the stronger and more capable steel and manufacturing industry that emerged from

1935 to 1940, was the engine of success in the years that followed it.

Tariffs, Protection and the end of free trade after 1940

A second measure, partly designed to propel a shift in the relative proportions of domestic and foreign investment by British capital, was a frankly protectionist tariff strategy that raised the rate of profit in the more important capital-intensive industries such as steel and shipbuilding. A subsidiary result was that the tariff restored a balance between the south, with its light industry and services oriented economy, and the north with its heavy industry. This was acomplished by raising profit margins in the latter.

For the rank and file of the Labour Party, many of whom believed strongly that free-trade was in the consumer's best interest, the prospect of tariffs, like the prospect of deflation, proved divisive. Support for the tariff was strong in sections of the Conservative party and again impelled closer cooperation between British finance and British industry.

Regions of informal influence also played a part in meeting Britain's goals in the international economy. Their contribution could be seen in the influence exercised over the smaller European members of the sterling bloc in the 1930s, as well as in the policies implemented towards South America and China. In these territories Britain worked tirelessly and with significant success in maintaining her financial interests. Commercially driven decisions, such as the backing given to Chiang Kai-shek in China, were made with such concerns in mind.

War brought with it serious challenges to the economic and social status quo. The war of 1914–18 had shaken the British notion of 'Gentlemanly Capitalism' this new conflict seemed set to all but extinguish it by questioning the stratified social order on which it had flourished.

The war certainly caused a shift in the balance of economic power from the City to industry and organised labour, because with national survival at stake, the status of the producing part of the nation was greatly enhanced. In fact, it can be said that the main result of the Labour government's involvement in capital and industry was to create a more politically aware and vocal group of vested industrial interests. These were dependent on cartelisation and protection, and their power was often used to forestall change rather than to encourage it, but the emergence of the large corporation in British industry promoted the growth of a more coherent, politically aware, industrial interest which had more influence than in the past and was closer to the centres of power in London.

After 1940 the advocates of free-trade were in full retreat. The world had separated into trading blocs centred on the sterling area, the Reichsmark area and the United States dollar area. Ironically, the type of Imperial Free Trade Area, championed by Mosley at the Ottawa Conference in 1932, had come into existence after he had lost office and by force of circumstances rather than as the result of Imperial Policy. Competition for trade in the remaining territories was fierce but the 'reconciliation' of industrial enterprise and City finance led to a fundamental change in the relationship between the principal segments of capital in Britain and, as a consequence, now had an influence upon the distribution of power though it was not yet capable of exerting a determining effect upon economic policy.

ANNEX 5: OPERATION MATCH-POINT

AND OPERATION SET-PIECE

From: 'The Battle of Britain' by Brian Winthrop and Basil Hanrahan, Tetrach Press 1968

The attack by aircraft of the RNAA on the German fighter bases in the Pas de Calais on the evening of Saturday 14th September 1940 was a singular success, in part because, unbeknown to the British, it was executed at an extremely fortuitous time.

From the point of view of British strategy it proved immensely useful for the United Kingdom to possess what was essentially a second air force. Fighter Command of the RAF was fully occupied with defending Britain from German air attack. Bomber Command was engaged in the twin tasks of preparing to interdict German invasion forces after the expected German landing in Britain and of destroying and disrupting German preparations for that invasion. Under these pressures it proved impossible for the Royal Air Force to undertake the necessary and obvious task of attacking the Luftwaffe at its bases in France. The success of such attacks in disrupting the cohesion of an aerial force had been bought home to the British by the success of German attacks on British bases and repaying the compliment in kind had been contemplated since mid-August. However, fully occupied as the RAF was, it proved impossible to spare the assets required to conduct such an operation. The Royal Navy Air Arm however, while principally a ship-borne force, had both the time and the ability to plan and execute one.

Since the commencement of hostilities, two British aircraft carriers had been lost, *Ark Royal* to a U-boat in the first days of the war, and *Glorious* to the guns of German surface units off the coast of Norway. Another carrier, *Courageous*, was being repaired after suffering damage in The Battle of Lofoten while both *Furious* and *Intrepid* were undergoing major reconstructions. This left *Fearless, Illustrious, Victorious* and *Formidable* of which *Illustrious* was operating in the Mediterranean and the other three were attached to the Home Fleet (*Formidable* was a new ship and was barely worked up).

The neutralisation of the Kriegsmarine's surface forces (most of which had been sunk or were under repair) in the Norwegian campaign, meant that the heavy units of the Royal Navy were engaged in waiting for the German invasion which was predicted to take place in September. This forced inaction did not sit well with many senior officers in particular Vice-Admiral Fredrick Bowhill. [159] Bowhill put together the plan to attack the German airfields in the Pas de Calais in late August though it was initially rejected by the Cabinet. Bowhill argued that in the event of a German invasion, the aircraft carriers would be of only limited use as their operation in the narrow seas of the English Channel would be extremely hazardous. Their aircraft however, were likely to be very useful if operated from shore bases.

It was noted very early in the Battle of Britain that the German bombers were extremely vulnerable when unescorted. As the battle entered its final phase, which was characterised by attacks on London, the chief restraint on the ability of fighter command to disrupt German formations and shoot down German bombers was again their escorting fighters, in particular the Messerschmitt Bf 109s. These aircraft had very short range however, and in consequence their bases had to be as close to the British Isles as possible. Several of the bases in the Pas de Calais were within sight of the English Channel, few were more than 5 miles inland and the exact locations of the airfields were identified by RAF reconnaissance aircraft in late August.

Operation Match-Point, as it was named, required the air groups of *Fearless*, *Formidable* and *Victorious*. These consisted of some 150 aircraft. Although the establishment of the three carriers was more than 200 aircraft this had been reduced by losses and attrition. As well as flights from the decimated *Courageous* air group, several squadrons from *Ark Royal's* air group (most of the personnel of whom had been saved when the ship sank after being torpedoed on 17th September 1939) and several squadrons from the *Indomitable* air group (the

---

[159] See Annex 9 and Appendices.

construction of *Indomitable* had been suspended in May when she was almost complete, her air group however had been partly formed and was training) two RAF fighter squadrons were also bought down from the North of England to provide extra cover.

The plan fell into two parts, Operation Match and Operation Point. Operation Match was intended to be an evening attack by RNAA aircraft timed to begin 30 minutes before sundown. The attack was to use large numbers of small bombs. At least half of the bombs were delayed action. Of these 25% were high explosive and the rest flares. The intention was not only to destroy enemy aircraft on the ground but to make the actual airfields unusable due to unexploded ordinance. The flares were on timers set to go off at five minute intervals commencing an hour after sunset and continuing for an hour after that. These were for the second part of the venture, Operation Point.

This consisted of a force of RAF bombers operating at around 5,000 feet who would then drop their bomb loads on the targets marked by the delayed action flares already dropped by the RNAA aircraft. By using a large number of delayed action flares it was hoped that the Germans would be unable to defuse all of them before the bombers arrived. These were also booby trapped to further inhibit defusing operations, the timers were simple and largely improvised in RAF ordnance depots in the weeks prior to the operation.

Some anxiety was expressed in Cabinet meetings that the operation was likely to result in the deaths of French civilians. Though it was noted that none of the airfields considered for attack were close to large centres of population, all were adjacent to villages. Bowhill argued that the situation warranted desperate measures and while deaths or injuries caused to French civilians would be regrettable, it was vital that the operation proceed.

The attack was led by Commander Eugene Esmonde. The airfields selected for attack were Audembert (which was home to I/JG26), Caffiers (III/JG26), Coquelles (I/JG 52), Guines (I&III JG53), Marck (Lehr Geshwader II), Marquise (II/JG26), Peupingues (II/JG52) and Wissant (I&II/JG51). The actual number of aircraft engaged was as follows:

Swordfish	55
Albacores	32
Skuas	47
Gannets	51
Gladiators	18
Sea Hurricanes	16
Spitfires	12
Hurricanes	12
Wellingtons	73
Hampdens	41
Whiteleys	54
Blenheims	48

Inevitably the attack did not go entirely as planned. There was some confusion over targets and three of the airfields (Guines, Marck and Caffiers) went almost unmolested while two, Wissant and Coquelles, were practically obliterated.

The RNAA aircraft coming from different airfields in the south of England arrived at different times over the target in the space of about 30 minutes. They were supposed to arrive at the same time generally however, it was the fighters that arrived first. Surprise was achieved and many German aircraft were destroyed by strafing on the ground. Despite this, some German fighters were scrambled to intercept and a large dogfight took place against the backdrop of the setting sun. During this action the first strike aircraft began to arrive consisting of two dozen Albacores from 869 and 851 Squadrons. Of these, eight were shot down, however this was only a small part of the strike force and believing that the attack was over the German fighters began to land when the British aircraft in the first attack withdrew. In consequence they were largely caught on the ground when the rest of the RNAA strike force arrived.

As well as the losses suffered by the Luftwaffe fighters to bombing, strafing and in the aerial actions; several more were lost attempting to land in the dark. At least one German pilot set off an unexploded British bomb when he landed his Bf 109 on top of it. In perhaps the most extraordinary incident of the day, a Swordfish piloted by Lieutenant Rupert Brabner RNVR, the Member of Parliament for Hythe and a future Prime

Minister of the United Kingdom, shot down the aircraft of German ace Major Werner Moelders, the commanding officer of JG51. Brabner was flying low over Wissant just as Moelders became airborne. The German pilot was unhurt, but the incident seemed to sum up the day's action for the Luftwaffe.

British losses were heavy, more than 25% of the attacking Albacores, Skuas and Swordfish were shot down by anti-aircraft fire and German fighters, but German losses were also severe. Many aircraft were destroyed, several pilots killed and injured and most important of all the airfields at Audembert, Coquelles, Peupingues and Wissant were rendered unusable.

Unbeknown to the British the following day, Sunday 15th September, was meant to see the largest attacks yet made on the British Isles by the Luftwaffe. Goering had ordered a maximum effort, though Kesslering – the commanding officer of Luftflotte 2 – after being informed of the damage and the losses to the Jagdegruppen based in the Pas de Calais area requested a postponement. Goering vacillated, but when Hitler was informed he flew into a rage and ordered that the attack go ahead stating that the Luftwaffe's own intelligence reports were claiming that Fighter Command was on its last legs. In consequence, less than half of the planned strength of the fighter escort for the German bombers was available on the following day. The results were catastrophic.

The weather was excellent and from mid-morning on very large formations of German aircraft began to mass over France and then to make their way towards London. These formations were met by RAF fighters and were mostly broken up before reaching their target. Some bombs certainly fell on London and the South of England but so effective was the defence on this day that the German attacks were panicky, uncoordinated and largely ineffectual. Only small numbers of Messerschmitt Bf 109s were met by the defending fighters and the losses of German aircraft were very serious indeed.

Fighter Command claims of 237 enemy aircraft destroyed proved wildly optimistic, nevertheless the actual German losses in the air fighting of September 15th were 87 aircraft destroyed. The RAF lost only 19 aircraft.

A second operation, Operation Set-Piece, was conducted on the night of 16th September, under the full moon [160] by 23 Swordfish aircraft again led by Esmonde. Many of the same Royal Navy crews that flew in Operation Match-Point returned for the mission and again the targets were the German airfields in the Pas de Calais – in particular those that aerial reconnaissance had shown to be only lightly damaged by Match-Point.

Unlike Match-Point, the RNAA aircraft for Set-Piece used only flares and again, half were delayed action. Their role was solely to mark the locations of the airfields for the main force and this operation was also a success. The airfields attacked in this operation where Audembert, Coquelles, Marck, Peupingues and Wissant (it was not realised that Wissant and Coquelles had been abandoned and the Luftwaffe units based there relocated).

This time the bombers of the main force also used a quantity of small delayed action bombs. This was on the suggestion of Vice-Admiral Bowhill who upon seeing the photographic reconnaissance pictures of the targets the following day, expressed some surprise as to how widely the RAF's bomb craters were scattered. He immediately grasped that their inaccuracy could be turned to advantage if delayed action bombs were used, surmising that if these continued to detonate throughout the night the noise would deny sleep to the German pilots in the vicinity.

The RAF were very impressed by the abilities of the RNAA's navigators in finding and marking the targets but it should be noted that;

1. The airfields attacked were close to the coast.

2. The very slow speeds and open cockpits of the Swordfish aircraft and the light offered by the full moon (the exhausts of the aircraft's engines were masked) meant that the countryside was clearly visible to crews who had already seen it in daylight and so had a passing familiarity with it.

---

[160] 16th September was the date of the full moon OTL too.

3. RN navigators were accustomed to operations over the featureless ocean where they were tasked with flying to and from small ships frequently in bad weather and so they tended to be extremely skilful – much more so than those of Bomber Command!

4. The Royal Navy trained for night actions and all arms of that service had reached a very high state of proficiency in night operations.

Again, on September 17th, the exhausted and demoralised German bomber crews were required to attack London with inadequate escort. Again, sustained and well-coordinated attacks by RAF fighters destroyed the cohesion of the Luftwaffe formations and many of the Germans dropped their bombs well short of the target and fled for home. Again Luftwaffe losses were heavy. On the 18th of September, Kesslering was forced to report to Goering that Luftflotte 2 would only be able to continue daylight attacks with great difficulty and recommended that the switch be made to night operations only.

So shocked and dismayed was the German high command by these reverses that operation Sea Lion (the planned invasion of the United Kingdom) was cancelled on 19th September and the Battle of Britain swiftly wound down until by the end of the month there were almost no German air operations being conducted against the British Isles either by night or by day.

ANNEX 6: A SUMMARY OF THE MOSLEY

REPORT OF 1941 AND ITS SUBSEQUENT

INFLUENCE ON BRITISH POLICY

From 'The British Empire from 1914 to 1948' by Ian Shaw, Longacre 2005

The Territories of the British Empire in 1940

The list below details the territories of the British Empire considered by the report of the Mosley Committee. It does not include the eight already existing or about to be created Dominions of Australia, Canada, Egypt, Eire, India, New Zealand, South Africa and Southern Rhodesia. Southern Rhodesia had a kind of 'semi-Dominion' status, being large enough to self-govern but too small to handle its own foreign and defence affairs. Both Ireland and Egypt had technically been dominions since 1922 but were not enthusiastic members of the Commonwealth.

Territory	Status in 1940
Aden	Crown Colony
Antigua and Barbuda	Crown Colony
Ascension Island	Crown Colony
Bahamas	Crown Colony
Bahrain	British Protectorate 1882
Barbados	Crown Colony
Bechuanaland	British Protectorate 1885
Bermuda	Crown Colony
British Honduras	Crown Colony
British Indian Ocean Territory	Crown Colony
Brunei	British Protectorate 1888
Bushire	Crown Colony
Burma	Crown Colony

Cameroon	British Mandate 1919
Ceylon	Crown Colony
Cook Islands	Crown Colony
Cyprus	British Protectorate 1878
Dominica	Crown Colony
Falkland Islands *	Crown Colony
Fiji	Crown Colony
Gambia	Crown Colony
Gibraltar	Crown Colony
Gilbert Islands	UK/US Condominium
Ghana	Crown Colony
Grenada	Crown Colony
Guyana	Crown Colony
Hong Kong	Crown Colony
Iraq	British Mandate 1920
Jamaica	Crown Colony
Jordan	British Mandate 1920
Kenya	Crown Colony
Kuwait	British Protectorate 1899
Malaya	Crown Colony
Maldives	British Protectorate 1887
Malta	Crown Colony
Mauritius	Crown Colony
Montserrat	Crown Colony
Nauru	British Mandate 1919
Nepal	British Protectorate 1816
Newfoundland	Crown Colony
New Guinea	Australian Mandate 1906/1919
New Hebrides	UK/France Condominium
Nigeria	Crown Colony
Northern Rhodesia	Crown Colony
Nyasaland	Crown Colony
Oman	British Protectorate 1800
Palestine	British Mandate 1920
Pitcairn Island	Crown Colony
Qatar	British Protectorate 1916

Saint Helena	Crown Colony
Saint Kitts and Nevis	Crown Colony
Saint Lucia	Crown Colony
Saint Vincent and the Grenadines	Crown Colony
Sabah (North Borneo)	British Protectorate 1881
Samoa	New Zealand Mandate 1919
Sarawak	Administered from Malaya
Seychelles	Crown Colony
Sierra Leone	Crown Colony
Solomon Islands	British Protectorate 1893
South West Africa	South African Mandate 1919
South Georgia and the South Sandwich Islands	Crown Colony
Sudan	Crown Colony
Tanganyika	British Mandate 1919
Togo	British Mandate 1919
Tonga	British Protectorate 1900
Trinidad and Tobago	Crown Colony
Tristan Da Cunha	Crown Colony
Trucial Oman	British Protectorate 1887
Uganda	Crown Colony
Zanzibar	British Protectorate 1890

*Including Graham Land, the South Shetland Islands and the South Orkney Islands.

The Mosley Report's General Conclusions

The British Empire, with the exception of very few of its territories, was a strategic and economic liability.

The terms of British military protection of the Empire should be renegotiated.

The profitability of the colonies of the empire should be maximised. Colonies that were, or could be made profitable should be discouraged from seeking independence.

Parliament in Westminster should exercise more political leverage with the protectorates and encourage the ones that were, or could be made profitable to become Crown Colonies. Territories with no hope of becoming profitable should be given independence within the Commonwealth as quickly as possible or have the terms of their dependence upon Britain for protection formalised and clarified as soon as was practicable and safe.

The report recommended a clear distinction between being a member of the Commonwealth and being a British Dominion. Being a British Dominion implied an obligation; that together with the United Kingdom and the other Dominions that all territories with Dominion status would co-operate on matters of foreign policy and defence. Furthermore, that the United Kingdom and countries with Dominion status would come to the defence of one another if any of them were threatened by an outside power. A Dominion would be a member of the Commonwealth, but membership of the Commonwealth did not imply that a country was a Dominion.

The report suggested that a Dominion should be defined as an independent country formally allied with the United Kingdom with regards to foreign and defence policy, while a member of the Commonwealth would be a Territory related to Britain without either polity having any specific obligations one to another. It further suggested that a Crown Colony should be defined as a Territory dependent on the United Kingdom for its government, foreign policy and defence.

Summary of Recommendations – Region by Region

NORTH AMERICA AND THE CARIBBEAN

Theses territories were; Antigua and Barbuda, The Bahamas, Barbados, Bermuda, British Honduras, Dominica, Grenada, Guyana, Jamaica, Montserrat, Newfoundland, Saint Kitts and Nevis, Saint Lucia, Saint Vincent and the Grenadines and lastly Trinidad and Tobago, all of which were Crown Colonies. It was recommended that all proceed immediately to full independence within the Commonwealth except Newfoundland which should either be granted Dominion status or encouraged to join the Canadian Federation.

SOUTHERN ASIA

These consisted of; Burma, Ceylon, The Chagos Archipelago (The British Indian Ocean Territory), The Maldives and Nepal. It was recommended that with the exception of Burma, all proceed immediately to full independence within the Commonwealth but that the bases at Diego Garcia (in the Chagos Archipelago) and Trincomalee (in Ceylon) be retained.

Burma was wealthy and potentially very profitable. It was the world's largest exporter of rice, produced 75% of the world's teak, had large reserves of oil and a wealth of natural and labour resources including a highly literate population. It was recommended that Burma be retained as a Crown Colony.

SOUTH EAST ASIA

These were; Brunei, Hong Kong, Malaya, Sabah (North Borneo) and Sarawak. Malaya was the richest of Britain's colonies. Before the recession of 1930–31 Malaya's total trade exceeded that of all Britain's other colonies combined. Even in 1938, during a slump in rubber prices, Malaya's trade was worth more than that of New Zealand or of all the British colonies in Africa put together. The Protectorates of Brunei and Sarawak also had large reserves of oil and Hong Kong was strategically important. The committee recommended the retention of all five of these territories within the structure of the British Empire, Malaya as a Dominion, the rest as Crown Colonies.

OCEANIA

The territories concerned were; The Cook Islands, Fiji, The Gilbert Islands, Nauru, New Guinea, The New Hebrides, Pitcairn Island, Samoa, The Solomon Islands and Tonga. It was recommended that all proceed immediately to full independence within the Commonwealth or alternately become territories of either Australia or New Zealand.

EAST AFRICA

These were; Kenya, The Seychelles, Sudan, Tanzania, Uganda and Zanzibar. It was recommended that all proceed immediately to full independence within the Commonwealth.

WEST AFRICA

The territories concerned were; Cameroon, Gambia, Ghana, Nigeria and Sierra Leone. It was recommended that all proceed immediately to full independence within the Commonwealth.

SOUTHERN AFRICA

These were; Bechuanaland (Botswana), Mauritius, Northern Rhodesia, Nyasaland (Malawi) and South West Africa (Namibia). The committee recommended that Bechuanaland and South West Africa be incorporated into the Union of South Africa, while Southern Rhodesia should be amalgamated with Northern Rhodesia and Nyasaland to make a single Dominion. Mauritius should proceed immediately to full independence within the Commonwealth.

THE SOUTH ATLANTIC TERRITORIES

These were; Ascension Island, The Falkland Islands, St Helena, South Georgia and the South Sandwich Islands and Tristan Da Cunha. These tiny remote Islands were either astride or near shipping routes of strategic importance or too small to be independent. South Africa was asked to accept a transfer of the sovereignty of Tristan Da Cunha but declined. It was recommended that all be retained as Crown Colonies.

THE MIDDLE EAST AND THE HORN OF AFRICA

The Iraqi revolt of May 1941, although ill co–ordinated and desultory, was an unpleasant shock to British interests in the Middle East. Members of the Mosley committee travelled to the region several months after the revolt had been put down and it was the Middle East and the prospects of its British territories that took up fully a half of the final report. These were; Aden, Bahrain, Bushire, Iraq, Kuwait, Oman, Qatar and Trucial Oman. [161]

The section on the region opened with some general comments about British dependence on foreign sources of oil and foreign companies for petroleum products. It noted the rise of the aircraft, the oil-fired ship and the motor vehicle and pointed out how essential these were to Britain's national life, and indeed the life of every developed nation. The report quoted a French Senator, Henri Berenger, who wrote on December 12th 1919 in a letter to Clemenceau;

> "He who owns the oil will own the world, for he who will rule the sea by means of the heavy oils, the air by means of the Ultra refined oils, and the land by means of petrol and illuminating oils. And in addition to these he will rule his fellow men in an economic sense by reason of the fantastic wealth he will derive from oil – a wonderful substance which is more sought after and more precious today than gold itself." [162]

The committee's recommendations were stark, unequivocal and highly sensitive. Of the territories concerned, only Bushire and Aden were Crown Colonies and the rest were protectorates or mandated territories. However, it recommended the immediate annexation of all of them except the Kingdom of Jordan as Crown Colonies, either because of their proven oil reserves or because of their strategic position. Indeed the committee advocated the acquisition of the entire Trucial coast (the southern shore of the Persian Gulf) except that part of it belonging to Saudi Arabia.

---

[161] In OTL and TTL the Iraqi revolt was supported by the Germans. In TTL the Germans have bigger fish to fry and support will be limited to diplomatic and political support. There will be no Luftwaffe expeditionary force for instance.

[162] Quoted passim in 'The Oil War' by Anton Mohr, 1926.

The report also mentioned the loss of British Somalia to Fascist Italy in the war of 1940 (an issue far beyond its brief) and noted that Italy now controlled one of the jaws of the southern entrance to the Red Sea. It went on to recommend the importance of resolving this problem but coyly made no suggestion as to how.

THE MEDITERRANEAN LITTORAL

These were Cyprus, Egypt, Gibraltar, Jordan, Malta and Palestine. The Committee did not recommend any change in the status of Malta or Gibraltar, but advocated for Cyprus either independence within the Commonwealth, or 'enosis' (union) with Greece while Britain maintained sovereignty over the bases at Akrotiri and Dhekélia.

The recommendation of complete independence for Egypt, Palestine and Jordan came as no surprise, neither did the proposal to retain the Suez canal zone.

The report also suggested the possibility of transporting oil from the Middle East by pipeline across Iraq, Jordan and Palestine to Jaffa but expressed doubts as to whether such a pipeline would be worth the necessity of hanging on to these fractious and unprofitable states.

The Post-Mosley Committee Policy – Region by Region

The debate in Parliament on the Mosley Committee Report was overtaken by the changeover of government in February 1941, though few changes to the policy outlined by the outgoing Labour Administration were embraced. However, the ones that were embraced were very significant indeed. What changes there were, were driven by the need to finance the commitment to the vastly expanded and vastly expensive welfare state that the Liberal/Conservative Coalition inherited from Labour.

The new Government was able to make much propaganda at the expense of the outgoing Labour Administration, by pointing out that while their social welfare plans at home sharply increased the financial commitments of the British Government, they had not identified a way to cover the bills. The thrust of the new Government's policy was to broadly continue with the retreat from Empire except where opportunities existed to maintain and or increase the revenues gained from it.

NORTH AMERICA AND THE CARIBBEAN

The Government eventually decided on few changes in the status of Britain's North American or Caribbean possessions. Due to the proximity of the United States and the latter's adherence to the Monroe Doctrine there was no pressing requirement to keep more than minimal garrisons in these territories and little need to worry about their defence.

The only exceptions to this were Jamaica, Guyana, British Honduras and Newfoundland. Jamaica was an economic basket case with few prospects for the future. Frequently riven by strikes and uprisings it possessed a nascent parliamentary system and independence within the Commonwealth was to be sought at the earliest feasible date. Guyana and British Honduras had small populations, minimal economic activity and outstanding boundary disputes. Independence within the Commonwealth as soon as possible was the preferred way to proceed.

The committee's recommendations on Newfoundland were taken as policy by the Government.

SOUTHERN ASIA

The recommendations of the committee were followed for all territories except Burma. It was decided to proceed by offering to grant Burma Dominion status. However, it was realised that Burma was a discontented Colony that might very well reject the notion of Dominion status and push for complete independence or even demand the severance or all ties with the Commonwealth. In that situation the country could easily fall into the orbit of Japan. This, obviously, was not regarded by London as a favourable outcome. A secondary protocol was sketched out whereby Burma could be re-occupied by British forces in a crisis, because it was realised that if whatever leadership emerged in Burma were to decide to draw closer to

Japan there was very little the British could do to prevent it short of military intervention.

SOUTH EAST ASIA

The committee's recommendations were followed in outline with some important detailed changes. It was decided to continue Hong Kong and Malaya's status as Crown Colonies until (if and when the time came) these territories produced agitation for independence. No such agitation presently existed so there seemed little need for any alteration in the status quo.

It was decided to amalgamate Sarawak, Brunei and North Borneo into one administrative region to be known as the British North Borneo Territory. Sarawak was the fiefdom of the Brookes family – the White Rajas – and North Borneo was administered by a Chartered British company, both were amenable to British overlordship. Brunei was the fiefdom of Sultan Ahmad Tajuddin who was 30 years old in 1943. The Sultan was quite understandably worried about Japanese expansionism and wished to continue with Brunei as a British protectorate.

The British, however, had decided that they were no longer willing to extend the vastly expensive protection of their armed forces to states from which they gained little or nothing. While they acknowledged that they could not compel the Sultan to allow his tiny country to become a British Crown Colony, if he refused to do so, then all three of North Borneo's states would be given independence from Britain within the Commonwealth. This was because Brunei was the only one from which significant profits could be expected and the other two were not a bargain without it. The Sultan balked at this, but was immediately subjected to political pressure from both Sarawak and British North Borneo.

In the 19th century, Brunei had lost much of its land area to Sarawak. The White Rajahs had only been restrained from further predation of Brunei's territory by the direct intervention of the British Foreign Office and Sultan Tajuddin had every reason to be concerned that if the restraining hand of British rule were removed, then the same process would be repeated until his kingdom was entirely consumed. He was also, understandably concerned about the threat from Japan.

The British offered the Sultan a deal whereby he would reign but not govern. His accumulated personal wealth would be untouched and he would continue to receive revenue from taxes and trade but the country's foreign policy, defence and internal administration would be undertaken by Britain through the medium of a colonial government structure, and the lion's share of the country's revenues would be retained by the Crown.

Essentially it was much the same deal that was offered to many of the Indian princes in the 18th and 19th centuries as British power expanded into the vacuum left by the collapse of Mogul power and, perhaps in part because of his youth and inexperience, perhaps in part because the life of an international playboy was more attractive to a young man than the dull work of government, like the Indian princes, the Sultan was glad enough to take it.

OCEANIA, EAST AFRICA AND WEST AFRICA

Because of the world geopolitical situation, any change in the status or sovereignty of any of the territories covered by the report was deemed to be extremely inadvisable.

SOUTHERN AFRICA

The recommendations of the committee were followed for all the territories mentioned except Mauritius. In this case, no change of status or sovereignty was considered advisable because of the world geopolitical situation.

THE SOUTH ATLANTIC TERRITORIES

The recommendations of the committee were followed.

THE MIDDLE EAST AND THE HORN OF AFRICA

This was the one region where the Coalition government extensively revised the policy of the Labour administration. Labour had taken the view that annexing any of its territories to profit from their oil wealth was immoral and wrong. This stood in stark contrast to Oswald Mosley's opinions, but Labour had snapped back to a more leftist 'internationalist' attitude under Attlee and Dalton. The Coalition's Foreign Secretary, Anthony Eden, was somewhat more pragmatic – he noted that the only real losers if such a policy were pursued would be the Sheiks, Emirs and Princes who governed them and these were not a particularly savoury group of people, were not at all benevolent and were frankly incompetent as governors. The vast majority of the ordinary citizens of the territories in question would be better off in every way under British rule. Britain's Prime Minister, Sir Archibald Sinclair, was uncomfortable with this policy in principle but realised that pragmatism in this case, favoured not only British interests but those of the ordinary people of the region. Consequently, he was quite prepared to leave it to Eden.

It was decided to attempt to bring only the smaller, less populous Persian Gulf states into the Empire as full colonies. These were Bahrain, Kuwait, Qatar and Trucial Oman. Their total populations in 1940 amounted to roughly 300,000 people. This compared to Britain's Caribbean possessions whose populations amounted to roughly one million people. Trucial Oman did not at that time have any proven oil reserves but was composed of a number of small emirates with a total population of just 60,000 people and had a large land area that had not been comprehensively surveyed. Oil had been discovered in Kuwait in 1938, Qatar in 1939 and Bahrain in 1932. Of these, only Bahrain had begun to export oil, Kuwait and Qatar were not then earning any revenues from oil.

The British planned to institute a greater degree of democracy including the addition of elected assemblies and functioning judicial systems. The government and administration of British colonies was generally more thorough, less arbitrary and significantly less corrupt than the regimes then in power in the Middle East tended to be. The sovereigns of the region were absolute rulers who governed according to their whims. The concept of government accountability was an alien one and the apportionment of justice both haphazard and liable to be swayed by bribery.

In addition, the British planned the introduction of universal medical and dental care on a level similar to that being undertaken in Britain as well as significant investment in infrastructure. It was felt to be essential that the people of these territories should not be materially worse off than the people of the United Kingdom and it was also planned to grant them British citizenship.

The most important consideration with regards to the status of the region however was the continuance of the British commitment to defend it from hostile powers. Defence from the Axis, a resurgent USSR or the other sometimes predatory states of the region such as Iran, Iraq and even Saudi Arabia was central to the well-being of the Gulf States. That this protection now came at a price surprised no one in the region, though of course there was opposition to the change in the status quo from the more romanticised pundits of Empire in Britain.

It was decided to encourage Oman to proceed to full independence within the Commonwealth while the British retained the Musandam Peninsular which jutted out into the Persian Gulf forming the southern 'lip' of the bottleneck of the Straits of Hormuz. Ra's Musanda, an arid rock that would have been an island were it not connected to the mainland by a narrow isthmus, had several natural harbours suitable to be turned into small naval bases, the most promising of which seemed to be Kumzar.

By controlling, Kuwait, Bushier, Bahrain, Qatar, the Musandam peninsular and Aden, the British also controlled the passage of oil to the Suez Canal. This further mitigated against the suggestion by the Mosley committee to build a pipeline across Iraq and Jordan to Palestine.

As previously noted, Aden and Bushier were already Crown Colonies. Iraq was self-governing and had essentially achieved independence in 1932. However, as the Iraqi revolt of 1941 had shown, the country was being wooed by Germany and Britain retained its protectorate status to warn the Germans off. In spite of this, Iraq was regarded as a territory to be got rid of as soon as the German issue was resolved. Jordan was economically backward but Britain retained protectorate status rather than court the possibility of the country falling into the orbit of the Axis powers.

This left only Italian-occupied British Somaliland. While the outgoing Labour Administration seemed content to accept the status quo, Eden declared that 'Somaliland would be returned to British Administration as soon as was practicable.' a statement of intent that attracted an outburst of derision from Benito Mussolini.

THE MEDITERRANEAN LITTORAL

The recommendations of the committee were followed for Malta and Gibraltar – the two territories were too strategically important to forego. Cyprus presented an altogether more difficult problem. It was estimated that 16% of the population of the Island was of Turkish origin and this minority were bitterly opposed to the implementation of enosis (union) with Greece. British withdrawal from Cyprus would mean that four unpleasant prospects would have to be contemplated, these were: civil war; invasion by Turkey; invasion by Greece and invasion by another hostile power (most probably Italy). None of these were deemed to be acceptable outcomes, and Cyprus was retained as a British colony 'for the time being'.

While Egypt without the Suez Canal was a largely worthless territory economically, there was no prospect of British withdrawal from any part of it with the Italians in Libya ready to pounce.

Palestine was perhaps the knottiest problem of all. The Balfour Declaration of 1917 had bound the hands of successive British Governments by committing Britain to actively supporting the setting up of a Jewish homeland in Palestine. This had caused growing immigration to the Territory by Jewish people, many of whom had been driven from other parts of Europe by hostile regimes and endemic anti-Semitism. However, before this immigration began, Jews were in a minority in Palestine, making up approximately one-sixth of the inhabitants and the majority Arab population viewed the influx with disquiet. The text of the Balfour declaration read as follows:

I have much pleasure in conveying to you, on behalf of His Majesty's Government, the following declaration of sympathy with Jewish Zionist aspirations which has been submitted to, and approved by, the Cabinet.

> *"His Majesty's Government view with favour the establishment in Palestine of a national home for the Jewish people, and will use their best endeavours to facilitate the achievement of this object, it being clearly understood that nothing shall be done which may prejudice the civil and religious rights of existing non-Jewish communities in Palestine, or the rights and political status enjoyed by Jews in any other country."*

I should be grateful if you would bring this declaration to the knowledge of the Zionist Federation.

Yours sincerely,

Arthur James Balfour

The Arab revolt of 1936 to 39 had been suppressed and Hajj Amin al-Husseini, the Grand Mufti of Jerusalem, one of the instigators of the revolt and a Nazi sympathiser, had been driven out. He had found refuge in Nazi Germany where his anti-Semitic views received a warm welcome and he became a leading advocate of the 'Final Solution'.

It was believed by the British Government that the way to proceed was by dividing the country between its Jewish and Arab populations. The Mosley Report had intimated that there was no prospect of reconciliation between the two sides and had basically taken the view that Britain should wash its hands of the entire territory and let them fight it out until one or other emerged as the stronger. This radical, indeed cynical approach, was characteristic of much of the Mosley Report. It seems that the former Prime Minister, freed of the responsibilities and restraints of office, allowed his broad imagination, love of conflict and overwhelming respect for strength to have free rein in guiding the committee's recommendations. However, this was too extreme a measure for the British Government to support.

Once again the British decided that the best way to proceed was to divide a population along religious lines. As in Ireland and India, this meant that population transfer would leave fractious and discontented minorities in place. However, as in Ireland and India, it was a sincere attempt to avoid the worse problem of civil war.

For the Palestine/Trans-Jordan issue, the Government largely ignored the conclusions of the Mosley Committee and drew heavily on the plan that had been discarded by Winston Churchill in 1922 when he was Secretary of State for the Colonies. This fulfilled, at least in part, the promise of the Balfour declaration by the creation of a Jewish homeland west of the River Jordan (including Gaza) while Jordan (the nation) became the Arab Moslem homeland with its capital in Amman.

Of course, the Zionist movement had not contemplated that they would share the new state with Arab Christians also. To minimise the inevitable friction the British decided to encourage immigration by Christians and by Jews into separate parts of the country. By and large the Christians were encouraged to move into Galilee and Eastern Samaria while the Jews moved into Western Samaria and Judaea.

The Moslem Arabs were largely to be resettled in Jordan except for the Moslem Arab population of Jerusalem, which would be left in place to care for the Moslem holy sites (such as the Dome of the Rock) in that city. Jerusalem would become a free territory under international mandate (which in the short term meant the British) with Christian, Moslem and Jewish quarters. There were to be no restrictions on pilgrimage to the holy sites of all three religions.

The policy marked a decision by the British to come down on the side of the Jews and Christians and to act on the spirit of the Balfour declaration rather than attempt to satisfy all three competing factions. This carried three potential advantages. Firstly, it gave strategic depth to the British base on the Palestinian coast at Haifa. Secondly, it was designed to implant a pro-British population in that strategic zone. Thirdly, it publicly punished the Arab groups who had sponsored the Arab revolt of 1936-39 and then openly sided with the Nazis in 1939-40. The other Arab countries in the region raised no complaint about the Arab population displacement out of the Jewish zone, in part because they were able to evict their own Jewish populations into both it and later the new British Colonies of the Persian Gulf. [163] The new state was to be called Israel and was established in 1943.

Conclusions: The Implementation of Policy in the Middle East

Much of the policy set out by the British government in light of the Mosley Report was of a long-term nature and could not be implemented in full while the world situation remained unstable. Nevertheless, it provided a blueprint from which the British proceeded in the post-war era.

The British immediately began the task of persuading the rulers of the small Gulf States to allow the territories over which they reigned to become British Crown Colonies. The process moved slowly, required considerable patience and was a mixture of persuasion, coercion and finesse that would have gladdened the heart of Lord Palmerston himself.

Firstly, the British made much of their plans to withdraw from the region, making a convincing case that peace had only reigned on the Arabian peninsular because of British suzerainty. This was an argument that had considerable force, considering that it was only the British who succeeded in restraining the Saudis in their attempts to subjugate the entire region in the 1920s. The British made it known that they had every intention

---

[163] This is essentially what happened in OTL but the policy is writ larger and the Borders of Israel are different. Many Jews were evicted from Arab states and the governments of those states that were not British controlled, asset-stripped them as they left. They made large profits which their leaders pocketed. So from their perspective, the population transfer means that they make money and empty their countries of Jews at no cost except to the Arab populations displaced to the east of the Jordan whom they don't care about anyway. Unlike OTL, this does not occur at the same time as the British trying to satisfy all parties in the region. The Arab Moslems are the definite losers because of the Arab revolts in Palestine and Iraq and their support for Germany.

of granting Iraq complete autonomy and intimated darkly that they would not attempt to restrain any subsequent Iraqi regime should they be asked to forego the sovereignty of the areas minor states. There was also the problem of the German occupation of the Caucasus and the possibility that the Nazis might continue their expansion southward.

The force of these arguments was lent weight by the British withdrawal from India, the granting of Dominion status to the former 'Jewel of Empire' and the subsequent lack of British intervention in the resulting Indian civil war. If the British would allow India to 'sink or swim', what would they do to the rest of their territories?

The British offered the sheiks much the same deal they had offered the Sultan of Brunei, under British overlordship they would reign but not govern, their accumulated personal wealth would remain under their control, they would continue to receive revenue from taxes and trade but foreign policy, defence and internal administration would be undertaken by Britain through the medium of a colonial government structure and the lion's share of the country's revenues would be retained by the British Crown.

This outwardly generous offer did not, however, prove to be enough to overcome the sheiks resistance and the British fell back on some old-fashioned gunboat diplomacy. Using the valid pretext of the necessity to counter the menace of piracy along the Trucial Coast, a problem that had existed since time immemorial but had never been fully eradicated, the British moved large forces into the region and began the construction of bases at Kumzar on the Ra's Musanda peninsular in Oman, at Manama in Bahrain and at Fintas in Kuwait.

There was some opposition to the new direction in British Middle East policy from the Willkie administration in Washington, but these objections were overcome by a firm British response backed by the always powerful voice of American business interests. These were extensive in the Gulf region, particularly in the oil business, and supported the British stance because of the continuity and stability British governance would bring.

In the end it was not so much British diplomacy that helped usher Kuwait and the Trucial states into the fold of the British Empire so much as the racially-charged pronouncements of the Nazi leadership. But this was only to occur under the pressure of war.

ANNEX 7: THE PARTITION OF INDIA

From 'The Indian Independence Movement' by Herbert D'souza, Hamish Horton, 1995

In December 1941, a senior member of Britain's Liberal Government departed London, bound for India. This was Frederick Pethick-Lawrence who, dismayed by what had happened to the Labour Party, had resigned the Labour whip before the 1941 election and returned to the Liberal Party that he had been a member of in his youth. [164] He led a cross-party delegation and was accompanied by two younger MPs, one Liberal and one Tory who were to assist him. The political situation in the UK meant that the Prime Minister could spare only one senior man for the job that had to be undertaken.

Pethick-Lawrence had been appointed Secretary of State for India by the incoming Coalition government in 1941; he possessed a brilliant mind and was a man of high principle. The task of his mission was to give away Britain's empire on the Indian sub-continent, but he was to find his every offer, idea and proposal blocked and frustrated by the intended recipients. For the next six months, Pethick-Lawrence and his team tried to talk the representatives of the various Indian political parties they met with into reaching an agreement. But as one observer put it 'He is no man to negotiate with the tough Hindu politicians. He is no poker player.' [165]

India's politicians might have been good at poker, but they could also be egotistical and naive. Jawaharlal Nehru, leader of the Congress Party, said: 'When the British go, there will be no more communal trouble in India.' An assertion denied by Indian history both before and after British rule. Also around this time

---

[164] In OTL Pethick-Lawrence did not resign the Labour whip. He was however, the chief negotiator of the British Government's 1946 Cabinet Mission to India.

[165] In OTL these words were spoken about Pethick-Lawrence by the Viceroy of India, Archibald Wavell.

Mohamed Ali Jinnah, leader of the Muslim League, made a remarkable comment for a man who ruthlessly employed religious feeling for his political ends.

"You may belong to any religion or any caste or creed – that has nothing to do with the business of the state . . . Indeed, if you ask me, this has been the biggest hindrance in the way of India to attain freedom and independence and but for this we would have been free peoples long, long ago."

In addition to this misconception, Jinnah completely failed to see what would happen if the country was split, despite the fact that the British were telling him of the danger on every occasion that he deigned to meet with them.

Pethick-Lawrence was outmanoeuvred in negotiations by all the Indian politicians. They had no time for his woolly idealism and Britain's chief negotiator was a man who thought in terms of little else. They would put up with a few minutes of tedious platitudes about the 'welfare of the world' or 'the welfare of the Indian people', without showing the slightest sign of interest before changing the subject. The only thing the two sides could agree on was that the British should go away. This left the country ripe for serious trouble.

India's Hindus and Moslems had mostly lived separate lives, usually in separate villages and clearly delineated areas of the major towns and cities. They had their separate faiths and followed their separate customs. It is a myth that the Moslems and Hindus had got on peaceably for centuries before the British arrived. The British had done little to unite India's peoples over the centuries, but then it was an impossible task. Divide and rule was not a deliberate policy of the British Indian Empire. Rather than being a result of deliberate planning, it had evolved because of the exigencies of circumstance. British military and political strength had held India together for two centuries, suppressing communal violence and moderating racial and religious hatred. It was about to be removed.

In the end, the British quit India as quickly as they could. The British plan to quit India was called Operation Madhouse.

[166] Only strong rule could unite India, this was provided by the Moghuls and then, for a time, by the British, but the increasing reluctance of the British to govern forcefully combined with Gandhi's notion of peaceful non-violence extrapolated to become an Indian political philosophy, doomed the country to break up and propelled it toward civil war.

In conflicts between groups, it is invariably true that if one side is willing to use violence and the other is not, the side willing to use violence will prevail. The view that the Indian independence movement proceeded solely in a spirit of peaceful non-violence is quite incorrect. It is certainly true that Mahatma Gandhi propagated this idea and that many Indians followed it, but the Indian Nationalist movement had a radical wing that was quite willing to use brutality to further its ends.

When the war of 1940 began, the British Government promised the Indian National Congress (INC) that India would be granted Dominion status as soon as the war was over. However, at this time, the INC was far from unified. In fact, the British promise of independence and the rapid steps towards that end that were taken in 1941 did much to fragment it. The separation of the Muslim League under Jinnah was one example of this.

Subhas Chandra Bose was from a wealthy Bengali family that hailed from Cuttack in Orissa. He attended Fitzwilliam College, Cambridge and in 1920 took the Indian Civil Service entrance examination placing fourth overall – a considerable achievement. But in April 1921 he resigned from the Indian Civil Service and joined the Indian National Congress. Bose's political outlook stood in stark contrast to that of Gandhi. In particular, he had no time for the notion of non-violent resistance to British rule.

Bose became the President of the Haripura branch of the Congress party in 1938. This was contrary to Gandhi's wishes, and he commented "Subhas' victory is my defeat". His continued opposition led to Bose's resignation and subsequent formation of an independent party, the All India Forward Bloc.

---

[166] This was true in OTL also.

The formation of the Forward Bloc was announced at a rally in Calcutta on 3rd May 1939, Bose believed that a free India needed authoritarianism, on the lines of Kemal Atatürk's Turkey. Bose was elected as the President of the party and advocated a programme that would take advantage of the political instability caused by British engagement in the war. This was contrary to the view of Gandhi, Nehru and the rest of the Congress Party leadership at the time who were content to wait for the British to grant India independence after the conclusion of hostilities. But the Forward Bloc passed a resolution urging militant action against British colonial rule and on the outbreak of war in September of the same year; Bose advocated a mass campaign of civil disobedience against the British.

On July 2nd 1940, Bose was arrested and detained for a time in a Calcutta Jail, though later this was reduced to house arrest. In January 1941 he escaped and fled India travelling to the Soviet Union via Afghanistan. He sought Soviet support for the Indian independence movement but Stalin rejected his request, so he then travelled to Germany. The German Ambassador in Moscow, Count von der Schulenburg, had him flown to Berlin in a special courier aircraft at the beginning of April where he received a warm welcome from Joachim von Ribbentrop and other Nazi leaders. There he set up the Special Bureau for India with Adam von Trott zu Solz and began broadcasting on the German-sponsored Azad Hind Radio. He also founded the Free India Centre in Berlin and became greatly enamoured of the Nazi party and its leadership who informed him that they saw Indians as Aryan. They didn't mention that they saw Indians as debased Aryans, and appeared to welcome him into their circle enthusiastically.

Bose's political philosophy and that of the Nazis was very similar. As early as the 1930s he seems to have decided that a democratic system could not hope to overcome India's poverty and social inequalities and he wrote that an authoritarian state would be needed for the process of national re-building. In that sense he could certainly be considered a fascist and his alliance with the Axis was based on more than just pragmatism mixed in with an admiration for Germany's humiliating defeat of the British. [167]

Upon India's being granted Dominion status in 1942 and with the exit of many of the British, Bose returned and once more took up the leadership of the Forward Bloc. This greatly annoyed Nehru, the new Prime Minister and certainly hastened the break-up of the country. Far from being mellowed by his time away, Bose had become a strident advocate of Indian nationalism and in an attempt to broaden his political appeal he embraced alliance with Hindu nationalist groups that sought to expel Moslems from Hindu-dominated areas and fuelled the growing internecine bloodshed in India.

British Cabinet documents recently released under the 50-year rule show that by early 1943 this violence was becoming so bad that Nehru actually appealed to the British to send some of their troops back to India to help keep order. Sinclair's Government rejected the request and it was shortly after this that Nehru began to seriously consider Jinnah's suggestion for dividing the country into separate Moslem and Hindu states.

The leadership of the Congress Party was largely secularist and disagreed with the division of India on the lines of religion. Gandhi was both religious and irenic, believing that Hindus and Moslems could and should live in friendship. He opposed the partition, but his appeals for calm and a two-week hunger strike did little to ease the situation and the ever-rising toll of violence increased the pressure to implement partition in the hope of avoiding a full–scale civil war.

In April 1943, with constant rioting, looting and fratricidal slaughter a daily fact of life, Nehru met with Jinnah and Bose to decide on the break-up of the country. Due to the situation, it was necessary to complete the process with great haste and one of Bose's demands was that India should reject British Dominion status and become a Republic. Bose believed that India should be in alliance with the Axis rather than with Britain though he does not appear to have made this point at the time of the conference. Nehru acquiesced to this demand on the

---

[167] This was true in OTL also.

condition that Bose would endeavour to calm the situation and persuade his supporters to pause in their attacks on Moslems. Gandhi opposed partition but had become side-lined politically by that position. He proved largely ineffective in stemming the tide of religious carnage, his resorts to sulking and refusing food in protest at the failure of the people of India to rise to his expectations being the limit of his power in the matter.

The decision was finally made on the 21st of April 1943 and the announcement of the borders was made two days later as public order broke down all across northern India and Bengal. In the next few days a massive migration got under way and in the months following partition almost 15 million people left their homes and moved to what they hoped was safety.

Based on the 1945 Census of displaced persons, 7.2 million Moslems went to Pakistan from India while 7.3 million Hindus and Sikhs moved to India from Pakistan. 78% of the population transfer took place in the west, with the Punjab accounting for most of it. Politicians and community leaders on both sides whipped up mutual suspicion and fear, culminating in dreadful events. Far from causing an immediate end to the violence, partition in the short-term made matters dramatically worse. Part of the problem was that these enormous movements of people took place in the hot season when travel was hard and tempers easily frayed. The newly formed Governments were not equipped to deal with migrations of such a staggering magnitude, and massacres took place on both sides of the border. Estimates of the number of deaths incurred in partition range from lows of roughly half a million, up to as many as 1.5 million.

The Civil war itself was precipitated by Bose's demand for the expulsion of all Moslems from India but was mercifully brief. The Indian and Pakistani armies (both of which still had many British officers) remained loyal to their respective governments and by and large tried to protect civilians. Atrocities were committed by military formations on both sides, but these were isolated incidents and few in number. Bose himself was assassinated on 3rd May 1943. The persistent allegations that he was killed by British intelligence at the request of Prime

Minister Nehru have never been substantiated; however, the MI6 files pertaining to him are closed until 2044.

The two self-governing countries came into existence at midnight on 15 September 1943 almost 3 months to the day after the last skirmishes of the Civil War. Pakistan became a Dominion with Jinnah as its first Prime Minister. [168] The job of Governor General went to Sir Mohamed Zafarullah Khan.

The idea of India becoming a republic would have been quietly dropped after Bose's death but for the fact that The Congress Party had already announced that this was to be the way forward. Gandhi rejected the notion of becoming India's Head of State and until his death no head of state was appointed.

*

The princely state of Jammu and Kashmir had been divided up by Jinnah and Nehru based on the religious inclinations of the population. This plan had the Moslem regions of Kashmir, Gilgit and Baltistan absorbed into Pakistan, while the Hindu region of Jammu and the Buddhist regions of Ladakh and Aksai Chin went to India. The Maharajah of Kashmir was named Hari Singh. He was a Hindu, though the majority of the people in the state were Moslem. Nehru and Jinnah both disliked him and he was not consulted on the division of his realm. This was typical of the high-handed approach that Jinnah and Nehru took during the independence and partition process.

In consultation with his Chief Minister, Kailash Narain Haksar, as well as Sheikh Mohamed Abdullah, the leader of the Kashmiri Muslim Conference Party; Singh rejected the suzerainty of either India or Pakistan. An incursion by tribesmen from Pakistan on the 22nd November 1943 was repulsed by Singh's forces and he declared independence four days later.

---

[168] In OTL Pakistan became independent in 1947 by which time Jinnah's advancing tuberculosis made him take the ceremonial position of Governor General.

His timing worked in his favour. Not only was winter about to make military operations in the mountainous state tricky, but there was little appetite for further bloodshed in either Delhi or Karachi. Jammu and Kashmir was a poor state and neither India nor Pakistan were sufficiently recovered from the agony of partition to go to war over it. Under international law, Singh had every right to declare independence, but the leaders on both sides of the border were convinced that the state would fall into their hands without a struggle sooner rather than later. Jinnah was encouraged in this belief by Sheikh Abdullah and Nehru by Haksar. Kashmir became a member of the Commonwealth in 1944.

Unsurprisingly, the Nazis started to try to court both Pakistan and India diplomatically almost as soon as the countries became independent. Nehru rebuffed their diplomatic overtures but Jinnah hedged his bets and strung them along, talking reasonably to the Germans while cannily giving them concrete assurances of nothing. Jinnah played the Germans as effectively as he played the British. As he is reported to have remarked to his wife; "For most of 1941, I had to listen to British hacks talking rot about idealism, then for much of 1944 I had to listen to German hacks talking even more rot about race and eugenics." [169]

---

[169] Not a genuine quote.

ANNEX 8: GROSS DOMESTIC PRODUCT AND DEFENCE SPENDING OF THE GREAT POWERS 1944 [170]

From 'The Economy of the Third Reich' by Wilhelm Offenbach, Macallister 1962

Axis Powers

THE GERMAN REICH

Germany [171]	453.5
'Vassalzustande' [172]	179.2
French Colonies [173]	38.1
Dutch Colonies	102.8
Belgian Colonies	1.0
Protectorates [174]	106.1
German total	**879.7**

---

[170] The figures in this section are given in billions of 1990 Geary-Khamis international dollars. The information is largely derived or extrapolated from Mark Harrison's *The Economics of WW2* Cambridge University Press 1998 and Angus Maddison's *Monitoring the World Economy 1820 to 1992*.

[171] Germany within 1938 borders plus Austria, Czechoslovakia, Poland and 4/5ths of Switzerland. For Germany and Austria the OTL 1942 figure has been used then an annual growth of 2%. For Czechoslovakia and Poland the average figure for GDP shrinkage in the 5 major western European countries occupied by Germany in 1940 – 44 OTL for the period 1942 – 44 TTL has been used. For Switzerland, the 1943 figure has been used, then the average for GDP shrinkage for the period 1944 TTL.

[172] France, Holland and Belgium. The OTL figures for 1943 have been taken as a base line and then the average OTL shrinkage 1940–43 for TTL 1944 used.

[173] The colonies have been either taken or deduced from Maddison. Territories not occupied by the Axis have been deduced using a backward extrapolation from OTL 1950 – 55 figures. Territories occupied by the Axis have used a forward extrapolation from the 5 years before occupation where available.

IMPERIAL JAPAN

Japan [175]	252.7
Japanese Colonies [176]	140.1
Japanese total	**392.8**

THE KINGDOM OF ITALY

Italy [177]	160.3
Italian Colonies [178]	34.2
Italian total	**194.5**

THE REPUBLIC OF SPAIN

Spain [179]	60.4
Spanish Colonies	0.8
Spanish total	**61.2**

---

[174] The Baltic States, Ostland, Muscovy, Caukasus, Norway and Denmark. For Norway and Denmark the actual OTL figures for 1943 have been taken as a base line and then a figure of 2% growth for the TTL period 1943–44 used. For the Baltics and the former Soviet territories I have assumed 50% GDP shrinkage.

[175] 1936–40 annual growth rate (5.4%) is used for 1941 – 44 taking into account TTL factors.

[176] Manchukuo, Korea, Pacific territories, FE Russia, former French Indochina and Chinese conquered territory 1933–38 growth rate taking into account TTL factors.

[177] Italy 1942 plus 1/5th of Switzerland plus 2% growth per annum.

[178] Albania, Algeria, Eritrea, Ethiopia, Greece, Libya and Tunisia.

[179] OTL figures have been used.

MINOR AXIS POWERS

Bulgaria	10.5
Hungary	26.1
Romania	23.1
Yugoslavia	25.4
Minor Axis total [180]	**85.1**

AXIS TOTAL   1612.3

Other Great Powers

THE UNITED STATES OF AMERICA

United States [181]	912.1
US Colonies [182]	29.2

---

[180] For Bulgaria, Hungary and Romania plus Moldova the OTL figures for 1943 have been taken as a base line. For Yugoslavia the OTL figures for 1939 has been used. A figure of 2% growth for TTL 1944 has then been used for all.

[181] In TTL some of the factors that drove American growth are not present. The massive injection of British money into the American economy that took place OTL 1937-41 does not happen. In OTL 1938-41 Britain expended its entire gold and dollar reserves, a sum of £700,000,000 (about $3,500,000,000). Most of it was spent in the US. To give an idea of what that means, US GDP for FY1938-39 was $5,165,000,000. The British spent $2,000,000,000 on the purchase of tanks and aircraft and $171,000,000 was put up in capital for munitions factories. The British government met two thirds of the cost of building a factory for Packard in which they could manufacture Rolls-Royce Merlin aircraft engines. This cost $25,000,000 and the royalties on the engines were waived! $8,000,000 was spent in building the M3 Lee/Grant tank factory, $17,000,000 went on new shipyards and $87,000,000 on ships. On the other hand the French spent roughly $600,000,000 before June 1940 so that money will flow into the US economy as it did OTL. Also significant is that in TTL the US does not secure the £5.3 billion worth of high-yield foreign investment assets the British were forced to sell to American interests after 1941 for about 20% of their book value. For the figure arrived at here I have started in 1935, used a growth rate of 4% until 1940 (slightly below the OTL average for 1933–36), then –2% for 1941 due to TTL recession then 3% pa 1942 – 44.

US total	941.3

THE BRITISH COMMONWEALTH [183]

United Kingdom	394.2
Australia	44.5
Canada	53.2
New Zealand	11.5
South Africa	16.6
Other British Territories[184]	102.6

Commonwealth total	**622.6**

THE REPUBLIC OF CHINA [185]	259.9

THE REPUBLIC OF INDIA[186]	215.4

RUMP USSR [187]	133.4

ALLIED TOTAL	**2172.6**

---

[182] The OTL 1938 figure is used plus a growth rate of 2% per annum.

[183] UK GDP is started from an assumed 1938 baseline figure of 352.1 (up 23.9% from OTL) because of the decision not to return to gold in 1925. Growth has been steady at just over 2% per annum on average after the Treaty of Leamouth. For the 4 'White' Dominions the 1946–50 growth rate has been used for 1942 – 44. For Britain the 'White' Dominion average has been used. For the colonies the OTL 1950 figures have been used with a backwards extrapolation.

[184] Including Pakistan

[185] Estimated.

[186] OTL 1948 figures have been used minus an estimate for Kashmir.

[187] Estimated.

Proportion of National Income (GDP) Spent by the Powers on Defence (Percent)

	UK	Germany	USA	Italy	Japan	Spain
1935	4	8	1	5	?	?
1936	6	13	1	11	?	?
1937	6	13	1	11	15	?
1938	6	18	1	10	24	?
1939	15	32	1	8	22	2
1940	43	49	2	12	22	5
1941	17	56	2	23	27	11
1942	7	60	2	22	28	10
1943	8	17	3	9	29	9
1944	8	16	3	10	28	10

GLOSSARY

AA	Anti-Aircraft
Ack–Ack	Anti-aircraft fire (slang)
BIA	Burmese Independent Army
CO	Commanding Officer
CPUSA	Communist Party of the United States
DNC	Democratic National Congress
FDR	Franklin Delano Roosevelt
GOP	'Grand Old Party', the American Republican Party
GRU	Glavnoye Razvedyvatel'noye Upravleniye, (Main Intelligence Directorate) the foreign military intelligence agency of the Soviet Union
HMS	His Majesty's Ship
IJN	Imperial Japanese Navy
INC	Indian National Congress
KMT	Kuomintang
MI5	Military Intelligence, Section 5, the UK's counter-intelligence and security agency
MI6	Military Intelligence, Section 6, the UK's foreign intelligence agency
MP	Member of Parliament
MN	Marine National – The French Navy
NEI	Netherlands East Indies
NKVD	Narodnyy Komissariat Vnutrennikh Del, (The People's Commissariat for Internal Affairs) Stalin's secret police
NRA	National Revolutionary Army, the military branch of the Kuomintang
OCU	Operational Conversion Unit
OTL	Our Time Line
RAF	Royal Air Force
RM	Regia Marina – The Italian Royal Navy
RN	The British Royal Navy
RNAA	The British Royal Navy Air Arm
SA	Sturmabteilung (Storm Detachment) the Nazi Party's original paramilitary wing

SS	Shutzstaffel (Protection Squad) A Nazi paramilitary organisation
TTL	This Time Line
USAAC	United States Army Air Corps
USAAF	United States Army Air Force
USN	United States Navy
USNI	United States Naval Institute
USS	United States Ship
USSR	Union of Soviet Socialist Republics

ACKNOWLEDGEMENTS

Part of this story was posted by me under the title *The Dark Colossus* on the Alternate History Discussion Board in 2006-2007 but has subsequently been completely re-written and given the title *Drake's Drum*. I feel it is only fair to acknowledge my sources of inspiration, while emphasising that the intent and substance of these sources has been changed by me to serve this story, which is a work of fiction.

It started life in 2001as an idea stimulated by a post on the Battleship vs Battleship message board of warships1.com entitled *The Peace of Amiens 1940* by Steffen Jorgensen. This came together with a critique that I began writing on the version of Stuart Slade's novel *The Big One* that was posted on the 'History Politics and Current Affairs' board in 2004. I had written about two foolscap pages before I realised that I was not so much writing a critique, as suggesting a completely alternative plot! These two strands of thought came together to form the outline of the story.

Passages in chapters 5, 7, 11 and 15 are based on the work of Ed Thomas who posted a scenario entitled *A Greater Britain* on the Alternate History Discussion Board in 2005. It was published as a book by Sea Lion Press in 2017. Parts of the *Drake's Drum* story, as I originally wrote it, had a similar intent to Ed's but differed from his work in one crucial respect. Ed's was really good and mine wasn't. The passages in question are credited to 'Tom Shaed'.

The lines of poetry in chapter 10 are from T.S. Eliot's *The Waste Land*.

I have been tinkering with the notion of alternate Washington Treaties for nearly thirty years but the version of the treaty presented here was partially inspired by the Washington Treaty Renegotiation Exercise. This was debated out on the Battleship vs Battleship message board of Warships1 in 2001. Richard Hawes, who negotiated for the British Empire, wrote an appreciation of that exercise and was good enough to share it with many of the participants and spectators including myself. It will be noted that the treaty presented here is markedly different from the final treaty agreed in WTRE.

The final passage in chapter 13 is adapted from *'The USSR and Total War: Why the Soviet Economy Collapsed in 1942'* by Mark Harrison, in A World at Total War: Global Conflict and the Politics of Destruction, 1939-1945, pp. 137–156, edited by Roger Chickering, Stig Förster, and Bernd Greiner (Cambridge University Press, 2005) and is credited accordingly. Mr Harrison has asked me to emphasise that it is Copywrite © material and adapted with permission.

I would like to thank Mark L. Bailey and Shane Rogers for their comments and insights on many parts of this story. Their 'France Fights On - Alternative Point of Departure' (FFO-APOD) scenario is still an ongoing project, but is the most extraordinarily detailed, painstakingly constructed and comprehensively researched alternative history I have ever read. All errors are my own.

The maps have been created in Photoshop using the line tool. A few are scans of pen and ink drawings created by myself. Some of the photographs have been altered in Photoshop. The licensees are noted in the captions.

APPENDICES

www.drakesdrum.co.uk

Sea Lion Press

Sea Lion Press is the world's first publishing house dedicated to alternate history. To find out more, and to see our full catalogue, visit **sealionpress.co.uk.**

Sign up for our mailing list at **sealionpress.co.uk/contact** to be informed of all future releases.

To support Sea Lion Press, visit **patreon.com/sealionpress**

Made in the USA
Columbia, SC
15 October 2020

22879002R00224